Chasing Comets

by brandon spacey

Chasing Comets

by brandon spacey

Copyright © 2026 by brandon spacey
and SpaceBrew Publishing.

All Rights Reserved.

Second Edition

Cover art by brandon spacey.

Chasing Comets is a work of fiction. All characters
appearing in this work are fictitious. Any resemblance
to real persons, living or dead, is purely coincidental.

Novels by brandon spacey

Callie Simmons Novels

book 1: Midnight's Park
book 2: Resurrecting Mars
book 3: Into the Darkness
book 4: Red Bell

Shawn Stedwin Novels

book 1: A Flutter in the Window
book 2: Hello, World
book 3: Day of the Dogwood

Standalone Novels

Shedding Sadness

For Lisa. Thank you for sneaking me into my first real concert. That concert changed forever the way I view and appreciate music. It forged in me an appreciation for the art of the performance.

CHAPTER ONE
finding the rhythm

From *WhiskeyNeat* Magazine

Breaking the Sound Barrier
by Randall Cameron

There's a new band on the air waves. And by the time this magazine hits the stands, or—more importantly, your favorite reading chair in your parlor—you'll have no doubt already heard of them. And probably heard them as well.

Of course, I speak of One Last Orbit.

As does everyone else at this exact moment in human history. These things happen like tidal events. In the sixties, it was the Beatles. In the nineties, everyone spoke of Nirvana. We had our age of Taylor Swift and

Lady Gaga. But it looks like we are, at least for now, in the age of One Last Orbit.

And that's not a bad thing.

I've seen a few of their shows now, and this is without a doubt the best way to consume their music. The visual element of their performance seems to be every bit as important as the sonic side of it. We all have our favorite concert artists. The Barenaked Ladies, in their heyday, put on a great show. Garth Brooks. P!nk. Toto. There are too many to list—and they each have gargantuan followings who will swear it's the best live performance you've ever seen. And it's usually the front man who brings it over the top.

Enter the dazzling, spectral presence of Tanis Ransom.

The music itself, to start, is entrancing. When an artist is able to lock into the fundamental physics of sound, harmonic vibration and the way it interacts with the natural hardware in our ears, he is able to achieve more than just the sum of the parts involved. And I didn't get this from the album. Only when I stood in audience of the band did I feel it resonate deeper than just the ears. It seemed to tug at that part of your aura that resonates in your soul.

The band is Shannon Kennedy on lead guitars. He's the youngest of the bunch. You find Layne Billings on bass guitar, and he's the newest member—having replaced Mark Watkins after his sudden departure from the band last year, citing health issues. Kevin Vig, whom you may know from his days as a producer of such bands as Lost in Transit and Sweet Baby Rain, plays the drums. Benjamin Redding mans the keys and pad, sometimes at the same time.

The singer, one Tanis Solara Ransom, is the daughter of former NASA rocket scientist, Ezra Ransom.

You can see where this is going.

Mr. Ransom introduced his daughter to the cosmos at an early age, and—well, now you know the story behind their spacey sound. Most of their songs either deal with physics, space travel or alternate realities that might cross both plains simultaneously.

Originally from Bar Harbor, Maine, the band assembled itself over several years, playing everything from dives to dance halls and everything in between. Once they gained a sizable following, the band could be found headlining the Sally West and the Dixie Whistle, both fairly large live venues. The Sally became their home bar. OLO played there every couple of months in the younger days.

Now days, they all live in and around Bozeman, Montana, with three of the members—Kevin, Tanis and Benjamin—living within walking distance of each other on the same great swath of land between the Bridger and Gallatin mountain ranges. On days when they're not on the road, there's a greater-than-zero chance they'll all be in Kevin's home studio, where they actually recorded their first studio album, *A Walk Through the Stars*.

The album's opener, *Long Way Around*, could likely fit all of us more than we know. A woman driving to meet her man, "nothing but black top and

I'm surrounded by stars"… turns into a forlorn but misunderstood message, seeming to tap dance around playful naivety made endearing by the song's hook. "You said never in a million years, so I took the long way around". It's sad, almost pitiful, in fact, but the pleading and innocent gait of its protagonist works better than one might guess.

There are touches and notes of space-themed drama hidden in almost every song. Tracks like *Just Another Star, Super Little Novas* and *Calling Neptune* make it quite obvious, where others, *String Theory* and *Stardust Sunrise* are more covert in their message.

The album's sixth track, a bass-guitar-heavy rocker called *I'm Not That Girl* offers a tougher side of the typical sweetie pie front woman with the soft, sultry voice: Tanis actually screams some of the lyrics. Surprising, if not a little jarring.

Kennedy says of the scream, "None of us knew that was coming. She had never rehearsed like that. But come time for recording, she dropped that line in there – 'we'll hit 'em like a sonic boom!' – and we all just sort of froze…"

Heard, Mr. Kennedy. But strangely enough, it works.

The album features a heavy, sullen track called *Whisky* that touches on filling emptiness with alcohol and touts the hook, "It'll be your lover, but it can never be your friend." Poignant and powerful, as are most of Ransom's lyrics. And she does write them all. Every track.

I spoke with her a few days before writing this column, and asked her where she goes to find the words. "Not just space, or space travel, but cosmology and theory are passions of mine," said she. Clearly, she isn't just pulling ideas from Clarke or Asimov. She seems to know her stuff.

But whether or not the spacey lyrics and the cosmically-lost theme is scientifically sound doesn't seem to matter. Because the way the band presents them will make you a believer either way. When Ransom sings lyrics like, "I'm falling out, and Neptune's chasing me," you tend to forget you're on Earth at all. You're stuck out there, some several billion miles from home, trapped around a downgraded planet.

Hence, my saying I've never been to a concert quite like this one. It truly is something to behold, with more than just the ears. It's not your typical pop concert. In fact, it's not really pop at all—not in the conventional sense, at least. But what, then, you may ask, is it?

Ransom calls it Space Rock. Simple as that.

Okay, but what *is* Space Rock? "Well, it's more than just singing about space. It's about making the listener feel like he's *in* space. The music plays just as big a role as the lyrics." Not your typical rock instrumentation, in other words. We get it, Tanis.

Classically trained but not foreign to pop-rock in the slightest, Ransom's vocals are elegantly paired with the meticulous complexities of the music. While her range isn't itself remarkable, it should be noted that her ability to gain the higher register, though gravelly and rough, is chillingly pleasant – a raw, naked cry. At her upper range, this primal exposure seems to speak of the human condition – its pleading, insistent call gripping right at the core of an emotional experience. In short, she means what she sings. With lyrics to match, her entire presence is nothing short of spectral. Galactically forlorn and eerily poignant, Tanis Ransom is one of the last true sirens in the dying art of operatic trance.

You're lost in space; you're witnessing the dying of a star; a distant sun setting over the desolate ruins of a wasted planet; a far-off and lonely quasar spouting its cold energy into the dark space of the endless universe. An almost supernatural transition has taken place here, and only the OLO concert-goer can truly understand it.

This is not your typical concert. Fans don't come to see One Last Orbit with the intention of getting rocked by an arrogant guitarist, flailing arms and skipping across the stage.

They come to be transported to another dimension.

Throughout the duration of the show I was eerily aware that I was being taken somewhere. It felt like they were teleporting me with their music alone. We've all heard the songs on the radio. And while they're fabulous works of musical art, the radio—or even your home stereo system—is not its true final form. Hearing a pre-recorded rendition of their music just isn't the optimal way to experience this music. These guys, like Dream Theater or The Pineapple Thief or so many others who cherish the purist form of the art—these guys know how to get you involved. It's as much a feeling thing as it is a hearing thing. And a sight thing. Perhaps the smell of the crowd—the sweat, the breathing, the pot someone sneaked in—is part of it as well. But your other four senses are definitely at work together, hand in hand, and mostly overloaded.

With the decade coming to a close, people are once again scattering for theory on what the next era of music will bring. I would suggest you will see a lot more of this completion project. This mission to entertain through every sense simultaneously, rather than leaving it only to the ears. Because let's face it: if you're listening to One Last Orbit through your ear buds, you're missing half the show. Sure, the music is great. It's more than great. It's entrancing. Hypnotic. Enrapturing. But the thrill of having been part of the audience only enhances that sonic greatness. It finishes the experience. And whether you took the bus or drove to the show, you're sure to feel the same on the way home. There is an infinite sadness that abounds when the band signs off. Going home feels wrong. It feels like you've just left home. This sadness is for the unbending truth of the matter. And that is that it doesn't last forever.

1

Noah Wright stood leaning against the thick wooden rail on the back porch of The Sally West and watched as the water splashed against the rocks below, the same as it always had. In the deep evening dim, there was almost no white left in the caps as the saltwater ran long up onto the beach and crashed against the gigantic boulders strewn about the coast. The sun had set and the wind was whipping the flag in the parking lot to the south. It would not be fully dark for another half-hour, but its approach was almost palpable. The coming weather underlined the end of fall and made everything seem darker.

The Sally was an old restaurant-turned-bar that should have been knocked down two decades before, but somehow had escaped destruction. It stood on the eastern edge of Snows Point, Bar Harbor, Maine. Two decades before, when Sally West died and her family sold the estate, a new buyer swooped in and saved the restaurant, sparing its destruction and giving Bar Harbor a stand-up excuse for a nightclub. The best bands in Maine set their sights on The Sally. It was the Madison Square Garden of the local circuit, at least on the island.

A short glass of whiskey hung in Noah's hand as he stared out at the harbor. The parking lot lights clicked on, bringing to life a loud buzz and lighting up the south end of the wrap-around porch. Couples sat out here around fire pits filled with glass rocks, smoking and drinking when the music inside was too loud. Or when the atmosphere got a little warm. Noah took a sip of the warm whiskey and swished it through his teeth as he stood up straight. His phone buzzed in his pocket. It was Doug. He was late, as usual.

The text said he was exiting the highway and was only a few minutes away. A quarter of the roads on Mt Desert Island were closed for almost half the year. And there weren't many roads to start with. The old wooden door swung open and a young couple came out laughing, followed by Trixie, Noah's favorite waitress. It didn't matter what section she was working, she always made arrangements to take care of him and his friends when they visited. Maybe he was her favorite patron. It might have been an attraction. Or it might have been the fact that he tipped her really well.

"Hey, sugar. You want another one?" she said as she came to him, round tray propped against her flat belly.

He looked down at the empty tray, then shook the last sip around in his glass. He threw it back and wiped his mouth with a coat sleeve, then set it on the tray. "Does the pope shit in a funny hat?"

Trixie laughed out loud, slapping Noah's chest lightly. She pulled her hair back behind her ear, revealing a barbell through its widest part, and several silver studs in the lobe. "Where's Doug?"

Noah leaned against the rail on one arm, nodding toward the parking lot behind her. He pointed with the hand on the rail. "You know it's supposed to snow tonight?"

She turned and looked over her shoulder at the parking lot, to see a rugged Jeep Cherokee come barreling into an empty spot, popping up onto the curb with its right front tire. When she looked back at Noah, her eyes were smiling. "You guys ever going to take me out on the trails?"

Noah put his hand on her cheek, running his thumb against her high cheekbone. She turned her face into his grasp. "You're not afraid to get dirty?" he asked. She pursed her lips, but didn't answer. "You're so pretty. I can't imagine you being a friend of the mud."

"You'd be surprised!" she said, turning again as footsteps pounded against the boards on the other end of the porch. "Hey, baby," she said.

Noah watched as Doug came up and slung an arm around Trixie's shoulders, moving her roughly out of balance. Her diminutive frame was easily set off-track. "Who's playing?" Doug asked. He leaned his head down and kissed her cheek. Noah tilted his head.

"Are you serious, dude?" Noah asked.

Doug spread his hands. "What? What did I miss?"

Trixie was back between them, both hands on the outside rim of the tray. Doug was looking at her. "It's Mellow Nightfall night!" said Trixie.

Doug made a face. Noah chuckled, still leaning on the rail with one arm.

"Oh. And how the hell was I supposed to know that?" asked Doug.

"Be a better fan and keep up with the damn bands?" Noah said.

"Come on inside, boys, let me get you some drinks to warm your bellies!" Trixie said, bouncing toward the door.

Doug looked at Noah for a minute then shook his head. "Dude, we've got to get that girl hooked up with someone."

Noah widened his eyes, nodding in agreement. He stood up and clapped Doug on the shoulder, then turned him around toward the door, shoving him toward the tiny Trixie, who stood holding it open with a scuffed black boot.

They walked into a loud warmth that almost knocked them back. A band was on the stage playing dirty southern rock. It sounded like smoke and whiskey coming out of the speakers. Noah cracked his neck and looked around the place. The usual crowd was strewn about the bars and tables, talking, drinking. Heads bobbed. Women laughed out loud, men flirted. Most were facing the stage.

Doug turned to Noah. Noah came to a stop, looking at the stage. "What time they go on?"

"Probably nine-thirty."

"There's Scotty," Doug said, pointing at a nearby high-top. Noah followed him toward the tall table, his eyes scanning the crowd the whole time. Doug shook hands and hugged the guys at the table, nodded at the women. One of the girls came around and hugged his neck, kissing his cheek. These were Doug's friends. Noah knew them, but had he been alone tonight, wouldn't have gone to see them. Maybe a wave across the bar, maybe a nod at one of the guys on the way to the men's room. As he got closer, he spotted a girl with purple hair at one of the nearby tables, and recognized her. She was the singer of another band that played here sometimes. She was startlingly pretty at this distance. He couldn't remember her name though.

Some of the guys said *what's up*. A couple held out hands, which he shook, still glancing about the large room. Back when it had been a restaurant, there had been half-walls all about the place. Now that it was a nightclub, those walls had been removed. It was one wide-open space, occasionally spotted with wooden piers that supported the rafters. It smelled like old wood and smoke, though smoking was not allowed inside. Noah reckoned that might not just be the owner's preference, but a fire code. This place would go up in a flash if someone sparked near one of those piers. It was big, but not giant. Maybe five hundred feet squared.

The stage took up the middle of one wall.

Trixie came back to the table, a tray full of glass on her hand. Noah lifted his bourbon glass off the tray as she set a napkin on the table. "What do you think it takes to pick her up?" Noah asked her, looking at the singer at the table in front of him. Trixie turned to look in the direction of his gaze, then turned back, rolling her eyes.

"Dude, get in line," she said, still setting out glasses and bottles on the table. Half the tray was cleared when she turned to Noah. "You know there are other girls out there who would die for you to ask them out, don't you?" She looked up at him with big brown eyes that seemed always to be trying to say something on their own.

Noah looked down at her. "Honey, I'll take you out any time you want." He put his free hand on her bare shoulder, squeezing softly. "You just say the word."

"Ha! Okay, tiger," she said. "I've said the word many times!" she said, turning away, eyes wide with false humor.

"When are you going out again, Wright?" one of the guys asked. Noah couldn't remember his name. He just knew it was the guy who always said the same thing, even though they had never gone out on the trails together. Guy probably drove an H2.

"Ah, you know, whenever I can put up the work for a while," he said, taking a sip of the fire water.

"I hear ya, man! Dude, we've been so busy lately," the man was saying.

"I get you," Noah said. He clapped the man on the shoulder and excused himself, making his way to the next closest table. His mind was on other things. Other people. He walked casually up to the table where the purple-haired woman was talking animatedly to a friend – a short girl with glasses and mousy hair. The one with the purple hair looked maybe five-foot-seven, a hundred and twenty pounds. She was tall. Beautiful. Beautiful, but not unapproachable.

Noah walked right up to the two girls, standing between them where they leaned against the table on one arm. It was a perfect triangle. He took a sip of his whiskey. "Hi. Can I ask you a question?" he said, staring directly at the purple-haired woman.

She stopped talking. Looked at him. She was still smiling. "Sure. What's up?"

"Was your dad a thief?" Noah asked.

The smile she had been using to talk to her friend still hung on her face, though now it looked forced. "Excuse me?" she asked. She was forcing more than a smile. She was forcing politeness.

"I asked if your dad was a thief."

Her smile completely dropped away, and she swallowed, staring at him seriously now. She breathed in and lifted her chin, then said, "Yes. He's serving twenty years in Jersey City Correctional for armed robbery of a liquor store. Why do you ask?"

Noah felt his face flush and might have lost a few heartbeats. "I, uh..."

She stared at him a moment longer, a look of displeasure in her eyes, and finally said, "He did have time to steal the stars for my eyes, though. Is that what you wanted to know?"

Noah breathed again. This gal was good. Well, considering he had handed her a shitty line, how good did she have to be? It didn't take much to beat that one. She had been ready for him. "Hon, I think I'm the one with a star in my eyes, 'cause that's all I see right now."

She screwed up her mouth and held back a smile, again raising her chin, then slowly started nodding, letting the smile come out a little more. "Okay, that was a pretty good recovery."

Noah glanced at the mousy girl. She was staring at him with only the ghost of a smile on her mouth.

Patiently waiting for him to get done with whatever business he was trying to achieve here. He said, "Thank God, because I was about to ask for mouth-to-mouth."

The purple-haired lass opened her mouth wide, showing a whole lot of pretty white teeth. Her beauty, he realized, was hard to miss when she smiled. It looked like a laugh, but she wasn't laughing. She put her hand on his chest and leaned in a little closer, shouting so he could hear her. "I think you're trying to hit on me," she said.

He could smell the cinnamon on her breath, and looked at her short glass. It had red liquid in it. Her friend was looking at him too, but Noah paid her no real attention beyond a cursory smile.

"Am I? I'm not really sure. I don't know how this stuff works," he said, leaning in closer, putting his mouth close to her ear. "I do know, though, that I'm supposed to ask if you come here, or something like that."

The girl leaned back, mouth wide open again. It was a silent laugh. Maybe that was it. Whatever it was, it was gorgeous. The kind of smile you practiced for pictures, if you were lucky enough to have the pearls. "Well, I am here. So I guess that means we have established that I *come* here. So what's your name?"

"My name? I thought we were talking about you!" he said, holding his glass close to her chest, pointing at her with it.

She reached up and wrapped her fingers around the other half of his glass, shaking it slowly. "But you already know so much about me. Like that my father is an armed robber and such."

Noah lifted his chin, pursing his lips. "Yeah, I'm having trouble believing that one."

"Well, good. So we don't have to go through the awkward rigmarole of my telling you I was joking, you coming back saying you didn't mean to offend, and my saying no offense taken," she said.

Noah nodded again, and smirked at her. "Well anyone who actually takes offense at that, knowing the asker could not have possibly known the state of her father, well..." he shrugged and held up his hands as if to say what more do you want? "Of course, I could have asked you if you had a purse full of magnets," he said, looking levelly at her. The mousy girl was all but completely forgotten. She had found something to look at beyond the vicinity of their table.

Purple stared for a moment, her brow beginning to furrow. Then it dawned on her and her face lit up again in a smile. "Ah, because you're Iron Man and you were drawn to me. I got it."

"Bingo," he said, giving her a wink and sticking his thumb up. "How often does someone tell you you're remarkably and exquisitely put together?"

She opened her mouth yet again, tilting her head and looking him straight in the eyes. Then she slammed her mouth shut, head still tilted hard to one side. He had stumped her. That old fabled feline tongue trapper was close by. Noah smiled at her. He noticed the faint lip gloss she had applied, probably an hour before, staring into the dirty mirror of the women's room. She had left half the gloss on her tumbler. "Thank you. I..." she started, then picked up her glass, holding it close to her chest with both hands. She stared at him, dumbfounded and silent, mouth locked against words she probably couldn't come up with. Noah had finally gotten the best of her.

He took another step, moving a little closer. "Listen," he said, looking toward the stage as he spoke. "I'm not really good at this stuff anymore."

"Anymore?" she asked, pulling away to look at him. "Well I think you're doing just fine," the woman with purple hair said.

"Yeah, I used to be good. I actually used to be a professional pickup artist," Noah said.

"Is that so?" she asked, lifting her chin.

"Yeah," he said, scanning the crowd again. "I drew pickups. My specialty was the headlights."

This time she laughed out loud. "Oh my God, you're a dork!" She turned to her friend, obviously trying to include her in the conversation. But Noah didn't look at the bespectacled girl. She was cute, but she didn't have purple hair. And she wasn't the one he had set eyes on. It was too late for her. She was a wallflower. The purple-haired woman closed her mouth again, licking her lips. Her smile was genuine. There was no doubting that. If this gal was an actor, she couldn't have put on a smile this real. It was intoxicating, Noah saw.

He had seen her perhaps half a dozen times before, always from a distance, and only once up close. He remembered that one time very vividly. He had been here for one of her shows. She had just come off the stage, still glistening with a sheen of gorgeous shiny sweat. The band had gone backstage to cool off, to unwind from the stage buzz. And after maybe ten minutes, she had come back out, alone. She was smiling. The crowd had gathered around the doorway that led down the hallway to the Green Room. This hallway was separated from the main hall with silly bat wing doors. She came through those doors with her hands in the air. She looked like a million bucks as she passed right by him. Noah stood there clapping with the rest of the crowd. She had not looked at him, but had gotten close enough for him to see how real her beauty was. Even after a show, sweaty and tired, she looked lovely. And now, standing here close enough to smell her perfume, he was taken back to that night. Picking up where it had left off.

Noah realized that he had the advantage of her. For all the times he had seen her on stage, this woman had likely never seen him. If her eyes had breezed across him, she didn't remember him. He, therefore, decided not to let on that he knew who she was. Give her the benefit of the common folk. Wasn't that what these singers and celebrities always wanted? Someone who didn't know them? Someone who respected and liked them for who they were, and not the stage makeup? Well, she was far from a celebrity—just a local-circuit babe who fronted a pretty good rock band. He liked the band okay, and tried to make most of their shows, but couldn't readily think of anything earth-shattering about any of them. But she and her voice stuck out in his mind. So if the band stayed together, perhaps celebrity was something she would never have to worry about.

"So why'd you come over here? You noticed my headlights were on?" she asked, smiling lightly.

He shrugged. "Are they? I try to keep my eyes up here in places like this," he said, pointing at his face. "The hair though – that's really what got me over here. I had to see it up close."

She laughed easily. "Yeah, it's kind of a stage thing." She reached up and touched it. Part of it was piled up on the top of her head in big curls held by carefully placed pins. "Is it bad?"

He shook his head. "Nah. It's all right." Noah looked around again, then added, "I don't think it would work for me though," Noah said, reaching up and running his fingers through his own hair.

She giggled again and took a small sip of her drink. She licked her lips and stared at him, patiently awaiting the next line. She glanced at her friend. The mousy one with the glasses. That girl was looking at the stage, leaning against the table with both arms, bending her knees to the beat of the music. The band was putting on a pretty good cover of Don Henley's *Dirty Laundry*. Noah let the beat drive him a little, and found himself bouncing inside his shoes, just slightly. Just enough to let it rock the liquid in his glass.

Purple looked back at him. "Well you gotta get out of your comfort zone sometimes."

Noah knew that was right. That was, in fact, exactly what he was doing by coming and talking to this woman, with whom he had no real business consorting in the first place. This was almost a hobby for Noah, though. The fact that he already had a girlfriend didn't come into it. Joy Kennebell was wonderful. But flirting was fun. Harmless.

"It took some balls going purple, didn't it?" he asked.

She shrugged. "Nah. I like to change things up. Keep people guessing. You know, surprises." She shook her fists like she was getting ready for a boxing match.

He nodded, pursing his lips. "Yeah, I can dig on surprises."

"So what now?" she asked. She looked pleased with herself. "Now that you've seen the purple up close, what are we to do?"

He looked at her for a moment and shrugged.

"I don't know. I hadn't really planned beyond that," Noah said. He smiled at her, a shy number. It might not have worked.

She returned his smile, but did not say anything. She was letting him figure it out.

"Besides, it's hard to talk when you're out of breath."

She frowned. Then forced a smile. "Huh?"

"Seeing your smile sort of took my breath away."

She smiled widely. "You said you weren't really good at this stuff."

"What stuff? Bad pickups?" he asked, looking around again, briefly.

"Yes! The pickups! Did you come over here to woo me?"

Noah looked down at the ground and kicked at the stained concrete with the toe of one boot. "I, uh…" he started. "I don't know what that means."

"Ha!" she said, slapping his chest. But this time she left her hand there a little longer. "Did you come over here to try to pick me up?"

He looked her up and down, as if carefully assessing her. "I think I could. You couldn't be over a buck-oh-five."

She laughed out loud again. And again put her hand on his chest. It felt like she was pushing a little too hard with that hand. Trying to feel something beneath the thick fabric of his black Dickies shirt. "Oh, you're wonderful. I haven't seen one-oh-five since high school!"

"You weighed a hundred and five in high school? Good God!" he said.

"Hey!" she said, slapping his shoulder this time. She sure seemed to be touching him a lot.

Noah shrugged again. "Hey, you challenged me. Try to pick you up?" He straightened up and took a sip of his whiskey. "Honey, I could pick you up with one arm."

She laughed out loud again. "I bet you could," she said, raising one eyebrow as she took in a mouthful of her drink. Peripherally, Noah saw Trixie approaching, so he went ahead and downed the rest of his, then held the glass up at shoulder height, out to his side. Trixie came up and snatched it from him.

"Another one, Noey?" she asked, slipping up beside him and putting an arm around his waist. She was looking up at him from half a foot below.

"Surely. I'm not drunk enough to call a taxi yet," he said.

The girl with the purple hair smiled again. "Could I get another one too, please?" she said.

Trixie stepped away from Noah and took her glass as well. "Yes ma'am, you may. What were you having?"

"Fireball!" the girl said, raising a small fist in the air. "I have a tab with another waitress though. Is that okay?"

"Yup! This is Tracy's section. I'll just let her know to get you another one."

"Thank you, sweet heart. You're the best!" the woman said, and fumbled in her small black purse for a fiver.

"Thank ya, darling," Trixie said, walking away with the five-dollar bill sticking up between her two fingers.

"So I guess you know her?"

"Nope. Never seen her before," Noah said, raising his eyebrows.

She giggled again. "Well you get special service. So what kind of name is Noey?"

"That's what I keep asking her. It's not my name. No clue where she got it."

"So I guess you come here often," the girl said.

He held up a finger and nodded. "Nice. I do. I love the local music scene." And now here it comes. Here's where she says, *'Well surely you've seen my band play. I'm the singer, you know?'* And then he would have to act like he hadn't. Or that he had forgotten. And that's where he drew the line. The game would be up then.

But she didn't.

"I can respect that. I dig it too. I try to make it out to see the bands as often as I can," she said. "Well, thank you for the pick-me-up. I needed it."

Noah pulled his chin back. "Huh? I didn't get to pick you up, though."

She leaned in and put her hand on his shoulder again, putting her mouth close to his ear. "Not yet, you didn't. Thank you for saying hi to me tonight."

He bowed in her direction, bending a few inches forward. "It has truly been my treasure," he said, putting his palms together like he was about to bless her.

"The treasure is all mine," she said, that hundred-dollar smile painting her mouth again.

"I know it is. That's the real reason I came over here."

"You're in the top scores list now, darling," she said, smiling widely. "I didn't get your name though!" she said. She reached out and shook his hand, for real this time, since he no longer had a drink. Her touch lingered a while longer than standard protocol required for a handshake. Her hand was soft and warm. Dry. Small, but with long fingers. Her touch felt good to his palm.

He breathed in deeply, lifting up on his belt loops, looking around the room. "Yeah, most people don't. It's a lot like a James Joyce novel. You can read it a hundred times, but you never really get it."

She laughed out loud once again. "You are good," she said, shaking her head and furling her lips. You are too good." She clapped lightly, then added, "I should tell you though, I've read *Ulysses* and I actually understood it. So it's safe to tell me your name."

Noah pointed at her. *Damn, she's good.*

Doug appeared at Noah's right arm. "Hey man, Troy's here. We've got time for one game," he said, making the motion of running a pool cue. "Hi," he added, smiling at the girl with the purple hair. She waved merrily.

"Woop. Okay, gotta go," Noah said. He stuck his hand out again, awkwardly wiping it on his jeans first. "Make sure you tell Trixie that drink is on me, okay?"

"Okay," the girl said, looking a little lost. Clearly, he had achieved what he had wanted to. She was enjoying his company, and was crestfallen that this other guy could come up and take him away so easily. "So what is your name then, if it's not Noey?" she asked hurriedly.

"Oh. Sorry. It's Noah."

Trixie returned, a tray with only his drink on it. It looked to Noah like maybe she was trying to send a message to the poor girl with the purple hair. She couldn't have just gone ahead and brought her Fireball with his drink? He felt bad about that. Jealousy didn't have much room in his party. He took his drink off the tray then rolled his eyes as Trixie turned away. "Okay, I'm not sure what to do with this," he said, looking at his drink. "Do you drink Bourbon?"

She nodded quietly. "Sometimes."

He held it out to her between his thumb and forefinger. "You can have this one. Sorry she stiffed you."

"It's okay. I'll just wait for Tracy. I don't want to take yours!"

"I think they have more back there. Don't go thirsty. I insist." Noah still held it out to her.

She finally, reluctantly took it. "Thank you. You're very kind."

He shrugged and put his hands in his pockets. "It was nice talking to you, Lady with the Purple Hair."

"Nice talking to you, too!" she said, smiling resignedly. She tilted her head and held the drink up for a one-sided toast.

He smiled and leaned in close, then wrapped his hand over hers on the glass and tilted it to his mouth, taking a little more than a sip. He then released her hand and wiped his mouth. Meanwhile, she laughed and took her own sip. "What's your name, pretty lady with purple hair?" he asked, leaning in again.

"Tanis," she said. She slipped her arm around his neck. Perhaps his leaning in so closely had made her think that was what he was after. Whatever, she now had her arm round his neck and her mouth right in his ear. He could feel the moist warmth of her breath on his neck. "Tanis Ransom."

He looked up from his half-bent posture and kissed her on the jawline just below her left ear. "Stay cool, Tanis. You well define exotic." And then he walked away, leaving her standing there with a drink cradled between her hands, staring dumbfounded at the mystery man who had appeared out of nowhere.

2

The pool tables stood on the north side of the bar in an alcove off the main hall. There was no door, just a wide open room. Noah met Doug and Troy at the table and picked up a chalk cube as he leaned against the table watching Troy rack the balls.

"What's up, brother?" Troy said. When he finished racking, he came around to the side of the table and clapped Noah on the back. They shook hands. Troy was an old friend of his from high school. Not very good at pool, but he liked to believe he was. He would consistently play for money – sometimes ten or twenty dollars – but he never won.

"Howdy ho, bubs. Did you hear who's here tonight?" Noah asked.

"Yeah, Doug said you were making her giggle."

"No, dipshit. Not her. I mean with the band."

Troy frowned and began chalking his cue. "I thought she was with a band."

Noah sighed.

"Yeah, I heard," Troy finally said, a smile breaking into his otherwise plain features.

"You talking about Mikhail?" Doug said, rounding the table to collect the cue ball.

Noah nodded, leaning against his fists on the edge of the table. "Yeah. I guess it's a last-minute thing. He's supposed to stand in tonight. Should be interesting."

"In much the same way that Steve Vai standing in for Mike would be interesting at a Pearl Jam concert," Troy said, making a serious face.

Noah chuckled. "These guys used to suck, too."

Doug shrugged. "Suck no more. This is gonna be bad ass. Can I shoot yet?"

"Of course," Troy said. "Waiting on you."

"Would you like to move the rack then please?" Doug said, opening his hand over the table.

"Oh, shit. Sorry."

Noah reached over and plucked the rack off the table, tossing it underneath.

"So tell me," Doug said as he leaned over the table, "what's up with the purple-haired singer? Did you get her number?"

"Not yet," Noah said, glancing out into the main hall.

"Good luck with all that," Troy said, rounding the table to watch the break.

Doug broke the balls, sending two big ones into opposing corner pockets.

Noah shrugged again. "I don't know, man. She seemed pretty interested."

"Did you lay down a pickup line?" Doug asked, stepping to the side to take a shot on the eleven.

"Of course. That's the rule, right?"

Doug shrugged as he leaned over. "Just checking. That shit probably doesn't work with the rich and famous."

"Tanis Ransom?" Troy asked, frowning again. Doug made another shot. "You wanna leave me some balls to shoot, asshole?" After a moment, he said, "I think she's got a ways to go before you call her rich. Let alone famous."

"Well if they're not going anywhere, it ain't because of her," Doug said, hiking a thumb back over his shoulder. "

"So what'd she think of the pickup line?" Troy asked. He finally got a shot. And missed.

Noah shrugged. "I don't know, man. I kind of lost it when I started talking to her."

"Explain," Troy said with a frown. He was taller than Noah by about an inch, standing at close to six-four. He was skinny as a rail though. Noah guessed his waistline was probably close to Trixie's. And she only stood five-five. And weighed about as much as a bag of concrete mix.

"I don't know. I didn't really go over there to game her. I've always sort of been intrigued by her. So, yeah, I opened with a line, but I quickly tried to escape that crap. I want this to be real, but it kept falling back to smart-assery," Noah said, standing straight and running his fingers back through his hair. He glanced into the main hall again. Maybe there was a hope in there somewhere that she would be visible. Glancing occasionally into the billiard den. Trying to catch an unseen look at him. She wasn't.

"Uh oh. Getting a little deep, Wright brother," Doug said.

"Yeah, you might want to put the reigns on that, man. Don't want to see you get your heart broke. She's been dating some guitarist for about a year," Troy said.

"Guys. Guys, calm down. I'm not trying to date her. I just wanted to say hi," Noah said, holding his hands up.

"Whatever, bro. We're on your side," Doug said, taking a drink of his beer. He had switched from the liquor, apparently. "In fact, I'd love to see you pull that one in. She's a hottie."

"She's all right," Troy said. "I wouldn't say," he started, but Doug cut him off.

"What, dude? Says the man with no girlfriend?"

Troy held his hands up defensively. "I was just saying she's not even the hottest girl in the building."

"No, you started saying you wouldn't call her a hottie," Noah said.

Doug jumped in. "Yeah. Come on. She's hotter than anyone either of us has ever been with."

Noah caught Trixie's attention and waved her over. She waved back and flashed him a *hang on a minute* sign, then stopped at another table.

"Now there's a hottie, right there," Troy said, holding his glass up to his mouth.

Doug and Noah both looked back at her. "Trix? Dude, she's so available she might ask you out," Doug said.

"No shit. She hits on me all the time," Noah said.

"Give her to me," Troy said, then took a drink. "I would kill for a night with her."

Noah chuckled. "All yours, bro." She came into the room.

"Hey boys. What can I get ya?"

Trixie's black hair was long, maybe halfway down her back, but she kept it in a ponytail most of the time she was at work. She was in her early twenties, but looked like she had stopped growing in seventh grade. Some of the guys seemed to like that about her. Noah wanted more substance. Not to mention her annoying persistence. And he knew he wasn't the only one with whom she flirted regularly. She was pretty in a roundabout way. She carried herself well. Had a vibrant, bubbly personality, and that was attractive. She had brown eyes and dark eyebrows, which gave her sort of a mysterious look. But Noah, having turned 30 a few months ago, felt she was too young at twenty-three.

"A drink for me," Noah said. "What do you want, D-Rex? More sissy water?" he asked, pointing at Doug. The nickname seemed natural at the time Noah conceived it. His last name was Barker. They had been watching a dinosaur movie. The dinosaurs barked. A connection was made, and it stuck.

"Sissy waters for both of us," Doug said, waving between Troy and himself. "But we'll probably be on the floor."

Noah looked at his watch. "Shit. It's already time."

"That's cool, I'll find you guys out there," Trixie said, collecting the two empties. She looked around briefly for Noah's whiskey glass, then frowned. "Where's yours?"

He put his hands in his pockets. "Oh, I left it on Tanis's table."

"Oh. Okay," she said. Noah noticed she wasn't very good at hiding jealousy. And he didn't really know why she liked him so much. True, he had treated her nicely, and always tipped her well – always asked for her. But it had, when broken down, been a strictly business relationship. They hugged and squeezed each other's shoulders, winked, used pet names and all that. But there had never been anything beyond that. He had not, at least that he knew of, led her on in any way. Noah liked Trixie just fine as his cute little waitress. And yes, he did think she was cute. Cute as a basket full of kittens. That was always an added bonus, to have a fox come serve him and a table full of his friends a round of drinks. And maybe he had shown her off in that regard before. To friends who weren't regulars at the Sally, maybe he had tried to impress them with her adhesive nature. But God, he didn't want to lead her on. He liked it just fine when girls liked him, but he didn't want to lead anyone on.

Or maybe it was the new interest stealing all his adoration. Had Tanis really worked that deeply into his skin already? He shook his head as they made their way out to the floor. Clearly he had some soul-searching to do.

3

The crowd was already thick out on the floor in front of the stage. They were able to get close to the stage, though there were a few rows of bodies in front of them. The lights were still on and house music still blared through the high speakers, no low end on the sound range present at all. That was typical in rock concerts. When the act took the stage, the sound would therefore be a lot fuller and louder to the waiting crowd. Noah scanned the crowd occasionally, looking for his sisters as well as his new interest. His two little sisters usually came out for Mellow Nightfall gigs, but didn't always arrange to meet him. They would either run into each other, or not.

Noah thought back on his conversation with Tanis and wondered what he was really after. Why had he talked to her at all? It had been such a spur-of-the-moment decision that he didn't really have an answer for himself. He certainly hadn't planned it when he came in tonight. It almost seemed to him to have been a magnetic attraction. Like she had arrested his interest – fascinated him. The only interest he had previously had in her had been the standard share a man like him gave a woman like her. That was, a woman who sang for a band. There was just a certain amount of awe and intrigue there that he genuinely found interesting. Not being a music man himself, he was perhaps a little jealous of those who had it. He loved music down deep in his soul though, and found he could not live without it. He appreciated the talent it took to make it, and respected the hell out of those who did. He also attended a lot of live shows on that account. So of course, he had a special place for gals who could sing. Maybe everyone did, who knew? She was a singer. It naturally followed that he would be at least nominally attracted to her. But Noah had never spent any time thinking about her before tonight. Even on the nights he had seen her perform, there was only the passing thought. *What would it be like to have her sing to me during sex?* Things like that. Typical stuff. So why, then, had she attracted him so readily – so easily – tonight? She certainly had not been paying him any attention when he approached her. She had not, so far as he knew, even seen him until he walked up, out of the blue, and started making bad jokes. However she had done it, it had been successful. And now he could not stop thinking about her. The smell of the cinnamon on her breath; the few thin stray locks of black hair that had been too short for the hair tie falling against her pale neck; the way she opened her mouth widely, showing a perfect set of teeth when she laughed without really laughing… All of these things were attractive to him, but they were not the reason he had approached her.

The lights went down. The music dropped off. The crowd got loud in preparation for the coming show. Doug looked around and then leaned in real close, shouting in Noah's ear. "You ready, dude?"

"Hell yes!" Noah shouted back.

"Where is your sister?" Troy shouted.

Noah raised his eyebrows and shrugged. *Who knows? Furthermore, who cares?*

A whining guitar riff blasted into the noisy air, and then the spotlights started dancing. As the guitarist shredded strings in the relative darkness, fog blew in from the back of the stage. The rat-a-tat-tat of the drums kicked in and the show was off. The three men stood there tapping their feet and moving with the music.

There was something about these guys, Noah, thought, that kept him coming back. Their singer wasn't great. Not at all. But he had excellent presence on the stage. He knew how to keep the crowd involved and interested. They had been in the studio lately, and were supposed to have an album out soon.

Most of their music was dirty, grungy rock with hard-hitting beats and grinding rhythm guitar runs. When they broke down for the occasional melodic ballad, lighters and phones lit up the smoky air like stars over a foggy lake. The fans were definitely into it. The singer paced back and forth on the stage, leaning into the crowd, blasting out vocal melody, occasionally holding the mike out for the crowd to sing along. And sing they did. It was an amazing show, full of the ups and downs one got at a bigger venue, a national act band. But these ups and downs were more intimate. The smaller stage and closer proximity to the fans made it personal. After a ninety-minute set, they took a break, then returned for a three-song encore. In this return to the stage, they played two fan-favorites: hard rockers with lots of edge. And then they finished with a surprise.

Noah stood watching as the lights went down for the third song. And as they came back up, an acoustic guitar rang out in a sweet melodious chord progression that he thought he recognized, but could not quite place. He could now finally see in the spotlight, the guitarist sat atop a speaker box with a twelve-string. He strummed beautifully as the light faded from blue to purple to red and back. Then the bass player stepped up to the microphone. Where the hell was the singer?

"Ladies and gentlemen, we have a special treat for you. Please welcome my friend to the stage. She's gonna close us out with a little throwback to something a little softer."

What the hell? Noah frowned.

"Please welcome my friend, Tanis Ransom."

The crowd, of course, went wild. Noah's heart dropped to his stomach. Somewhere during that fall, it had also managed to stop beating momentarily. His jaw fell slack as he saw the tall slender figure of the girl he had been talking to earlier in the evening. She appeared like a specter out of the fog and stepped up to the microphone. Noah found he was shaking his head. He looked down and noticed Doug was looking at him over his shoulder. He had a smirk on his face. Noah shook his head, shrugged. He had no idea she had been planning to play with these guys tonight. As far as he knew, she never had. But then, he didn't know much.

He had certainly never seen it. And he had seen Mellow Nightfall several times.

He suddenly recognized the song as *Leaving on a Jet Plane*. He shook his head again. Unbelievable. Then he found himself clapping with the rest of the crowd. The rest of the suckers who hadn't seen it coming. She put on a classy British dialect as she accentuated each word carefully, holding up fingers as if to pinch the words out of the air in front of her. Her eyes were closed as she rocked slowly back and forth. It was a much slower version than John Denver's original. It was slow and melodic. The first verse was just Tanis and the guitar backed by a light drum beat. Then after the first chorus, the bass joined in. And for the second chorus, an edgy, dirty electric piano kicked in and grinded along as she rose to the song's climax. The guitarist and bassist both joined her in a third and fifth harmony on the microphones. Chills shot up Noah's spine. "Good God," he said to himself. "Incredible." He obviously wasn't the only one thinking so, either. The crowd was eating it up; singing along, raising their hands and swaying with the music. More fog. More sound. More instruments joined the fray. A cello? A harmonica was in there somewhere too. Noah found he was getting tears in his eyes as they ran Tanis's vocals through a vocal processor: for the last chorus, her voice was tripled through the speakers. A sweet, gorgeous melody broke through the night as the guitar screamed in the background in perfect clarity, a sad, lonely underline to the words it supported. It was perfect. Previously, Noah would have bet money no one would have made it sound better than John himself. Now he was sold. And he realized suddenly that tonight was probably the worst night for him to have seen her perform like this. He was already weak in the knees thinking about her. If he was wondering before if he liked her, this had just made it painfully obvious. As the vocals ended, the spotlight on Tanis faded out so one could only see her silhouette writhing slowly in the blue darkness, arms above her head, snapping soundlessly – a dark shadow of beauty and femininity moving with the liquid perfection of an art born of the blood. One could not learn this kind of fluidity. This was innate to the incredible being on the stage. This was her nature. And God, was she beautiful. He could see no actual details of her face or body. Just a perfect black void of light against the eerie stage light that shone from the back of the set. But that perfect shadow was more beautiful than anything he had ever seen. The way it moved – the music, the clarity of the sound.

When the hell had they planned this? She had, of course, known the whole time they were talking that she would be on this stage tonight. She had never let on a single hint. Not even a hint that she was a singer. Had he not already known he might never have. But he had had no idea this was coming. She was either that confident that he would stick around for the last song of the night, or simply didn't care. Maybe she just wasn't that person who tried to impress people with her music. Well, she didn't need to try. That, he realized, was an absolute. He shook his head again, stunned.

The song ended and the lights broke into the darkness. She smiled a wide, pretty smile. It forced a smile onto Noah's face too, but he realized it wasn't her special open-mouth smile. The one she had shown him several times earlier. Part of him was happy she had reserved that one. She reserved that one for more intimate settings. And maybe for him. He could pretend, anyway. Yeah, he was smitten. But now he was nodding as he joined the crowd, clapping, whistling, shouting. People were screaming, jumping, waving arms, chanting her name. She waved for a few seconds, then blew a kiss to the crowd and turned, disappearing into the darkness behind her, and off the stage. Only stayed long enough to say thank you with a wave, then disappeared. Classy. Not overdone. Noah took a deep breath. Wow.

Doug was looking at him again. "You okay?" he shouted, smiling wildly.

"No," was all he could say. He smirked and looked at his watch. The band was waving and saying their thank-yous and good-nights. Noah jerked his head toward the door. Doug pulled his head back toward the stage and raised his eyebrows. Noah shook his head. They made their way to the door, Troy following closely behind. He was busy on his phone.

Once they broke through the doors into the cold night air outside, Noah turned to Doug. "Well, that was a pleasant surprise."

"You seriously didn't know she was singing tonight?" Doug asked.

"Hey guys, I gotta run. I'll catch you tomorrow," Troy said, shaking their hands and heading for his Jeep.

They said their goodbyes and stopped behind their own Jeeps. Doug drove a Cherokee. Noah's was a two-door Wrangler. Both were lifted, big tires, huge clearance. A light snow was starting to drop. Noah held out his hand and caught a few of the tiny flakes. They melted as soon as they touched his hand.

"I had no idea, man. Did you?" Noah asked.

"Oh yeah. We talk all the time, bro."

"Whatever dude. Seriously, she didn't say anything about it."

"That's cool, man. She's humble."

Noah coughed. "You think? I think she played me like a fiddle. She knew I would stick around and see her on stage."

Doug shrugged, hands in his pockets. "Either way, man. That was completely bad ass. John Denver? Who the shit closes with John Denver?"

Noah pointed his keys at the club in front of their Jeeps. "Those guys. And they got away with it."

"No shit," Doug agreed. "See you at home, man."

"Yep," Noah said. "I'm gonna go home and shoot myself."

Doug laughed out loud then slammed the door of his XJ.

Noah sat in the seat of his Wrangler, letting it warm up, hands between his knees, rubbing some warmth into his palms. He shook his head again. This girl was going to drive him crazy.

He went right to bed. It was just after one o'clock when his head his the pillow. Not especially late for a Friday night. Certainly not unheard of on a night when he closed the bar to watch a band. But by seven o'clock when the sun started warming his blinds, Noah had not gotten so much as a wink of sleep.

4

"Did you see that show last night?"

"Yeah. I was there."

"You were? I looked but I didn't see you! Of course, we were packed in there like sardines."

"Where were you?"

"We were back about fifty feet from the stage, right in the center."

"Yeah, the boys and I were like three rows from the front," Noah said.

"You lucky dog! You should have texted me! I got there too late," Lennie said. Lennie was Noah's younger sister. The middle child of three, she and Noah had the most in common. They spent a lot more time together than did he and his baby sister, Lisa. Lisa was twenty-five, and two years Lennie's junior.

"I looked for you, but like you said, it was crowded. I figured you were catching it though."

"Oh yeah," Lennie said. "I caught it. Did you see the last song? That girl Tan-"

"Yes, I saw it, Len. Listen, I'm still in bed. Can I call you back in a little while?"

"Yeah, sure. Later, bubba."

"Later, sis," he said, and hung up the phone. The truth was, he wasn't still in bed. Noah was standing in his kitchen, looking out the window at the snow in the back yard. His grass was white with it. He held a steaming mug of coffee in one hand. His other rested on the granite counter top. He didn't want to be reminded of Tanis. He didn't need any help bringing her back to the front of his mind. She had scarcely left it.

The phone rang again. He sighed as he looked over at it, sitting there on his counter. He expected the bright screen to read "Lennie" again, but it didn't. It was Troy.

"What's up T-Roy?" Noah said. He took a mouthful of scalding coffee, swallowed, then leaned his head back. He ran his longish hair back with his other hand, then stared at the ceiling, where a cobweb blew lazily in a non-existent breeze. It stretched from the light fixture to the wall. The joys of a bachelor pad, he thought.

"The roads are icy," Troy said.

"No shit?"

"Yeah, man. Get your boots on."

"All right," Noah said.

"Is Doug home?" asked Troy.

Noah turned and looked over his shoulder into the living room. Doug was still asleep on the couch, the TV blasting silent light into the darkness. He had come to the kitchen through the dining room, as was his typical route on a late night, so as to avoid waking the cranky D-Rex. "Yeah, he's here."

"Wake him up! We've got work to do!" Troy said.

"All right, man. We'll meet you on the road," Noah said.

"Meet me at Oscar's. I'm gonna grab an omelet."

"Got it," he said, and hung up. Then, turning toward the living room again, "Doug!"

Grunts and moans emanated from the living room, and then Doug was sitting up, wiping his eyes. "What's up, dude?"

"Get dressed, fool. It's icy out."

"No shit?" Doug said, trying to locate a window. There wasn't one – nor had there ever been one – in the living room. He seemed surprised at this. "What time is it?"

"Almost eight. We're meetin' Troy."

"Where at? The Lamplighter?"

"Oscar's."

"That boy and his omelets," Doug said. He was already pulling his boots on. He had slept in his jeans.

"That boy and his everything. You know how neurotic he is with repetition. The safety of routine and structure."

"No doubt," Doug said. He tied a lace off and stood up. "All right, lemme throw a piss and gargle."

Noah turned to look at him. "You want coffee?"

"Does the Pope shit in the woods?"

Noah held up his hands. "All right, sorry."

Noah and Doug pulled up to Oscar's and got out, leaning against the hood of Noah's Wrangler, waiting on Troy to come out. They knew he wouldn't be long. He took his omelets to go, wrapped in a large flour tortilla. They had found the Jeep parking as soon as they entered the parking lot. It was a sort of unspoken code between Jeep owners. They parked together, whenever possible. Troy's rig, another lifted Wrangler, was a four-door. Between the three of them they had all facets of the Jeep trade covered. All three Jeeps sat running, staying warm for the task ahead. They were dressed in light waterproof orange jackets. Snow boots. Thick cargo pants. Dickies. It almost looked like uniform.

"Did you get any sleep?" Doug asked.

"No. Damned if I didn't try though."

"You're kidding."

"No. Dude, it's terrible. I'm not this emotional over girls."

"Oh, I know," Doug assured. "The last time I saw you crazy about a chick was in grade school."

"Heh. Yeah. Stella," Noah said.

"That little girl had you doing loops."

Noah leaned his head over, nodding with the memory. A pleasant smile on his face. "Yeah. Man, she was a looker. If you've never been thirteen, in love with a girl you've never touched, and listening to *Hysteria* to lock it all in, then you haven't experienced that craziness."

"I guess I haven't. Great song. I envy you that."

"It's the best feeling in the world. Every time that song comes on, it's hers. Stella owns it now. Every time I hear it, I think of her. And that new-love that never developed. She broke up with me before we ever even kissed. It's also terrible torture though," Noah said.

"Yeah, F that. When I fall in love, I want it to be once," Doug said.

"Dude, I was thirteen. I didn't know what love was. I do now though. That's sure as shit what it was."

"So that's where this girl Tanis is?"

Noah shrugged. "I don't know, man. I'm not in love with her. I can tell you that. But I'll never hear *Leaving on a Jet Plane* the same again."

They both laughed out loud.

"What's up tonight?" Doug said after a minute.

"Troy's house. Fire pit. Pirate Flag," Noah said. The three of them had brewed a batch of pale ale four weeks before. Troy had, apparently, bottled it a couple of weeks ago. It was ready to drink.

40

"Sounds like a plan. Where is that little bitch?" Doug said, turning just in time to see Troy's lanky, awkward frame come out the door. At nearly six-four, he was almost entirely made of legs. His jeans looked like stilts. He waved with one hand, a Styrofoam box in the other.

"Mornin' boys," Troy said as he got closer.

"We ready, omelet master?" Doug said.

"Meat and mushrooms and onions and cheese. And yet you find a way to make fun of it," Troy said, slinging open the door of his Jeep.

"Let's go find some damsels, shall we boys?" Noah said, climbing into his own rig.

"See you on twenty-three," Doug said, opening his door.

Troy was standing inside his door. He turned to look at them, a mouthful of omelet burrito. "Dennis is meeting us out there. Keep an eye out for him."

They closed their doors and backed out. Troy hopped in and drove forward over the grassy parking median instead of reversing. No need to be boring. And they were off. As they pulled onto highway 3 from Livingston Road, they were together, a single file of monster Jeeps rumbling up the highway. But over the course of the next few miles, each of them split off in turn, taking a u-turn under the bridge and heading back the other direction. All of them were looking for stranded motorists off in the ditches. These people would slide off the road and into a ditch, and then sit there waiting potentially hours for a tow truck. This small team of mercenaries ran up and down highway 3 and highway 233 looking for trouble. When they found it, they performed a rescue. Troy and Doug both had winches on the fronts of their Jeeps. Noah carried a long tow rope.

After an hour of scouting, keeping in touch with the others by CB radio, Noah spotted a blue TJ rolling slowly along in the right lane. He pulled up beside the Jeep and honked. Dennis looked over and smiled, waved. Noah picked up his handset and keyed the mike. "Find anyone yet?"

Dennis keyed his own. "Not yet. How long you guys been out?"

Noah replied, "About an hour."

"Where you at Double-D?" Doug said over the radio.

"Your boy Noah just found me over here by the Schooner Head. Where are you guys?"

"Think I got one, boys." That was Troy.

"What's your twenty, T-Roy?" said Doug.

"Meet me between Holland and Roberts. Mount Desert. It's a doozy, guys. We got a six-wheeler trying to rescue a Caddy."

Dennis held up a fist, then the moment broke and he showed his winning smile. His friend Randy was riding shotgun. He waved at Noah, then fell in behind him as Noah waved back and took the lead. They exited onto the 233 and made their way up to Roberts Drive. There on the shoulder was, sure enough, an exciting rescue. It was no damsel in distress, but, hey. Anyone in need was a good pull, they said.

Troy was out talking to a man behind a one-ton Chevy dually pickup. The man was short and stout. He wore a heavy jacket and a camouflage ball cap. He had a heavy mustache that covered his entire mouth. His pickup was down in the ditch just in front of a four-door Cadillac Coupe DeVille, inside which sat a man of about seventy with his family. Noah pulled up beside the truck, right behind Troy's rig and pulled it out of gear. He stopped and pulled the parking brake then rubbed his hands together.

"This is gonna be a good one!" he said on the CB.

"Amen, brother," Dennis replied.

Noah pulled on his gloves and got out. He shook Dennis's and Randy's hands and then headed down to Troy while the other two waited by Dennis's Jeep. "Where do you want us, boss?" Noah asked.

Troy turned to look at them, still talking to the man. After a minute, he turned and walked toward Noah. "I'm gonna turn around and winch him. You get behind me and rope me up. Dennis might need to come in beside you. We'll just have to see. This guy's empty weight is thirteen thousand pounds."

"Nice. D-Rex should be along shortly. I guess he can yank the Caddy?"

"Yeah," Troy said, hopping up into his four-door. He whipped it around and immediately started sticking in the snow.

Noah laughed and backed up, pulling up behind him. He hopped out and grabbed his tow rope and started strapping up, with about thirteen feet between their bumpers. He hooked the rope back onto itself and then got back in the cab. Dennis and Randy stood watching. Doug was coming from the other direction. He cut across the median and behind the line of rigs, dropping right down into the ditch and turning around. He pulled to a stop just behind Dennis and got out. Noah watched them as he listened for Troy's cue from the radio. After about five minutes of pulling the cable from the wench and strapping it to the truck's undercarriage, he gave the call.

"Pull, Noh," he said.

Noah dropped into four-wheel-low and slipped into first gear. He kept tension against the rope as Troy started backing up, pulling on the winch simultaneously. He had the long remote cord running through his window so he could control it while behind the wheel. He was pulling with the traction of his Jeep while the driver of the truck spun his wheels. Every time he would gain an inch of traction, Troy would tighten the slack on the winch cable so the truck wouldn't slide back. And Noah would pull up the slack in his rope, keeping Troy from sliding forward, back toward the ditch. It was a long, laborious process, but that was what these guys lived for.

After ten hard minutes of pulling and spinning, the truck got traction and tore off out of the ditch, throwing earth and mud and snow back into the ditch behind him. They all got out shouting and celebrating. High-fives and handshakes abounded. When they were done with the truck, Dennis pulled up in front of the Cadillac and attached his winch hook to the frame. Doug did the same thing Noah had done, backing up and throwing a tow rope between the two Jeeps. And within a minute, the Cadillac was back up on the road.

Both men – the man in the truck and the man in the coupe – tried to offer money to the rescue squad. No one accepted it. That wasn't why they were out here. For the Pull Crew, it was an opportunity to do a little winter off-roading on public property and roads. During off-road season, they had to go way out of town to hit the trails. Here they were actually performing a service. The police liked them. It made their job easier. It saved people a bunch of money, and made shorter days for the tow truck drivers. All around it was a win-win.

After three more light rescues, the Crew met at the Lamplighter for lunch and a cold beer. It had been a good morning on the roads, all around. As Noah finished his shark steak sandwich, he realized he had made it through a whole morning without thinking about Tanis. His heart jumped in his chest as he realized that. Then he took a swig from his beer and went back to forgetting about her again.

5

The fire was hot on their feet and bright in their eyes. They sat around it with boots propped up on the hot stone, spitting into the fire, staring at the flames, drinking beer and shooting the shit. A steel tray sat on one side of the pit, several brats still sizzling on it. They had burned the bratwursts in the fire and eaten them neat, no bun or dressing of any kind. It complimented the fresh-squeezed pale ale.

"Good beer," Doug said, holding up his bottle.

"Hell yes," Noah said, raising his own. "What was the yield?" he asked.

Troy was sitting forward in his chair, chewing on a brat. He licked his fingertips then studied them. "Fifty-four bottles. You boys drink up."

"Doing my part, man," Noah said.

"Yeah. Shit. This swill is going down like water," Doug said.

The three men had known each other since time out of mind. Noah and Doug had met before they could run in a straight line. The boys quickly became good friends: troublemakers who ruled the neighborhood. It was, therefore, surprising when Troy moved to town in the third grade and became the leader of the threesome. In a group of more than two, a leader naturally rises to the top. Troy was the smartest. The loneliest, nerdiest, most well disciplined. How he had stepped into the commanding position, no one could quite well define. But it sure had happened.

They now lived in an entirely different state from which they were born and raised. But their pact kept them together. They all went to college together then moved out to Maine together. Troy had gone into finance. He made more money than the other two, so he had his own house. Noah and Doug rented. Noah was a freelance web designer, working several hours a week from home while Doug worked as a maintenance supervisor for an apartment complex. Troy had opened a four-wheel-drive shop, outfitting Jeeps and trucks with big tires and lift kits. And so the spirit was born. They all found a passion for off-roading and big rigs. They all bought Jeeps – arguably the best off-road vehicle available – and started outfitting them. The goal was to defeat any challenge that might ever stand in their way. There should be, at the end of the day, no hill – no ditch, no wall, no ravine or mud hole – that could stand in their way.

"How long you think these times will last, boys?" Noah asked, staring at the fire. He was fascinated by the oddity of the human eye, and how it was attracted to the brightest point of light in whatever range of vision was available.

Troy looked up at him, his bottle hanging loosely between a thumb and forefinger. "You mean the fires?"

Noah raised his eyebrows, held his hands up, shrugged. "The fires, the rescue squad, the hanging out, the brewing beer… All of it. When do we grow up? When do we grow out of it?"

Troy made a face. "Why do we gotta grow out of it? I thought this was the point of it all. We busted our asses in school to get jobs so we could end up here, doing this."

Doug raised his bottle. Noah could see across the pit that he was staring at the fire as well. "True," Doug said. "That's some shit right there."

"You know, to me, the whole point of life is to get somewhere where you don't have to be anywhere."

Noah thought about that for a moment, dissecting it, rolling it around in his head. "You mean, like permanently?"

Troy shrugged. "Yeah. Sure. You maybe have a doctor appointment once a year. The rest of the year?" he held his palms up, beer bottle dangling. "Free. You don't have to be anywhere. Ever. That's the whole damn point of life."

"Man, that's some good shit," Doug said. He leaned forward, holding his bottle out. Troy clinked his bottle to Doug's.

"Don't you agree? I mean, isn't that what we all want, guys?" Troy said.

"Yeah, man. We agree. So in that case, it looks like we made it," Noah said.

"Okay, Barry," Doug said, smirking.

Noah looked up at him and chuckled. "You know, everything we say could be the lyric in someone's song, come to that."

"That's probably Elton John right there," Troy said, pointing at him. They all laughed out loud.

They all sat in silence for a while, staring at the fire, listening to its crackles and pops.

"You know what's best about these times?" Doug finally said.

"No girls allowed?" Troy asked, looking at him.

"No girls allowed," Noah said, holding his bottle up. The others held theirs up as well.

"Amen to that shit," Doug said.

They all shared a smile and a drink. "Dude, turn it up," Doug finally said. The bluetooth speaker they left out by the fire pit was passing on the tunes from Troy's phone like a musical messenger. Troy turned it up a few clicks. Bruce Springsteen was singing about the Glory Days. Apropos.

Music was the other major thing the three had in common. They had been attending concerts together since they had been old enough to drive. It didn't seem to matter what kind of music was playing: country, blues, rock – they were interested. As long as it sounded good, they would give it a chance. Troy seemed to be the least involved of the three of them, though he never said anything. It just seemed to Noah that if someone ever had to tell someone else to turn something up, then someone didn't quite get it. He and Doug certainly never had to tell each other to turn anything up. They could be riding together in one or the other's Jeep, in the middle of a heated conversation, and any one of a number of songs could come on, and one of them would turn it up, immediately pausing the conversation. Nothing needed to be said. It just was. And it was understood. Music was always playing in the background, and music trumped all. No conversation they could be having was so important it couldn't wait four minutes for a song to finish.

The three of them had seen several hundred concerts and shows together. And it seemed that Lennie, Noah's little sister, had the same bug. She begged Noah to take her to shows before she was able to go on her own. And even still, sometimes she would ask to ride with him, just to experience the effect of music on a group of friends. She would grab a few of her friends and show up at Noah's house an hour before downbeat, pumping him for information. "When are we leaving?" "Who's opening?" "What time is the headline?" He was proud to have her along.

Being three years his junior, there were many nights growing up when Lennie had watched her brother leave for a show, too young to get through the doors. But once, when Noah was eighteen, he had worked at a music store selling vinyl to college kids. He had some connections there. Bands would come through pushing their own material, or looking to browse the rack to support their peers. This put Noah in touch with the local talent. They were always inviting him to their shows.

One particular night, when Lennie's favorite local band was playing downtown, Noah had taken her. Lennie had been listening to the CD on repeat for months and months, just eating it up. Every time he would come home from work, Noah would hear the music blasting through her door. Noah arranged with the guy who would be working the door to let her in. As they approached, Noah had slapped the guy on the shoulder, holding out a ten-dollar-bill – twice the cover.

"Hey, buddy, how's it looking?" The door man had turned his head to look into the club while the fifteen-year-old Lennie shuffled right by him. She wasn't a problem. She didn't try to drink or cause problems of any kind. And she knew the songs better than most of the other people in there. It only made sense to Noah that she should get to see them live. She deserved it. She had earned it. When you spin a record that many times, when you know every word of every song before you've ever seen them live, you have earned your spot on the floor.

Noah finally took a deep breath and let a thought creep into his head that he had been holding out for a long time. He felt the cold slip down his spine as he considered it. Seven nights hence, One Last Orbit would be taking the stage at The Sally. Any time Orbit played, Noah, Doug and Troy – and usually Lennie – were there. So this particular date had already been on their calendar for a long time. But now it seemed to mean something more.

One Last Orbit was the official band for which Tanis Ransom was the singer. She stood in with other bands occasionally. She was, apparently, a hot commodity. The performance last night had been the first time he had seen her with another act, but he had heard about it several times before. She got around like a rumor in a nursing home. And he was trying not to be a girl about it, but something about her had captivated him. How would it be at the show? Would she talk to him afterward? What if she saw him from the stage? Would she look at him? Smile? Would she wave at him? Would she stick around afterward?

"Penny for your thoughts," Doug said suddenly.

Troy and Noah burst out laughing.

"Seriously? Did you just say that?" Noah said.

Doug was laughing too. "It just seemed like the thing to say. You got so quiet. So pensive!"

Noah took a drink of his beer, then dropped the bottle into a cardboard box between his and Troy's chairs. They kept the bottles so they could use them again. He cracked his neck. Troy's dog, a black lab named Chief, stood up beside Troy's chair and stretched his back legs, then moved a little farther from the fire. He was always near during a fire.

"Yeah, honestly, I was just thinking about last night."

"Figured," Doug said, not condescendingly. "That trip really got your thick, didn't she?"

"God, I guess," he said, shaking his head, scratching the back of his neck. "It's crazy."

"What about your girlfriend?" Troy said.

"It's not about my girlfriend, Roy. That's not the point," Noah said, looking at him directly.

"Then what the hell is the point?" Troy said.

"I just can't stop thinking about her."

Doug handed his bottle butt-first to Troy. Troy took it and dropped it in the box. Doug then got up and stepped over the edge of his chair to a dark spot to take a leak on the grass.

"So what are your plans with this gal, then?" Troy said. He was leaning forward, elbows on his knees, rolling his bottle between his palms.

"He was just playing the old pickup game," Doug said over his shoulder.

Noah looked up at him and made a sour face, flipped him off. "Okay, listen. When you spend thirty minutes talking to the hottest girl you've ever met and she actually seems very interested, don't you think that's worth fretting over a little bit?"

"And she is a singer. You're hot for the chirps," Doug said. He shook and zipped up, then turned back to the fire. "The man does have a point, Roy."

Troy looked up at him. "No, Doug." He was shaking his head. "No, he doesn't. He didn't even get a number. He talked to a girl in a bar. A bar! And he's acting like Dawndy at a wedding."

"Dawndy? What the hell?" Noah said.

They both looked at him. "Western Wagons. Every time Dawndy goes to a wedding, someone takes her home," Doug said. "Come on. Wake up, dude."

"Oh. Shit. Yeah," Noah said, leaning back, rubbing his sweaty hair back from his forehead.

"Man, this chick's got you all effed up," Troy said. He leaned over his chair and grabbed a couple of bottles out of the big ice-filled bucket, then handed them out. "Maybe you have a case here."

Noah cracked his bottle open and tossed the cap in the general direction of the graveyard. "That's exactly my point."

"So, we know he has a girlfriend," Doug said to Troy, then looked at Noah. "But seriously – answer honestly," he said, pointing his bottle hand at Noah, "how much time have you spent thinking about Joy in the last twenty-four hours?"

Noah leaned back, shaking his head. "That's not fair. Totally not a fair fight."

"I rest my case," Doug said.

6

"Wake up, sleepy head!" Lennie was shaking Noah's shoulders, bringing him up from somewhere deep and warm. The reality he was leaving was far preferable to this bright one where there were headaches and confusing noises and little sisters shaking him.

"What? What the hell?" Noah said.

"Okay, grumpy butt. Time go get up," she said. She leaned over and kissed him on the cheek then left the room. From the hallway, she said, "Made you breakfast," and now he could smell the evidence. Noah sat up and looked at his alarm clock. Almost ten. He rubbed his face and took a swig from the glass of water on his nightstand.

The kitchen was bright. Lennie had opened the blinds in the nook and the dining room, giving the sunlight complete access to the typically dim area. Noah came in and pulled a chair out with his socked foot and sat down, putting his face in his hands. "What are you doing here, Len?" he said, not looking up.

"How long has it been since we spent a Sunday together?" she said, scooping some eggs up onto a bed of toast on a wide plate. She slid it in front of him then sat down with her own.

"That doesn't answer my question. Thanks for breakfast."

"Sure, bubba. I miss you. I thought we could hang out and watch a movie or something."

"You don't think you should check my schedule or anything?"

"Well, no. I mean, I called Joy and she didn't mind, so I think I'm covered."

"Man, this shit's good. What'd you put in these eggs?" Noah said, frowning.

"Well, if I told you, then you'd be able to reproduce it yourself, thereby alleviating any need you had for me. So," she said, holding a piece of bacon up for emphasis, "I'll keep my secrets, thank you." She popped the bacon into her mouth.

"You rock, little sis."

"You don't know the half of it yet, big bro," she said, pointing her fork at him.

"What? What are you talking about?"

She winked at him. "Just finish your breakfast. You'll see."

"See what, Lennie?" he said. He looked around the room then held his hands out. "What the hell are you talking about? What's with all the mystery?"

Lennie laughed out loud. She was having too much fun with this, Noah thought. And he didn't even know what *this* was. She reached over and put her hand on his arm and leaned forward, a mouth full of eggs. "Mmm! Mmm mmm!" she said, trying to communicate without opening her mouth.

Noah leaned back rolling his eyes. "Dude, what has gotten into you? Are you on something?"

She widened her eyes and nodded. "Mmm hmm!" Lennie washed her food down with a gulp of orange juice then said, "You bet!"

When he finally finished eating, she took his plate and tossed it into the sink, then grabbed his hand and pulled him into the living room. She pushed him onto the couch and looked around the room, hands on her hips. She then pointed at a small decorative pillow on the couch and said, "There, cover your eyes with that. You can't look!" Noah sighed and did as he was told, obediently putting the square pillow over his eyes. He leaned back and kicked his feet up on the coffee table.

"Is this gonna take long?" he asked, growing tired of the charade.

Lennie whined. "Come on, booger butt. I'm trying to do something nice for you. Can't you just play along?"

"Okay, okay, sorry," he said. He heard shuffling and bumps coming from the dining room, just on the other side of the wall behind him. And then he heard her shuffling into the living room and felt weight move the table.

"Okay, open your eyes!" Lennie said. He did. She was standing there with her hands clasped under her chin, smiling like a new mommy. He had to smile back at her.

Then he shook his head. "What? What are we doing here?"

She widened her eyes. "Oh my God! Do I have to spell it out for you?" She pointed down at the table. He finally looked down, and the smile fell from his face.

Noah leaned forward, suddenly serious. There on the table sat a beautiful classic turntable, in what appeared to be perfect condition. "Is that… are you serious right now?" he said, leaning even farther forward and lifting the smoked plastic lid with tentative fingers.

Lennie was bouncing now, her grin back in full force. "I remember a couple of months ago you said you've always wanted a record player, so I saved up and got you one!"

Noah sat back on the couch and looked up at her. "Damn, Lennie, this is awesome. Thank you. You are the coolest sister on the planet."

She giggled with delight, still clasping her hands together under her chin, then started swinging her foot a little. He looked down at it. She was pushing lightly against a big cardboard box he had stepped over to sit down. And hadn't even noticed it. It was full of records.

He sat forward again and pulled it closer to him, then looked up at her, seriousness in his eyes. He was speechless. Noah shook his head, then started fingering through the records. Doobie Brothers, Gerry Rafferty, The Who, The Rolling Stones, Eagles – it was all there. All the good ones. He felt a little glassy eyed, so he stood up and took his little sister in his arms. Her hug was enthusiastic.

"I love seeing you so happy!" she said in his ear.

"I don't know what to say, Lennie. This is amazing. Where did you get all this?" he asked, turning back to the box on the floor. He sat on the edge of the table and started sorting through them again. Billy Joel was there. Back when he had the afro. Steely Dan was there. Pink Floyd and Yes and Eric Clapton and Edgar Winter were there too.

"I stopped by a few garage sales," she answered.

"This is the best gift ever, dude. Seriously. How much did you spend here, Lennie?" he asked.

"About three hundred dollars, all told." Her smile had faded and he was sad he had reminded her of the cost.

"Wow. Okay, well go get my wallet off the mantel. You shouldn't be on the hook for all that."

"Oh, that's the whole point of a gift, bubba! If you paid for it, it wouldn't be a gift!"

56

"Bullshit!" he said, standing up. He took her by the shoulders. "Listen, Lennie. I know you don't make a lot of money at the book store. The gift here is the time and energy you spent getting me something for no reason. Let me at least help you out with it."

She looked at him for a long time. Deciding. He went and got his wallet and pulled out a couple of hundred-dollar bills, folded them and put them in her shirt pocket. "Really. Thank you. I don't care about the money. This music – this gift – is priceless. You really are the best."

"Okay," Lennie said, a tear forming in her eyes now. "Let's hurry up and get it set up!"

Noah pulled the entertainment cabinet away from the wall a few inches, found a free socket and plugged in the turntable, then connected it to the stereo. They got the space cleared off for it and he set Lennie to packing the records on a bottom shelf while he tidied up the living room. Having a new component in his sound system got him excited about being in the room again, so he wanted it to look nice. Chip bags and soda cans, beer bottles, pizza boxes and magazines all got rounded up. Within fifteen minutes they had returned the room to sales-floor shape and Lennie made herself comfortable on the couch. Noah went to the kitchen and filled a six-pack cooler with bottles of Pirate Flag he had brought home. Then he dumped ice in it and took it to the living room where he set it at Lennie's feet. At the mantel he opened a smiling gnome statue and took out a small bag. Then he put on *The Stranger*, from 1977 – arguably Billy Joel's greatest album – and dropped in right next to Lennie on the couch. Lennie had argued with him about that. She would say *An*

Innocent Man was Billy's best. He packed a pipe and handed it to her.

"You get first dibs," he said.

"Aw, you're so sweet," she said, lighting the first hit.

Noah grabbed two bottles from the cooler, popped them open, then sat back and put his arm around his sister. She leaned her head on his shoulder, then blew out smoke and handed him the pipe. She kicked her shoes off and put her socked feet up on the table right next to his. And that's where they stayed for the next five hours, only getting up to take bathroom breaks and change out the record. They smoked pot and drank beer until nightfall. And then Joy arrived.

She came in around seven o'clock. The sun had just started picking up its things and vacating the kitchen, and the house was beginning to get that warm cozy winter feel. A fire danced in the fireplace, quietly warming the gas logs. Joy had a wide smile on her face. She had known about the turntable and records. She had also quietly stayed away most of the day at Lennie's request, so the siblings could spend the day together doing what they enjoyed the most in the world. The two were connected by more than just blood. They were attached by music.

"So how is it?" Joy said to a drunk and high couple on the couch.

"Come sit here and check on it," Noah said, patting the seat next to him. He was moving in slow motion.

She took off her coat and dropped her purse in a faraway chair, then snuggled in under his other arm. "Which one is this?"

"Sticky Fingers. Just started it."

"Fine. Very fine. Are we enjoying ourselves?"

"Yes, we are. We're listening right," Lennie said and handed her the pipe. Joy leaned forward and lit the pipe, then grabbed a fresh beer and leaned back under Noah's arm again. He had refilled the small cooler before he put the Stones on a few minutes before. They were set for another round.

After a few more hours of this, Joy made a request, put on *Aja*, then they sat back and dug themselves in for the final period of waking. The three fell asleep on the couch under the warm blanket of music, firelight, alcohol and cannabis, snuggling close and listening quietly to the cracks and pops of the 33-speed album.

7.

Lennie woke up first. She was still under Noah's arm. She sat up and let his arm drop to his side. She then pushed on his thigh and whispered in his ear. "Bubby, I gotta go to work."

As his eyes lazily came open, he realized he was missing his left arm. He looked down at it and saw that it was still there, but he had no control over it. He then tried to bring his right arm to the rescue, to find out what was going on. It was still over Joy's shoulder, but he couldn't move it either.

"Oh, God, my arms are asleep," he cried. "What time is it?"

"Ten 'til seven," Lennie said, sitting up straight on the couch and pulling her hair into a ponytail.

"So we've been sitting here for seven hours with my arms up like that? Shit. I might lose them both." He leaned far over to the left until his arm flopped down from Joy's shoulder, then leaned forward, dragging them off the couch. Blood started flowing into them bringing hard biting pinpricks all throughout his hands and forearms.

Joy leaned back stretching and yawning. "You getting out of here?" she asked Lennie, who was standing up and putting on her coat.

"Yeah. Gotta be at work in an hour," Lennie said, her mouth crunched into disappointment.

"All right. Well I had a blast hanging out with you guys. We'll have to do this again sometime."

Lennie pointed at her. "You got that right. Talk old Mr. Grumpy here into inviting me over sometimes and I'll make sure of it!"

"Sister, you're invited any time you want. You brought the music," Joy said.

"Damn right," Noah agreed. "What she said." His arms were slowly coming back to life.

His sister leaned in and gave him a peck on the cheek, then said bye and disappeared out the front door.

Joy turned and looked at him, pulling her own hair back over her shoulders, running fingers through it like a comb. "You have any work today?"

"Yeah. I have a couple of things. I need to finish this guy's shopping cart. Couple other things. No big deal. You work tonight?" he asked. Joy played hostess at a steakhouse, and was so good at her job that she actually got tips. It equaled out to be a fair amount of cash at the end of the weeks.

"Yup. Six o'clock," she said. It was always six o'clock for her. The steakhouse opened at seven nightly, so her hours – when she worked – were always the same.

"Cool. Well I should be done with my crap by noon or so, so we can go catch a flick or something."

"Sounds like a plan, hero. I'm gonna hop in the shower though," she said.

He looked her up and down. "I guess that's probably an all-around good idea."

He joined her.

When they were out of the shower, Noah sat on the bed looking at the calendar on his phone. He had enough work designing websites to keep him busy full-time if he wanted it. He opted, rather, for twenty or so hours a week at a higher price. If they were willing to pay it, why not? He excelled at what he did, creative and bright. He was also extremely fast. He could turn around a whole site in a day if he got busy on it. So they did pay it, and thus he made enough to work half-time. Noah settled, therefore, for half the potential income. But he made enough to support his drinking and music habits. That's all he really cared about when it boiled down to roots. He and his friends spent a lot of time in the bars, which did take a considerable portion of his income. Not entirely on alcohol, either. There was food for the nights when it covered the dinner hour, and there were always the lurking cover charges. It cost money to see music, to support the local bands. And then when there were good new ones, he liked to pick up a copy of the album. His drinking was only moderate when he was out, so his bar rent, as he called it, was a fund he set aside for the whole picture. And alcohol only took up a small portion of that picture.

He had enough work booked for the week to spread out and keep himself busy for all five weekdays, but he didn't like to work on Fridays. He moved a couple of projects around, estimating the amount of time it would take to complete them. And a lot of his code he had saved in text files that he could reuse. In cases where he was able to reuse code, a quick replacing of a color code and a graphic or two would get the job close to completion before he even started loading content. And in those cases, he could tell people he made in excess of five hundred dollars an hour. They were rare, but they did happen.

Noah dragged his Thursday appointment to Tuesday and his Wednesday one to today. That gave him two things to work on today, and two tomorrow. He'd have to bust his ass for a few hard hours, but he could get it done. And that would give him a four-day weekend. And that meant an entire weekend before Saturday. And that meant he could take his girlfriend out Thursday and Friday, and maybe take her deep into his system, thereby pushing out any foreign thoughts before the Saturday-night show. He had to remind himself, after all, that he was just spinning his wheels thinking about Tanis anyway. She was out of reach. Out of his reach, at least. Just one of those friendly girls who would make anyone feel important. She would make anyone feel like he had a chance.

When Joy walked back into the room, he looked up and tossed his phone on the bed. He called her over, where she came to stand between his legs. He laid his head against her bare belly. She was wearing jeans and a bra. The blouse would come after she had finished blow-drying her hair.

"I want you to take off Thursday and Friday," Noah said.

She stood still a moment, and then put her hands on his head and pulled it back so she could look at him. "Why, baby?" she said, frowning. She smiled through it though, unable to keep anything unhappy on her face when she was with him.

"I'd like to have a weekend with you." They both knew she would always work on Saturday nights. In retail, if you were any good at all, you worked weekends. She was good enough to make more than some of the servers, and all she technically did was seat people.

"I'm already off Friday, so that should be easy enough. What's on your mind?" she asked, tilting her head.

"Let's go camping."

Her face got serious. "Camping? Honey, it's absolute zero outside."

"We can get a cabin with one of those wood stoves in it. Light a fire and play cards. Make love all night."

She looked at him through squinted, thoughtful eyes for a long moment, hands still on his head. "You know, that sounds absolutely fabulous." She leaned in and kissed him on the lips. "You promise you'll keep me warm?"

"If not from cuddling, then from friction, for sure."

She slapped him gently on the face, then pushed him back onto the bed and climbed on top of him. She leaned down, letting her wet hair fall in his face and kissed him again. Then she rested her chin on her hands, elbows out beside his head. Her nose was almost touching his.

"You make me so happy, you know that?"

He looked into her blue eyes, trying to read the thoughts behind them. Her words seemed true enough. "That's good. You know, that's my goal, right?" He had said the words. But he wondered if he really meant them.

The next two days were a fog of work and coding. Noah woke at six-thirty both days, ate breakfast, showered, then put on his work clothes and poured himself a strong cup of coffee and got to work. Working from home tended to make him feel like he didn't have a job sometimes, so he occasionally forced himself into the grind by putting on khaki pants, loafers and socks and a button-up shirt. He even combed his hair. He worked from seven until about two in the afternoons, then took a lunch break. Then he worked from two-thirty until about four-thirty, tightening up loose ends and testing the sites he had built. Then he uploaded them to his hostage server for show.

The hostage server was just a server with a generic domain name registered to it so he could send customers to his domain dot com, slash, whatever their site name was. That way if they didn't pay him, he could take it down. He had heard horror stories of web designers updating sites live on the customers' servers, and then not getting paid.

When he shut off his computer on Wednesday evening, he had finished four sites. He sent links to the four respective customers and walked away from work for a long weekend. He would check his email on Monday and get back to work. But for now, for the next ninety-six hours, he was a free man. Not a slave to the pager or the on-call phone like a lot of his friends in the

IT industry. He scooted back from his desk, cracked his knuckles, then cracked the top off a cold beer.

There were no cabins available, as it turned out. Noah had waited too long to reserve one. They would have to find a way to keep warm in tents instead. As they sat around the fire pit, he wondered if he had screwed up by inviting his buddies on the camping trip, then had to remind himself that Joy knew him. She knew what she was getting when he made plans like this. That wasn't to say he never had get-aways without his friends. He did. He had taken Joy to New York for a weekend. To Austin once for a whole week. And occasionally they would go somewhere locally and spend the night in a hotel room. But camping was just not something he was prepared to do without his Jeeping buddies. And Joy knew that. Still, he thought he sensed a little disappointment in her eyes when Doug had pulled into the parking spot. It was only a flash though, because as the passenger door of the Cherokee had swung open and Alice got out, Joy's eyes had lit up. She stood and spread her arms, opened her mouth wide and started cooing like a little girl at a cotton candy kiosk. Alice, the ever-vibrant sub-fiver, as Noah called her, hopped down and struck a pose, her old straw hat covering her eyes, before finally running and jumping up into Joy's arms. She wore her jeans tucked into her cowboy boots and a flannel shirt unbuttoned but tied over a tank top. The girls hugged and then wandered off down the road talking quietly. As they got to the edge of the campsite, Noah whistled, then held out his arms.

"What the hell?" he said.

Alice came running back to him and jumped up into his arms like she had with Joy, kissing him all over his face before dismounting and returning to her position with Joy on the asphalt. Doug finally got out of the Jeep and made his way over to Noah, shook his hand, then slung his backpack off his shoulder onto the dirt. Noah already had the fire built. And Doug already had an open beer in his hand. They exchanged talk of the last couple of days then bumped their beer cans together and dropped into camping chairs.

Now they were all sitting around the fire, boots up on the stone like they did back home, but now with the added bonus of females. They all gambled out loud about who Troy would bring to the fire. He usually stayed at the store until an hour or so after it closed, and would have to go in to work in the morning to get the shop opened. But he would be back Friday evening as well. He was always good for the evenings. And he always brought someone. Sometimes it was hired help. A stickler for the rules, he would not show up to a couples' event empty-armed. He did not have a steady girlfriend, but he had several friends who would stand in for the part on short notice, and, of course, the escorts when that was necessary. If nothing else, the boy was reliable.

"I bet he brings Daisy," said Alice. "We haven't seen her in a while. Plus, she's the loneliest."

"That's effed up. You think he brings her because she's lonely?" Doug said, looking over at his girlfriend in the darkness.

There was a period of silence that lasted about six seconds, followed by three voices saying, "Yeah," in unison.

Doug looked at them all. "Really, guys?"

"The guy has a soft spot for her," Noah said, shrugging. He took a pull from his beer. "He's said himself that she's annoying and clingy. He only keeps her around because he feels sorry for her."

"Come on, man," Doug said, looking out at the silhouettes of elms past the edge of the fire's influence.

"Hey, none of us is talking shit. But would you bring her for any other reason?" Joy asked him. Doug looked at her for a moment, looking like he was going to object, then finally made a face and looked down at his beer. Took a drink.

"I guess not."

They all laughed.

When the round headlights of Troy's Wrangler Unlimited finally pulled up, dust clouds wafting away in their gleam, they all got quiet, looking expectantly toward the brightness. The lights and engine stayed on for a long time before shutting off. Then a door popped and Joy said, "Oh!" quickly and they all giggled.

The suspense was thick.

But they all thought they had a pretty good feeling they knew who it was. Troy was a quiet enough guy that he never announced ahead of time who he was bringing, so it was always a sort of surprise. But this time it was a surprise of a different type. A silhouette came walking into the light of the fire with Troy, hands in her pockets, ears covered with a fluffy beanie cap.

"Hi, guys!" said Trixie.

"Hey, darlin'!" said Joy, standing up. Alice shot a glance at Doug, then Noah. Noah shrugged and widened his eyes. *No idea.*

Doug made a face then stood up, still staring at Noah until he finally turned around. "Hey ho! It's the girl with the tricks!"

Alice laughed out loud, but got up as well. They all took turns hugging and welcoming Trixie, then shaking Troy's hand. Noah remained seated. He reached into the cooler and pulled out an icy bottle, held it out to Troy.

"Thankee, sai," said Troy. He pried the cap off and tossed it in the fire. "What time did you guys get here?"

"This morning, fool. I took off today and tomorrow," Noah responded.

"Oh yeah. I think you told me that. Must be nice."

"Dude you own the shop. If you'd stop micro-managing, you could get away occasionally," Doug said, then took a pull from his beer.

"You don't know what it's like. I work with a bunch of imbeciles. I'm going to have to go through and clean house soon. Just start all over. Well, except for Blaine. That guy is coming up. He's the one guy out of fifteen that I can count on." Troy took a long drink of his beer, then set it on the stone next to the fire and walked to the back of his Jeep to get chairs.

Trixie made her way over to where Noah was sitting and stood in front of him just off to one side. "Hi," she said, hands still in her pockets.

"Hey, lady," Noah said. He half-stood and gave her an awkward hug, then dropped back into his chair. "Glad you could make it."

"Thanks. Glad to be invited," she said. She turned to look at the fire.

Noah looked over at Doug. They made eye contact. A knowing glance. *This could get weird.*

When Troy returned with the chairs, they set up in the open spots and everyone got settled back in around the fire.

"Ken Baxter died today," Troy said.

"You're kidding," Noah said. "When did you hear that?"

"Who the heck is Ken Baxter?" Trixie asked. Joy looked at her and frowned, nodding.

"The guitarist from Land Never Claimed," Troy said. "Heard it on the radio on the way in."

"Good grief," Doug said. "That sucks."

"How did he die?" Alice asked.

"Apparently he has been battling cancer for a long time," Troy said.

They all sat in silence for a few minutes.

"Terrible," Noah finally said. "It's been a rough year for music."

"Yeah. Syd Marx from Dreadwire, Will Street from," Troy started, then snapped his fingers.

"High Rise Fire," Doug offered.

"High Rise Fire," Troy agreed. "Hank Warner from Blue Street Beggars," he added.

"Yeah, rough," Noah said. "That was like the year all those other artists died real close together. David Bowie, Natalie Cole, Glenn Frey. Terrible, terrible couple of weeks."

Doug said, "I'll never forget the night Glenn Frey died. Man, I cried. It really hit me hard. I was coming home from work, and I tuned in the Lone Star. Well, they were playing *Take it Easy*. And I thought, cool. So I turned it up, leaned my seat back and dug in. It was a pretty evening.

"Then the song ended, and *Tequila Sunrise* started. And I looked at my radio. I stared at it for a moment. There wasn't a double-shot evening going on. Nothing like that. I mean, I know that station, right? We all do. They don't do shit like that. My stomach immediately dropped. And I knew something was wrong. I wondered who it was. The obvious thought was Joe Walsh. But after *Sunrise* the DJ came on and said they were paying tribute to Glenn. And my heart broke. I went home and cracked open a bottle of scotch and we sat back and listened to Eagles all night. Firelight and scotch, record player clicking and popping. It was a sad night, but we turned it into one of those memories you keep forever. It was fabulous."

A few of the group nodded and voiced their agreement. Then Noah said, "Yeah, that was a good night. Sad, but good. The entire landscape of rock and roll changed forever that day. Once all those rockers are gone, that's it."

"I agree," said Troy. "Music just doesn't have awakenings like it did in the seventies, man."

"The sixties and seventies. Totally," Doug said. "Well here's to Kenny Baxter," he said, and held his bottle toward the fire.

"Here's to all of them," Noah added. They all held their beers toward the fire for a few seconds, then drank in honor of the fallen heroes.

8

After a couple of hours around the fire, the girls got the idea to play hide and seek in the woods. It was dark, all the other campsites around them had long since grown quiet, and it just seemed like the thing to do. It took a while to convince the boys. The girls were begging and pleading, listing all the reasons why it was a good idea, but the guys just wanted to sit and drink. Then Troy saw an opportunity and texted the other two guys.

"Guys… we can scare the shit out of them," he sent.

As Doug and Noah read the text, several glances were exchanged, but the obvious underlying sentiment in that look was that they were sold. They finally agreed with the girls, reluctantly, and stood up stretching and warming their hands in the fire.

"So who hides first?" Doug said, pulling up on his belt loops.

"We do," said Joy and Alice simultaneously. The three gals were standing together, arms around each other.

"Yeah, it was our idea," Trixie said. "Right girls?"

"Totally!" they agreed.

"Okay, so you boys stare at the fire and count to a hundred. Then you holler before you come looking," said Alice.

"A hundred?" Doug said. "What the hell shit is that?"

"Yeah, seriously?" Noah agreed. "It shouldn't take you ten seconds to find a hiding place out here. It's darker than the inside of a cow."

Troy laughed out loud.

"We have to get far enough away, dork," Joy said.

"All right, snap to it, boys. Turn around and check on the fire," Alice said. Then they were off. Three sets of sound trekking off through the leaves and sticks in quick fashion.

"They don't even have flashlights, dude. Remind me how this is a good idea," Noah said.

"That means they won't go out far," Troy said. They have to stay where they can see the fire. Should make it easy."

"Yeah, and that way is a straight drop-off," said Doug, pointing at the cliff behind their campsite, about twenty yards back from the tent. The drop was about forty feet and went straight down to creek, which was probably frozen over.

"Piece of cake," Troy said, looking at Noah.

"All right. Have we counted to a hundred yet?"

"Close enough," Doug said. "I don't hear footsteps anymore."

"Let's do it," Noah said.

They took off in separate directions, walking quickly and as quietly as was possible through winter's bed. Noah went along the road, looking back toward the drop-off, scanning the dark trees as he walked. Almost immediately, he saw movement. He took off running and found himself chasing Alice. She started screaming as soon as she saw him coming, and ran away from the fire. Toward where it got darker.

"Where the hell you going?" Noah said, running through dangerous terrain, dodging branches just before they took his face off. "Fire's back the other way!" he shouted, taunting.

"Then go chase someone else!" she screamed, but kept running. They cut through another campsite, the embers of a fire still glowing in the fire pit. Alice ran around the picnic table but Noah jumped clean over it. He landed badly and almost twisted his ankle, but recovered before he went down. He caught Alice by the coat tail and pulled hard. She spun and screamed and they both went down. She landed on top of him laughing and screaming about how unfair it was.

"I got you, punk!" he said in her ear. His arms were tight around her.

"Let me go, creep!" she said.

"Hey! What the hell is going on?" a man said behind them.

Noah let her go and helped her stand up. He got up and brushed leaves off his jeans. "We had a runaway. Had to come capture her. She's not supposed to be loose in the wild; sorry about that," he said.

Meanwhile Alice laughed wildly and tried to go back the opposite direction, toward the fire. But Noah held her arm tightly. The man was staring at them, arms bowed out slightly, looking like he was ready for a fight. But Noah stood staring right back at him, a grin half-painted on his face.

"Let me go, bastard!" she shouted. And Noah could hear the play in her voice. But her words, he realized, sounded all wrong to the other man.

Then suddenly there were footsteps. Doug was there. "Did you catch her?" he asked as he ran up.

"Yeah, I got her. Might want to double-lock that cage tonight, Claud," Noah said.

Doug walked up and took her by the arm then looked over at the man. "Sorry about that. Hope she didn't piss on your tent or anything. She's a wild one."

"Stop it! You're not putting me back in that cage!" Alice shouted, slapping at Doug's chest and arms.

"Y'all have a good night," Noah said, touching the tip of his cap at the man. They started walking back. The other man just stood there speechless.

Alice was giggling as they re-entered their own campsite.

"Okay, clearly we need some ground rules before round two," Noah said.

"Yeah, like don't cut through other people's campsites?" Troy asked.

"And no screaming. Dear God, you were loud!" Doug said.

Alice giggled. She wrapped her arms around Doug, head coming up to about his shoulder, and held on like he was holding her up.

"Hey, where's Trixie?" Joy finally said.

Trixie wasn't far away. They could hear her laughing. And she wasn't trying to be quiet, either. She was just having fun. The girls looked at each other, then turned toward the sound and jogged off into the cooler darkness beyond the ring of the fire's light. The guys looked at each other chuckling. The girls had taken over the hide and seek game to the point where they were both the good guys and the bad. The men were free to stand here and drink. Score.

Shortly, they heard the girls call out again saying they were ready to be sought. All good things must end. They were on duty again. The men took a big drink from their bottles of beer, then set them down on the aluminum folding tables they had spread around the fire pit.

"Who's going where?" Noah said, rubbing his stomach, trying to ready a belch.

"Shit," Doug said, shaking his head. "I thought we were off."

"We all did. You go north," Troy said, pointing with the two shortest fingers of his left hand.

Noah was a little too high to be seriously considering the art of hiding so as not to be found. He felt like he should be doing everything in slow motion, with careful deliberation. Troy was spouting all this military-like authority and command and it wasn't going over well. "Wow. Dude, you're serious," Noah said.

Troy looked at him. "What, you're not?" he said, holding his hands up. "I'm not going to let those girls show us up out here," Troy said, throwing his finger against the ground respectfully.

Noah looked at Doug, then widened his eyes. "Wow!" he said under his breath.

"Yeah, dude, you're a little intense right now over a grade-school game. Let's click it down a notch. I'm not running anywhere," Doug said.

Troy's shoulders dropped and he inhaled deeply. They could see the fire drop out of his eyes. "Okay. Sorry. I just don't like to be beat by girls."

"Ahem," Doug actually said.

"Dude. Yes, you do. That's the whole entire meaning of life… is to get beat by girls," Noah said.

"You know what I meant, dipshit. I'm not into the S and M stuff," Troy said.

Noah held his own hands up and rolled his eyes. "Dude, I didn't mean slave and master. Beat, like bested. Like getting beat by a woman at something. You say you don't like it."

"No. Hell no. They're girls," Troy said, arm waving toward the woods into which the girls had disappeared.

"Trust me. That's the whole point in life is to get beat by girls."

"I just said that," Troy said. "I don't like to get beat by girls."

"Yes," Noah replied, "you do. Getting beat by a girl is a win for both of you. One, because she knows you let her win. But she acts like she doesn't. And you act like you don't. And two, she's winning. She's getting the gold medal. That makes her feel special. Any time a woman gets the best of a man, she's likely to celebrate."

Troy frowned at him. "Don't you think that's a little sexist?"

Noah laughed out loud. "Ha! Of course! That's the whole point!"

Troy gave him a look. How could this possibly make sense, it said.

"It's a primal thing, dude. In our DNA as humans. Not something a feminist will be able to beat down just because she doesn't agree with it," Noah said. He put his free hand in his pocket, and took a drink of his beer. "A female was built to be inferior in physical strength. Think about it. It's true. So down deep in her cells, her wiring, she wants to beat the other half of the species at it. She wants to be stronger." He took another drink of beer and waved his other hand around again.

"Like I said, it's primal. So, like I was saying, if you let them win, then that primal part of their nature – that part none of us can control – that primal part feels satiated. It achieved something only a man is supposed to be able to do. And if she feels like she won, you win. And you know that, Roy."

Troy furled his mouth. "I guess that makes sense on a scientific level."

"Totally," Noah said, making a fist. "That's the only way it works. Fuss about women's lib and gender equality until the cows come home. But this is fact. Not opinion. Man, you give them that, the world is yours, bro."

"How do you let someone win at hide and seek?" Troy said, holding his hand up in a questioning manner.

"Well, you," Noah said, holding his hand out toward Troy. "I, uh," he started, "I don't know. I guess to let them win is to never find them. Who's gonna do that?"

"Yeah, screw that," Doug said, waving his hand at the fire then putting it back in his pocket.

"Who said anything about never? Let's just take our time," Troy said.

They all dropped into camp chairs and picked their beers back up.

"You're cheating!" one of them shouted.

"You can't drink beer if we don't get to!" said another.

They boys looked at each other and finally stood up again. "Let's do it," Doug said and stuck out his fist. They all bumped them together, then started off in opposing directions.

Noah walked the opposite way from where he had gone last time. Alice probably had gone the opposite way again, so he could just catch her again. Knock her ego down a little. To hell with the rhetoric he'd just been preaching. He wasn't going to lose to any girl either. Alice wasn't his girlfriend anyway. He could beat her safely. No repercussion to worry about. If she punishes him, it's only when they're together. He doesn't have to go home with her. Sleep with her. Share a bed with her.

He walked down the edge of the road again, moonlight begging to peek through the clouds. The clouds weren't listening though, so they stayed puffy and white in the black sky. Even in the complete darkness, the clouds around the moon were stark white and beautiful. They muffled the light though. Muddied it. Made it queer and untrustworthy. Tents lit only by this twice-reflected light were awkward looking and didn't seem to be the right shapes. Just the wrong amount of light to see.

Finally, he saw something sticking out from behind a tree. It looked like an elbow. He placed the height at thirty inches. That meant she was short. It was either Alice or Trixie. And since Alice had gone the other way the last time, this was bound to be her. Noah looked behind him, then stepped over the stone wall, built to keep people from parking too far off the road. He walked through the darkest path he could find – the one with the least amount of leaves and dry dirt. His shoes were quiet. Noah's stealth was strong. He crept past a tree and up toward where he had seen the elbow. A huge elm, about ten feet in front of him matched the description in his memory. He crept up around to the left side of it. He was definitely at the right tree. He stopped for a moment, staring at the elbow sticking out from the tree. As his eyes finally started to focus in the low light, he realized it was just a branch. He gasped with annoyance and someone took off running from behind a tree about twenty feet away, now giggling as she ran. At least she was being more considerate of their neighbors this time.

Noah, of course, took off after her. She ran across the street and back into the trees. She had run right under a streetlight though. It wasn't Alice. And she was too short to be Joy. That only left Trixie. He felt a tinge of excitement at that, but didn't have time to dissect what it meant. He ran across the street, under the light, then disappeared back into the darkness. His sight had not readjusted to the absence of light yet. Trixie got away. Just far enough out of reach to make a juke and evade him entirely. He stopped and listened. He had to force his breath down. As he stood there, he heard a few more footsteps, and then a stifled giggle. He looked up and concentrated on the darkness. *That* had sounded like Alice after all. Maybe he had been wrong.

"Alice?" he asked, whisper-shouting into the darkness.

"What!" she said, respecting the quiet rule. Answering to her name seemed to lay the mystery to rest, at least.

"Dude, just come out! I can't see enough in here. I might step in a bear trap!"

She laughed out loud and slapped her hand over her mouth. "Shut up, dork, just come get me! You don't win until you catch me!" She was saying all this in a loud whisper with very little vocal involvement.

He stepped forward, stretching his arms out, hands scanning the complete darkness. His eyes were still adjusting. Now there was a dying fire about thirty yards to his left. That made the darkness nearby even worse. "Alice! Dude, just come out!" he said. Noah was now completely still. He was in a perfect balance of dark and light. Not evenly distributed amounts of each, but a perfect balance that made it impossible to carry on. If he went any farther, he would have to break out his flashlight. He heard footsteps again, but they sounded more relaxed. They sounded like she wasn't trying to hide anymore. She was giving up the charade.

"Come get me!" she whispered. She sounded like she was just on the other side of the tree to his right. He turned and reached his hands out. At least the distant fire was behind him now. Noah could feel his vision improving. Suddenly, a hand reached out and grabbed his hand. She was pulling him in, behind the tree.

"Alice!" he said, a loud whisper. But her mouth was on his. He felt the firm warmth of her body as she pulled him to her, and they were embracing in the darkness. That cleared the mystery once and for all. After the initial shock of being kissed at all, Noah realized that there was no way Alice would be pulling such a stunt, and the height was all wrong. While Trixie was short, she was still several inches taller than Alice. She still had his hand and was now pulling it up between them.

The thought that there was something sexual being discussed in the darkness before, he had completely missed. But now they all came back to him. *Come get me!* That was blatant. How had he missed that? This wasn't tag, this was hide and seek! He didn't have to make contact with her for the gig to be up. She was clearly playing her own game.

"What are you doing?" Noah said, pulling away.

"Nothing! They won't know! Just kiss me! My lips are so cold!"

What the hell was *he* doing? He had questioned her motives. What about his? Had he really missed all the innuendo she had been putting out while he sought her? Or was he being modest? Was he unconsciously trying to create plausible deniability? Consciously? But her tongue was warm against his lips, his own tongue. He kissed her. She smiled, breaking the connection.

"There you go," she whispered, and returned to the action. She sucked lightly on his lips, running her tongue across them and biting gently on his tongue. She licked his teeth and pulled him in closer, tighter.

He strengthened his embrace. Her hand on his, she slid his grasp up a little farther, and he felt the thick padding of her push-up bra. He squeezed gently, then moaned. Apparently she took that as a complaint, because she reached up under her sweater, inside her coat, and unhitched her bra.

"Dude," he said quickly, realizing where he was, suddenly. This couldn't be happening. He had no desire to betray Joy. Why was this happening? He reckoned he was just high and drunk enough to let something slip into reality. "What am I gonna tell Joy?" he asked stupidly. He knew she had no investment here. Nothing to lose. Why would she care what he did or didn't tell Joy? Noah reckoned Trixie would be just as happy if Joy found out, and left him, than if she didn't find out.

"Tell her you like the way I kiss!" she whispered between kisses.

She tightened her hands around the back of his neck, pulling him closer. She took long laps, kissing the inside of his mouth, pulling him tighter and licking his lips like a Popsicle. He finally got control of his neck muscles again and pulled away from her.

"Dammit, Trix, stop!" he said, loudly.

She stood there in silence for a moment. "Was that like your safe word? You know you're enjoying this!" she said, then reached down and grabbed a handful of him through his jeans. "Ah! See? I told ya!" Then she pulled him just close enough for her nose to touch his.

Was she right? Obviously he was responding favorably to the heavy kissing. But he might still get away with this based on his being so far from sober. But he would have to stop right now. She quickly removed that option though as their lips locked together. She licked the top of his tongue like she was stroking a dog's back, and he began to get weak in the knees. He tightened his grip. She had to be right! Drunk and high or not, he could easily stop her. Noah was bigger and stronger than Trixie. And he was the man in this situation. The man with something to lose. He could easily stop her by taking control of the situation. But yet… Her hands were on his back pockets, pulling him in tighter. Her bra was now out of place, above her chest, creating funny shapes in her sweater. His hands were on her waist, inside her sweater. He had not yet gone far enough north on the map to reach the Arctic. At least not skin to skin. *Still somewhat innocent...*

Trixie pulled away slightly and he could tell in the dark that she was smiling at him. She wiggled back and forth and pulled her sweater up above her bra, forming a shelf above her breasts which cast everything below it in perfect darkness.

"Go ahead!" she whispered. She was definitely smiling. He could feel the puff of breath she had expelled with her H against his nose. And it was in the shape of a happy face.

He frowned at her in the darkness. "With what?"

"What do you think?" she said, tilting her head.

What about Joy? Where was his heart? His mind? His mouth, for that matter?

"I don't know what you mean," he said. He might have been lying. But he wasn't sure. He didn't know how to tell. His head was swimming from the adrenaline rush of running, mixed with the alcohol and the cannabis.

"You can feel my tits, Noah," she said. She grabbed his hands again, and now was squeezing them against her, willing them into the perfect shape to grab handfuls of her tiny breasts, taking away any space between their two fleshes.

He could feel himself getting warmer, pumping more blood. She pulled his head down again and sucked his mouth into her own. Their tongues tangled.

"Noah, I want you to try something with me," she said. Trixie pulled his face next to hers, resting cheek to cheek against him.

"What's that?" he asked, perhaps a little too curious. There was no more deniability to be had here. This had moved way past innocent fun, and far beyond anything that could be explained away by the alcohol. Suddenly there were footsteps behind him. Rapidly, he retrieved his hands from her sweater and turned around. He heard her turn as well, the sound of dirt being scuffed as she darted away from the tree to deeper darkness.

"Who is it?" he asked, then tried to cover with names. "Doug? Roy? That you?" Then he thought a little further and decided he seemed pretty suspicious. "You find anyone?"

Why would he be whispering? Walking? Wandering? Noah realized he was really bad at this. He was caught. It was Doug.

"Huh?"

"What?" Noah said.

"I said, 'huh'," Doug said.

"Huh? What the hell? Where were you?" Noah asked.

"Where was I? I was chasing down your girlfriend! That bitch is a cheetah!"

"Yeah? I could have told you that!"

"Where the hell were you?" Doug asked, turning to look around their immediate area.

"Right here, fool," Noah tried. He turned and looked for the elbow branch. "See that?" he asked, pointing. "I thought that was your girlfriend. Doug leaned in closer and saw what he was pointing at, then stood up straight and laughed, quietly.

"Damn, dude. Well, Joy came over here somewhere. You didn't catch her scent?"

Noah smirked. "Dude if I had caught her scent, we'd be in the tent together."

10

The fire was smoking badly as Noah came out of the tent and dropped into one of the chairs. He leaned forward to tie his boots, feet freezing in the thick socks, hands like ice blocks. Joy and Trixie were cooking breakfast over the fire, a steel grill folded down to hang over it.

"Morning, sleepy head!" Joy said, smiling at him as she made motions in the skillet with a spatula.

He sighed and smiled back at her, a weak little number. He had a hard time pretending he was a morning person in any situation. Trixie looked at him too. She was almost smiling. She might have been sending a message to him. *I'm here cooking with your girlfriend. But you had your hands all up in my kitchen last night.* He looked away quickly. They had apparently gotten away with their little foray. She was the enemy. Noah had been annoyed by her before. Now what would she be? Was he going to have to watch out for her the entire camping trip? Was he seriously going to have to fight her off of him? His stomach sank as he remembered putting his hands up her shirt. Her willing participation – nay, her insistence on the event. She was a totally different person than Joy. She felt completely different. And he couldn't find anything in his memory of the experience to associate with a negative feeling. So was that how this worked? She had been coming on to him for years now. Dropping not-so-subtle hints almost every time he saw her, practically begging him to take her out. So she tricks him into kissing her and that was all it took? Had he just been missing what all the fuss was about before? Now that he had his palms on her chest, he understood? He now knew something extra, and therefore, wanted her?

Noah had, of course, more questions than just that to answer. Why had he allowed himself into being tricked into kissing her? Why had he pursued her like that in the first place? Because of the high? He knew cannabis was a great aphrodisiac, but he didn't think it made him want strange women. And now, thinking back about the instant, he wondered again what made him take that last step. Because now that he was sober, he knew he *didn't* want her. And it wasn't like he had thought it was Joy he was chasing. Plausible deniability would have been available if he could have said with any real conviction that he thought it was Joy. Lots of alcohol, lots of weed. It could happen. Not likely. But at least it made more sense than just chasing Trixie down and letting it all happen.

Meanwhile, Joy was talking to him and he had been in a different dimension. "Huh?" he said, looking up when he heard his name.

"I asked if you wanted them runny or scrambled. What's on your mind, babe? You look lost in another world," Joy said.

Noah shot Trixie a glance. She was looking at him, half-smirking. She was obviously not as scared of being found out as he was. Was this a game to her?

"Scrambled is fine. I'm not ready yet though. I think it's gonna be a while before I'm hungry," he said, staring at the fire.

"Okaaay," she said, "suit yourself."

"Where are the others?" Noah asked, already knowing the answer – just dying for a subject change.

"Doug and Alice are still asleep, I'm guessing. Their tent's pretty still. Troy got up early and went to work," Joy said.

He nodded noncommittally, then stood up, putting his hands in his pockets, to get closer to the fire. He picked up another dry log from a nearby pile and slipped it in under the grill, then threw in a handful of dry weeds to kindle. The smoke was starting to burn his eyes.

"Sorry, we're not boy scouts," Trixie said. She was smiling widely now, and Noah realized this was the first he had heard her speak since his coming out of the tent.

He put his fingers together, forming a small diamond, and blew at the fire from where he was standing. Trixie started laughing at the gesture, but stopped quickly, when the fire caught the air and whooshed to life. Noah smirked at her and winked, then regretted it. At this point, it was entirely possible that she would take that as a sort of continuation of the events from the night before. He then made an effort to bend over and kiss Joy on the lips before walking to a stand of trees to relieve his bladder.

The rest of the day was uneventful. They all sat around the fire drinking; orange juice, then water, then eventually beer. Noah got a text from Troy in the early afternoon saying he would not be able to make it back this evening. He had two employees call out, so he was needed in the shop. They would be working late, so he was going to go home and crash afterwards. He sent another shortly after though, saying he would be back in the morning to help pack up the tents and collect his date for the weekend.

When Noah relayed the message to the group, Trixie took a deep breath and looked disappointed. But when no one was looking, she looked at him sideways and furled her lips. As if she were trying not to smile. *Oh, shit. She'll have an empty tent tonight.* As the meaning of her near-smirk began to make sense, Noah looked up at the clouds and silently shook his head.

11

That night was an interesting juggling act for Noah. He tried to accommodate Trixie, who no longer had a couple here, but also maintain his position as Joy's date. Joy understood that he was trying to keep the girl entertained, and was mostly cool with it. It did put a small damper on things though. They had to forgo couples' games, for instance. And Noah actively shot down any attempt the three girls brought forth about playing another round of hide and seek. So instead, they spent most of the time sitting around the fire telling war stories and drinking beer, passing the pipe.

Noah thought he had covered all his bases. He had done really well trying to keep Trixie at arm's length. She had made passing comments to him, and there had been the glances and the knowing nods. But he mostly ignored her. He hoped that Doug hadn't seen any of it. Because all the guys in the group knew who Trixie was, and who she really liked, it was no secret that she followed Noah around like a lost puppy when they were at the bar. The girls weren't there enough to have witnessed it. And Joy almost never made it to the bar at all because she worked almost every weekend. That freedom he had was a blessing and a curse. A girl on the arm, he thought, was a lot like a ring on the finger.

So it all went as well as could be expected, until Trixie finally stood up and said, "I need to go to the girls' room. Anyone want to walk me?"

Noah breathed in and stared at the fire. That job was typically reserved for other girls. He was usually safe. But no one else was getting up. It looked as though Trixie would be on her own. But Noah himself had been one of the founders of their group rule – no one walks alone. A buddy system, at least for the girls, because campgrounds were not always the safest of places for singular women at night.

"We just went a few minutes ago," Joy said. "Hon, why don't you walk her? It's probably better for a man to do anyway."

Noah tried not to show his frustration – or his hesitation. But inside he was shaking his head, rolling his eyes, sighing loudly, and everything else he could do as a cry for help. Outside, he was a gentleman. "Okay. Let's go," he said, bounding up out of his chair. He put his hands in his pockets and they walked out of the fire's light. She was a perfect angel, too. They walked along the road, both of them with their hands in their own pockets, and a foot apart at the shoulders. When they got far enough away not to be heard, Noah said, "I don't know what your game plan is, but if Joy breaks up with me because of you, I will not soon forgive you."

She looked at him in the near-darkness. "What, you didn't have fun last night, Noah?"

He stopped in the middle of the road and turned to look at her. He put his hand on her shoulder. "Trixie, I don't know what you want from me. You know I'm with Joy."

She looked around, then began wiggling her sweater up.

He reached down and stopped her. "Seriously, just stop!"

"You didn't answer my question," she said, pulling the sweater right past his hands. Then she pulled it back down over his hands and stepped forward. Why his hands were still up her sweater, he could not have answered. But they were. And now she pulled them in. "Oh my GOD!" she almost shouted. "Your hands are so effing cold!"

"Whose fault is that?" he asked. But he didn't pull away.

Trixie squeezed his hands hard and scrunched her eyes shut real hard for a minute, then finally breathed in deeply. "There. See, I left the bra back in my tent this time! Now isn't this fun?"

Noah stood staring at her in the low light. Then he shook his head. "Why are you doing this?"

"Because it's fun!" She stepped even closer, and looked straight up at him. "Look, I know you have a girlfriend. But you're not married. If you were, it would be different. But you're not!" She tilted her head a little, then swallowed. "So why not have some fun?" Trixie stood up on her tip-toes and kissed him on the mouth, leaving his lips wet.

Noah pulled his hands out of her sweater and started walking again. "Not here. Not in the middle of the damn road." But his mind was still where his hands had been. Why did it feel so nice? Why did it *have to* feel so nice? She was little bitty compared to Joy, but obviously size didn't have anything to do with it. She felt lovely under her sweater. The shape… the size, the texture, the pert response of the firm flesh… it all felt perfect to his hands. She was working on him, driving him crazy.

Trixie skipped along beside him until they got to the bathroom, then she separated and darted into the building, disappearing while he waited outside, leaning against the cinder-block wall. It was dark. He could see the light through the screen above the brick but below the steel roof support. But there was no light in this makeshift hallway outside the bathroom.

Noah looked down at his feet, then looked back toward the direction from which they had come. It was quiet tonight. There were very few campers at this time of year. And since this was a private campground, rather than a state-sponsored one, it was open all year. He and his group were the crazy ones. The guys who didn't care if it was summer or winter – as long as there was a fire pit, they were camping. A good rain would keep them away, but not much else. He saw no other fires besides their own, and that was a good quarter-mile up the road. Only a tiny orange flicker from here.

He leaned his head back against the brick and took a deep breath. What was he going to do about Trixie? Clearly, he had determined, he was interested. At least in the fooling around she was administrating. He heard the toilet flush, then a few seconds later, the sink thunked on and off. He heard the offensively loud hand dryer. And then he heard nothing. Noah waited a few more seconds, then called out.

"Trix? What's up in there?"

No answer. He shook his head. She was playing games again. Well, whatever, did she actually prefer the stinking, damp, cave-like feel of the bathroom to the darkness out here? If she wanted to mess around, this would actually be the safer place. They could hear people approaching. Not to mention that he wouldn't be inside the women's room if someone came to use it.

"Trixie!" he said a little louder. Still no answer. And no sound. He closed his eyes and shook his head. Then he pulled open the door and looked inside. She was standing there with her clothes in a pile beside her, in nothing but her boots. Her hands were on a part of her body he wasn't supposed to see. Technically, he could not see it. But she was looking at him seductively. She still had the features of a teenager – the flat belly, the slender thighs and arms. Gravity had not yet begun to attract itself to the usual parts of her. He envied her of that. Noah himself was already starting to develop a beer belly. He stared at her in the eyes for a moment, then, inhaling deeply, trying to calm himself, allowed his eyes to drift down, realizing he had not yet actually seen her naked chest. He was very familiar with the way it felt, but was surprised by the look of her. Her features, her colors – her shape – was all different than Joy. It was all he could do to keep his cool.

"Trixie, dude, you're killing me. I can't do this," he said.

"Do what, Nono?"

"Stop calling me that!"

"Do what, Noah? What can't you do? You're just looking right now!"

He swallowed, trying to form words in his mouth that just wouldn't come. He held his hand out toward her, as if to show her an example of herself would answer her question. "Trixie, seriously?"

She bit her lip and stared at him. She was working herself up. Noah looked down and came to the realization that she hadn't a single hair below her eyebrows. He watched her with intense fascination for a minute, then looked back up into her eyes.

"We have to go back. It's gonna start looking suspicious pretty quick," he said.

"Okay. Just a sec. Come here for just a second, Noah."

He dragged his feet up to where she was standing. Then she took one of her hands and put it on the back of his head, pulled him in for a deep kiss. She licked his mouth and tongue passionately as she continued to twitch and roll with the other hand. He could hear her breathing deeply through her nose. Then she broke the kiss and looked up at him again through half-closed eyes. Trixie pulled his head down to her chest. He followed the orders he had been given by her hands; no words needed to be exchanged. She moaned as he licked and kissed and explored her chest. His hands were around her, pulling against her back. Pulling her into his mouth. Then she put her hand on his head and started pushing him south. Noah backed away and stood up.

"No!" he said, a little too loudly. "I can't do this!" Then he turned around and walked out the door. Once outside, he leaned against the wall again, looking up, then closing his eyes, breathing deeply. His heart was slamming in his chest. And his blood was flowing hot into his groin. He wondered if it would be obvious. "I'm leaving in thirty seconds. If you don't want to walk back alone, I suggest you hurry!"

He heard her moan a little more loudly, and then cry out. "I'm coming!" she said. He squeezed his eyes shut. Shook his head. Then he walked out of the small hallway and back to the front of the restroom building, where a soda machine stood behind a black wrought-iron gate. "I'm coming, Noah," she said again. He swallowed. He took the obvious meaning – the surface meaning, opting out of the alternative for his sanity's sake.

After another minute or so, the door opened, and there she was, completely dressed, hopping in her boot, trying to pull it up with one hand while she balanced herself against the wall with the other. His relief was instant. Noah had feared she would do something stupid like come out here naked.

When she got her boot on completely, she joined him at the front and they headed down the dirt path to the road. "Whew!" she said, wiping her forehead with the back of her hand. "Thank you for waiting. That was amazing!"

"Good. Glad you enjoyed it," he said, staring straight ahead as they walked.

"Ah, Noah, why are you mad at me? I'm just trying to have a little fun!"

He shook his head with determination. "I told you, I can't do this. I'm a man. You're a woman. I won't be able to control myself around you for much longer, so I suggest we probably shouldn't spend time together outside the bar."

"Aww, that breaks my heart, Noah!" she said. "Hey, wait!" she begged. "Stop! Please!"

He stopped and looked at her. "Look, I'm sorry. I didn't think it would bother you that much. If you just want to be friends, that's fine." Trixie looked down the road, a little sadness creeping into her countenance. "I always just thought maybe you were interested. It seemed like you looked at me sometimes."

"I'm sure I do, Trix! You're hot! You look amazing!" He shook his head as if to clear it, and added, "Especially naked. Good grief. But man, I'm just not that strong, okay? I can't resist a hot naked woman throwing herself at me like that!"

"Then why even try?" she said, stepping a little closer.

"Because, I'm loyal. I have something pretty special with Joy. I don't want to screw that up just to 'play around'," he said, making quotes in the air, "or whatever it is you're doing."

"She doesn't have to know," Trixie said, leaning her head over to one side. Then she took his hand with one of her hands. The other hand, she raised to his chin. She grabbed his chin with that hand and shook it back and forth, gently. Then she slipped two of her fingers into his mouth. He could taste her, and finally realized what she was doing. She was staring at him seductively, through half-lit eyes, licking her lips. It felt as if she were controlling him like a puppet. He kept her fingers in his mouth for a long moment feeling the energy drain from him. And then she pulled them out and put them in her own mouth.

She squeezed the hand she was still holding then pulled her fingers out of her mouth. "Did I taste good?" she asked.

Noah swallowed again, shaking his head slightly. "Why are you so mean to me?"

Trixie smiled widely. "Next time you should cut out the middle man and go straight to the source."

12

Back at the campsite, Noah sat uncomfortably in his chair, trying to act like he didn't feel like he was hiding something huge from everyone. How the hell Trixie was able to be so nonchalant about it, he couldn't begin to guess. But apparently her like for him was so intense as to put her into a different reality – one that had a different set of rules. A reality, in fact, where Joy didn't even exist as a counterpart to her target. Trixie interacted with Joy like there was nothing going on. Like it was completely natural. But she interacted with Noah as if there simply was no Joy.

He had to think deeply to get to a point where he recognized Trixie at all. The *her* he thought he knew was no longer anywhere near the surface. She had seemed so much like a normal, fun, sweet-spirited waitress at a popular rock bar. They were nice to everyone. Hugs and winks and flirts were all part of the job, and it was accepted from both sides that most of it was bullshit. It got them bigger tips. The men knew the gals would most likely not be going home with them. But flirting was safe. It was as adventurous as most of the men ever got anyway. It just felt good to have someone look back at you and wink. It was all an act. To get away from the wife and pretend like there was something going on. And so Noah had thought as well. She was rather forward with her bounty a lot of the time, but he didn't really know how realistic that was.

Well, he hadn't. Now she had proven her case. She was for real. And he was in real danger. At least if he continued to know her outside of the bar.

Trixie sat in her chair talking with the other girls and looking at her phone occasionally, but otherwise acting like a completely normal girl out with the couples. Looking at her sitting by the fire, no one would ever suspect she was up to anything. And right now she wasn't. Maybe her climax had killed the monster for a while. She was looking at Noah occasionally, but with no special attention. He was thankful for that. She looked very relaxed. Maybe she had conceived a brilliant idea: He should take care of business, get it out of his system, and then be good for the rest of the night. Free to think his own thoughts – not those owned and controlled by the succubus that apparently lived inside him.

She would occasionally pick up her phone and smile at the screen, make motions on the screen for a moment, and then put it back in the chair's little pocket. Noah saw all of this, but tried to act like he wasn't paying any special attention to her either. He was really just curious how she was so easily able to exist in two separate universes.

It was when he looked down at his pocket and saw his phone blinking through his jeans that he started to realize what she had been up to. Noah slipped his phone from his pocket and unlocked the screen. There were texts from an unknown number. He didn't have to guess who they were, but wondered how she had gotten his number. He guessed Troy was the obvious answer. Some innocent, passing comment about needing all the guys' numbers for the camping trip, she would have said. And Troy would never have questioned her. There would have been no reason to.

The texts were dirtier than her mind, tempting and taunting him, and he had to reconsider his previous assessment that her monster had gone to sleep. He shut off the screen and slipped it back into his pocket without responding. And when he finished his beer, he excused himself, claiming he was whipped, and slipped into the tent with a goodnight to all.

There were no dreams. There was no sound, either, so Noah wasn't sure what had woken him up. But he sat up and listened. He could hear nothing but the soft crash of water against rocks past the edge of the cliff. Noah climbed out of his sleeping bag, kissed Joy on the forehead, and then stepped out of the tent in his tennis shoes. He walked to the edge of the clearing, putting the smoldering embers of last night's fire at his back and unzipped his jeans. He watched as steam rose up from the frozen grass as he urinated. The sun was not yet visible itself, but it was already making preparations for its arrival. He could see a warm glow out over the ocean.

Acadia National Park has the emblem of being one of the best places in the entire United States to watch the sun rise. The gorgeous landscape of rocks, trees, oceans and cliffs is one of the selling points. Another is the fact that it is the easternmost point in the country – so the sun becomes visible there a few minutes before anywhere else along the entire eastern seaboard. Noah and his group were out here enough and had seen enough sunrises that it was no longer an event for which they felt they needed to wake the whole group. But it was still beautiful enough to warrant catching it every time he got the chance. As he zipped his fly, he put his hands in his pockets and walked out of the campsite, down the road to the end of the campground, a hundred yards away from the tent.

Here was the cliff at which the continent came to an end in a tumultuous, crashing congregation of land and sea. As Noah looked down at the crashing waves, he thought it looked a lot louder than it was. It looked like it should be roaring. It was only a soft, peaceful waterfall of a sound though. He breathed in deeply in the cool morning air and looked out over the sea. The lighthouse just north of his position stood against a dark backdrop of landscape that had not yet been graced by the sun's early light.

He sat down on a rock and pulled his knees up, clasped his hands around them. The sun reached the point where it lit up the heavens before it became visible, sending orange and pink lines across the distant landscape of the sky. The splashes of color through the sparse clouds at the edge of the horizon made it look like the ocean just came right up into the sky. There was no clear separation between the two, and it was fantastically gorgeous.

Noah felt a small hand on his shoulder and flinched, turning to see Trixie standing there. His stomach sank instantly. "God, you scared the shit out of me!"

"I'm sorry! I thought you heard me coming," she said. She sat on a rock a few feet away and stared out at the distant sky. Noah studied her face for a minute in the odd luminance of a sun that had not yet come out from behind the corner of the world. She had thin eyebrows and light eyelashes, making her eyes and everything around them look pale. This gave her face the overall appearance of oneness – of plainness. But not at the cost of beauty. On most faces, he thought, the eyes stood out as darker, more pronounced areas because of the darkness of the lashes, the pupils, the irises, the eyebrows… Her whole face seemed to be awash in pale detail. He felt his heart skip a beat as he realized how pretty she was naturally. Noah was a fan of women who did not need makeup to look good.

She looked over and caught him staring at her. She smiled, a very pleasant, sweet smile, and he thought she looked like an entirely different person than he had seen in the bathroom last night. Trixie now did not look like she was capable of that kind of x-rated behavior. Not with this smile. This was a smile of purity, of chastity and love.

"Why are you staring at me, Noah?"

He sat for another moment, then looked back at the sunrise. The entire eastern horizon was now orange and growing hot and wild with light and beauty. Then he looked back at Trixie.

"I've never seen you without makeup," he said, and shrugged.

Trixie lifted her chin and swallowed, looking seriously at him – like she might be embarrassed or shy about her face. Timidly, she said, "Do I look okay to you?"

Noah smiled. "Yes." He didn't want to say too much – to betray his true thoughts. He didn't want to give her the idea that he was considering her for more than friendship. "I was just thinking how different you look than the girl who put her fingers in my mouth last night in the middle of the street."

Trixie smiled again, and turned to look east. "Sorry, Noah." She sat there staring at the sunrise, then finally said, "I guess I was just trying too hard to compete."

"Compete?" Noah said, almost laughing. "Who were you competing with?"

"Tanis," she said, almost absently.

"Ha! What the hell does that even mean? She's not my girlfriend!" Noah said, shaking his head.

"Because you came in that night and asked what it would take to pick her up," she responded.

"Oh my God, Trixie. That's not even..." he started, then looked back at the skyline where the sun was finally becoming evident. A small orange bump on the edge of the sea burning up the atmosphere, distorting and warping the line of the horizon with blazing white lines. "Listen. I'm a flirty guy. I flirt with just about everyone. All the time."

"Well I guess I thought that meant I had a chance," she said soberly. She was still looking at the sunrise. Her eyes looked glassy.

"Well I'm sorry to have lead you on. Joy and I have a sort of agreement. As long as I don't bring someone home, there really are no rules. That doesn't mean I can make-out with someone in a bathroom. But yeah, I flirt. A lot. I sometimes might make it seem like I'm available. But I'm not. And that's really not my intention. I'm sorry."

She shrugged. A small, humiliated gesture that showed her softness. Her humanity. Here sat a real person, with real feelings. And her feelings had been hurt. Had he really been leading her on that much? Had his fronts, his hugs – his tips – given her pause to think she had a chance?

"She's never there with you. I don't know," Trixie said. It seemed like she was grasping at anything now just to reach him. Or rather, just to keep clinging to that rope, dangling out over the edge of hope. And that rope was unraveling.

"Listen, Trixie. Joy works at Paul Alan's. She's a hostess there. She is very good at what she does. Which translates to her almost never having a Friday or

Saturday night off. We almost never get to go out together on the weekends because of it. So I go out with the boys. I hang with the girls, too. Whatever," he said, shrugging.

The entire hemisphere above the horizon was now pale orange, fading to pink, a galactic light show. It was beautiful as it was sobering. To watch it rise from here, from this point, it had the tendency of reminding one how small he really was. Reminding him that this wasn't just a light, but a star cutting through almost a hundred million miles of space to decorate their morning skyline.

"Well, I'm sorry, Noah. I took a shot. I failed. It's okay. I'll move on."

"Trixie, there is no shot to be had! It's not that you failed. You didn't fail. What you did last night was the hottest thing I've ever seen. Literally." He looked back at her and noticed that now a tear had developed, run down her cheek. He had to resist the urge to wipe it away for her. That was a forward gesture that she might once again mistake for an advance. It was perhaps made easier though, by the fact that he wasn't within reaching distance.

"Really?" she said, finally looking over at him.

"Yeah. If you were just trying to get laid, it totally would have worked. I can't imagine being able to resist you. I only did because I had to."

"That's not even me," she said, screwing up her mouth. "I don't come onto guys like that. I just," she said, and wiped her eyes, "I don't sing or anything. I don't do anything special like that. So I thought I had to come out and do something crazy to get your attention." She tried a weak smile then breathed in deeply, looking long at the horizon. "You know Trixie's not even my real name?"

Noah stared soberly at her for a moment. "Seriously?"

Trixie looked over at him again, her eyes now full of glass. Then she looked back at the sunrise. It was full – a giant disk, shimmering and orange. She finally nodded. "Yeah. Tricia Belle Clifton."

"That's a nice name. I like it," Noah said. "Where'd you get Trixie then?"

She shrugged, avoiding eye-contact with him for the moment. "Just sounds cooler, I guess."

Noah finally sighed, nodding his head. "Well, I'm a loyal guy, Trixie," Noah said. "I'm not maybe the strongest guy, but I try to be loyal. I do like to flirt. And I admit," he said, looking back over his shoulder to make sure they were still alone. "I admit that I like the hint of sexuality. I like to walk that edge sometimes. I've done more with you in the last two days than I have in years, though. I just don't really ever act on it. I flirt with it. I love thinking about it. I'm a man." He shrugged. "But I try to keep my hands to myself."

"Well, I'm sorry I came onto you. I have always just liked the way you treat me at the bar."

"Well that's all I have, Trixie. Think about it. All our interactions until this weekend were only at the Sally West. You bring me my drinks, I throw an arm around you, I try to be generous with my tips – try to take care of you. That's all we have."

"So that's all I am to you. A waitress," she said.

"That's not what I said," Noah replied, avoiding the temptation to sink into a fight. "We've just never hung out outside of the bar. It's been a real pleasure getting to know you this weekend. I like you. You're fun. You're zesty and bouncy and beautiful and witty. I enjoy being around you. But I'm just not in a place where I'm available."

"I understand," she said, sighing. She stood up and brushed off her rump, then hopped down off the rock and came over to him. She looked him hard in the eyes, standing there chewing the inside of her lip like she was deliberating a difficult life choice. Then she put her hands on the sides of his face and kissed him. She put her mouth hard against Noah's, not moving, but holding their mouths together for what seemed like a long time. Then she broke the kiss and walked away.

As he turned to watch her trudging up the path back toward the campsite, he swallowed. He looked down and realized his hands were trembling. He also realized that she had just done a lot more than kissing him. She had sent him a very complex message not backed by any words. He understood suddenly that she had been telling him something hard. Something strong. That had been a goodbye kiss.

CHAPTER TWO
staying on pitch

From *WhiskeyNeat* Magazine

No Stranger to the Reign
by Randall Cameron

Pop sensation Tanis Ransom of One Last Orbit says she's ready for Europe. Having just completed a 170-day North America tour, the band is energized. They are now back in Bozeman, Montana – their new home town – regrouping. Next spring they will begin their first European tour in Frankfurt, Germany. As of now they have forty dates confirmed for their concert calendar. They expect twenty more to be added by March, says Ransom.

Shannon Kennedy, the guitarist, said, "We spent six months on the tour bus. You think you'll get tired of each other. But when there's that much energy on the stage, that much power holding you together, you don't. It electrifies you. We could keep going. Winter is when we like to get back to our roots though. We'll play a bunch of small venues, mostly unannounced."

Over the last four years, the band has made a sort of cult roots calling card out of the practice. Invading small clubs under pseudonyms. The false band names change every month or two, as well, so no one knows where they'll turn up next. Some of those names were Pop Fancy, Dark Tide, Group Assault and Famous Last Word. Their manager, Josie Coker, will send a demo CD to club owners with the fake name on it and a set of three or four songs that have not been released by the band. These songs are, of course, good enough to get them the headline at these venues. Then they'll play Friday- and Saturday-night shows, usually for free, to unsuspecting crowds.

What do they get out of it? "It's amazing," says Ransom. "They all know us, but the surprise is in their eyes. It's a great feeling. We feel appreciated on a whole other level when we do the small shows. It's one of our favorite parts of the tour."

Kevin Vig, the drummist, as the band calls him, agrees: "That's the rich part. You get to connect with home crowds. Maybe people who couldn't make the big shows. Or people who couldn't get close to the stage. Whatever the story, those are some of the most rewarding shows."

With their second studio album just a month away, the fans are getting anxious. Ben Redding has been carrying pre-press copies to shows, tossing them out like Frisbees into the crowd. It's already been posted all over YouTube, and other royalty-free sites. The band doesn't mind though. Why else would they hand out free copies?

"No one likes to talk about money. But truth is, the biggest money comes from the tours themselves. We just want our music to find its way into homes. We're not worried about piracy. In fact, it's kind of an honor to see a song making its way across the internet before it's been officially released," says Layne Billings. Billings is the newest member of the band. He joined when Mark Watkins was diagnosed with brain cancer. The fans have taken nicely to him.

The new album, *Makeshift Planet*, hits the shelves in May. Pre-order numbers already put it in the platinum status – the first time that has happened for One Last Orbit. Front-woman Tanis Ransom shows no emotion when we ask her about it though. "I'm extremely excited. I'm very happy. Humbled that so many people want to hear our music. But I try not to get caught up in numbers." We don't either, Tanis. After selling out every single show over a six-month period, there doesn't seem to be much point. If you build it they will come. Likewise, if One Last Orbit plays it, they will listen.

"Excited? Hell yeah, I'm excited!" says Coker. "You'd think I'd be used to their success by now. But it just keeps getting better." Coker has been their manager since the local days, when they filled small venues like the Dixie Whistle and The Sally West, in Bar Harbor. Those are their favorite clubs to play. The ones where the original fan base still exists in shocking numbers.

And they try to get back there several times a year.

They picked up and moved to Bozeman from Bar Harbor as a unit after the success of their first album. Though they all have their own homes, three of the five members live on the same acreage, within walking distance of the studio in which they record their tracks.

"It's not as easy as I wish it were," says Ransom. "We love coming home, but it's sometimes tougher than the travel itself." She chews her lip as she deliberates. You can tell she means it. She's still got a lot of that small-time girl in her. "Maybe someday we can retire back to the home bars."

Retirement may be a dream they can accomplish. But it's not likely to be any time in the near future. Right now they're on top of the world. According to the numbers about which they don't like to talk, they're higher than that. They're in orbit.

1

The crowd was streaming in steadily. It was almost nine – about an hour before the headlining band would take the stage. It was not yet late enough to miss part of the show, but late enough to be fashionable. Noah and Doug stood outside looking over the railing at the water crashing against the rocks below. Doug had a bottle of beer in his hand, Noah had the short glass of bourbon he preferred when he was out. It forced him to drink a little more slowly, to not over-indulge.

"How's Alice?" Noah said, putting the whiskey up to his lips.

"She's good. She's just not used to staying up that late for that many nights in a row," Doug said.

"Two. Two nights. Good wow, are we getting old or what?"

Doug smirked, shrugged. "I know, man. I don't recover nearly as quickly as I used to."

"I know that's right," Noah agreed. "You seen Trixie yet?"

"Nope. She's probably busier than a one-armed paper in a leg-kicking contest," Doug said.

Noah chuckled.

"Bro, did something happen with Trix the other night? You were acting a little distant around the fire," Doug said. He turned to look at Noah, leaning against the railing as the crowd filed in behind them.

"You caught that?" Noah said. He looked Doug straight in the eyes. Here was a guy he could completely trust. But if Doug had noticed something, it was possible – even likely – that some of the others might have as well.

Doug nodded faintly. It was almost imperceptible. "Yeah, man. I could tell something was going on."

Noah took another sip of the whiskey and took a deep breath, then set his drink on the railing. "She came onto me, man."

Doug widened his eyes. "Yeah? Like how?"

"Like physically." He shook his head as the image of Trixie reentered his head. The contrast of a soft, pale female figure standing naked amid the brutalist architecture of the concrete bathroom was one of the sexiest things he had ever seen. "She all but raped me," Noah said.

Doug shook his head, squinting? "When the hell did this happen? Good Lord, man."

"A couple of times. Remember when you found me at hide and seek standing there by that tree with the elbow-shaped branch?"

"Yeah, sure," Doug said.

"I was recovering."

"She was there? Wait. You found her? What the hell happened out there?"

And here, Noah entered the land of contradiction. He had just reminded himself how he could trust Doug. But here he was about to cover up a little of the truth – to keep it from him. "I didn't know who it was. I just knew I'd caught someone. I thought it might be Alice, actually," he said, and looked away. To keep his hands busy, he took the glass off the rail and took a sip. "Anyway, I slipped around a tree to grab her, and she just, I don't know. She grabbed me. Started kissing me."

"Whoa. No shit?" Doug said.

"Yeah. Like full tongue and everything. I mean..." he started, then turned around and looked at the crowd for a minute, trying to compose himself. The memory was awakening parts of him that were better left asleep. "Dude. I haven't been kissed like that, ever. It was like when you're thirteen – grabbing your first kiss. It feels like you can't get enough of her into your mouth. Like you're so excited and so overwhelmed with that new passion – that new feeling, that you just... God. It's like you try to eat them alive."

Doug stared at him wide-eyed. He did not say anything. He was listening.

"That's what it was like," Noah said, turning to lean on the rail again. "That's how she was kissing me. Like she was burning, and the only thing that could put her out was to swallow me whole."

"God, that's sexy. Holy shit, dude," Doug said. He put his elbows on the rail next to Noah. "Lucky son of a bitch. I guess you got away with it."

"Yeah. But I… Dude, that's not what I want. I am happy with Joy."

"Well of course. Duh. But if someone comes onto you, that's like a freebie. I mean, you can't keep going back, but I think that one time is forgiven. Totally not your fault, man. And if it was at least enjoyable, then hey, man," he said, opening his hands, "shit. Count yourself lucky. She's a firecracker!"

"Yeah, I guess," Noah said with a sigh. "It was pretty exciting. But dude, I can't be hanging around her if she's gonna be doing that shit. She's way too hot to resist."

Doug stared at him for a long moment, then took another drink. "So what are you gonna do?"

"That wasn't it, man," he said. He told Doug all about the trip to the bathroom and what had transpired thereafter. Doug was staring at him, mouth open, clearly entranced by the erotic story. It wasn't something that happened all the time, to either of them. It was easy to get sucked into the mood.

"Damn, dude. That is rich. Wow. I had no idea she was like that," Doug said. He was staring out into the darkness, eyes unfocused and lost.

"Yeah, me neither. That morning when we talked, she said that it wasn't her, either. She's never like that. She just thought she had to come across as this wild, bold, libertine-like fox to be able to get my attention," Noah said.

"Well whatever, but if she was capable of it, then that's who she is. It's hard for shy, timid girls to imitate shit like that," Doug said.

"I hadn't thought about that. But yeah, I guess you're right."

Doug turned to look at him, one arm still on the rail, the other hand holding his bottle. He was smirking. He pushed Noah's shoulder with the fist that held the bottle. "Dude, if that's who she is, can you imagine dating her?"

Noah turned to look at him. He stared for a long time into Doug's eyes. Doug lowered his chin, cocked an eyebrow. *'See what I mean?'* that gesture said. Noah found himself shaking his head. This was probably going to get worse before it got better. He was dealing with a dangerous woman. It was unlikely she would hurt him or stalk him or anything intrusive like that, but just the act of avoiding her would prove to be difficult. And if he allowed her in… The sex would be stellar. He had to look away. To clear his mind. To think of other things. The excitement always lay strong behind 'door number two'. That elusive attraction you only read about in cheap dime-store novels or saw on blue movies… it was all too sexy to completely walk away from. It was the American dream. Every man wanted a woman like that. Someone crazy. Someone so explicitly raunchy she had no boundary at all – at least not that existed in this dimension. He imagined all the paths she could take him down. What it would be like to hold her, naked, in the privacy of a bedroom with no rules. No boundaries, no watching eyes, no chance of being caught – it was fantastic. Literally, the definition of fantasy. It seemed almost too hard to avoid. To walk back to his normal – albeit phenomenally gorgeous and outstanding-in-bed – girlfriend. She was completely awesome. Damn near perfect. But Joy wasn't a science experiment. She was more *People*, less *Rolling Stone*.

Noah turned back to the crowd, now thinning out, that streamed in through the open doors. Loud rock blew out like a stiff wind, the opening act putting on its climax. It was a soulful bass-heavy rock beat with melodic vocals. A lot of strength came through those doors. These guys sounded pretty good. "Let's go grab us a spot," he said.

Doug hiked his chin and followed Noah as they pushed into the warm, red darkness of the bar. Almost all the ambient light came from stage fixtures. The crowd was bouncing and moving with the beat. The sudden loudness was exciting, and almost a little overwhelming. They flashed their wrist bands at the doorman and slipped easily into the crowd. It was packed. They had to be close to capacity tonight, Noah thought. If not over it.

Noah moved slowly through the crowd, turning his shoulders to slip between the people, who separated like water around him as he made his way to the side bar. As he got closer, he caught the eye of Clive, one of the bartenders. Clive recognized him, nodded, then raised his eyebrows. Noah nodded, then held up his finger, and pulled Doug in close. Pointed at his bottle. Clive returned the nod, then bent over, popped the cap off a bottle with the deft hand of an expert and grabbed a short glass from a shelf under the bar. He poured several fingers of brown liquid in the glass, then dropped the bottle back into place and slid both of them across the bar just as Noah reached it. He picked them up and mouthed *thank you*, then headed back out into the forest of people.

Doug took his bottle. They held their drinks close to their chests as they squeezed through the throngs of humanity. It was slow going, and occasionally stunted with short stops where friends and acquaintances would wave them in. They'd shake hands and clap each other's backs, say what's up and move on. They got past all the tables and into the main body of the concert crowd, where the energy was somehow even higher. Writhing, sweaty bodies blocked their progress. Slipping between these bodies, there was a lot of promiscuous skin contact. Sweat was transferred from chests to hands. Girls with their hands up in the air, twirling in their own little space made way for the two men, but tried to steal a dance as they passed. They would press up against an arm here or grind their rears against a hip there. It was a sexy crowd, no doubt.

They finally made it to about the center of the floor, and had a pretty good vantage point from which to see the stage. The revelry around them was intense and indiscriminate. There seemed to be no clear lines of demarcation between one body and the next, or even between groups. It was like everyone had come to the show together, in one gigantic bus. One big family. When they settled into their new space, Doug leaned in and told Noah he was going to hit the head.

The drums were well miked. From here, Noah could feel the bass drum vibrating his chest bones, shaking his very lungs. The Sally West had an incredible sound system. He began to feel the excitement of the coming show. The current band would be leaving the stage within the next few minutes. Then the house music would come on for a while – perhaps a little southern rock, maybe some blues – something to set the mood for the final act, but always something disparate. One Last Orbit would come on between nine-thirty and ten.

Noah pulsed with excitement. His nerves were on fire. He had not seen Tanis in the last week and wondered how she would look tonight. It was a dumb line of questioning. She only ever looked one way. He wondered a lot of things though. Would she remember him? Would she see him from the stage? Would she look at him? Would he see her after the show?

He felt a pinch on his elbow. He turned to look and saw Tanis standing there, staring at the stage, a drink in her hand, bouncing slightly, bobbing her head to the offbeat cadence of the drums. Noah's heart skipped. Possibly more than once. It was almost as if his thoughts had called her; his desire for her to appear on the stage had summoned her. To avoid betraying his surprise, he took a quick sip of his drink, looking up at the stage with her. He leaned in close to her ear.

"You like these guys?"

She pursed her lips and nodded, stirring her drink with the thin black straw and long, pretty fingers. It was almost as if they had been standing together all night. Like they were siblings. They were here together. Used to each other's presence. There seemed to be no urgency in the conversation. No need to be excited. Nothing new. Nothing to see here, move along. But inside, Noah was trembling. It made him feel important to have the singer of the headline act standing beside him. And she had gotten his attention. Had he slipped up to the spot where she had been standing without even noticing her? No. No way. He would have seen her. Her hair was piled up atop her delicate head, purple shiny strands reflecting the crazy lightning from above. She wore a black leather jacket zipped all the way up, and black fishnets below a black skirt. The toes of her soft black boots were tapping the concrete.

"Well you look good," he said, and she finally looked at him. She was still stirring that drink. Completely relaxed. He had wondered what it felt like to be in the band that was about to go on. Wouldn't there be nervousness? Apprehension? Not for her, apparently.

"Thank you, Noah. Looking pretty hot yourself," she said. He felt her hot breath against his ear as she spoke loudly enough to be heard, but not loudly enough to be considered shouting.

He turned and smirked at her. At this close tolerance, he could see her makeup. He could see the depth of the brown in her eyes. The tiny lines around her mouth – those things people couldn't see while she was on stage. "I didn't say hot. I said good. An altogether less fancy word, but true nonetheless."

She tilted her head and shook it, standing up on her tiptoes to speak in his ear again. "Yeah, and I said hot."

Noah stood up straight and swallowed. He had to bring himself back down to earth. Did the lead singer of the strongest band in town just say he was hot? Twice? Was he even *on* earth? Was this real? He felt like he was floating. Maybe the whiskey was starting to kick in. Still, Tanis stood staring at him. She put that tiny straw up to her lips and took a sip from her clear-colored drink. She winked at him before returning her attention to the stage.

Noah tried to change the subject. To get his mind off of what was taking place. He had been away from her for a week. His emotions had begun to normalize again. Well, until Trixie had played her tricks with him, he had almost started feeling normal. Noah was part of the world again, not on top of it. Then Tanis comes up and pinches his elbow and sends him into orbit again. Just like that. Was it that she was popular? One couldn't say famous. At least not yet. It wasn't inconceivable that her band would go somewhere. They were very good. But for now she was still small-time. Tanis was definitely well known around these parts, though. He was actually surprised she wasn't being bothered here in the crowd. Maybe they just hadn't noticed. Or maybe her fans were just respectful.

"You ready?" he asked, then immediately felt stupid. Of course she was ready. All one had to do to know that was to glance at her.

Straw still in her mouth, she looked up at him without moving her head, then nodded. The other band hit their last note. The crowd erupted.

"Thank you guys! We're Ten-Foot Woman. Good night!" the singer screamed from the stage. The lights went out for a few minutes while the band left the stage. And then they came back on. It was suddenly bright. Everything looked different. The house music slowly rose to audible. It was nowhere near as loud as the band had been.

"Ten-Foot Woman," Noah said with a smile. "I like that."

Doug returned and punched Noah lightly in the shoulder. "Hey man, I'm gonna grab another drink. Want one?" he asked, then looked down at Tanis. "Hey, Tanis. How you doin'?"

"I'm well, thank you," she said, smiling with the straw still against her teeth. She was twirling it in her slender fingers, clicking it against her teeth, occasionally closing her lips around it for a drink, occasionally licking it.

"Yeah, I'll have one," said Noah. Then to Tanis, "Want a refill?" he asked.

She looked at him for a minute, eyes going back and forth between him and Doug, then said, "Yeah. Sure. Vodka tonic, please."

"You got it," Doug said, then disappeared again. Noah watched him fight through the crowd. When he was ten or twelve feet away, Doug glanced back over his shoulder, obviously knowing that Tanis could no longer see him. Noah and he stood above most of the crowd. She was tall for a girl, but not above-the-crowd tall. Doug and Noah made eye contact. Doug raised his eyebrows and made a face. Then he turned back toward the bar. That look had said everything. *Dude you've got your hands full if you're wanting to keep Joy around.* It wasn't a guess. Noah knew that was what he had said. Lifelong friends had that kind of language.

He returned his attention to Tanis, who was staring at him with easy-going eyes. There was nothing there that spoke of anything sexual. It was just a patient waiting look. One that said, *'I'm here when you're ready to keep talking'.* Noah took another sip of his drink and looked around at the crowd, which was loud, but not rowdy. They were all waiting patiently for the woman beside him to take the stage. And most of them didn't even know she was here. Noah noticed a couple of the guys – and even gals – turning in place to observe her, to see her, and hope she saw them. Maybe hoping for a nod or a smile or a wink. Some kind of acknowledgment that she knew they were seeing her. She gave none. Tanis wasn't stuck-up. She was just completely given to Noah at the moment, and was not spending any energy or time looking around at the crowd. No one was being rude or intrusive though. They all kept their space.

"How was your week?" she asked him, and momentarily, Noah wondered if she knew. Did she somehow know that he had suffered for a good portion of the week, over her? That she had wrecked his normally structured and routine way of life by just talking to him like she was interested a week ago? Was she asking in mockery? No. There was no way she could have known. And what if he had disrupted her even flow as well?

He shrugged, trying to keep his cool. "It was all right. Went camping. Got away for a couple of days, reconnected with nature."

"Oh, cool," said Tanis. "My friend Carrie and I used to go camping all the time growing up. Haven't beeen in ages." She looked at him, still chewing on that damn black straw. Sideways, he suddenly thought how he would love to be that straw. Just to be in her mouth. He let the thought pass before it developed real roots.

"Yours?" he asked, and took a sip of his own drink. His sips were getting smaller and smaller as the level of the liquid in his glass dwindled away to near nothing.

She shrugged. "It was okay. I had to drive to Prospect with Kevin to get some equipment."

Noah stared at her for a minute, wondering if he was missing something. "That it?" he asked.

"Huh?" she said, looking up at him as if he had just awakened her from a daze.

"I mean, that's it? You had to drive to Prospect? That's the extent of your week?"

"Well, that was the only interesting thing that happened," she said, and then blinked. It was almost like she suddenly realized the conversation was a lot more stunted and unnatural than their first, a week ago. "Sorry, my mind seems to be in another world right now."

"Lost in orbit?" he said.

She looked at him sharply, then grinned, a mischievous number. "You've got it." She then stood there for a moment just looking at him, rocking from one foot to the other, back and forth, almost as if she was sizing him up. "So you're here to see Orbit?"

"I know," Noah said, putting his hand on her shoulder.

"Okay," she said, nodding. "You gave no indication last week," she added.

"But then," Noah responded, holding a finger up, "neither did you."

"Ah, I guess that's so. It didn't seem to be important at the time."

"It's still not," Noah said.

"Isn't it?" she asked, eyes a little wider.

"I don't see why it should be. I knew before I ever approached you. That's not why I approached you though," he said.

She stared him in the eyes again, reading him, again. Then she started nodding, slowly. Like she was beginning to accept this.

"Look," Noah said, holding his glass up like it still had liquid in it, "I think it's cool. It's hot. I love that you're a singer. But no, that's not what made me come up and talk to you. It really has no bearing on the case, at least to me."

"I guess that's good?" she asked.

"Not sure I take your meaning. I'm not starstruck, if that's what you're asking. I think that yes, it's good."

"Okay," Tanis said, nodding again. "You know, my music is pretty important to me."

"That's great!" Noah said, swinging his arm round to her shoulder again, where his hand rested once again. "I'm just saying I approached you because of your staggering good looks. Not because of the fact that you sing."

She laughed out loud, then took another sip from her chewed-up straw. "I thought it was my purple hair though."

"No, that was just a beacon in the darkness," Noah said.

She laughed again. "It just seemed a little weird that you knew all along and never asked me anything about it. You know?"

"How is that?" Noah said, pushing his head in a little closer. "Or, why, rather? Does that offend you?"

"No!" she said, finally reaching the bottom of the glass. "Not at all. I'm just not used to it."

"Well, like I said, you didn't bring it up either. Were you trying to hide the fact that you were about to get on stage and slay us all with John Denver?"

She leaned forward, putting her hand on his chest, and suddenly it seemed like it had been before. Like it was supposed to be. She was laughing silently. "Oh, yeah."

"So did that just, uh, slip your mind?"

She shrugged. "I don't know. It just seems like if I bring it up, I'm bragging or something. I don't know. I just usually don't talk about it unless I'm asked."

"Fair enough. Well I didn't know if you wanted to talk about it or not, so I just left it alone. So here we are," Noah said.

"Here we are," she agreed, raising one eyebrow. "Both standing here with empty glasses."

"Oh yeah, shit," Noah said, looking over his shoulder for Doug. There was no sign of him yet. It would probably be a long time coming tonight, busy as it was.

"Okay, so now that the awkward part is out of the way, did you come to see our show tonight? Or were you here for Ten-Foot Woman?" Tanis asked. She looked amused.

"I think we both know the answer to that. This isn't the first Orbit show I've caught," Noah said.

"Yeah, well I have my purse full of magnets backstage, Iron Man!" she said.

This time he laughed out loud. Doug reappeared, balancing three drinks in his arms. "Here you go, guys," he said, handing them off.

Tanis smiled and winked at Doug as she took hers. The three of them clinked their glasses together, and the lights went out. The crowd got loud. Tanis pulled her phone from a back pocket with one free hand and slid her thumb across the screen momentarily, then slipped it back into the pocket.

"I guess this is it?" Noah asked, tilting his head toward the stage.

"What?" she asked, looking up at him with wide, innocent eyes.

"Isn't it time for you to go?" he asked.

"Oh, no, I've got time." She turned her whole body, not moving her hands off the glass or the straw. Doug took her empty glass and spun right in time to catch a waitress walking by. He set their empty glasses on the tray. She smiled at him. Tanis turned to face the stage, still sucking on the vodka. She looked like a child with a treat from the drive-through.

The band came out and began playing a rumbling number with a lot of far-out notes and loops, a lot of echo. It was very spacey. After the initial roar of approval, the crowd was once again bouncing in their shoes, and the people in their general vicinity seemed to have forgotten that the singer was in their midst. They were enjoying the show.

The three of them stood there watching it for a moment, Noah bobbing his head to the beat. "Digging this," he yelled.

"Yeah, I like it too. We wrote it last week."

"Seriously?" he asked.

"Uh huh," she said, looking up at him. That straw seemed to be attached to her teeth.

"Are there words?"

"Yeah. Of course," she said.

"I only ask because their singer seems to be missing," Noah said. Doug looked at them with amusement in his eyes.

"Well it's not quite the singer's time yet," she said, then squatted down slightly, resting there for a moment as the music came to a dead stop and the lights went out completely. After a long pause, the lights and music slammed back to life simultaneously and she popped up like a jack from a box, throwing her head forward – the most Noah had seen her move with the music yet. It was clear she knew the song, if nothing else.

"Here, hold this," she said, holding her drink out to Doug. He took it obediently. Then she unzipped her jacked and leaned in close to Doug's ear. "Thank you for buying me a drink, sweetheart," she yelled.

"Don't mention it," Doug said in return.

She smiled at him, then pulled her jacket off. Now it was clear that she was dressed for the show. She wore a high-neck blouse that covered her entire front with shimmering satin and total class. But her sides were completely exposed. Noah saw nothing but skin under her arms, and as she turned to pull the leather jacket off the other arm, he noticed her back was almost completely exposed as well. She wasn't wearing a bra.

A risky getup if she did not want to expose herself, but it seemed to cover her adequately. And there was part of it that tied around her back at about the chest level. So maybe it was safe.

She held the jacket up and let it drop over Noah's arm, folding itself in half. "Okay. Let's go," she said, and wrapped her arm through his. She started leading him up to the stage, then stopped, turned back toward the drink Doug still held, and reached out with her neck. Doug's hand moved and met her halfway. She took a long drink through the straw, then licked her lips and smiled again. Then they were off. Noah knew where she was going, but wasn't sure what he would do when they got there. So he moved through the crowd clearing a way for Tanis, until he got to the front of the stage. She came to a stop beside him and put her arm around his neck, pulling him close.

"It was extra cool talking to you again, Noah," she said in his ear. Then she grabbed her coat and put it over his shoulder and turned around. She reached back, looking over shoulder and grabbed his hands, putting them on her narrow waist. She squatted and he caught on. Noah hoisted her up where she stepped gracefully onto the stage to ear-splitting applause. Being in front of the first row of bodies, Noah realized how loud it really was from up here when the crowd got into it. Tanis turned and grabbed the microphone with her left hand and walked across the stage singing her first notes through amplification. They were true and beautiful. Noah looked up and smiled, then shook his head and turned to walk back to where Doug was waiting.

2

His questions having been answered about whether or not he would see Tanis before the show, Noah felt relaxed and high with excitement. He had been her primary target before she went on stage. He had put her on stage. Surely that had to mean something. He still had her leather jacket draped over his shoulder. Doug fingered it when Noah got back to his place, in a show of acknowledgment. The unspoken word was that it meant she would have to meet up with him after the show to retrieve it. Noah smirked and nodded, then shook his head. *Unbelievable.*

"And all you did was walk up and talk to her last week?" Doug asked, pushing Noah's ear closed so he could hear against the war of music and crowd going on around them.

"Yeah," Noah said, shrugging. "Crazy. Right place, right time? I don't know."

Doug shook his head, then said, "You got ninety-nine problems, bro."

"I know, man," Noah said.

Tanis marched across the stage like she owned it, speaking to the crowd in her sweet, emery-board voice. She would stand with her foot up on a stage monitor, throw her hand into the air, pointing at the sky and hit a high note that brought everyone to applause and shouts, then in the next song, crouch down at the front of the stage, wrapping her arms around her knees pleading in a sorrowful voice to have them follow her into a dream. It was a lot like a dream for Noah, who was beginning to believe that what he had said earlier might have been perhaps a little disingenuous. The fact that he was not starstruck, that was. But he didn't feel like the term was entirely accurate, either. He had, after all, approached her away from the stage. This was many months after seeing her perform the last time. And in his memory, he could not recall anything particularly moving about the show. He had seen them a bunch of times, and they were always good, but he did not think that her talent had influenced his decision to approach her that evening. But now, watching her on the stage, she looked like an absolute professional. The way she would stand there, biting her lip and looking at the bass player while they got a rhythm going, shaking her hips, snapping with her right hand, the way she would single out someone in the crowd and sing to them for a moment, the way she would sling her arm around the guitarist's neck and lean her head on his shoulder... it was all making him weak in the knees. Just talking to her last week had been enough to rent a large portion of his mind to thinking of nothing but her almost constantly. Now seeing her perform was not helping that at all.

After one song when the lights went out, a soft strumming of the acoustic guitar brought the crowd to loud cheers. Noah recognized the song in a distant memory of the last time he had seen them perform. This was the crowd's favorite. It was a soft, melodious number with a tragic, lonely chord progression, heavy on whining, pitch-bending guitar riffs and deep on the rumbling lows of the floor tom and bass drum. It was very pretty – chill-inducing, in fact, and Noah stood there rocking lightly back and forth between toes and heels as he watched her croon, a goddess in the spotlight, some of the prettiest vocals he had ever heard.

Out on the road, I've been driving all night;
Sleep keeps threatening but I put up a fight...
I need to pull over, been cooped up too long;
The radio's on, but I've not heard a single song.

Noah looked over at Doug to gauge his interest level. He was more than just listening. He was into it too. A lot of the crowd was singing along, in fact. Noah had missed too many shows to know the words to it, but it sounded like one he could enjoy turning up in the Jeep's expensive sound system.

Well I'm coming to get you,
feels like I'm driving to Mars;
Nothing but blacktop,
and I'm surrounded by stars...
I roll down the window,
let the stardust catch my hair;
Just a little while longer,
'til I burn up in your atmosphere

I'm on my way, baby, I think I'll be there soon!
Another quarter-million miles, then I'll slingshot round your moon...
I'll take you up on your offer now!
You said never in a million years,
so I'll take the long way around.

Doug shook his head and nudged Noah with his elbow. Noah looked at the floor, shaking his head. The music was almost entirely crying guitar notes, stretched into long decaying melody that went sour before the note changed. It supported the lonesome lyrics Tanis sang while the guitarist and the bassist sang low harmonies with her, creating a choral element to the music that brought tears to Noah's eyes. Many others, he was sure, were glassy-eyed by now as well. It was spooky in its beauty.

Foot on the gas,
 I nudge it up another notch;
No one's around,
 my hand, it warms a short of scotch…
Blazing through nowhere on this short infinity,
Aiming for one with whom I've strange affinity.

She sang on, swaying slightly in the darkness of the stage while thin streams of blue light circled around her – not quite what one would call a spotlight, but just bright enough to let the crowd know she was there. The bass player, during the chorus, played chords on his guitar. It grabbed Noah's attention and he found himself nodding. The rarity of such a thing tainted his thoughts.

I think I'll catch him just the other side of the sun;
I've invested millennia and now he seems the only one…
He's the music roaming through my soul so free,
The starry song in a stellar symphony, played just for me.

Putting stars behind me, I'm hot on his trail
But I feel so slow, a relativistic hyper-snail.

I'll take you up on your offer now!
You said never in a million years, so baby, I've
taken, I've taken the long way around!

She repeated the last line, getting higher in range and louder, more passionate, holding her hand up and grasping at the words in front of her, hurting with the imagery her lovely voice produced. The pain in her eyes was believable. Noah felt chills up his spine as she sang the line one more time, then the band stopped as she held out the last word, then kicked back in, the guitar a siren that dwindled down to soft background noise. It was incredible. And as the cymbals finally stopped ringing, the lights went out and the crowd answered.

Noah had to set his glass down to give the applause its appropriate respect. He clapped so hard his hands hurt, and whistled. "Dude that was bad ass," he said to Doug, matter-of-fact. It was a haunting, lovely song that pulled at his emotions with just its melody alone. The words and her performance of them had only enhanced it to unbelievable levels. That song would stay with Noah long after the last note rang out.

3

After the show, the crowd thinned quickly, leaving Doug and Noah standing mostly alone in the middle of the floor. There were a couple of dozen die-hards left. A waitress – not Trixie – came by and took their glasses from them, asked if they wanted another round. Noah affirmed that they did, then as she was walking away, reached out and touched her elbow. "Hey," he said. She stopped and turned to look at him again, smiling. "Can you bring a vodka tonic too please?"

"You got it," she said, and fluttered away to the bar.

"Good thinking," Doug said. He stood looking down his nose at Noah. "So what the hell is going on with her, dude? Are you guys like a couple now?"

"Boy it sure feels like it, doesn't it?" Noah said, shaking his head.

"I wouldn't know. How does it feel?"

Noah looked at him. "You know, I don't know. Am I crazy?"

"How do you mean?" Doug said, taking a pull from his beer bottle.

"It's like she puts Joy on hold," Noah responded, rapping a fist against his chest. "How can someone just swoop in and shut me down like that?"

"It doesn't sound like she's shutting anything down but your feelings for Joy. Sounds like she's lighting you up," Doug said.

"Dude, I'm in love with Joy. How can I just forget that so easily?"

"You said it yourself, you love that 'new-love' feeling. We all do, I guess," Doug said, looking around. He stepped away a couple of feet, indicating bodily that the conversation was over.

Noah looked up and saw Tanis approaching. She was getting stopped by the usual groupie girls who hung out after every show, waiting their turn for selfies and shirt-signings. She was smiling and personable to everyone who stopped her. She looked like she was interested in everything they were saying to her. A genuinely nice gal, she was.

Noah stood there with his hands in his pockets, her leather jacket hanging through one of his arms while he waited, shifting his weight with the house music, back and forth between his boots. He glanced over at her occasionally, checking her progress. It was slow going. She had a lot of fans. Occasionally, during the middle of her own talking, she would look over at him as if she were talking to him, staring long at him before finally returning her eyes to the person with whom she was currently engaged. It looked like classic new-love behavior. Could she be feeling the same things he was? Was she smitten by him like he was of her? Surely not.

The thought lingered in his mind though. What, really, was love? It was when two humans struck each other just the right way, with just the right amount of mystery and fancy, causing the covet to creep to the surface of thought. After a good conversation – even just a single one – if one's mind was stuck thinking about that other person, then it was possible for it to grow wings. To develop. To mature. To turn into constant thought, constant craving for more conversation, more interaction, and – thus, more thought. Could that have been what happened here? Well, he couldn't know her side of it. Not yet, at least. But he did know that what he knew about her so far, and the interactions they'd had so far had been enough to keep his mind occupied with her for a long time. Had he been single, or at least sans Joy, Noah had no trouble believing he would be asking Tanis out already. At least for a coffee date. Why not? That's how these things started anyway. A simple conversation turns into the desire for a date. A date turns to interest, to holding hands over the table, those deep looks into each other's eyes, and before you knew it, well... maybe he was getting ahead of himself.

"Hey!" said Tanis as she approached.

Noah blinked himself back into the current universe and looked at her. "Great show, Tanis."

"Aww, thank you!" she said, and sounded genuinely grateful. Either she was really good at faking it, with years full of plenty of practice saying thank you, or she was truly what she advertised – the real thing. She put her hand on his elbow while she spoke. That made it a little more likely, in his mind, that she was the latter. "Wow, I'm hot," she said.

"Yeah, you know, I could have told you that before you got up there and wasted all the time trying to figure it out," Noah said.

She opened her mouth wide, showing her teeth – that lovely silent laugh-smile of hers – and squeezed his arm where her hand rested. Her hand rested on his arm. Noah had to think about that for a moment. She was standing here talking to him with her hand resting on his inner arm. The only time women did that, at least in his experience, was when they were hitched. Tanis was definitely acting like they were a couple. "Was it good?" she finally said.

"Oh God, yes," Noah said.

"Dude. Seriously?" Doug added, making a fist. He took a drink of his beer, then held that fist out.

Tanis giggled, then leaned across Noah to bump her tiny fist against his large one. This put her on the toe of one boot, using Noah as a support for just a brief instant. She pulled her weight back to both feet, using his elbow as the crutch, and ran her other hand back through her hair as she looked about the emptying hall. She was now inadvertently standing a lot closer to Noah. And her hand was now literally hanging from his elbow. Noah didn't dare say anything about it for fear of alerting her to it if she was perhaps unaware.

"We should get a drink, guys!" she said, looking up at Noah. She looked excited. Energized.

Noah glanced over Doug's shoulder in time to see the waitress returning. "Got ya covered, sister," he said, just as the girl appeared from behind Doug with a tray of drinks. When she saw that it was Tanis who was standing with the guys, her eyes widened. She looked a little starstruck herself.

Tanis's mouth dropped open and her eyes widened as she saw the third drink – her drink, complete with a lime wedge – standing on its own napkin on the tray. "You got me one already?" she said, leaning in closer to reach over and take her drink. Her arm slipped fully through Noah's now, and suddenly she was his. Her hand was no longer on his elbow. It was now looped through his arm, wrapped back toward her chest, holding onto her coat. Was this really happening? For a moment, Noah's heart was caught in his throat. He looked over at Doug with wide eyes, checking his reality.

Doug lifted his eyebrows briefly, then he returned his attention to Tanis. "He figured you'd be thirsty," he said, raising his bottle. *Nice aversion. That's what good friends are for.*

Tanis looked up at Noah and smiled, then stood up on her tiptoes and kissed his earlobe. His stomach took flight with butterflies. "Thank you, Noah. I'm ever grateful," she said, then took a long sip from the glass. She glanced at the waitress as Doug flipped his wallet open to pay for the round.

Noah followed her gaze, read her mind. "Oh, can you bring her a straw please? One of those little stir-stick ones?"

"Sure!" the girl said.

"Hey, sweetie, what's your name?" Tanis asked her.

"Joyce," the girl said.

"Thank you, Joyce," said Tanis.

"Oh, sure. No problem," the girl said. She was blushing a little. Noah smiled, amused. Cute girl. "By the way," she said, after working up the courage, "that was a great show tonight!"

"Aww, you're a dear," Tanis said, holding out her arm. She had to let go of Noah to complete the action. This relieved him slightly. At least when they were separated, he knew how to act. "Thank you, darling," Tanis said, pulling the girl in for a hug. Joyce was trying to hold back a legitimate face-splitter by the time Tanis released her. "Hey, why don't you let me get a picture with you, Joyce," Tanis said.

The waitress's eyes widened and her jaw dropped open. "Seriously?" she said timidly.

"Absolutely," Tanis said, pulling out her phone and smiling. She wrapped her arm around the younger girl and pulled her in close, reaching out with her right hand and snapping a photo. "Excellent!" she said when they separated. "That's one for the Insta!"

"Oh my God, thank you, Tanis!" said the girl. She hurried away smiling from ear to ear.

Noah giggled at the exchange.

"Wanna grab a seat?" Doug said, throwing a thumb back over his shoulder.

Tanis looked up at Noah, raising her eyebrows. "Sure!" she said.

"Let's do it," agreed Noah.

They pulled up seats around a high-top and Noah checked his watch. It was almost midnight. City ordinance allowed for bands to play until twelve on Fridays and Saturdays, though the bar stayed open until two. The Orbit crowd had mostly left, and now there was the usual nightlife crowd left in the bar. The pool tables and bars were full, but the hall floor was largely empty. It was a great time for people watching. Joyce found them and brought Tanis her straw, then disappeared.

"What are you boys doing tomorrow?" Tanis said, elbows on the table and twirling the ring on her index finger.

"Washing clothes," Noah said.

"Well that sounds like a real hoot," said she.

"You've waited all week to do laundry?" Doug said, chuckling.

Noah flipped him the bird.

Doug looked at Tanis and said, "We went camping last weekend. Everything we took smelled like a camp fire."

"Ah," she said, raising her chin, then looking at Noah. "That sounds fun. Acadia?"

"Yeah. Fire pit, beer, sunrise. The usual."

She was shaking her head. "Nothing like it in the world."

"Why, what are you doing?" Noah asked.

"Band rehearsal," she said.

"Good word. You guys don't take a break after a show?" Doug said, frowning.

"No doubt. Have you not earned it?" asked Noah.

"It's like football. We always watch the tapes the day after," Tanis said. She picked up her drink and began her fidgeting with the straw.

"You watch tapes?" Noah said, smirking.

"Totally." She looked around the room, then smiled at him. "No, you know we all make these little mistakes during the show though, and the guys are always sure to remind me where I messed up. We work on those parts."

"God, that sounds ruthless," Doug said.

"It's hard work. But it's so worth it. When you have a crowd out there waving to your music, singing your words, it's probably the greatest reward I can imagine. It only makes me want to get better."

"That's awesome," Noah said, shaking his own glass a little. "Well it has definitely paid off. What was that spacey song?"

Tanis leveled her gaze at him. "Mmm, you're gonna have to be a little more specific."

Doug laughed out loud. "That's like asking Tom Scholz which Boston song has the clapping in it."

Noah laughed too, realizing his mistake. "The slow one. The real melodious one about drinking scotch and driving… 'You said never in a million years'," he said.

"Ah. Long Way Around."

"Yeah. That was perfect. Really, really well done."

Tanis reached across the table and squeezed his arm, then retreated. "Thank you. That's very sweet," she said. She smiled and then studied her fingernails.

"It's one of my favorites too. Can I tell you a secret though?"

Doug looked at her and said, "What, you can't stand scotch?"

"Ha! No! I wish that were true!" Tanis said. "No. I wrote that song in like ten minutes."

Noah shot her a look. "Are you serious?"

She nodded, still looking at her fingernails. She blew on them then looked at him again, putting her hands beneath the table. "Yeah. I think some of my best music is the stuff that comes to me really quickly. The ones I deliberate on for hours, or days, just never really seem to materialize. The ones that come fast, that one, *Ode to Night, Calling Neptune*... Those seem to be the peoples' favorites."

Noah frowned and asked, "Owed tonight?"

She put her fingers in the air and pointed at each word. "No. Ode. To. Night. Like it's an ode I wrote to the night."

He raised his chin and his own finger. *Got it.*

"So let me get this straight," said Doug, "you wrote all those songs yourself?"

She looked at him, tilting her head slightly as if to try and judge if he was serious. She chewed her lip for a moment. "Yeah. You're asking if I personally wrote the songs?"

"Well, yeah!" he said, holding a hand out, palm up.

"Yeah. I wrote them. Sorry, I thought you were..." she started. She shook her head then grinned. "Sorry. Never mind."

"That's pretty remarkable," Noah said.

"Thank you. It seems to be the one thing I am able to do consistently, is write music. I can't cook to save a starving child. I can't iron a shirt without creasing it in a bad place. But I can write a song," she said, holding her hands up. Then she leaned in and took Doug's arm with one hand and Noah's with the other. "I hope that doesn't sound arrogant..."

Noah frowned at her, then looked at Doug. Doug was shaking his head. "No. Not at all."

"Okay. Sorry, sometimes it feels like I'm bragging, and I really don't want to brag. We don't choose our talents," said Tanis.

"You know, it must be hard to find audience to talk about the things you love without being judged, or deemed arrogant. But I know people like you, people who are talented – they love to talk about their art," Doug said. "I know a guy who writes books. He's great at it. And he loves to talk about it. The way the characters come to him, the way the chapters like, I don't know, write themselves... He just loves to talk about the craft. But it sounds arrogant. I know he's not. He's just excited about it. He loves to share the behind-the-scenes stuff, how he got where he was in the book, whatever. He just gets excited filling you in on the art side of it. But he can't really do it much because people think he's bragging. And trust me, he's the farthest thing from a braggart. So I think I know where you're coming from."

She was nodding slowly, staring at him intently. "You pretty much nailed it. I would love to tell it all sometime. To sit there and just spill my guts about how I wrote this song or that. I would love it!" she said, looking up to the ceiling, putting her hands against her chest. "But yeah, I think people will think I'm arrogant. I talk about that stuff to my mom, my close friend, Jennifer. But not to many others. Scary."

"Well, we're a safe audience," Noah said. "I'm fascinated by art. I would love to hear about it sometime."

"Well thank you, Noah. That's very kind. I'll fill your ears with my awesomeness."

"I think you already did that tonight, sugar," Doug said, putting his bottle to his mouth.

"You guys are so sweet. I'm glad you enjoyed the show," said Tanis, grabbing their arms again.

"So what's the deal with all the space-themed songs?" Doug said. Noah looked at him, then rolled his eyes. "What?" Doug said.

"Nothing. Just seems like a silly question. So they write about space."

Tanis smiled. "Well, it's not some big mystery or anything, I can tell you that. I didn't get abducted by aliens or anything."

Noah and Doug laughed.

"I've been fascinated with space ever since I was a little girl. My daddy and I watched a Discovery Channel thing about an alien planet or something. It was all computer-gen stuff. But it proposed what life might look like on another planet. It grabbed me hard." She took a drink and shrugged. "I guess that was it. I found a niche. I love to write about it. There are such great distances and gigantic things out there," she said, holding her hands apart like she was grabbing something out of the air. "It's just so eerie and big and lonely – there's just so much to write about."

"That's really, really cool," Noah said.

"Well, not all of my songs are about space," she said and shrugged again.

"Now, you keep saying your songs. Did you write them all?" Doug asked.

"Sorry. I meant our songs. But yes, to be honest, I did write them all. That's one of the things that makes us a tight band. We never fight about who's gonna do the writing. It's just what I do. It's my job. They don't ask, I don't complain… It just sort of works."

"That's amazing," Noah said. "How many songs have you written?"

"Ha! Gosh, I don't know," she said, twirling a lock of hair around her finger as she stared at nothing, thinking. "I would say probably over fifty though. Not all of them have stuck. Like I said, some of the ones that start taking too long to make happen, those just sort of fizzle out and get left behind. Like comets that couldn't keep up," she said, showing that mischievous grin again.

"Is that a lyric?" Noah asked, turning his hand over, offering her the opportunity to explain if she liked.

"Yeah. Could you tell? *We all turn, running, our senses on fire, but not all comets keep up with desire. Those we seek can burn us the most; I'm burning in lethargy, my own solar ghost,*" Tanis rattled off. She then smiled to herself and took another sip of her vodka.

"Effing wow," Noah said. "That was amazing."

"Truly," Doug agreed. He held his bottle up for a toast. The other two tapped his glass.

She smiled again, looking down at the table. "Thank you, guys."

Tanis reached out and dropped her hand on Noah's wrist again – this time his alone. If Doug noticed the exclusion, he did not show it. He paid no attention. Just looked about the place, feeling the vibe.

Noah considered flipping his hand over and taking her hand, but thought it might be a little presumptuous. He wasn't sure why he felt that way. It had been she, after all, who had made all the forward movements so far. But then she reached one hand under the table, grabbing the bar stool, he guessed, and looked around the room herself. She was tapping her foot on the bar stool, causing her upper body to bounce with the rhythm of the music. She also started patting the back of Noah's hand on beat. This was most likely a completely absent-minded rhythm she just had running through her. But now that it was on his hand, he felt a little more emboldened. Noah finally kicked his courage up and flipped his hand over, nonchalantly turning it over onto its back on the table. The next pat came down and dropped her hand in his, and they were suddenly holding hands. She stopped the patting and looked at their hands. He worried briefly that she would pull away now that she realized what was going on. But she didn't. She stared for a moment, then said, "You have really nice nails."

"When I left the house this morning I would not have believed I would hear those words today," he said.

Doug and Tanis laughed out loud. Noah felt relaxed as she clasped his hand a little more firmly. It seemed to be happening so quickly – so *automatically*. He could not well describe it. And was thankful, therefore, that he didn't have to. Doug had noticed the movement too, but said nothing, and didn't look at either of them. He was being politely ignorant.

Noah hunched his shoulders, feeling the discomfort of the bar stool, and cracked his neck. As he moved his head to the left, he saw someone out of the corner of his eye, leaning against the bar, perhaps looking at him. He let his eyes focus. It was Trixie. She was staring with a blank expression. As soon as she saw him looking, she tried a little smile and wave, then turned her head away.

Noah looked up at the ceiling, closed his eyes and silently cursed himself.

4

Doug's was the first phone to vibrate. This was pretty typical, as Alice did a lot more checking up on him than Joy did with Noah. And since Joy didn't typically get home until late she usually went right to bed. She would sometimes send Noah a goodnight text. But she almost never asked where he was. Alice did. Still, there seemed to be a competition between Doug and him in which they monitored who got called home first. Doug was always a good sport about losing, but Noah knew he was jealous.

Alice was plenty of fun to be around. A cowgirl who knew how to hang with the guys. She drank beer and had a mouth like a sailor, and loved to be scooted across a dusty dance floor. Noah adored her as a friend, and was happy for Doug having landed her as a girlfriend. But when it started getting late, curfews always seemed to be enforced.

Doug looked at his phone, then screwed up his mouth and sighed. "Well, friends, this is where the night ends. At least for me," he said.

"Hey, nice rhyme!" Tanis said, smiling widely. "It was great meeting you, Doug. I hope to hang out with you guys again sometime."

"I would be sad and astounded if that did not come to be," he said, putting his hand on his chest. "Fantastic show tonight. Really. I'm a fan."

"Thank you," she said, smiling again, a humble one that showed none of her teeth. "I'm so glad you liked it." Tanis stood as he rounded the table, wrapped her arms around his neck and leaned her head against his chest for a hug.

Noah and he shook hands, slapped each other's backs and said goodbye. And then there were two.

When Doug had left, Tanis looked at Noah and said, "Girlfriend calls?"

"Yeah. She's cool as all hell. But when it starts to get late, she starts getting possessive," Noah said.

"A possessive woman," Tanis said, raising her chin for a moment. Like she knew something she was about to share, then decided not to. Noah couldn't read the inflection she had put in the words, either. He could not tell if her comment had been meant to convey a negative feeling or a good one.

"So, I notice you're not reaching for your phone," Tanis said, tilting her head. She had a mischievous smile on her lips. *Sly*. He realized that was an elegant way of asking if he had a girlfriend, but leaving him an escape if he preferred not to answer.

"I am definitely not reaching for my phone. Everyone I want to talk to right now is right here," he said.

She giggled. "Aw! I like that you said that. I've had a really good time talking to you." Tanis reached into her coat pocket and got her keys out.

Noah looked at them briefly. "Yeah. Me too. Just didn't want it to come to an end so soon," he said.

"Who said anything about it being the end?" she said, looking surprised. She began pushing stray locks of hair back behind her ears. "I was hoping you would be a gentleman and walk me to my car."

Noah tried not to let his disappointment show. "All right. I guess it is about that time," he said, and finished off the rest of his drink. After they had stood up and put their coats back on, they mingled toward the front, hands in their coat pockets. There was no more sign of Trixie, but Noah felt nervous walking out, like he was being watched. Why did he feel so guilty? He had not done anything wrong.

Once outside, she directed him toward the 'Jeep parking' that always seemed to form when Jeepers parked in the same lot. Noah frowned momentarily, then looked at her as they walked. "Wait. What? You drive a Jeep?"

"Yeah!" she said, smiling widely again. "She's sparkly purple."

"Of course she is," Noah said, smirking.

She slapped his shoulder playfully. "I call her Mally."

"You know, I've seen that Jeep here! I would never have guessed it was yours though," he said.

"Why not?" Tanis said. She held a hand up and pointed at her purple hair.

"Okay. So that matches. But you'll have to explain the importance of the name Molly."

"Mally. With an A. Because she's a mall crawler. I don't think I could ever take her off-road."

"Oh, get out of here!" Noah said, turning toward her. "Are you serious?"

"Oh yeah, totally! It's not because I'm afraid I'll scratch it up or anything. I'm just scared to drive on rocks and stuff," Tanis said. They arrived between her Jeep and another. It happened to be his. Hers was backed in, so their driver-side doors were only a couple of feet apart. What were the odds, he wondered, that they would be parked right next to each other?

"Why, what do you drive?" she asked

He reached behind him and knocked on the door.

"Uh-uh!" she said, shoving him on the shoulder. He actually had to put his foot back to keep from being pushed off balance. "You're kidding!"

"Nope. Meet Amber Waves."

"Hello, Amber!" Tanis said. "Well, I'm sorry, love, but I'm going to have to see you start her to believe you are parked right next to me."

He shrugged, then popped the door and climbed up into the seat. He engaged the clutch and pulled it out of gear, then turned the key. His Jeep purred to life.

"Oh my God!" she said, that wide-open smile painting her pretty face in the light of a nearby street lamp. "That is crazy!" Then she turned and hopped up into her own cab, which was actually a couple of inches taller than his. He reckoned hers was sitting on thirty-seven-inch tires. Noah felt a little inadequate. She turned her key and got Mally warming up, then jumped back down and shut her door.

"This is so crazy," she said.

Noah's stereo suddenly blared to life. The satellite sometimes took a minute to come on. He realized it was very loud. Kings of Leon's *Arizona* was blasting out his open door. It had just started. Noah flinched and reached to turn it down, but Tanis reached in and grabbed his hand.

"No!" she said, pulling his arm. "Leave it!"

He stumbled down onto the parking lot with his door at his back. "You like these guys?" he asked, nodding his head toward Amber Waves.

"What, are you kidding?" she said. She was still holding his hand, swaying back and forth on her feet. "Dance with me, Noah!"

Noah swallowed and assessed the woman in front of him. He stepped forward and put his right hand on her waist. They rocked back and forth on their feet while Caleb sang about his heartbreaking encounter in the desert. He looked down at her while they moved slowly from foot to foot. She wore deep black eyeliner, accentuating the depth of her brown eyes. Noah looked at her full lips, beautiful and thick, slightly spread as she stared at him. Her nose was thin, chin small and pointy. He thought she had the face of a doll. How had he thought she was anything less than staggering before? Of course, he had never been this close to her. Behind her, sparse, weak snowflakes were coming from a pitch-black sky. The winter fog made the glow of the street lamps seem confined. It made the sky feel close – like they were in a small shell of existence, safe from the rest of the world. Other people were walking to their cars in the distance. Some looked over, some smiled. None had anything to say. Tanis stood with the toes of her boots up on Noah's own toes. As they shifted their weight to one foot, the other would scoot this way or that, just slightly. The snow was too scarce to amount to anything other than tiny silver sparkles in the air. The few dots that landed on Tanis's hair stood out like stars for their brief, tiny lifespans, before disappearing. Noah reckoned that if there were to be forgiveness for a stolen kiss, it would come now. Right here, right now, he could kiss her. She would let him. He could feel it. They stood rocking to the slow percussive beat from the Jeep's speakers, that meandering bass line, the reverb-heavy guitar… It was perfect. But he didn't want to be the one to break that boundary. Not yet. They said nothing. Just looked at each other. He slipped his thumbs through her belt loops, his fingers fell on her back pockets. She moved her hands up to clasp them behind his neck. The music was only loud enough to dance by, loud enough to make whispering a task – but from a distance, it wouldn't be a bother. No one was disturbed. And Noah felt like if this song were to accidentally repeat twenty or thirty more times, the snow could come down as hard and thick as it liked. He would be happy to stand here dancing with Tanis all night. But as the drums dropped off and then kicked back in, he knew it was to be short-lived. He swallowed. She took a deep breath. The song ended. Another began. She dropped her hands and turned, looking around the parking lot.

"Well. Okay. Not sure this parking lot has ever felt so beautiful," she said.

"It has never been this beautiful. It may never be again," Noah said.

"You're right. We have to make sure of that."

He looked at her for a moment, wondering what was running through her mind. Her hands were back in her pockets and she was licking her teeth behind closed lips.

"What does that mean?" he said, finally.

"I mean we can never let it be more beautiful than what just happened."

"Oh. Would you not like that to happen again?"

"Not here, no," Tanis said. She was looking at him with mysterious eyes. "We have to spread the beauty to other places. Parks. Water towers. Bridges during rush hour. Pastures full of running horses in the rain."

She looked up at the falling snowflakes and closed her eyes, a smile spread across her face. "Alleys between old gray fences, the roof of an old abandoned shopping mall at midnight, under the long shadow of a windmill..." she trailed off, then looked at Noah.

Noah shook his head, a smile almost finding his lips. He was too stunned to speak.

She looked around again, then sighed. "Well, I think it's probably time for me to say goodnight."

"How did you get to be so poetic?"

She leaned her head to one side and smiled lightly at him. "Poetry is music for the deaf." She touched his chest with a pointing finger. "You be the music, I'll be the words."

He wanted to think of something clever to say, but could not come up with anything. It was too late anyway. She was climbing up into her Jeep. "See you around, Noah. Thank you for the dance tonight."

He lifted his chin. As he stood there with his hands in his pockets, watching her through her open door, he felt like something big was about to drive out of his life. "I'll be your music any time you want to dance," he finally said.

Tanis sat completely still for a minute, eyes struck with fascination. "That was beautiful, Noah." Then she smiled. "Good night," said Tanis Ransom. And then she closed her door and pulled slowly out of the parking space, brake lights creeping away as he stood watching, dots of snow collecting on his shoulders.

5

Noah lay in bed, sweating in the dark. The music was loud. He had the mp3 player on his phone set to a 70s rock station, playing nothing but solid hits. The high-end stereo that stood atop his dresser pushed music through the floor speakers at either side of it, loudly enough to wake the house, had there been anyone else home. Doug had gone to Alice's tonight, so Noah had the whole house to himself. To get stoned, to get drunk, to listen to music way too loud and lie in bed, kicking himself in the teeth for not kissing Tanis Ransom. He hadn't even gotten her phone number. Joy's pretty, freckled face kept creeping back into his mind, but he kept pushing her down. He knew he would have to think about her at some point. He would have to face the music. But for now, he avoided it. He was just thankful they still lived apart. That gave him his bed. His queen-sized den of torture. The ceiling fan might have been on. If it was, he couldn't feel it. He knew only that he was hot, he was high, and he had an old fashioned glass in his hand, resting on his chest. It had some amount of liquor in it. He couldn't remember how much, or when the last time was that he had taken a drink. He had refilled it several times when he got home. Thoughts of Tanis and the streaks of purple in her hair danced maddeningly through his head. Why did it have to be like this? Why did she have to come along when he already had someone? Why did it have to pour when it should only be raining?

He rolled his head to look at the clock. It was three-thirty-three. "Make a wish," he said aloud, hand flailing in the air toward the clock. "I wish I had never met her." Noah lifted his head as much as his chin would allow, to take another tongue full of the whiskey. It dribbled down his chin, onto his neck, down to the sheets. "I wish I had never freakin' met her," he said again. Then his head fell back on the pillow and he stared at a spinning ceiling lit only by the absurdly bright orange display of the stereo. And he wondered who *her* was.

Noah reminded himself that he had not had any intention of stirring anything up with Tanis. He had not even given it any thought. He tried to relive the evening he had met her. It was mostly a fog, but he thought he had most of it right. He had been talking to one of the vapid idiots at a nearby table about work or something. One of those small talk conversations that was getting too big. He remembered that much. And he had seen Tanis standing there at the next table. What was it that had made him want to go talk to her? It was true what he had told Trixie the other night: it really was in his nature to flirt. That was just what he did. He never pursued anything with it. He never went beyond the wink and the smile. Just having fun, that was all. So he knew that night had been no different. Noah had not seriously considered he would actually have a chance with Tanis Ransom. He was a good-looking guy. He didn't have that sharp, chiseled movie-star face like Doug, but nor did he have the puffy-cheeked innocence of a baby face like Troy. He was comfortably in the middle, right where he could avoid it forever if he wanted. If he breezed through life avoiding women, he would never get any attention at all. But if he made any moves, used any smooth words at all, he could have them smiling pretty quickly. And so he had made a hobby out of collecting these smiles from women. Not phone numbers, not marks on a bedpost. Just smiles. The kind of smile that means something. He was good at it. That had to have been why he approached the singer. Maybe she had looked like a challenge to him. Maybe he thought he would have to work hard for that elusive smile. Well, that had not been the case. He remembered clearly how quickly that smile had shown up. As the strings section burned into the warm darkness from the Stones' *Moonlight Mile*, he remembered clearly that first smile. It had looked like she was about to either laugh or say something big. That smile was powerful. More powerful, perhaps, than any word she could have said. He had collected his smile. So… Why was he still talking to her? Why had he not just moved along, happy with the acquisition? He leaned up and took another swig of liquor, a little more carefully this time.

Noah rolled his head to the other side and found his phone on the spare pillow. He picked it up and woke the screen up. No messages. No missed calls. Nothing. What had he been expecting at almost four in the morning on a Sunday? Well, he knew what he was wishing for. But he had already made his wish, hadn't he? He wanted to change it. *I wish I had gotten her number.* He rolled his eyes and put his hand on his sweaty forehead. Atlanta Rhythm Section came on the stereo. *So Into You.* Noah stared at the ceiling and sang along, tapping his foot against the air, shaking his leg with the swing. *Why the hell didn't I get her damn number?*

During the keyboard hook, Noah raised his whiskey glass with his left hand, and played the air piano with the other, singing the notes loudly. He made a pact with himself. Tomorrow. Today. Whatever the hell day it was. He would wake up and get started on his life-changing decision. Sunday. Noah would spend at least half the day thinking about what he wanted. *Who* he wanted. Was he prepared to break up with Joy, potentially ruining her life just for a shot at this girl he didn't know? When it came down to it, he knew one thing about Tanis Ransom. She could sing. What if she was no fun off the stage? What if she was just a regular girl – which he already had? Well, he knew they were all regular gals underneath it all. But what if there was truly nothing special about her? What if she was a terrible lover? What if, what if, what if? Who cares? He couldn't stop the tide of his heart. It was pulling him deeper into the allure of mystery. He had to find out. Regardless of what he knew or didn't know, he had to find out what she was all about. Ruin Joy's life? Very simply, *so?*

Oh God, *Dreams* came on. Stevie scorning a player. At the very base of it all, was that not all he was? Whatever decided to do – whatever he did – if he broke Joy's heart just so he could find out who Tanis really was, then he was no better than that player Stevie Nicks was singing about.

Noah took the fingerprint-spotted glass off his chest again and rolled to the side, setting it on the nightstand. Then he sat up on the edge of the bed, hands gripping the disheveled comforter under him and staring at the floor. What was he doing? Why had he gotten so serious about this? Nothing had even happened yet. What if she was just a really sweet girl? One of the types who was just that nice, that touchy-feely – that *dancey* – with all her friends? He laughed out loud at that. No way. He stood up and dragged his feet across the carpet, looking at the display from the stereo. The warm, orange glow telling him he was listening to *STREAMING* music. It illuminated the room with a beautiful aura. He went past it to the bathroom to take a leak and stumbled into the wall before finding the toilet. While he stood peeing, he looked up at the picture above the commode, a painting his grandmother had let him pick off her wall when he was a child. A small house sitting on a lot of land. His hand on the wall for support, he stared at that stupid little print and wondered what it was like to live in that little house. No women to screw with his emotions. *Eye in the Sky* by The Alan Parsons Project came on and he had to sing it out loud while he stood there.

"Damn, what a great song," he said after finishing the first chorus. He flushed the toilet and made his way back to the bed, playing air guitar on the way. When he hit the edge of the bed, he toppled into it, face down. He sang the next chorus too. But beyond that, he couldn't have told anyone what song was even playing. The next time he was aware of anything, it was hard to remember how he had even gotten there.

6

Noah became aware, in a far-off, disconnected sort of way, that it had suddenly gotten quiet. Much like a sudden noise can be startling, this sudden silence was disorienting. But he was still unconscious. It was just the edge of awareness. Somewhere over the distant hills, he had heard something being loud, and now it was silent. He thought his ears might be ringing. Then he thought his shoulder was against a wall. He felt pressure there. He rolled up and tried to push himself away from it, but his hand met with something soft instead of the hard resistance of the wall. "Uhnn," he grunted and rolled his head over. It was a belly. A woman's belly. He lifted his head.

"Good morning, baby," said Joy.

"Uuuuhnn," was all he could manage.

"Have a little too much last night?" she asked.

Noah managed to roll over and cover his eyes. Everything above his neck hurt. He couldn't feel anything below it. It was like his body had been cut off below the head. "What time is it?" he moaned, hands still covering his eyes. He felt weight settle on the bed beside him.

"It's almost noon, sweetie."

He felt fingers in his messy, sweaty hair. "Oh my God," he said.

"I brought you some aspirin," she said.

"Huh?" Noah said, sitting up.

"You look like you could use some, baby," she said and handed him several white spots and a glass of cool water.

"Oh, God, thank you. You're amazing."

"You'd do well not to forget that," she said and leaned in to kiss his forehead. "You could probably use a shower, too." Joy fingered the hair off his forehead.

"I'm sure," he agreed. He dropped back onto the bed and rolled to the other edge. It was easier than crawling. There, he stood and almost crumbled under the ache in his head. He cried out again and made his way to the bathroom. He reached in and started the shower, then sat on the toilet, resting his head in his hands.

"Why did I do that?" he asked.

From the other room, Joy said, "I'm sure you mean about the drinking so much."

"Yes. The drinking so much. I could have been fine with half of what I drank. I'm miserable."

"True. Or I guess you could mean dancing in the parking lot. I might be asking myself why I did that," Joy said.

Noah looked up sharply. "Huh?"

"Hon, your sister goes to all those concerts, too. She said she saw you dancing in the parking lot with some woman."

Noah's vision began to blur. He could hear his heartbeat pounding in his ears. His blood felt like sludge – like concrete not yet dried, pumping through his head. The pain of his headache was trebled. Why had Lennie told on him? What the hell was she thinking? They were so close.

"I'm not mad, Noah," Joy said after a minute. "Kind of interested to know who it was. And maybe why. Maybe even what this means for us, but…" she trailed off.

"Nothing. I don't even know why she told you. It wasn't a big deal. And it wasn't planned or anything. Just one of those weird things," Noah said.

"She thought it was me at first. She was going to come say hi and dance with us. Then she realized the woman was taller than me. And had purple hair."

Good God. Noah shook his head, closed his eyes. Not only had he been spotted, but if she didn't already know who the other woman was, it wouldn't take long to figure out. He finished draining and stepped into the shower.

"Who was it, Noah?" Joy said as she came into the restroom. She lowered the lid and sat on the toilet so she could talk to him while he showered.

Well, she didn't know who it was based on the hair alone. Not yet, anyway. "No one, babe. This gal drives a Jeep. We just walked to our cars together. We started them to let them warm up and a song came on so we danced for a minute. It was all in fun."

"That does sound fun!" said Joy. "See, I think I miss out on so much of the fun stuff just because I'm always at work."

Noah closed his eyes and let the scalding water wash away the night. It would be a while before he felt human again. He had lived yesterday on credit, and the bill was due today.

7.

Over dinner, Noah and Joy sat at the table talking, and surprisingly enough, drinking. They had run to the market and split up when they got there. He had hit the butcher's counter while she went to the wine aisle. So they shared a bottle of Moscato. Slicing into rare beef that jiggled when their forks touched it, they enjoyed one of their finest meals together. And then they moved to the back patio, where they sat in Adirondacks looking out at the sky. It was unseasonably clear out, and the moon was new. There were billions of stars to be seen.

Noah looked over at Joy and was reminded of why he had always been attracted to her. He squeezed her hand and thought about what they had developed together over the last three years. It seemed silly now, in the warmth of her presence and the sweet wine to be pining for a girl he didn't even know. Tanis was full of mystery. But at one time, so had Joy been. At one time, he reminded himself, he had gone just as crazy over her.

It had been three years ago. Noah had just turned twenty-seven. His sister, Lennie, had still been full of her teenage spunk at twenty-four. That spark and liveliness that was so attractive to everyone, and that Noah himself adored. The two of them had been at a Renaissance Faire together. Lennie was walking behind Noah, hiding herself as they walked along the dirt avenue. Doug had been there too, with his girlfriend of the time, Lacy. Noah had begun to ignore his little sister, growing tired of trying to keep up with her energy. She was darting into shops and trying on headdresses, wielding wooden axes and making mean faces, picking up wooden tankards and acting like she was sloshing ale all over her. None of this was out of character for her. Lennie had enough energy, Doug had once said, to power most of Los Angeles County for several days with just a good night's sleep.

So there was little Lennie, walking behind Noah as he and Doug and Lacy walked in a single rank line, the latter two holding hands. Lennie wasn't bored. She was just burning off loose energy. Grabbing his belt loops and squatting behind him as they walked, she scooted along. Noah, being used to her behavior almost never grew impatient with her anymore. He just simply ignored her. She finally got bored of walking behind him, and popped out to his right, to bounce along beside him for a while. And when she did, she slammed full into a woman coming the other way. In this collision, the woman's nearly full mug of beer went all over her chest.

"Nice," Noah said, stopping and turning to look. "God. I'm so sorry, ma'am. She's off her meds."

The woman's hands were up and she was looking down at her chest and the dirty wooden mug at her feet. But when she looked up Noah, she was smiling. "I'm just drinking too slow," she said softly.

Lennie had disappeared. Noah turned to look for her, but she was just gone. "I am so, so sorry. I don't know about that," Noah said, pointing at the soaked blouse, "but I can replace the beer for you."

"It's really okay," she said, and glanced away.

Lennie was back. And just like always, instead of saying sorry and wasting words, she spent it on actions. She had towels in her hands. Not paper towels, but real towels. Noah could only have guessed where she had gotten them. Resourceful as ever, little Lennie. But she was patting this strange woman down, straight face full of concentration and concern. The woman stood there with her arms spread, smiling slightly. Noah gathered that she was trying to come up with the words to say it was okay, or not to worry about it, but was just stunned speechless.

"God. Dude, Lennie? Really?"

"It's okay, really," the woman said, and gave Noah a wide smile. It was then that he had looked at her for the first time. Really looked at her. Her wide smile was very wide. Her lips were only a shade darker than the pale, white skin of her face. She had striking orange hair and about a million tiny freckles on her face. The milk-white skin of her face complemented the white teeth in her smile. Shiny, straight row on top, crooked on the bottom. She was obviously not self-conscious about this jagged run of bottom teeth though. She was showing them off in the most beautiful way. Noah was instantly smitten. While Lennie was in robot mode, not talking, not apologizing, just moving up and down the woman's body with one towel while the other hung over the woman's shoulder, Noah shook his head again.

"Sorry. She's on a mission."

The woman closed her mouth, never stopped smiling, and raised her eyebrows. She looked like she was actually enjoying it. "She's a keeper!" said she.

Noah raised his chin. "Uh, she's my sister."

The woman's eyes widened and the smile finally dropped. "Oh. Oh, really?"

"Uh huh. What's wrong?" asked Noah.

"Nothing at all. Can I change my mind about that beer though?"

When they had first met, Noah and Joy had spent nearly every waking moment together. They talked all the time when they couldn't be together. Talked late into the night until their cell phones were hot against their faces, batteries complaining of low charge. At that time, Joy had worked as a marketing lead for a catering company, so her hours were strange, but typically only busy around lunchtimes. She would show up at his house before and after lunch in work clothes and let him take them off. If she couldn't come by his house for whatever reason, he would sometimes meet her on one of her routes and they'd find a parking lot. She drove a company van. It had a large cargo area. They made use of this on many occasions.

Now, after almost three years, they were settling into routine. Everything was still great, but it wasn't new anymore. It didn't have that new feel about it that turned Noah on so much. This was, he reckoned, why he liked the hunt so much. Regardless of if he took home the game, the hunt was so much fun. It was a thrill just getting a look or a smile or – on rare occasions – an actual phone number. Though he never did anything with the numbers, just the rush of adrenaline in a victory was all the reward he needed. But when the dust settled, and he found himself at home again in her arms, or sitting here on his patio holding her hand, he was always glad he had Joy. She truly was a catch.

Tanis *might* be a catch. Joy, he knew, without a doubt, *was*.

As he looked over at her, his feelings of dread and dismay began to slip away. The wind blew in through the screen, whistling lightly and bringing the scent of honeysuckle from the neighbor's fence with it. It was cool, but not unbearable.

"You okay?" she asked, smiling lightly at him.

"Yeah. Think so. I think I'm going to live now. Earlier, I wasn't sure."

Joy smirked at him and leaned her head back against the wood of the chair. Her feet were up on the seat, knees up near her chest. She squeezed his hand. "I may be able to get off next Friday night again. Who's playing at the Sally?"

Noah looked out at the fence at the back of the yard, the night sky above it, took a deep breath. "Oh, let's see. The tenth?" He thought for a moment. "Dusty." He looked back at her. "Dusty's playing."

"Oh. Are they good?"

Noah shrugged. "They've got like a southern rock, bluesy style. Like Don Henley meets Warren Haynes with a dash of Elvis thrown in."

"That sounds great! I've always had a thing for Elvis."

Noah nodded for a moment, taking a sip of his wine. Then he frowned. He looked over at her. "Really? I've never heard you say anything about him."

"Oh yeah. I used to love him when I was a little girl. Love Me Tender?" she said, and nodded, pursing her lips.

"Costello, honey. Not Presley."

"Oh," she said. She stopped smiling and looked straight ahead. "Oh. Yeah, I guess I should have known that."

"I'm an Elvis man, baby. Just not *that* Elvis."

"Got ya," she said, pointing at him and taking another sip of her own wine. "Still."

"Still," Noah agreed, pointing back at her.

"You know, I always thought how cool it would have been if Michael Jackson and Lisa Marie Presley would have had a child. Can you imagine that legacy? The King of Pop is your dad, the King of Rock is your grandpa?"

"Good God, yes," Noah said, frowning again. "Never thought about that."

They slept together that night. Joy did not always, nor automatically, stay at Noah's house. It was a strict counsel she kept with her good side, she claimed. She liked exercising her willpower, and would sometimes leave after a heavy make-out session just to be sure that they still had control of themselves. Noah wasn't all that sure he agreed with that part of it, but it was rare enough that he didn't fight her on it. On the nights she left, she would remind him that once he married her, he could have her all the time. If he wanted to end this unsure charade of not knowing how long he had her, he had to put a ring on her finger.

When she did stay, they did not always, nor automatically have sex. If she stayed, they slept together in the literal sense. He would never make her, nor would she agree to, sleep on the couch or anything as silly as that. But sleeping together did not mean anything would happen. Joy explained that she had to save some part of her for him, in the hopes that one day she would have all of him. And instead of one particular body part, she saved herself entirely on certain nights. But once again, there was no schedule, and sometimes he would be driven to near madness and intense discomfort because of her leaving.

Doug, when Noah brought it up to him, didn't seem to see anything wrong with it. "Man, she kind of has a point. She's giving you occasional tastes of what you're gonna get if you marry her. I can't really blame her." And he got nothing out of his sisters. Lennie, the closer of his two sisters, would make a face and say, "Ooh, Noah! I don't want to imagine that you even do that. Ever." And that was that. Lisa, well, there were just some things he didn't bother bringing up with her. They had their distance, set about by the age gap for one, but a completely different set of interests for another. Lisa and he would hang out every few months, sometimes as infrequently as two or three times a year. And it usually felt like it was only because they were related.

Lisa, rather than going to college like her sister Lennie, or the Air Force like her brother Noah, had gone to beauty school and learned to cut hair. Straight out of high school, she had gone to live with a group of friends in a house in Portland. Noah called it the compound. No fewer than twelve people were living there at any given time. And after seeing her for the first time in half a year back then, she came home covered in tattoos and piercings. They did not have much in common, but she was full of wisdom even for her young age, sometimes getting Noah to see things in a way no one else could, and sometimes helping him to solve weird problems, therefore.

Lennie was a bubbly, free-spirited and selfless person. She worked at a bookstore, even though she had a degree in Psychology. After finishing school, she tossed her degree on a side table and went to look for a job that made her happy. Being around books made her a lot happier, she said, than sitting in some chair with her legs crossed, taking notes on someone's feelings. When people came into the bookstore, she knew what they were feeling based on what they were looking to read. And she had met a lot of great people doing it. Lennie and Joy had grown very close over the last few years as well. Lennie loved her as much as Noah did, and was sometimes the glue that held them together. There had been several fights from which neither Noah or Joy did not think they would recover. But Lennie would come in and talk to one or the other, and like magic, they would always find a way to work it out.

Lennie would sit on the table holding Joy's hand, presenting her case to Noah, or show up at Joy's apartment begging Noah's case when that's what she felt the situation called for. They both knew how important she had been to their survival on more than one occasion. They really didn't fight like that anymore, but Lennie was still thought of as the peace bringer.

Tonight, Joy lay on her side facing Noah, her forehead against his chest. His arm was behind her back, toying with her hair, twirling it in circles round his finger. She was staying tonight. But tonight, he was lucky Joy was still here. And this time, he thought, it could have ended because of Lennie. Her little tattle trick had almost gotten him in trouble.

As he lay thinking about the peace he now felt, he decided he was in the right place. Noah stared up at the ceiling, only barely visible with the dim orange glow from the stereo and thought about how happy he really was, and what a mistake he had almost made. Then he thought of Trixie, and his heart skipped a few beats. He shook his head. He couldn't believe she had come onto him like that. So within two nights, he had almost lost Joy because of as many women.

Lennie was there when they woke. She was sitting on the couch reading a book and listening to classical music. When Noah came into the living room, she bounced up and squealed with excitement then ran to hug her brother, and asked him if he wanted breakfast.

"I can cook for two!" she said.

"You mean three?" Noah asked. "Joy's here, too."

"No. I included her," Lennie said, turning and holding a finger up at him, staring at the floor. "I already ate."

"Oh, well look at you little gangsta!"

"Look at me!" she said, waving her hands and shaking her hips.

Lennie turned the stove back on and started cracking eggs into a dirty skillet. Noah sat at the table and looked out the window at the backyard.

"My friends and I are going out tonight. I want you to come," Lennie said. She stood at the stove with one hand on a spatula, the other on her hip, facing him.

Noah looked over at her. "Why? Where are you going?"

"The Devil's Rainbow," she said.

Noah stared at the salt and pepper shakers on the table. He blinked. Then he looked up at Lennie. "What the hell is that?"

"Oh come on! Just trust me for once, will ya?" Lennie said pleadingly.

"You want me to trust you when you say you and your friends, who I don't even hang out with, are going to a place called the Devil's Rainbow. Yeah, that sounds awesome. Count me in," Noah said. He got up from the table and went to the coffee maker to start a pot. There was already a pot there. Lennie was on top of her game.

"Yes! I do! You've taken me many places in my life, and a lot of the times I had no idea where we were going. And you said those exact words."

"Devil's Rainbow?"

"Trust me."

"Trust you about what?" Noah asked.

"No. Trust me. Those are the two words," Lennie replied.

"What two words?"

"Jeez, bubba, you're dumber than a sack of brown lettuce when you haven't had your coffee."

"So why would you ask me things before I've poured my first cup?"

After breakfast they sat out on the patio for a while with coffee and tea while Joy got ready for work. Noah was trying to get himself in gear for work as well, knowing he had four clients he had to check on today. It had been a big weekend, and seemed like weeks since he had even thought about work. It was hard to get motivated again. So instead, he sat in an Adirondack chair and let the sun hit his face through the screen. It was cold outside, but one wouldn't know just by looking. The sun was out, the breeze was blowing, and it looked like a spring morning.

"So who were you dancing with the other night, Noh?" Lennie asked him after a long silence.

Noah looked at her over the top of his shades. "You don't know?"

"No! I couldn't tell. It was too dark. I could tell she had purple hair though."

"Why are you so interested in it?"

"Why were you doing it?"

"Look, it's not something I planned on. It just sort of happened. I walked that girl to her car, and a song came on when we started them to warm them up. So she grabbed my hand and we danced," Noah said. He held his coffee mug up to his mouth but didn't drink. "Anyway, I've already talked to Joy about it."

She grunted. "I don't care about that. I wasn't trying to get you in trouble, Bubba. I was just curious who you knew that had purple hair."

He glanced at her again, then shook his head. Then he sighed. "Our little secret?"

"Secret? Why does that matter, if it didn't mean anything? Was it Joy's sister or something?" Lennie asked.

"No. It was Tanis."

"The singer of One Last Orbit?" Lennie said, eyes wide.

Noah looked away, nodded.

"You dog! Oh my gosh! I wish I would have known that!" she said, slapping his shoulder over the small table. "I would have totally came over there! I didn't know you knew her!"

"I don't, really," Noah said. "Like I said, I just walked her to her car. Not a big deal. And we didn't plan it."

"Aww, well I still think that's really sweet and romantic."

"Of course you do. You're a girl," Noah said.

"You introduce me to her and I'll keep your secret," she said, playfully biting her lip.

"Why would you do this to me?"

"What's the big deal about it? Just introduce her to me. No harm, no foul!" Lennie said.

The screen door swung open and Joy came out. Her hair was wet. She wore the black skirt and white blouse of her uniform, but was still barefoot. "What's up, guys?" she asked, coming to a seat beside Noah.

Noah looked at Lennie one more time. She squinted her eyes at him like a threat, then smiled. "Hey, babe," he said to Joy. "I think I'm going out with Lennie and her friends tonight. Not sure when we'll be back," he said. Then he looked at Lennie. The breeze whipped in through the screen and blew her hair into her face. She leaned her head back. She looked like she was enjoying it. "When will we be back, sis?" he asked her.

"I'd say no later than midnight."

Noah nodded, then returned his attention to Joy, who sat on his opposite side, hand on his wrist. "Cool! Where are you all going?"

"The Devil's Rainbow, apparently," Noah said, waving his other hand lazily.

"Ah, cool! That'll be fun!" Joy said.

"What, you've been there?" Noah asked.

"Yeah! Of course! Have you not?"

Noah shook his head and got up to go back inside. He had work to do if he was going anywhere tonight.

A single-file line wound its way through the brush and branches on the trail toward where the sun had been just minutes before. The sky was a deep orange up ahead over the trees, but faded quickly to the dark, cold colors that spoke winter in the mountains. Though there were not many mountains out here, there were a few. And down in the trails within them, there could have been thousands. As long as there were two beside them, Noah thought, they were lost in the mountains. The air was a lot colder out here than it was in the city. City being a loose word for where they lived, of course.

The trail was only wide enough for one person, and it was dark enough that its color nearly blended in with the grass on either side of it. The only way one could tell the difference was by the texture. Noah could see his breath. He walked at the back of the line behind three girls, one of them being his sister, Lennie. The only other guy in the group was at the front of the line. They all had backpacks on – Noah had been handed one when they got out of the car – and they were all heavy. He was playing along, having no idea what was in store for the evening, but not wanting to let his sister down. It was a funny favor game, feeling like he owed her for all the things he had ever done for her. Now he had to let her do something for him. Let her run the show, to show him a good time. And there had been rumor that there might be a fire somewhere in their future. Noah could definitely get behind that.

On the car ride out here, Noah had sat in the backseat by the window. His sister sat in the middle between himself and another girl her age named Cagney. The other guy was driving. There was another girl in the passenger seat up front. He didn't know her name. He thought the guy's name was Trent or Brent – something like that.

The only thing that made it tolerable, besides the loud music, was that the girl up front was liberal with passing around her flask full of Canadian whiskey. The sun had begun to set just as they were finally nearing the end of the road trip. The window was cold against Noah's temple. His sister had kept grabbing his knee and shaking him, trying to get him excited about the trip, but refused to tell him anything about what they were doing.

When they finally pulled into a parking lot, Noah had been about to drift off. The comforting noise of the road with the consistency of the wind against the glass near his face and the mono conversations had made him drowsy. Then it was quiet, and doors were popping open. Now they were here. Wherever here was. He knew Acadia National Park. But he had not been to any place called the Devil's Rainbow. At least not that he was aware of.

The firs and the spruce trees stood like silhouetted statues against the night, dark against the darkening sky. As they stumbled over rocks and holes in the trail, they finally came to a point where there was an opening. A slight rise in the trail went between two trees, and looked as if the world just dropped off, or came to an end. Lennie turned around smiling, and quickly got behind Noah, putting her hands over his eyes. He stopped in his tracks.

"What the hell, sis? I'm not walking anywhere like this," he said.

"Oh, just like two steps; not far. I promise," Lennie said.

Noah took a deep breath and sighed for effect, then scooted his feet forward, until he felt his arm being grabbed by someone else entirely.

"Stop!" Lennie said. "Brent, make sure he doesn't fall," she added.

Noah stood stark still, then shook his head under her small hands. "Fall? Lennie, dude, this is getting uncomfortable real fast."

"You'll be all right," Brent said. "Let him see, Len."

Her hands dropped away, and Noah was staring at a gap between two parts of the mountain. Not a very impressive view. But the sun was completely gone now, and everything was getting dark. He wondered if it would be prettier with a mist or sunlight or something. And then he looked down and realized what he was supposed to be looking at.

A rope bridge drifted lightly back and forth in the breeze, stretching about sixty feet across a chasm to the other side. Noah quickly grabbed the two wooden posts that served as tie points and steadied himself, then looked wide-eyed at Lennie.

"See, bubba? An upside-down rainbow. Hence, Devil's," she said, bouncing her head around.

"You don't expect me to cross this do you?" he said, looking levelly at her.

Lennie's smile never faltered. She clapped her hands together and bounced up and down excitedly. "Yes, Noey! Of course! It's the only way across."

He shook his head. Then he looked down into the chasm. The chasm itself wasn't very intimidating, in fact. It was only a couple of hundred feet to the bottom. But thinking about being on a dinky rope out over it made it intimidating. His hands were trembling.

"You're serious? You guys do this shit?"

Brent smiled at him. "Oh hell yeah. Mad rush, man."

Noah was still shaking his head. Then he put a hand on his forehead and backed up a step. "Man. I just need a minute to process this."

"Take your time bro," Brent said, putting a hand on his shoulder. "But you'll love it."

Noah stared at him for a long time. A little presumptuous to be thinking he knew what Noah would love, having spoken less than a paragraph to him in all of history. The other two girls were sipping from the flask, giggling as they watched the exchange. Then one of them finally shouted and raised her fist in the air.

"Long live the pirates!" she screamed and darted out onto the rope. It swayed crazily under her, bucking back and forth like a living thing.

Noah looked over at Lennie. "Pirates?"

Lennie shrugged. "It's just sort of tradition. You have to shout something when you get onto it." Then she leaned in real close so the others wouldn't hear, and whispered, "Doesn't really matter what."

The other girl waited until the first one was across, then got out onto the rope herself. She looked back at Brent and said, "Safe?"

He nodded.

"You bet your sweet ass I'm a turtle!" she shouted.

Noah frowned and looked at Lennie again. "What's her name?"

"Cagney. Cagney Baris. Cute, huh?"

Noah pulled his head back. "Yeah, I guess. Not really what I was thinking though. I don't know either of their names."

"Well that's Cagney. The other one," Lennie said, pointing, "is Ashley. But we call her Fish. They're sisters."

"Ah. Why?" Noah asked.

"Well," Lennie said, frowning and looking down, "I guess because they have the same parents?"

"No, dumbo. Why do you call her Fish?"

Lennie shrugged.

"So this is what you do in your spare time? All these years, I've never known you did shit like this, Len," Noah said.

She smiled and kissed him on the cheek, then turned and said, "My turn." She leapt forward with a startling lack of caution, causing Noah's heart to skip a few beats. He jumped forward instinctively to protect her, but it was too late. She was already out on the rope. "To the moon and back, Noah!" she shouted at the top of her lungs. A breeze kicked up a little and he looked up into the sky. The moon was almost non-existent – just a tiny thin sliver, like a thumbnail clipping in the heavens. Noah's eyes glassed over as he looked at the sky – its sheer beauty. A wash of stars was now visible. And in that instant he was looking up, he saw a meteor tear green across the sky and disappear somewhere south of them.

Lennie was halfway across the rope when Brent looked over at him. "You next, or you want me to go?"

Noah shook his head and mouthed a curse to himself, then said, "I'll go."

"Good man!" Brent said, clapping him on the shoulder. His hand against Noah's coat made a dull, lifeless sound.

Noah's feet felt warm in his shoes as he put his first foot on the rope and felt it give sickeningly under his weight. "What the hell am I doing out here?" he asked himself. His hands were tight on the guide ropes, but the foot rope swung maddeningly – dangerously – under his feet. He was ten feet out on the rope when he looked down and noticed the drop below him. Then he looked up at Lennie – a dark spot against the darkness ahead of him. It wasn't far, but it looked like miles from here.

"You're supposed to shout your battle cry, bro!" Lennie yelled from the rocks.

"Into the wild!" Noah said, but only halfheartedly. He was breathing heavily. It was too dark to see the depth of the abyss below him, but he knew it was no short fall. From this height, at this level of light, it could have been right beneath him. The colors all blended together.

"You're doing good, bubba! Keep coming! Don't look down!" Lennie shouted.

"Too late," he said. He was halfway across and the wind picked up again. The foot rope swung out again and his legs buckled while his arms stayed still. The rope was doing its own dance beneath him. He didn't feel he was in danger of falling, but the idea of having to do this with only his hands fluttered across his mind a couple of times. It didn't appeal much to him.

He looked up again and stood still for a moment, watching the moon. A thin wisp of cloud passed between Noah and that moon. And suddenly he heard shouting. Wailing, whining, cries like lost souls. Quickly, he was shaken back to the present. And those three girls waiting on him at the far end of the rope. They were now shouting and wailing and whining and crying, and he realized it had not been their voices he had been hearing. It was distant.

"Woo woo woo!" Lennie shouted, mouth a small ring pointed toward the heavens while she spun in a circle betwixt the other girls. They were all dancing and shouting with the coyotes. It was chilling and beautiful. A sort of ethereal connection with the wild. They could have been in Alaska, out in the bush. Noah felt that chill run up his spine, then heard Brent crying behind him, shouting with the coyotes. Noah was forced by his own nature to join them. He stood there on that rope, swaying lightly in the crisp breeze, wailing that forlorn cry of the wild while the animals seemingly screamed from all directions at once. It was everywhere!

And then it stopped. Just as suddenly as it had started, it was quiet again. Brent shouted from the far side of the deadly crossing, "Tonight we dine in hell!" And the girls were off clapping, dancing, shouting – human shouts this time. Woo-hoos and yee-hahs and high-five-type shouts of glee and victory. Noah joined them, smiling as he bounced across the last thirty feet of tenuous cord strung between the mountains. As he got to the rocks on the far side, the girls welcomed him in with their dance. They were holding his hands, dancing in circles and shouting and jumping up and down. And somewhere in there, a silver flask was getting passed around. The warm whiskey burned his dry throat. But it felt wonderful going down. Faster than he could have imagined, Brent was there with them. And they were all singing at the sky, shouting from the top of the mountain.

They did have a fire that night. They all lay around resting on elbows and backpacks, looking at the stars, smoking a joint and passing around the whiskey flask and pulling from the cans of beer they had stashed in their backpacks. It wasn't good beer, and it wasn't cold. But tonight, Noah wasn't being snobbish. It was beer. He was with new friends, and they were making new history.

After a few hours, the excitement was beginning to die down. Noah realized that the have-him-home-by-midnight promise Lennie had made to Joy was not going to happen. They were here for the night. There was simply no way any of them were driving home. He did look forward to seeing that rope bridge at morning light though.

"You know what's spooky to me?" Lennie said, looking at the fire.

"What's that?" asked Brent.

"The fact that we literally know more about the surface of the moon than we do the bottom of the ocean," she said.

"Yeah. That is spooky. All that water. All those millions of tons of water. There could be shit down there that we can't even imagine," said Cagney.

"That's it precisely," Lennie said, pointing at her.

"Caves. Caves are spooky to me," Ashley said.

"How about a cave at the bottom of the ocean?" Brent said.

The girls giggled. "Yes!" Cagney shouted. "F that."

"You know they have them," Brent said.

"They? Who has them, Brent?" Ashley said. They all laughed.

"They do exist. There simply have to be caves at the bottom of the ocean that no man has ever explored," he said.

"Of course," Lennie said. "So yeah, I have to agree. Imagine if you could get down to one of those caves – in the deepest part of the ocean. And you surfaced inside it and were able to breathe and stuff. Imagine how dark that would be. And you have to spend the night in there."

The other two girls laughed out loud and Cagney fell toward Lennie, hugging her, almost knocking her over. "No way, dude! Okay you're freaking me out. That is some spooky shit."

"No scarier than out here, right?" Brent said, waving his hand out toward the darkness around them. "You heard the dogs earlier. They could be right here enjoying this fire, just outside our vision."

"Nah," Cagney said, sitting up. "They don't scare me. I like coyotes. Now if there was something else, like a serial killer out there, that would have me running for the hills."

"You're in the hills, sister," Ashley said. "Where would you go?"

"Across the Rainbow?" Lennie asked.

"Okay, yeah, that's my entry for spookiest thing I can imagine. Being trapped in the middle of that damn bridge with someone coming after you," Cagney said.

"He could cut the rope!" Lennie said, grabbing her arm.

"Why does it have to be a he?" Brent said, tossing his can into the fire.

"Oh come on!" Cagney said. She slung the remaining mouthful of beer out of her can at him. Only a few drops actually made it that far but her point was made. He wiped his forehead, smiling.

"Seriously. You know there have been plenty of female serial killers throughout recorded history," Brent said.

"Oh yeah?" asked Lennie. "Name one!"

"Nannie Doss?" Brent said. He tossed a stick into the fire. "The Giggling Granny. She giggled maniacally during her interrogations after they caught her."

"Yeah, that's pretty damn creepy," Ashley said, looking over at her sister.

"She killed several of her husbands. I think she killed her mom and her sister, too. Crazy bitch," Brent said.

"Okay, so how do you know so much about her?" Cagney asked.

He shrugged. "It's just something I'm fascinated by."

"Weirdo," Ashley said, tossing a pebble at him.

"I also had to write a report about her in college. So yeah, I think she goes down as one of the creepiest things I can think of," Brent said.

"I second that," Ashley said.

Cagney looked over at Noah and tilted her head. "What about you? You sure have been awful quiet."

Noah smiled and looked at the fire.

"Yeah, bubba. What's the creepiest thing you can think of?"

He took the last swig of his beer. Then he looked at Brent and held his can up.

"You need another one?" Brent said, reaching into the backpack behind him.

"Yeah. We're picking these up in the morning, right?" Noah asked.

"Oh yeah. Negative footprint, man."

"Cool," Noah said, and tossed the empty into the fire. He took the fresh one and cracked it open, then sucked the foam off the top of the can. Then he breathed in and looked around at the expectant faces lit eerily by the red glow of the fire. "The spookiest thing I can think of?"

"Yeah!" Lennie said. "I bet you've got a good one!"

Noah chuckled. Then he looked up the stars and rolled onto his back. He threw a finger to the sky and pointed. "Right there. Or anywhere. But I'm saying right there."

They all looked up. Noah rolled his head to look at the other four.

"No. Lie back like me. Look up at them and watch with me."

They all obediently rolled onto their backs and looked up into the stars. As if by design, a green streak shot across the sky. The girls cried out and then giggled.

"That was pretty eerie," Cagney said into her hand, stifling a cough.

"They're suns," Noah replied.

They all lay silent for a long moment.

When he felt like it had been built up enough, he continued. "But that's not it. The spookiest thing I can think of is that there's a star just like any of the ones you all are looking at. It's about three light-years away."

They all waited patiently for him to continue.

"Well, scientists have been watching the light that a lot of these close stars produce. You can see little blips go across them occasionally. When these little blips transect the star on a regular basis with a regular pattern, that's how we know there is a planet orbiting them."

"Oh, shit yeah. That's bad ass!" Cagney said.

"Well, this one in particular that I'm talking about, it has a blip crossing in front of it. But it's not regular. Not regular in time or dimension."

"Like from another dimension?" one of them asked.

"Not that kind of dimension. I don't mean like Twilight Zone. Like space. It's not a regular shape. Its pattern and timing and everything is irregular," Noah said.

"That is kind of spooky," Ashley said. Noah could tell she was just being polite.

"What's spooky about it, Fish, is that it's not producing radiation like a comet passing through the system. It's not a planet, either."

"Well what is it?" Brent asked. He had turned his head toward Noah.

Noah rolled his head up to look at Brent. "They've been watching this star for over four years. And best they can tell, it doesn't fit the pattern of anything we're familiar with."

"What could it be?" Lennie asked.

"It appears to be a superstructure of some kind," Noah said.

"Oh my God, I just got chills up my spine," Cagney said.

"Oooh God, me too!" shouted Ashley, and they were scrambling for closeness.

"What does that even mean?" Brent said.

"It looks artificial. Like someone built something in orbit around this star."

"Wow. Yeah, that is pretty damn creepy."

"For what, Noah?" Lennie asked.

"To collect light? A gigantic space colony? Someone needed more space? Who knows?"

"Collect light? Why would anyone collect light?" asked Ashley.

"Why do we collect light?" Brent said.

"Solar power!" Cagney said.

"Oh my God!" one of them shouted.

"So you think there's a civilization out there more advanced than us?" Lennie asked.

Noah shrugged. "Dunno. Seems pretty likely though."

"And so what we're seeing probably happened a few thousand years ago, huh?" Cagney said.

"No. It's only a few light-years away. What we see is pretty recent."

"Oh my God. Okay. I have to get up," Cagney said, standing up. She walked around the fire brushing the dirt off her backside. "You win. That's the spookiest shit I've ever heard."

CHAPTER THREE
marking time

From *Front Row Magazine*

Orbit Finally in the Lineup
by Rod Agnew

One Last Orbit is finally being considered for a Grammy award for their latest album, *The Solar Mind*. And there seems to be two very distinct parties at work here. Those who think, "Why has it taken so long?" and those who think, "Why this album?"

It's not in my nature to join these frays. I personally like their music quite a bit. They have such an eclectic and ethereal sound on some of their tracks, while on others, it's just good solid rock. But one can experience all seven stages of grief within the duration of one album. Their musical style is so disparate and diverse it's hard to slap a genre on the record.

So, into the fray.

The Solar Mind delves into a sort of thought experiment about the protagonist's desire to find love – and control it – at any cost, even going so far as to experiment with Salvia or to employ an AI boyfriend to handle the task. Presumably the protagonist is Tanis herself, though one would expect her not to be quite so open with the concept of being incapable of keeping a lover.

The album is split about evenly into two musical endeavors: one (the Solar Mind arc) where she seeks this forever love through any means, and the other where she tells us how she got here. And as far as I can tell, these autobiographical tracks appear to be true to Tanis Ransom's coming of age.

The track, *Different Cells*, for instance, speaks of her decision to chase the astronomy path her father took. She was mocked and bullied in high school for being "a geek girl with her telescopes" as the song emotes. And then *Really Wanna Know Me* tells of where she is now. "There's no more room on my tour bus." And yet another – *Earthbound* – describes the moment the music found her and pulled her away from her schooling.

The album ends with three tracks that fall back on the Solar Mind arc of the album. *Singularity* – you can leave, but if you stay, she'll stay true. *No Need to Move* – this one appears to describe a settlement of sorts. "We can orbit each other where we are... no need to move." And ending with *Let the Universe Decide* – as if she's finally resigned to giving up hope in trying to control her love and letting fate have its way.

The entire album is a fascinating journey through the mind of Tanis Ransom—whether it's fictional or actual snippets from her life. I found it deep and engaging from the start, almost too much to handle emotionally. One gets a little relief for the third and fourth tracks, and then the poppy, upbeat *Robot Boyfriend* breaks the cry streak like that scene in *Steel Magnolias.* You know the one.

And for an album about finding love, there's only one true love song on it: *Who's to Say?* And yet—she's still arguing with someone.

So, yes, I can see both sides of the fence. Why has it taken so long for the Grammy nomination to find this band? But also, why *this* album in particular? It's certainly not their signature gamut of fruit-stand song selection. And maybe therein lies the answer: they've finally found their sound. And with two songs near the six-minute mark (one is actually slightly over it), it's a sound you don't want to leave.

I highly recommend this album. I greatly encourage you to seek it out. To put on your best headphones and engage with it – however you consume music – and listen to it, uninterrupted, start to finish. Then you'll see what all the noise is about.

One Last Orbit is making a *lot* of noise with their sound.

1

Wednesday evening, Noah was sitting at the bar by himself. Doug had some work he had to get done. Troy was preparing for end-of-month at the store. Just to sit there alone was a nice break for Noah. He was drinking his usual scotch, listening to the house music and casually watching the pool tables where there was a pretty good amount of action.

It was nine o'clock when Trixie came through the double doors at the front and darted to the back to put her personal things in a locker. Then she was out on the floor, picking up bottles and glass from the high-tops and wiping up beer. Noah watched her with interest, wondering how long it would take for her to notice him sitting there. Her cheeks were red from the cold outside, and then from the heat of her fast movement about the tables. She had sweat on her brow when she finally looked up and saw him. Then she smiled, a genuine smile of surprise. Noah was forced to smile back.

"Hey Trix," he said.

"Hey, love. How are you?"

"None of that really matters as long as the whiskey is cool," Noah said, raising his glass.

She wiped the bar beside him, then came around and gave him a hug. He leaned in and hugged her with one arm, trying to balance his drink.

"Well? Is it cool enough for you?" she said, then stood with her hand on her hip.

He nodded, then took a sip. "Yep. That's why I always come back."

"Oh. And here I thought you came here for me."

Noah held his glass up a little higher and looked at it. "Yes. And that. There is that." He felt a sudden jab when he remembered seeing her at the bar watching him as he sat at the table with Tanis. Trixie had caught him holding her hand. Noah was thankful that she was being cool about it. Part of him felt sorry for her, as it seemed like she had fallen for him, at least a little bit. She was being very grown-up about it if she had. She had made a very forward advance on him, and he had shut her down. And here he was worried what she thought about him when he was holding a woman's hand while his girlfriend was somewhere else.

After she had cleaned up around the bar and gotten settled into her shift, she came to him again, from across the bar, and leaned her elbows on the wood and sighed.

"You the only floor girl tonight?" Noah asked her.

She nodded and looked about. There was only one other guy at the bar, and he was busy on his phone. There were several other patrons at the tables around the bar, but maintenance was easy. They talked for a few minutes, Trixie worked for a few minutes. It was like that for almost an hour, when Joy finally walked into the bar. Noah's heart skipped a beat, then he had to remind himself he wasn't doing anything wrong. It seemed like he had gotten so used to keeping secrets that when one life cross-faded into another, he had to look over his shoulder. He shook his head, then smiled at Joy as she came around the bar.

"Hey, babe," Noah said.

"Hi, sugar!" Joy said, kissing his cheek and slinging her purse off her shoulder to drop it on one of the hooks under the bar. She looked up and smiled at Trixie. "What's up, Trixie? How are you?"

They leaned over the bar and gave each other British kisses, then Trixie asked her what she would like to drink.

"Chardonnay, please."

"How was work?" Noah asked, turning to face Joy.

She clasped her hands over her crossed knees and took a deep breath, then turned and slung her hair back over her shoulders. "It was good. I made four hundred bucks."

Noah's eyes widened. "On a Wednesday night? What the hell?"

"I know. Well that's not all me. I get part of the servers' tips. When they declare them, that is," she said, rolling her eyes.

Noah smiled and put his hand on her knee under the bar.

"Quincy had a big table. That was about half of it. But yeah, so I had a guy come in with two little girls. He asked for a seat."

Noah squinted at her. "You really still have people come in asking for seats?"

Joy chuckled. Trixie set a glass of yellow wine in front of her. "Thank you, dear." Then, to Noah, "I know, right? I told him politely that we had a two-week wait for tables, and it was reservation only. He looked really sad. He was cool about it. But he said his daughters were there with him for a daddy-daughter night, since they had missed the father-daughter dance by accident the night before. So I felt really sorry for him. But when I told him we didn't seat off the streets, he just looked disappointed, but he was cool. He told

his girls 'Sorry, girls, we'll get something else though!'
It was sad.

"So anyway, this couple is out in the airlock
arguing. And the guy just looked like a punk. Like a
real asshole. He had earrings in both ears and a flat-
billed cap on, and just looked like a real dick. So when
Clark came up and told me we had a two open, I just
decided, screw it. I'm gonna bump that guy. So I
dashed out through the airlock and onto the sidewalk.
That man was buckling his little girls into the car. It
was like a Subaru or something. Nothing fancy. But I
called over to him and told him we just had a
cancellation."

"Really," Noah said. He shook his head.
"Command decision, huh?"

"Totally," Joy said, and ran her hair back behind an
ear, then took a sip of her wine. "So he came in and he
and his pretty little girls ate a steak dinner. It was so
sweet, Noh. Watching him treat them like princesses.
And they were so pretty in their little blue and pink
dresses! It was the sweetest thing! Just warmed my
heart! So I knew I had made the right decision.

"Well when they finished, he stopped by the hostess
stand and patted the wood with his hand telling me
thank you. He said I made his little girls' night. And
Noah, you could see it on their faces! I don't think
they've ever ate at a steak house. It was so sweet!" she
said, covering her heart with a hand. "Anyway, when
he pulled his hand away, there was two hundred dollars
there."

"Dude. Slick."

She smiled broadly and took another sip of wine.

"Cheers to that!" Noah said.

"Cheers, baby!" Joy said. They clicked their glasses
together.

"Feel like dancing a little bit?" Noah said after a few minutes.

Joy shrugged. "No. Not physically. But I'll never turn down a dance!" She took a big swig of wine and set the glass down, then stood up.

They moved out onto the floor near the bar and embraced, then Noah kissed her hand and they started swaying back and forth to whatever music was playing. It wasn't dancing music, Noah noticed, but it didn't matter. He was just trying to be romantic. But he also knew that if he was actually out on the floor, the powers that be would see him, and probably play along. Someone had to be watching him.

And sure enough, after Supertramp went off the speakers, the hidden DJ spun *The Lady in Red.* Noah looked up at the ceiling and rolled his eyes, but they slowed down a little, and started taking their dancing a little more seriously.

"Thank you for asking me to dance, sweetie," Joy said in his ear.

"I'm glad to do it. Well, when they're not playing Chris de Burgh."

She slapped his shoulder lightly. "Stop it. The music doesn't matter to me."

Noah sighed. "I wish you wouldn't say things like that."

Joy giggled in his ear. They were attracting some attention. The only couple on the floor. Several people were turned sideways in their seats, just watching. There were some smiles, some sways, and some people acting like they were on stage singing the karaoke version of the song. Noah smirked and shook his head. She was right, in a way. The song really didn't matter. He was trying to get back to where he had been a few weeks before. Before he had met Tanis Ransom. He was trying to remind himself how much he was in love with Joy. Joy with the red hair. Joy with the pale smile and the freckles. She was no singer. But neither was he. For someone who loved music so much, he sure couldn't play a lot of it.

After the slow song, the DJ spun Journey's *Faithfully.* That was more like it, he thought. As a side note, Noah wondered how many couples had danced to this song on their wedding night. Probably enough to make it cliché. There were songs like that. What song would he dance to at his wedding, if it ever happened? These were things he would have to think about. Of course, before he got to the wedding song, he would have to think about things like when he was going to propose to his girlfriend. And perhaps a wedding date. Music seemed more important than all that to him, though.

Joy pulled slightly away and looked him in the eyes. "We're the stars of the show!" she said.

Noah tried to smile. Tried to feel like he meant it. But it just wouldn't come.

Later, he sat with Doug at the bar, alone. Joy had gone home to take a royal bath and get out of her work clothes. After a few long silent moments, Doug finally turned to him and said, "Look, man."

Noah looked up, then glanced about the bar. Then, to Doug. "What?" He met Doug's gaze.

"You've got something on your mind. And I think I know what it is."

"You do?" asked Noah.

Doug nodded, sipped his scotch. "Listen, man."

"Looking. Listening."

"You need to pick one."

"Pick one?" said Noah, frowning.

"Yeah. This just isn't you. And it's not scalable," Doug said.

"What the hell does that mean?"

Doug breathed in deeply, never taking his eyes off Noah's. He smiled without any humor. "I know you. I know how your heart works. Your mind," he said. He said this last while tapping a finger on the side of Noah's head. "You won't hold up when the pressure starts rising."

Noah started shaking his head, and was about to speak, but Doug held a hand up. *Wait. I'm not done.*

"You remember Shelly Taft?" Doug said after a moment.

Noah nodded and smiled. "Of course!"

"And Rebecca de Jesus?"

"What's this about?" Noah said, the smile fading fast.

"Dude, that was, what? Sixth grade? Loving those two girls at the same time nearly killed you."

Noah leaned back a little, put his hands on his legs under the bar. His palms were sweating.

"Only, this ain't the little leagues, bro," Doug continued. "We're older now. We share more than just love notes in class. We share beds and apartments. Record collections. People can get hurt."

"Look," Noah said, finally. He turned to face his friend. "I'm not trying to get involved in anything extra-curricular." He closed his eyes, shaking his head when he saw Doug raise his eyebrows. "I'm not! This shit just keeps happening to me, and I'm not good at fighting it off."

Doug faced forward and took another drink of the scotch. "Lucky bastard."

Noah ignored the comment. "With Joy?" he said. It sounded like a question. "It's just not new."

Doug nodded, a look of defeat in his eyes. "Ah, the old 'lost its spark' argument. That's right." He shook his head.

"And, dude. Remember when we were shooting pool that first night? You and Troy and me? You said you were on my side. Something about hoping I could snag her or something," Noah said. Was he pleading with Doug? Why did it feel like he was trying to plead his case? Ask permission?

"Yes, I remember," Doug said, turning to face him again, his drink hanging loosely in his left hand. Doug stared at him for a long, silent moment. Assessing him. "I don't have any problem with your being with this chick, bro. She's bad ass. I just think Joy deserves to be let go if you're not going to keep her. Don't string her along, man." This last he said while putting his right hand on Noah's shoulder.

Noah shook his head. "Man. Why does this shit have to be so hard?"

"Tell me this though, Wright." Doug stared at him for another long moment. Noah noticed the glaze in his friend's eyes. He was clearly creeping close to that line that separated the sober from the not.

"What's that?" Noah said, taking a sip from his own.

"What happens when it gets old with the chirp?"

Noah laughed out loud. He turned back to face the bar again.

"What?" Doug said. He wasn't laughing. "They all get routine. Look at Joy. Joy Renee Kennebell. The red-headed angel. You called her that, once upon a time. Straight down from heaven," he said, raising his almost-empty glass and lowering it dramatically, never taking his eyes off of the fine precious liquid inside. He returned his glassy gaze to Noah. "Pale skin, red hair, perfect rack. She was new to you once."

Noah swallowed. He was right. Joy had been the catch of the century when he had first met her. He would never have bet she could ever 'become routine'. Not her. Not Joy.

Doug quaffed down the last swallow of his golden whiskey then put his glass down on the hardwood of the bar and waved at Clive, the tender. "Cut me off, my man."

Clive rang him out and slipped the invoice down in front of Doug. "Thanks, guys," he said, trying not to intrude.

Doug turned and stood up, stretching. Noah turned to face him. "What the hell do I do then?"

"If you're going for new, then you're playing hopscotch. You have this weird dichotomy going on inside you. You're built out of parts from different suppliers, bro. You got a heart from The Relationship Factory and a mind from *Fifty First Dates*."

2

Noah lay in bed watching the ceiling fan make its slow, lazy rounds in the dark. The room was lit with the blue light of a half-moon. Joy was snoring softly beside him, her breath warming his ribs from the right side. He had his arms up, his hands clasped behind his head. *What is this I'm feeling?*

He felt the torturous, haunting pull of the unsure digging its tendrils deeper into his psyche. There were more than one of them though. More than one *unsure*. There were many. They were legion.

Unsure why he was feeling anything other than bliss about the perfect love that was Joy. If he were to draw a notepad from his nightstand drawer – the same notepad within which he recorded bits and snippets of his dreams for later recollection – and list all the things he wanted in a woman, Joy Kennebell would check all his boxes. Every last one of them. So why was he unsure about her?

Another unsure was the feckless, reckless Trixie Clifton. She was adorable, sure. But not anywhere near the top of any list Noah would consult when looking for a partner. And Doug had been right: he *was* born with the heart of a lover. He needed companionship. He craved it. Trixie did not even seem the type who was into settling down. Not with anyone. And she was, what, six or seven years his junior? Did that not represent a portion at least of the reason he considered her feckless? Most of the reason she was reckless? She was just a college-age kid. She still drank to get drunk. She was too much party.

And was that it? Was Joy too much business? Not enough party? Noah didn't think so. She was fun to be around. A mature kind of fun. And get this: almost a year older than he. Did that not represent some sort of maturity? Responsibility? The reasonable choice.

The other unsure, of course, was the spectral Tanis Ransom. What was she all about? Holding his hand as if they were old lovers. Dancing with him under the snowfall in the parking lot? Who does that? God, someone he wanted to admire. That's who. But those who do that don't just do that with anyone. Do they? He didn't think so. He felt special for that. There was definitely something going on there. Something about which he was most assuredly *unsure.*

If Noah had it right, then he had his pick of the three women. But if he screwed this up, he would lose the one who surely did love him. That was perhaps the *only* surety in the whole equation. His mind kept going back to that question though: was Tanis really one he could choose from? Was she available? Was she interested? Well, she was a reckless soul herself if she just threw herself like that on anyone she was around. That was the definition of reckless. Pretty women had to be careful about shit like that. And somehow, they inherently knew it.

Noah blinked. That question seemed to be answered. She *did* have something for him. Something. No friend zone was he in. She wanted something. What Tanis had been doing had definitely been flirtatious. It had meant something. He had a feeling she knew exactly what she was doing. Her flirtations, though every bit as forward and remarkable as the young

Trixie Clifton, were just classier. Just more *mature*. More... modest. Isn't that what it all came down to? What if it *all* means something?

Trixie was the fun backseat tryst after the Friday-night football game. High school. Not college. High school. It was not that he didn't feel anything for Trixie. Why would he not? She was able to turn his dials. Only not the right ones. And certainly not for the right reasons.

Noah got up as softly as he could, grabbed his half-empty glass of whiskey from the night stand, and scooted across the room to draw the curtain back and look outside. He lifted the old wooden frame of the window and raised it a few inches, immediately feeling the cool air come pouring in. He stood in his pajama pants, shirtless, and stared at the road outside. The shadows of the trees danced beneath the moonlight. He took a swig from his firewater. And as the burn crept down his throat, warming him from the inside out, he had a spark of intuition. A thoughtful glance toward the horizon of knowing, away from the guesses of the last several sweaty hours of the night's wandering wonderings. Like a lighthouse swinging its beacon light in his direction, he caught a glimpse of the *right*. Maybe that wasn't the right word. Maybe it wasn't *right*. Proper? Appropriate? He took another swallow, finishing the glass.

Whatever the answer, he felt some clarity. *It might not be 'right', but it's what I want. It's correct.*

Noah turned and looked at Joy as he set his glass on the dresser. She lay on her left side, facing away from him, snuggling the blankets in front of her, exposing her entire right side, bare leg to panties, white tank top to bare shoulder. Her red hair looked dark and magical in the low light of the moon. She was nothing less than exotic. Why was his heart not in it?

"No!" he shouted in an inner whisper, unheard to the rest of the room. "My heart is in it! It's my *mind* that's not in it."

He shook his head and leaned his head all the way back, closing his eyes as he trudged to the bathroom.

Splashing cold water on his face, then looking in the mirror, Noah took a deep breath and stared. *What are you doing, Noah? Where are you going, gunslinger?*

He wiped his face with a towel, then made his way to the kitchen and grabbed a fresh glass, filled it with bourbon and dropped a giant sphere of ice into it, then padded out to the back patio, where he had a deck that overlooked a forested green belt, and a wet-weather creek. The moonlight played beautiful tricks with the shadows tonight. He heard a voice from the far side of the deck and jumped, spilling half his bourbon. Chills shot hard up his spine as he stopped and pointed the glass toward the voice.

"Dude, what the hell? You scared the ever-loving shit out of me!" Noah whisper-shouted.

"Sorry, bro. I didn't want to scare you, but I had to let you know I was here."

Noah breathed out through pursed lips and let his heart settle as he made his way across to the lounge chair where Doug sat. As he approached and dropped into the chair, they clinked glasses.

"What are you doing up?" Doug asked him.

Noah looked at him in the dark. Then slowly, after a long, pregnant pause, he shook his head. "Thinking about what you said last night."

Doug nodded his head thoughtfully, a look of almost-amusement on his face. "So you've come out here to ponder the question in an appropriate environment," he said, waving his glass across the expanse of the creek as if in a gesture of offering it to Noah.

Noah looked out at the creek, listened to its gentle roar, and shrugged. "I guess." He started shaking his head, then looked back at Doug. "Why am I thinking about it at all? Joy is perfect, man."

Doug chuckled, then reached over and grabbed his friend by the thigh and squeezed. "Hey bro, no one is going to fault you for being a romantic."

"Shit. You think that's all this is?" Noah said. "You know that's bullshit."

Doug laughed out loud. "No. It's not, Noh." He turned to look at Noah and squinted. "A romantic always wants it to be new." He shrugged and returned his gaze to the creek. Took a drink of his cold liquor.

"And you think no one is going to fault me?"

Doug raised a hand, palm up, as if about to offer something to Noah, and said, "Well, it..." and raised his eyebrows. After a moment, he dropped his hand and said, "Yeah, never mind. I guess they all will."

They both had a laugh.

"Just not your boys. We understand who you are." He shook his head slowly, then made a show of setting his glass down carefully on the frosted tabletop beside him. "Though I will admit it does sting a little to see the trail of broken hearts you leave in your wake."

Noah shook his head this time. "I know. But I want that newness to stay. I hate that it has to wear off."

"Dude, you are not unique in that regard. You're no snowflake."

3

Though he couldn't remember going to bed, Noah didn't think it was an ungraceful affair. None of his toes felt broken, and he was wrapped in the soft blankets as if he had meant to end up there. Joy was gone. He turned and slapped his arm down on the cold side of the bed where she had lain only a few hours ago. Hours? Had it been that long? There was sunlight streaming through the window now. He looked up at the ceiling and took a deep breath.

"God, I've got to quit doing this shit," he thought aloud. When was the last time he had been truly sober? October? He swung his feet off the side of the bed and rubbed his toes in the carpet, scratched his head. Two empty bottles stood on the dresser. One scotch, one bourbon. One glass sat atop his nightstand, and two more on its bottom shelf. The bottles weren't both emptied in the same night, but they did stand together, painting a pretty serious picture.

He turned and looked toward the bathroom and took a deep breath. It was Thursday morning. He made a small promise to himself that he would not drink again until Friday night. It was small but it was a start. From there, he could promise himself not to drink Sunday night, and from there, take the rest of the weekdays off. If he could keep it on the weekends, he'd be doing something.

When Noah made it to the kitchen, Joy was sitting at the table with coffee, reading a book. She smiled and looked up at him. "Good morning," she said. "I made coffee."

"Thanks," he managed as he made his way to the coffee pot. He grabbed a mug from a hook below the cabinets with his left hand as his right found the rough familiar plastic of the carafe handle. He lifted the pot. It was heavy. When he dipped the carafe to make his pour, the bulbous bottom of the glass hit the granite of the counter top and popped like a light bulb sending a pint of hot coffee splashing out over the front and scalding his legs. Joy yelped from her seat at the table, and he took a deep breath, then tossed the handle with partial glass still attached into the sink.

Joy looked at him over the top of her glasses above her book, but remained silent. Noah leaned against the counter. "Sorry," he said. But was he? What was he sorry for? Clearly, it had been an accident.

"You can have the rest of mine," she said, sliding her mug forward a few generous inches on the table. He stared at her, feeling the heat of the large stain spreading down the legs of his pajama pants.

She stared back at him, doe-eyed, obviously wondering what was bothering him. "You okay, honey?" she tried.

Noah puffed air out his nose, shook his head. "No. Don't think so."

Joy fingered the hair behind her ear and swallowed, setting her book down quietly on the table in front of her. "You didn't get much sleep, did you?" He shook his head. "What kept you up?"

"Just thinking."

She looked down as she stood up and scooted behind him, pulling the dish towel off its rack by the sink. He realized he was standing sentry, watching her perform the ministrations of a woman scorned. As if this were her duty – some previously agreed upon ceremony on which he was to depend. They had no such agreement. So why was he punishing her? Well, the scab was hanging by a corner now. Why not rip it off?

He turned to look at her. Joy. Arguably the love of his life. Isn't that what he had called her when he had been talking to Doug and Troy that night at the bar? Here she was, soaking up the coffee – his spill – and wringing it out in the sink. A real, live human being standing here in front of him – so close he could touch her. Smell her. Soft flannel animal-print pajama pants. Tight white ribbed tank top a little small around the midsection, riding a few inches above the belt line of the pants, exposing her belly and sides. Those soft, fleshy bits he loved so much. The real parts of a woman. Breasts were great. Ass was wonderful. But what about those hips? That belly? Those parts you were allowed to touch in public and not be considered distasteful? The parts considered classy when exposed in public, if not a little risque? Here she was. Her hair was pulled into a messy ponytail atop her fragile head. The strands running up the back of her head had lumps and loops that hadn't quite made the pull with the rest of the hair when she had pulled it up. Her face was devoid of any makeup; still puffy with last night's sleep. No doubt nothing on her breath but the morning coffee. She was staring down at the counter, both arms engaged in the process of removing the hot coffee.

He leaned back against the counter now, crossing his arms as he watched her doing what he knew damn well he should be doing for himself. She didn't owe him anything. Here she was, beautiful in her vulnerability, innocent of all charges, serving him.

"I said I'm sorry," he said, knowing that wouldn't make anything better. In fact, he didn't even know why he had repeated it. He wasn't even sure he meant it. Nor, come to that, was he even sure what he had been sorry for.

"It's okay. Accidents happen," she said softly. He watched her working, moving. Braless and beautiful, and his heart hurt. Why did he have to hurt this blameless woman?

When she had finished wiping the coffee off the cabinets and floor, she rinsed the towel out in the sink and turned to look at him, crossing her own arms. Her right hip found the counter top, where it met and melded, forming a perfect lean.

"Will you tell me what's wrong, Noh?" she asked, and there was no mistaking that fear – that unsure – in her voice. He had made his point that something was wrong here and she was walking on eggshells. That part of him that loved for the love part, his heart, reached out to her. His brain told him to punish her for every mistake that she had never made though. His brain *wanted* to punish her, to make this *her* fault. Would that not make it easier to do the final deed? If there was some real reason to be leaving her, would that not make it bearable?

"I just don't think this is working."

Joy blinked, her face a picture of confusion but confidence. She wanted to stand strong. She wanted perhaps to impress him with her will, her ability to stand up against wrong – especially coming from someone within whose arms she should find nothing but solace and comfort – protection. She breathed in deeply and her eyes went glassy.

After a moment of standing there contemplating, she sniffed and wiped her nose, then managed, "Is it someone else?" She tried a weak smile. It didn't look genuine, but he had to give her credit for trying.

"I think so," Noah said. He had to look away then. He cracked his neck and stared straight ahead, unable to look his mark in the eye. He knew this was wrong. But it was also wrong, as Doug had reminded him, to string her along if his heart wasn't in it any longer.

"Is is the girl with the purple hair, Noah? The one you danced with?"

He turned to look at her again, surprised by her intuition. Slowly, he nodded. "Yes," was all he said.

She gulped hard, squinting back tears. Somehow, she was able to maintain. Her face cleared. She sniffed again, then nodded. "I'm so sad, Noah. I thought we had it all." And then the tears came.

That hit him hard. He felt it in his chest, and knew she was right. And knew she was right for him. But he was on a track now, ruining the greatest thing he had ever known. As he was wont to do. As was his pattern. Afraid of comfort, the natural flow and rhythm of regularity. *Routine.*

"Maybe we did," he said.

Joy breathed in sharply through her nose, now no longer trying to hold back the tears. She swallowed, but still did not back down. God, how he wanted to hold her! Tell her he was proud of her! What a gal! Way to stand up to the asshole! Well, his heart did, anyway.

"I'm sorry I couldn't be your everything," said she. "This breaks my heart. I really wanted to be the one."

She uncrossed her arms and dropped her hands to her sides, then raised them slightly, as if she were about to hug him, then dropped them again. She emitted a forced half-smile, very strained, tears openly pouring down her cheeks now, then she walked past him and out of the kitchen. She grabbed her book from the table and disappeared.

Noah stood there in the same position, staring out the back window, for a long time. What had he just done? Was this sadism of the soul? He heard drawers slamming and movement from the master bedroom, then, finally, the front door slammed. The distant whisper of a car engine starting and driving away was the last of it. There. That's it. It was done.

He stood there gazing unfocused at the leaves on the back deck, still unsure what had triggered what he had just done.

"Dude, that was brutal."

Shocked, Noah turned and looked over the bar at Doug, who was pulling up a bar stool four feet from him. He rested his arms atop the bar above the sink, then said, "Can I get some of that coffee?"

Noah looked down and remembered he had broken the pot. He reached over and grabbed Joy's cooling cup off the table, then slid it across the counter-top bar.

Doug took it held it up to his mouth.

"So how much of it did you hear?"

"All of it."

"Was I too harsh?"

"Did you accomplish what you wanted?"

"Hell, I don't know," Noah said, spreading his hands on the counter and shaking his head. He stared at the shards of glass in the sink.

"This business ain't easy to run," Doug said.

"What the hell are you talking about? This ain't a business! I'm… I'm just trying to..." he spread his arms for effect, then had to drop them when he couldn't decipher in his own mind *what* he was trying to affect.

Doug looked up at him through the tops of his eyes, mouth still hidden behind the mug. "Dude, there is no easy way to break off a perfect relationship. Maybe you should ease up a bit, and consider what you were going for." He held one hand out toward the general direction of the deck out back and added, "I think you achieved it. A clean break."

Noah stared at him for a long time. "Why am I so screwed up, man?"

Doug almost shrugged, made a face. Didn't say anything.

"I'm not even sure that's what I wanted."

At this, Doug met his eyes again. "I thought you wanted new."

Noah let out a yelp that tried to be a laugh, caught in his throat, then backed up. It quickly became a lump that brought tears to his eyes. His hands, atop the counter, now had the slightest tremble about them. He brought them a little closer together. He might need them soon. For what, he wasn't quite sure yet. Always these unsures.

Doug was staring at him. He tilted his head. "Hey man, this is your curse. You knew if you ever wanted free of the current swing, you'd have to ditch in the leaves." He stared for a long moment, then took another sip of the coffee, then added, "I'm not judging you, bro, but that shit's gonna break hearts, man."

Noah did something like a hiccup, but it didn't resolve. It left another lump, and more tears. Then, before he knew it, they were welling up – overflowing. Stinging his eyes and pouring down his cheeks. He brought his hands together. Ran them through his hair. Then he dropped, his elbows on the counter in front of the sink, and collapsed on the floor. As his back hit the cabinet behind him, the shower became a storm. Doug was there beside him in a flash, arm around his shoulders, pulling him in.

"That's good man. Let it out, bro." He patted Noah's shoulder with one hand then tousled his hair with the other. "Pay your penance."

4

Noah walked slowly, arms resting on the shopping cart, as Lennie glided along in front of him dropping her items in the basket. It was Saturday morning, before the normal throngs of people filled the aisles.

"So you're saying you broke up with her because it was routine?" Lennie asked. "Please tell me that's not what you're saying. I know you're not that shallow."

Noah looked up at her but did not say anything.

Lennie stopped in her tracks and turned to look him in the eyes. "You are saying that. Brother! What the hell is wrong with you? That's such a dick move!" she said, slapping the end of the basket for effect. It had none.

"Len, I just have to be true to myself. Staying with someone to make them happy is not being true to myself."

She chewed her lip for a moment, then turned and started walking again. "Dick move, bub."

"Yeah, well, maybe. But I haven't been happy in a while," Noah said.

"What?" said Lennie, a frown creasing her features. "I thought you two were in absolute bliss!" She took a bag of rice from the shelf and let it droop over her hand, swallowing it.

"Nah. Besides, that's only half of it. Remember when you caught me dancing with Tanis in the parking lot that night?"

Lennie's eyes got real big. Her mouth fell open. Then she threw the rice at Noah, almost hitting him in the face. It instead slapped against his chest, as he was too slow to bat it away, and fell into the seat of the basket. "No way! You've been seeing Tanis Ransom?"

"Not quite," he said, smirking.

Lennie walked round to his side of the basket and stood next to him, her hand on his shoulder. "Spill it, Noh. What does that mean?" She had a genuine look of curiosity in her eyes.

"Well, I keep running into her. We seem to get along well. I think there might be something there. But I can't really say I've been seeing her."

She bobbled her head for a moment, looking him in the eyes. Studying him. "I want to hate you so bad right now. But I do have to admit that would be pretty cool if you were dating her." She reached up to put her hand on Noah's face. He backed off and kept a distance though.

"Whoa! What are you doing? Get that hand away from me!" he cried.

"Huh?" Lennie said, dropping her hands to her sides.

"Don't be putting your germs on my face."

"Oh yeah, you and your germ phobia," she said, wandering off down the aisle in search of the next item.

"Supermarkets and pizza buffets, Sis. The two dirtiest places in the world."

She stopped, and turned to look at him once more, the back of her pen between her teeth, arm frozen in place. "I get supermarkets. What's with the buffets?"

Noah shrugged. "I've gone into the bathroom in those places and seen the soap dispenser completely empty. People don't wash their hands after they do business in a public bathroom, in a place that serves hand-food?"

Lennie made a face then shook her head. She grabbed a tin of something heavy off the shelf and dropped it in the basket, crossed it off her list. "Okay, but their hands aren't touching *your* pizza. How does that affect you?"

"Their hands are touching the spatulas that serve the slices. And so are mine," Noah said.

"Okay, that's gross. Thank you. I'm never going there again. So are you going to introduce me to Tanis, big bro?"

"I love how you think I have that option. I don't even have her phone number."

"I'll tell you what," she said, returning to his side once more. "Next time you're with her – in whatever capacity that is – you introduce me to her."

Noah frowned. "Was there a bargain in there somewhere?"

"And I will hate you a little less for breaking Joy's heart," Lennie said.

"You know, Len, it could be very helpful for me if my favorite person in the world would try to understand what I'm going through here," Noah said, seriously.

She studied him for a long minute, holding a jar of olives under her chin like a prop. "It's not easy for me to understand, bubba. But I forgive you. I don't really hate you."

He held his hands out and said, "There. Thank you."

5

Saturday evening, Noah's hopes were high as he and Doug walked through the doors of the Sally West. He knew Tanis spent many of her evenings here catching the bands. And it seemed there was at least a greater-than-zero chance she would be showing up in the hopes of finding him here as well. She might have been here every Saturday anyway, and he just had not been paying attention until he had met her. That was a little more unlikely, he thought. That would be saying she was easy to miss. Easy to miss, she was most definitely not.

Dreadwire was the main act tonight. Noah was a massive fan of their music. Their music was dark and moody, quite a bit like One Last Orbit's, but with a little more of a dirty edge. Almost grungy. Troy had once called them a mix between Alice in Chains and Led Zeppelin, and Noah thought that was about as good as one could get with the simile.

Troy was already at the billiard table, the balls racked, leaning against the rail checking his phone. Hands and hugs, words exchanged, they all settled into their night. Trixie was blessedly not working their section this evening, if she was working at all. Noah knew she would find him and serve him wherever he was if she were here. But tonight it was a new gal.

"So how you holding up?" Troy asked him when they had gotten into the game and he found a moment where he was standing with Noah. A dirty rock band was blasting out a pretty good rendition of CCR's *Commotion*. Noah was tapping his foot with the beat.

"I'm okay. Every time I think about her I feel a sinking feeling in my stomach, like I've done the wrong thing," he said.

Troy looked at him sharply. "Every time you think about Joy?"

Noah was about to say something smart-assed, like 'who else?' but quickly realized it was a good point. A fair, legitimate question. "Yeah."

"Well you probably *did* do the wrong thing. But it doesn't mean you did it for the wrong reason. Or at least not as a means to the right end."

Noah nodded and took a pull from his beer. "Dude, that's exactly what my thoughts were last night. Almost word-for-word."

They finished their game and started another. A new band took the stage and opened with a killer. The conversation between the three had come to a dead end. Nothing new to cover. They had talked it all out. Noah was chalking his cue as he turned to look at the stage.

The band broke into the first chorus of *Southern Cross*. "Good God, these guys are fabulous," he said.

Doug had rounded the table at this point and took Troy's stick from him. "Yes, they are," he said. "It doesn't hurt this guy sounds just like Stephen Stills."

Troy pointed his beer bottle at Doug in agreement. Noah was still staring toward the stage when Doug came back to his end of the table once again. "Your shot, bro." Then, after a thoughtful pause, "She here?"

Noah shrugged and brought his cue up, bringing his concentration back to the table. "I don't know. Haven't seen her yet." He took a shot on the 8 ball and dropped it in its proper pocket. He dropped the cue on the table and looked back toward the floor. "You guys can keep playing. I'm gonna go get close to this band."

"Who are they?" Doug asked, following his gaze.

Troy grabbed the cue off the table and started pulling the balls back together. "They're called Iron and Fire or some such."

"Nice," Noah said. He and Doug clasped hands in the air, then he made his way onto the floor, where it was surprisingly cool, and the music grew louder as he neared the stage.

Noah twisted easily enough through the crowd and found Lennie center stage, right about in the middle of the floor. She had both hands wrapped round a brown bottle of beer, and was twisting in place, singing along with the last chorus of *Cross*. He slipped his arm around her and felt her dig in for an armless hug, still singing loudly about how love can endure.

"What time did you get here, sissa?" he asked, his mouth close to her ear. He had to squat half a foot to get down to her level.

"Seven-thirty," she shouted back. "Love these guys."

Noah raised his chin. He could see why. They stood there swaying and rocking to the beat of several songs before the front man finally addressed the crowd.

Thank you! We have a few more for you. Hope you guys are diggin' the grooves tonight. We're gonna play a slower one now. Find someone special and put your arm around 'em.

Then they tore into a minor riff that Noah instantly recognized as Neil Young's *Cortez the Killer*. But this guy could actually play the lead guitar. He shook his head and closed his eyes as he followed the singer's instruction, dropping his arm around Lennie's shoulders. This time she moved the beer to her left hand though, so she could slip her arm around his back too. She sang along with this one too, and it made Noah proud in his heart that his young sister knew all the greats from the seventies. She knew her music better even than most of his friends.

Noah could smell smoke coming from somewhere in their neighborhood and took a deep breath. He sipped his beer, trying to make it last so he wouldn't have to leave the audience of this band. He was a new fan. And he had even forgotten, for just a little while, what he had been unable to stop thinking of for the last several weeks. Fully immersing himself in the sonic comfort blasting from the perfectly matched sound system off the stage.

Lennie leaned in and relieved his stress by offering to grab him another beer. She was going to refill at the bar and trade some in at the loo. He handed her a twenty, which at first she tried to refuse. But when he held it out and looked away, she finally took it, then stood tiptoe to kiss his cheek. The band broke into a rolling bass line that sounded familiar. And as they came into the first verse of *The Air That I Breathe* Noah found himself closing his eyes again, singing along. It was then that he felt that touch right in the middle of his back. He turned, expecting to see Lennie, and so was already reaching out to take the bottle from her. Only it wasn't Lennie.

He turned full around and found Tanis looking up at him with wide eyes. There was a look of seriousness in her eyes that he found chilling. "Hey!" he said, trying to mask the surprise.

She lifted her chin and waved him closer with her right hand. He leaned in and put his ear near her mouth. Tanis asked, "Was that your girlfriend?"

Noah stood up, smiling at her. She did not return the smile though. Noah thought she looked legitimately concerned. He leaned back down and put his mouth to her ear. "Little sister. Her name is Lennie. Funny, she's dying to meet you, too." He stood back again and watched Tanis's face break into a relieved smile. Then she nodded. He leaned back in and said, "I'm single, Tanis."

The smile got a little bigger, a little more relieved, he thought. Then she stood tall and said, "I have to get another drink. I'll come meet your sis when I get back!" Noah gave her a thumbs-up and watched her slip off into the crowd. He returned his attention to the stage, feeling a buzz flow through his veins. That smile had looked like relief to him. Happiness. Want. Was this really happening? Was it really that easy to get her? He shook his head, smiling.

As the song finished, the front man called out, *One more for you guys. Thanks for jamming with us tonight. Stick around for Dreadwire!* The guitarist began strumming a familiar chord progression, and *Peaceful Easy Feeling* came to life from the stage.

"God, what a great song," Noah said aloud. He glanced around the crowd, hoping Lennie would hurry back with his beer before the song got too far. And as if his will had summoned her, he saw her pop out from the crowd and smile as she wedged her way toward him, two bottles held out in front of her. She was, of course, already singing along. He took his bottle from her and put her back under his left arm, and there they stood swaying, singing along. The entire crowd was singing along. It was hard not to, he reckoned, when there was alcohol in the glass and Eagles on the air.

About the time the second verse started, bringing a harmony vocal to the mic, another appeared at Lennie's left side, sandwiching Lennie between Noah and herself. It was Tanis, and she, too, was singing along. Noah instantly felt the tension change in his sister's shoulders, then she twisted her head to look up at him wide-eyed and full of excitement. Then she turned to her left, never letting her arm come off her brother's back, and kissed Tanis on the cheek. The three stood their swaying and singing as the song ran its course. *How's that for an introduction, little sis?*

6

During the band's cleanup and exodus from the stage, the house lights came up dim and the crowd exuded a new sound. This was the mellow noise of patient anticipation, laughter, light talking and some singing along with the house speakers as they cranked out *Can't Buy Me Love*. Formal introductions had been made and the three of them had talked a while before Lennie had finally stalked off in search of her own group of friends. Before she had departed, she gave a sly little smile to Noah, screwing up her nose. He read it perfectly. He was forgiven.

Noah was alone with Tanis for the first time ever as an officially single man. He felt the wound still trying to scab over, but the pain was numbed by the alcohol and Tanis's exotic eyes. "So I guess you do come here often after all," Noah said. It was much easier to be heard over the crowd and house music between bands.

"I do," she said, then looked around, almost shyly and added, "At least I do now." After a moment, the shy wore off and she looked up at him and smiled. He nodded his understanding.

"So you like Dreadwire?" he asked, hoping he already knew the answer.

"Yeah, but I also love Iron Fire. It's hard to miss a ticket like this."

"Iron Fire, you say?" Noah said, leaning in a little. "I thought was Iron and Fire."

She shook her head. "Nay. No 'and'." Tanis was still looking around, as if she were searching for someone. A few people had noticed her and tapped her shoulder, saying hi as they passed her, but no one had tried to interrupt them.

"Looking for someone?" Noah asked.

She looked up at him and screwed up her mouth, then shook her head. "Nah. Just anxious for the band to start, I guess."

After a few minutes, the lights dropped again, but the house music still played. Janis Ian singing *At Seventeen*. Noah could see Tanis mouthing along with the words, but not singing aloud. She finally looked up at him and said, "You know, that was me."

"What was?" Noah asked.

"I was one of those with 'ravaged faces, lacking in social graces'." She said this while making quotes in the air with one hand.

Noah chuckled. "That's hard to believe."

Tanis nodded, wide-eyed, as if to affirm her honesty. "Oh yeah. I was an ugly duckling." And without warning, she suddenly leaned into him and said in his ear, "Do you remember that time we accidentally kissed right in the middle of the concert floor?"

Noah laughed out loud and leaned away from her to get a look at her face. "No!" Still chuckling, he added, "When was that?"

Tanis leaned in again, mouth against his ear, and said, "Like right now?" and her hand was on the back of his neck. She only let him lean back far enough for their eyes to make contact, and he saw her brown eyes switching back and forth between his left and right. His body flooded with chills, and then her lips were covering his. It was suddenly very dark. Noah closed his eyes and found the back of her head with his own hand, pulling her tighter against him. One arm each hung out to the same side, grasping their drinks. The other of their hands were slipping into the hair on each other's heads. Her mouth was all over his, her tongue actively playing his own and he could feel her breath from her nose against his wet upper lip. It was a heavy breathing. Her mouth tasted like the grapefruit she was drinking. He understood momentarily that she was getting the short end, tasting the pale ale on his mouth. It did not, however, cause her to pull back on her reigns in the least.

Noah did not know how long they stood there in that first kiss. It was unbroken. It was not a series of many shorter, smaller kisses. It was one long one. All he knew was that the song finally finished and a sudden electricity found its way into the crowd as it got louder. The band was obviously making its way onto the stage. And then it was confirmed by several percussive beats he could feel in his chest, from the bass drum. And then she finally pulled away. They had now kissed exactly one time. For more than half of Janis's iconic ballad. He had a feeling he would not soon forget that song.

They stared at each other for a moment, both breathing heavily and looking longingly into the other's eyes. Then he leaned into her ear and said, "I do remember that now." And when he pulled away, her face was wrapped with a soft, pleasant smile that showed no teeth. Her hand slid down and took his own as they turned to look at the stage.

About halfway through the first song, Lennie and her friends came bouncing back to join them, and she made quick, shouted introductions. Once that was done, the group of four girls turned and left Noah and Tanis to their own, but didn't go away. They remained just in front of them, dancing and singing, bouncing and throwing the occasional hand into the air. Lennie being Lennie, in other words. Her friends were just like her. And they were all perfectly in their element.

During the intermission, Noah led Tanis by the hand out into the tavern where he found the boys still at the same table. It was well obvious they were arguing about something as the two approached, but quickly fell silent. Troy still had a hand in the air, out in front of his chest. It hung there and finally fell limp as he cleared his throat and looked at Doug, then back to Noah.

"Hi there," he said lamely.

Tanis's face lit up with a wonderful smile. Noah presented her as Ms. Ransom and Troy stepped around the table to shake her hand. Doug lifted his hand in a wave. "Good to see you again, Tan," he said.

She looked at Noah and grinned. "He's already calling me Tan, Noh. How do you like that?"

"What are you two lovebirds up to?" Doug asked, not a little awkwardly.

"They're watching the band, idiot," Troy said, still trying to find something to do with his hands. "How are they?"

Tanis looked at Noah again, as if for permission to handle this one, then quickly shot back, "They're very good, Troy. Are you guys not able to hear them from in here?"

Doug and Noah both chuckled. Troy did not. He cleared his throat again. "Yeah, but I bet they sound better up close."

Doug rolled his eyes and took a swig of his beer. Tanis responded, "Well, you should come join us for the second batch!" Then, to Noah privately, "I'm going to see myself to the ladies' room." She squeezed his hand and winked at him, then slipped into the back hall.

"What the hell is wrong with you, Roy?" Doug said when she was gone. "You're acting nervous as a cat in a bath."

"I'm not nervous! What are you talking about?" Troy shot back.

"Dude, you are acting a little strange. What's that all about?" Noah asked.

Troy straightened his glasses, then put both his hands on the edge of the pool table and appeared to study the balls. When he finally looked up, he said, "I think I spoke out of hand last time. I need to revise my statement."

Noah leaned on his own side of the table. "What statement is that?" Peripherally, he saw Doug finish off his bottle and ask the waitress for another round. Noah didn't need to ask him if he had ordered enough for all of them.

Troy took a deep breath. "She might be the most gorgeous woman I've ever actually laid eyes on," he said seriously. Noah and Doug laughed out loud.

Doug clapped him on the back. "See? That wasn't so hard, now, was it?" he said, pulling Troy in for a side hug.

7.

After the show, Noah turned to Tanis and asked her what her plans were. She breathed in deeply and looked thoughtfully about the clearing concert hall. "Well, you know Orbit is playing here at the end of the month. So I guess I have to get ready for that."

"How much do you really have to do to 'get ready' for a show? Isn't this old hat by now?" Noah said, smiling.

She tilted her head and took both his hands in hers and said, "No. It is never old hat for me. I feel blessed and privileged to be on that stage every time I'm up there."

"Well, that's not what I meant," he said, a little embarrassed. "I just meant, you're so used to it that it doesn't take much prep work anymore. Does it?"

She was nodding before he finished. "Yeah. I like to be my best. The whole band does. So we kind of treat every show like our first one. We rehearse even the oldest songs. We like to stay tight."

"I would love to hang out at one of your rehearsals some time," Noah said.

Tanis stared at him for a few seconds and said, "Well, we'll have to see about that. I don't usually allow visitors to peak behind the curtain." As they approached the bar, she turned to him still walking, and said, "It's nothing personal. I just think as dirty as rehearsals are, they steal the magic from the desired effect of the songs."

"Dirty?" he asked. He leaned against the bar, then raised a hand when Clive noticed him. Clive dipped his chin and got two cold bottles from the cooler, popped the tops and slid them to Noah.

"Yeah. There's a lot of stops and starts. A lot of redoing one part over and over until we find the exact sound we want from it. It's very disconnected. It hardly feels like music sometimes. And I think once someone sees that, they lose perspective a little. Or, well, maybe, rather, they gain perspective." She pulled out a stool and slipped atop it with a slight bounce. "They see the whole big picture of how it comes together." She took a sip from the bottle, then added with a shrug, "Maybe it's just me. Maybe it would make it better for some people."

Noah shrugged, a little disappointed. "Yeah, I think it would be cool to see how it all comes together. But whatever you decide is fine." Then he turned to her on his bar stool and looked at her closely. "You know, I don't even have your number yet," he said, and felt a slap on his shoulder. He turned to look, expecting Troy's mug standing there behind him. His heart sank, therefore, because it was Trixie.

"Hey, Trix," he said. "How's it going?"

"Ah, pretty good," she said, hopping up onto the bar stool to his right, completely ignoring Tanis on his left. "How's Joy doing?" she said, putting her hand on his wrist on the bar.

Noah lifted his shoulders and pulled his hand out from under hers, reaching for his bottle as a cover. He leaned back so the ladies could acknowledge each other. Maybe that was it. Maybe Trixie just hadn't seen

Tanis. He glanced to his left and saw Tanis had a curious look on her face, her elbow resting on the bar top, twirling a lock of her hair on a long finger.

"Uh, she's good, Trix. You know we broke up, right?"

Trixie, ever the drama queen, slapped a hand over her mouth and said, "Oh no! Noey, I'm so sorry!"

"No, it's fine," Noah said, trying to force a smile. He knew it looked every bit as stilted as it felt. "I'm actually happy."

"That's so sad," she said, putting her left hand on his right shoulder, trying to engage him more fully. "You two seemed fine at the camp-out the other weekend!"

Noah cleared his throat and threw another glance at Tanis. She was chewing her lip, but maintaining her polite exclusion from the conversation. She knew who Trixie was. She should, therefore, he thought, know how much of a twat she was being. "No, it's over. Solidly," he said, raising a victorious fist a few inches above the bar. The halfhearted gesture might have done more to show his disappointment in her line of questioning than it did to alleviate any concern that might have flowered in Tanis's mind.

Trixie was shaking her head, a mournful look on her face, as if she were wishing the bereaved well at a funeral. "Well I'm still sorry to hear it. You two made such a sweet couple. Call me if there's anything I can do, okay?" She leaned in for a hug. Noah leaned his head back making the whole thing look awkward. "Take care, now, okay?" she said, then patted Tanis's shoulder slightly as she made her way back into the milling crowd.

Noah took a deep breath, then a pull just as deep from his bottle, shaking his head slightly. Tanis, he noticed peripherally, straightened on her stool, returning to face-forward. After a long silence, he turned and said, "I'm sorry about her."

"Oh she's fine, Noey," Tanis said. There was, however, no malice audible in the comment. It still stung, though. "Maybe you're the one I should be worried about. Are you sure you're okay, so soon after a breakup?"

Noah closed his eyes, shaking his head almost imperceptibly. "Look. We had been circling the drain for a long time."

Tanis raised her eyebrows and tilted her head, a quick gesture that showed her surprise. *Well, if you say so,* that look said. But she didn't say anything. Noah realized the amount of stress she was probably feeling about the situation right about now, and took a moment to note the way she was handling it, with such grace.

"I'm serious, Tanis," he said, turning his stool top to fully face her. And a small jolt of relief surged through his chest when she turned hers to face him. She clasped her hands in front of her and swallowed. She was ready to listen. Only, he had not been prepared to have to talk about it. Not yet, at least.

"When did you break up, Noah?" she asked, with, again, a great deal of grace and character.

"Thursday morning," said he. This time the surprise that registered in her eyes looked more like pain. Her face fell and she had to look away. She reached for her bottle, but did not put it to her lips. She only looked at the label, as if to study it.

After an uncomfortable silence, she finally met his eyes again. "Two days ago. Noah, tell me I'm not some rebound girl."

Noah dropped his shoulders and took her hands. She pulled them away after only a second though. *Shit!*

"Tanis. Do you remember how I flirted with you before? When I first met you? And how we danced in that parking lot?"

"You mean, when you were still actually strongly with Joy? Yeah I remember." She finally took a sip from her bottle.

He took a deep breath and tried again. "That was real. That was all real! I promise!"

"Noah, according to Trixie, you two were strong as an oak at your camping trip the other weekend! Why would she say that?" Tanis said. Noah could see tears forming in the corners of her eyes.

He shook his head again. "Come on, Tanis, can't you tell she's just being vindictive? She's jealous!"

Tanis exhaled, "Oh! Ha, really! Here we go."

"I'm not trying to brag here. If you can't tell she has something for me, then you're not looking close enough," Noah said, maybe a little too loudly. It bought him a stern look in the eyes though, and that wasn't bad. He hoped his eyes were sending the proper pleading message.

She cleared her throat, then said, "Noah, I have no doubt that she, and probably twenty other girls in here," she said, waving a hand out at the crowd, her gaze following along, "think you're hot. I know I do. But… But…" she trailed off and dropped her hand, then spread her hands in her lap. The tears broke free. Just the two of them, for now. Noah needed to work to make sure those two tears weren't chased by any others.

"But nothing. I could say the same thing about you, Tanis. You're the hottest girl in here." He saw her eye twitch at that, but she maintained her straight face.

The lights went down again, and the booth cranked up the music. It was Saturday night at the Sally. Now the people would dance. The thick, driving beat of a bass drum kicked in with the warbling, spacey bass line of a Kings of Leon song. *Great. Just what we need right now.*

"Look. I didn't want to tell you this, but she *came onto* me at that camp out."

Tanis's face became a pained expression of incredulity and fear. "Who, Trixie?" she asked, tossing a thumb over her shoulder. A bracelet jingled as she did so.

Noah nodded. Tanis didn't. She shook her head. She was breathing in slowly while she did so. And the shaking got a little more defined. Then she gathered her purse and stood up. "Noah, it was nice meeting you," said Tanis. Then she turned to walk out of the bar.

"Fuck!" he said under his breath, turning back toward the bar. Thinking quickly, he reached back and grabbed his wallet from his back pocket. He fished out his credit card and stood up as he held it up to get Clive's attention.

Almost immediately, Clive looked up at him from the end of the cooler and shook his head, then waved him away. He mouthed the word *Go!*

Noah waved and stuffed the card and wallet back in his pocket and turned, almost jogging for the door, silently thanking God that he knew what she drove. At least there was that. As he burst through the doors and out into the night air, he was assaulted with a snowy wind that instantly stung his cheeks. He glanced about and saw her walking away at a quick pace, about thirty yards away.

He ran after her, shouting as he started, "Tanis! Wait! Please, wait!" And God Almighty, she did. She stopped in her tracks and turned to face him as he jogged up to meet her there under a street lamp. He

226

could see her breath in the air in front of her. He could also see, by the light of the lamp above, that he had been unsuccessful in his attempt at making those first two tears lonely. Her cheeks were wet with them now.

Tanis stood looking at him with a kind of pleading in her eyes that he felt good about. Maybe there was hope yet. As he came to a stop, he reached down and pulled her hands out of her pockets. She let him this time. And he held them. "What was that in there?" he asked her.

She frowned at him, shaking her head ever so slightly.

"I mean, that kiss you planted on me in the dark!"

She took a deep breath and looked around the lot, then back at him. "That was me being a fool. Taking a huge chance on something I felt a little too confident about." After a deep breath, she said, "I should have listened to Carrie."

"Carrie? Who the hell is Carrie?"

"She's my best friend. I've known her since second grade," she said, looking up at him. Clearly, her patience was wearing thin.

"Tanis!" he said, shaking her hands. "No! It wasn't foolish!" He took his turn at looking around the lot. They were still the only two braving the incoming snowstorm. "God, Tanis! If you only knew!"

"So tell me!" she said, raising her voice for the first time.

"I came here to see you." He saw her chewing her bottom lip again, maybe a little more aggressively this time. He sighed. "Ha! You want to know the whole truth?" He looked around again. She was nodding, looking at him solemnly with her eyes leaking. "I broke up with Joy to take a chance with you."

Tanis tilted her head. Her lips parted but she didn't speak. She looked like she had just gotten the breath knocked out of her.

Noah nodded emphatically, squeezed her hands again. "Yeah. Talk about taking a chance."

"Why would you do that, Noah?" she gasped.

"Because." He took a deep breath. He was still catching his breath from the sudden run, in fact. "Because, I couldn't imagine living the rest of my life knowing that a girl like you was walking around out there, and I hadn't given her a proper chance. That I hadn't tried my very hardest to see what it would be like to call you mine."

Tanis trembled as she drew in breath, clearly holding back a cry. Her lips trembled. But then she was kissing him again, her arms around his neck. She pulled away once, holding his face tightly in her hands, staring at him through tears, and asked plaintively, "Are you sure, Noah? You're sure you don't want to be with her anymore?"

He nodded, showing her a comforting smile.

She pulled him back in, finishing the kiss. They turned slowly in the snow under the dreary halo of light cast upon them by the yellow lamp above. Noah felt electricity in his very soul. And when she broke the kiss, she laid her head on his chest, crying and laughing at the same time.

"Noah?" she finally said, barely breaking the silence.

"Mmm?"

"I want to give you my phone number. I think you should have it."

CHAPTER FOUR
instrumental

From *WhiskeyNeat* Magazine

The Orbit Staying Grounded
by Randall Cameron

Progressive rock band One Last Orbit is celebrating ten years together by throwing a party. And you might just be invited. They released their fourth album last month, "In Your Atmosphere", and their label is picking up the tab for the celebration at The Sally West in Bar Harbor, Maine – the band's old stomping grounds.

The band is offering free tickets to the first 2000 people to respond to an online invite, according to Josie Coker, the band's manager. Early indications suggest the venue would overcrowd quickly if there weren't limitations. "We put feelers out to gauge the interest level, and it was overwhelming. Most people were willing to shell out up to a hundred bucks a head for the party," said Coker. These respondents will be excited to learn that the tickets will be given away. And furthermore, will include drink coupons and door prizes.

Every guest will be given a goody bag at the door as well. Rumors put the value of this bag at well over a hundred dollars, but we've gotten no word as to what's actually in it. Suffice it to say, One Last Orbit is spending a ton of cash to show their appreciation for their fans.

You caught that. Right?

Yes. They own the label that puts out their own records. KNV Studios, run by Kevin Vig and his wife, Candace, does the heavy lifting.

"We love our fans. They feel like family," says Shannon Kennedy, lead guitarist. "This is the best way I can think of to show our love for them." Nor is this the first time the band has done such a thing. Not mentioning their secret concert series, where they played local venues under the cover of fake band names, there have been at least two other times where the band surprised their fans with valuable rewards.

Two years ago, after closing out a successful summer tour, they gave away free copies of two of their CDs (*Makeshift Planet* and *The Solar Mind*) to everyone who paid the door cover at the Dixie Whistle, a hometown bar.

In August of last year at a show in Dallas, Texas, the band was upset with how the security at Triplex Stadium had treated the fans in the assigned seating section. As a token of their respect and love for their fans, the band sent their own staff out into the crowd, throwing t-shirts, hats and other band-labeled swag into the audience. They emptied fourteen boxes of merchandise, worth well over sixty thousand dollars to the band's bottom dollar. It is no surprise that their fan base is so loyal.

It wouldn't upset me to find an invitation to the upcoming party in my inbox.

1

It had been two weeks since they kissed in the parking lot, following night after night of long phone calls and falling asleep apart. There had not yet been anything more intimate than the kissing; Noah had the feeling she would let him know when she was ready to move beyond that. Tonight was the first night either of them had been to the other's place. And it was to her apartment he had come.

Around two o'clock, after he had finished his work, he had called Tanis and asked if he could surprise her. She had made the verbal equivalent of a frown. "Of course," she had said. "But how would one go about surprising me by permission?"

"Well, one would slip unannounced over to the other's apartment and knock unexpectedly on the door, then hope to be invited in, even though she had no idea he was coming, and therefore was completely out of sorts, and not dressed for company."

"That sounds amazing! Though I could only see it working if she were to tell you which apartment on the east side of building three she actually lived in at Preston Glen Apartments. You know? Because there's the one she lives in, and then one below it. So how would you ever know where to go to knock on the right door?"

"There is that. I had not considered it. But say, just for the sake of argument," Noah had said, scratching down a note while he talked, "that he had been able to overcome all odds and obstacles, and by sheer majestic detective work had actually found where she lived… Just what if he were able to pull that off?"

"Well," she had said, and paused for a really long time, "I think that would probably work then. I bet she would truly be surprised if he did all that, and was able to knock on her door at, say, five o'clock?"

"I bet that would work for him," he had conceded.

And at four seconds after 5:01, he had knocked on her door.

The door opened on a chain, and she yelped, then quickly closed it. Noah heard the sound of the chain being drawn, then the door was flung full open. Tanis covered her heart with one hand while the other pulled stray locks of hair behind her ears. She was wearing a silk robe that seemed to be missing its sash.

"Oh my God!" she screamed, taking him in for a hug with one hand while the other kept her robe closed. "What are you doing here? I'm so embarrassed! I'm totally not dressed for company!"

Noah shrugged and smiled at her, then said, "Ah, well, I was just in the neighborhood and thought I would drop in to check on you."

She shook her head, a look of disbelief in her eyes. "Oh my God! How did you ever find where I live? You must have been stalking me on OuterCircle or something."

Noah giggled as he stepped inside and she closed the door behind him, once more going to work on stray hairs. He then whipped a full bouquet of yellow roses out from behind his back and handed them to her. "There happened to be a kid on a bike selling roses out there. So I thought, what the heck, why not get you some?"

She covered her mouth as it dropped wide open. The other hand still maintained closure of the robe. When she was finally able to pull her hand away from her mouth, she took them and embraced Noah again and kissed him on the cheek. "How swell it was that the little boy on the bike even had the thought to wrap them in the green plastic paper! They are gorgeous!"

Tanis took his hand and led him into the kitchen, where she quickly produced a vase – this, by taking one off the top of the cold box that held an old bouquet of fake flowers and dumping it into the trash beneath the sink – and dropped the roses into it.

"You will have to excuse the mess," she said, looking around quickly to make sure she had not left anything draped over the back of any chairs. She, of course, had not. The place was perfectly and immaculately clean, and ready for company. "The place is a wreck. I was not expecting company!"

After settling the business with the flowers, here they stood in the living room where a fat candle stood burning in the middle of a neat coffee table. The place was small and cozy, almost bare of decoration, but attractive. A large TV sat atop a cabinet opposing the small love seat, taking up most of that wall. Noah quickly noted the rather immodest sound system that surrounded the television. He guessed she took her movie-watching very seriously. Kindred spirit.

During the next hour, she showed him around the apartment, a guided tour that showed him a perfectly made bed stacked with more pillows than he could count, her laundry room that smelled sweetly of fabric softener, and the small bathroom that – oddly – had no shower, but only a large garden bath tub, where stood another series of tall candles that flickered in their own dreamy conversation.

As they stopped in her dining room, she introduced as the music room, he saw a very simple arrangement of musical persuasion. Beside a table littered with notebooks covered in blue inked words, a dark colored guitar stood on a stand. It was a little dusty but otherwise beautiful with its fancy pick guard and Mother of Pearl inlays on the neck. He noted it was an Ovation. He was surprised by that, for as far as Noah knew, most musicians stayed away from the composite-body guitars like that because they were hard to hold, and sounded terrible to boot. Standing by the window was a small electronic keyboard of the Casio variety. Full-size keys, he noted, but not all eighty-eight of them. There might have been half that. He began to wonder how much music she really played with this budget musical setup.

She turned to him, smiling, and waved a hand across the room, obviously very proud of her setup. "This is where I do my writing," Tanis said. She had a look of excitement in her eyes, and he felt a pang of embarrassment for her. Suddenly, he wanted to make a large donation to her musical cause. She needed better than this starter setup; these were like a child's beginner equipment.

"Is that your only guitar?" Noah asked, trying to keep his smile genuine.

She breathed in deeply, staring at it, almost longingly, then sighed and said, "Yeah. Sadly." Then she turned to look at him and he saw all she was neither embarrassed or unhappy about it. "I can't play guitar, Noah, so it doesn't matter," she said, slapping his chest lightly. "Heck, I can't even play the keyboard," she said, turning to look at the sad, truncated instrument.

Noah frowned. "What do you mean?" he said.

She sighed and smiled. "I've never learned an instrument. I'm just not musically inclined beyond the vocals." She shrugged, then added, "I mean, well, I understand theory. I played the cymbals in high school marching band."

Noah nodded, returning her smile. "So what do you do with these then?"

"If the boys are here and we find a mood, we might write something." She put her hands in her pockets and twisted back and forth subtly. "It's cool. Shannon comes over here to write sometimes. So he uses the guitar." She turned to look at the sad instrument, then back at Noah. Then she said, "Benji won't play that Casio though," and laughed. Noah laughed with her.

"You could still learn to play, Tanis," Noah said, taking her by the shoulders.

Tanis lifted her left hand up, palm toward his face, her long fingers all perfectly together. She had a monochromatic tattoo on her wrist that went well up onto the palm of her hand. It was beautifully done, but with no color other than the black, long since faded to blue. On her wrist was a hummingbird, wings blurred in flight, with its long beak disappearing into the open end of a trumpet vine flower. The flower itself ran across the ball of her hand and turned to vine, which ended in the middle of her palm. She pointed with her other hand to the skin beneath the artwork. For the first time, he saw the the ropy, ugly scar that clashed so badly with her beautiful pale skin. It was hidden very well beneath the tattoo that ran from wrist to palm. Noah wondered how he had gone this long without noticing the ink.

"My God," he said, taking her delicate hand in his fingers, studying it, touching it. He looked up to meet her eyes. "What happened?"

She tried to chuckle but it didn't come out as planned. It just made his heart sink deeper. "I stepped into the bathtub with a glass of wine one night. I lost my footing, and… Well, this happened."

Noah didn't understand. He was shaking his head slightly. Tanis must have read this. She added, "The glass popped in my hand as I hit the side of the tub. It sliced me open and did a lot of nerve damage. I had to have two surgeries to repair all the damage, not to mention all the therapy." She kept her hand up, allowing him to continue holding it. He was still shaking his head. "Yeah, it was terrible. Anyway, I'll never play guitar now."

"So…" Noah started. Then he cleared his throat and started over. "You can't play because of the nerve damage?"

Tanis shook her head, but was still smiling lightly. "I can't feel the tips of all my fingers but the pinky. I've tried so hard, but I just don't have the strength in my hand, and without feeling, I always get the wrong strings. Most of the time I couldn't even beat the action on them, either. So they would just get muted."

She looked over her shoulder at the piano and said, "That's why I got that piano. I can at least play some chords while I write, so I'll know where I want the music to go. At least I have that much."

"That's seriously one of the saddest things I've ever heard. Your music clearly hasn't suffered though," Noah said. "Does it come out the way you like it? The way you *hear it* in your head?"

She nodded and smiled. "Yes. I rely very heavily on Shannon to read my mind when it comes to that."

Noah, still holding her hand, stepped up and kissed her where the bird's beak disappeared into the fluted end of the flower. When he pulled his lips away, he let go of her hand and she closed her fingers, then dropped it to her side.

"What is the significance of the hummingbird?" Noah finally asked.

"It's what my daddy used to call me when I was little. I used to hum all the time. Constantly humming."

"That's sweet," Noah said. "Does he still call you that?"

She bit her lip and nodded quickly. "Uh huh!"

"Your dad sounds like a cool guy then," Noah said, nodding himself.

She breathed in and looked him in the eyes and said, "He's the best. Best dad ever."

"Well, I'm glad he's not actually serving time at Jersey City Correctional," said Noah. Then he sighed and shook his head. "Sorry about the bad 'dad' joke," he said.

Tanis giggled and said, "Ha, ha. I see what you did there." She took his hands with her own and stepped closer. They were almost nose-to-nose. "It's okay, Noah." she said, a sly smile creeping into her eyes. She stepped into his embrace and rested her head against his chest. "It's what got you here. You literally picked me up that night with your great sense of humor and confidence."

"It was a bad joke. Cheesy pickup lines. My friends and I used to have contests with them. I'm so sorry."

"You know how many men have given me lines?" she asked. But she didn't wait for him to answer. "Hundreds." He hugged her tighter. After a moment, she said, "Know how many have kissed my tattoo like you just did?"

Noah suddenly felt more foolish. The last thing he wanted to be was predictable. Predictability could have been his nemesis. He breathed in, ready for the embarrassment. "How many?"

"Not a one."

2

After the tour, she finally showed him back to the living room, where she invited him to have a seat on the couch, while she went and tossed a bag of popcorn into the microwave. And throughout the entire first hour he was there, that damned right hand had kept her robe closed, except for the brief moment she had pointed at her scar, and then he had been too distracted to notice. He began to wonder if she had played the part of a surprised hostess a little too well, and was hiding nothing but nakedness beneath. But when she came back to the couch with a giant orange bowl filled with the popcorn, she bent to set it on the coffee table, where he finally saw it break at the neck, and learned the truth. He saw the high neck of a shirt within the shadows of her robe.

"Tell me something about yourself that I wouldn't think to ask," she instructed, taking a bite of popcorn. She then took a second puff and held it between thumb and forefinger on a cocked wrist.

Noah caught on quickly, and, after taking his jacket off, he turned to face her and opened his mouth wide. She made the first shot, and clapped excitedly. "Yay! It's an omen!" she exclaimed.

"I save turtles in the road every time I ever get a chance," he said.

Tanis stared at him for a long time, lips pursed, nodding ever so slightly in approval of this answer. And then they were off.

"I chew on my nails when I get nervous. I don't bite them, though."

"I will rewind a song and listen to it a second, and sometimes a third time if it really hits me the right way."

"I've never been to Paris. But I don't really want to go. What's so romantic about a tower?"

"My mouth gets all itchy if I eat certain vegetables raw or under-cooked. But those same vegetables I can eat cooked with no problems."

"My mother says I used to talk in my sleep when I was a child, reciting what sounded like scientific formulas."

"I can tell if someone would make a good friend just by looking them in the eyes."

"For most of my life, I misused the word novelty, thinking it meant something totally different. I seriously went through a small depression when I learned I had been misusing it, and had probably embarrassed the shit out of myself in so many cases that I would never be able to remember."

"I have what is considered the rarest blood type, at least in the United States."

"I believe in the afterlife, but I don't believe in ghosts."

"That's funny, I don't believe in aliens. I think we're alone in the universe."

"I used to burn ants with a magnifying glass and pretend I was God."

"I can talk about anything while I'm eating. *Anything.* But if someone blows their nose while I'm eating, it's over. Appetite gone."

"I used to chew sunflower seeds and suck all the salty flavor out of them and then spit out the mess, because I hadn't learned how to separate the seed from the shell."

"I have never been afraid to fly, but the thought of being on a cruise ship makes my palms sweaty."

"For my first job, I worked in a bicycle shop. I know everything there is to know about bicycles."

Now, after the last response had been spoken, a mess of popcorn littered the carpet near and around the couch. A lot more of it had settled into the folds and creases of the blanket between them that covered their feet. They sat facing each other on the love seat, pitching popcorn into each other's mouths. So far, they had discovered that neither of them was actually any good at it. When one actually made a shot, there were hollers and celebration. They had been going back and forth for over an hour, rattling off autobiographical trivia with no riposte. No challenges or requests for clarification had been allowed. It was, perhaps, to be used as a test of their respective memories.

"Can I get you a drink?" Tanis asked, clapping her hands together. Then, suddenly, she turned and fetched the stereo remote off the table, turned up the music that had been previously inaudible, and dropped the remote on the carpet. The apartment came to life with soft pop music.

"Do you have whiskey? Bourbon, especially?" he asked.

"In fact, I do," Tanis said, getting up and letting the blanket fall to the couch. After a minute of hollering back and forth from the kitchen, she returned with two glasses. One held the golden-orange fire-water Noah loved so dearly, the other, a clear and bubbling liquid and a slice of lime.

"So, I guess we've established that bourbon is your favorite drink," she said, crossing her legs beneath her as she adjusted the blanket again, one hand in the air with the glass.

"I guess you could say I have a love-hate relationship with it," Noah responded, taking his first sip. How fortunate he was that she kept a bottle of bourbon in her home. Was she fully stocked? Did she have a shelf full of Canadians, Scotches and Ryes as well?

"Oh yeah?" Tanis said, licking her lips. She looked at her drink with a fair amount of pleasure. "How's that?"

"I love it very much. And I hate it when I don't have a glass of it in my hand."

Tanis laughed out loud and had to cover her mouth to keep from spitting the remains of her last sip onto the blanket between them. She leaned forward and dropped the hand from her mouth to her chest, coughing. "Don't do that!" And then they were both laughing.

After the long fit of laughter, Tanis finally caught her breath and wiped tears from her eyes. "God, that wasn't even that funny," she said.

"Hey, you started it," Noah responded.

She looked up at him suddenly, her eyes full of mischief. "Do you like the butter on the bottom of a popcorn bowl?"

"You know," Noah said, "I've never given it much thought."

She swung her right leg off the couch and turned to grab the bowl that held the popcorn. She dumped the remaining kernels on the coffee table and turned, rising, and swept her left leg over him, straddling him. And here, he saw the pink boxer shorts she was wearing ride high up her thighs. She leaned over and swiped her long index finger across the bottom of the bowl, then put it to his lips. Noah opened his mouth willingly enough and took her finger in, all the time watching the expression on her face, which imitated the face she thought he should be making, he guessed. Unless she thought his taste buds were at the back of his tongue, her finger was a lot farther into his mouth than it had any need to be. And it remained long after the butter had been cleaned completely off her finger. He didn't mind.

She bent down further and licked his lips, finger still in his mouth, then turned her face and kissed him, slowly removing the finger as she replaced it with her tongue. Her robe hung open around him. He reached up and put his hands on her waist, feeling the soft knit material of her tank top, and beneath that, the softness of her flesh.

Tanis sat astride his hips, her pale thighs spread wide around him, and he had cause to realize, just for a brief instant, that he had never seen any evidence of her chest at all – no idea what she had kept hidden for the entirety of his knowledge of her existence. Not that it mattered – not in the least – except as a curiosity. She reached up and took his face in her hands, her elbows only inches apart, eyes closed, and began moving back and forth on him very subtly, very slowly.

Noah, looking at the lids of her closed eyes with something like wonder, raised his hands in her robe to her shoulders, and pushed it off her back. She complied, swinging her shoulders back and let it fall down the length of her arms. She broke the contact with his face just long enough to remove her arms from the sleeves and let it drop around her. He saw the shape of her beneath the thin fabric of the black tank top, realizing she was not wearing a bra. She was playing the part, after all.

Her hands crept beneath his chin and took inventory of his shoulders and his chest, working from the middle out, then back in. Her hands then moved to his stomach, feeling the soft evidence of his too-many beers, then back up to his chest, which still had thick muscle her hands seemed to relish.

Noah took this as a cue, and did the same to her. He felt the thin femininity of her long neck, moved across her shoulders, small and thin, then down her slender arms. They clasped hands momentarily, then she squeezed and let go, and he understood she was signaling him to go on. He ran the backs of his hands along the insides of her arms up to the creases where they met her rib cage and heard her breathe in deeply. Her tongue darted again, deeper into his mouth and her kiss intensified. He spread his fingers wide and ran his hands back down her sides, slowly, and this time with his thumbs wrapped round the front of her. He felt the soft but firm resistance of her breasts, broken by the hardness of her nipples beneath the fabric and her shoulders came in, instinctively. He could feel the chills that sprouted down her arms with the backs of his hands. She bit his bottom lip, sucked it into her mouth. His hands returned to her chest, and she collapsed on him, her hands finally coming off his cheeks and wrapping round the back of his head. She broke the kiss and slid up, putting his mouth against her throat, moaning loudly, and trapped his hands between their chests. He could feel her heart pounding against his knuckles. He pulled his hands out and slid around to her back, feeling the bones of her spine, pulling her tightly against him. She was moving like a liquid thing, squirming on him, chin atop his head, bare feet tracing up and down the length of his inner thighs.

It continued like this for countless long minutes, her squirming and rubbing on him, but nowhere near his pelvis. Then she put her mouth to his again, lowing her position until she was straddling his waist again and began moving a little less erratically, more slowly, and more rhythmically, until he realized she was trying to finish him like this. Instinctively, he tried to resist, but only in thought – not physically. And before he knew it, Noah realized he would not be able to stop the train. It was on a downhill track, and running fast.

Her breathing grew as heavy as his, her kissing more and more passionate, more deeply than he would have thought it possible. This was not just kissing. Tanis was trying to swallow him from the inside out. Her hands found the sides of his jaw again, and she broke the kiss, putting her chin against his mouth. He watched her as she opened her mouth and cried out with no sound, rubbing her thumbs against his chin and cheeks and she grinded into him below. Her train was running free as well.

When it reached the bottom of the hill, as it were, she rested her face against his and became still. She turned her face away and sighed audibly, just the once, and he rolled his face around to kiss the back of her head. Then she lay still. She lay like that for a long time. The music had been accompanying their endeavors for the last half-hour, but he had scarcely had a chance to pay attention. Now as he lay sweating, panting with the woman on top of him like she was trying to hide him, he noticed *Wolves Without Teeth* had been the song to which they had come together. He closed his eyes and shook his head lightly. *How appropriate is that?*

Without a further thought, together, they fell asleep.

3

There was no way to gauge how much time had passed, but his t-shirt was completely soaked through with sweat. The heat of Tanis's body atop his was something akin to molten metal, but he did not want to move her. She lay with the back of her head against his left cheek, her hands curled up under his arms and her knees bent out, which put her feet right inside the backs of his knees. He could feel her heavy breathing, hear the sound it made as it escaped between her lips. Noah reached up and wrapped his arms completely around her, embracing her like a papoose, relishing the heat, the intimate perfection of her body against his.

He could not remember ever having an experience like that before. No zippers had been run down, no buttons undone, no belts unbuckled. No boundary created by clothing had been broken. No physical lines crossed. Yet both had experienced the full release that comes with friction against a friendly surface. Noah squeezed Tanis tight and heard her cooing pleasure return. He could hear her, feel her waking up against him. Tiny adjustments were being made all over her body. An ankle here, a wrist there, here a wriggle of the hips. After a full minute of this, her arms shot out and made perfect straight lines. She held the stretch and wiggled, moaning loudly before finally leaning back and putting her elbows on his chest. She arched her back and looked as if she might try to touch the bottoms of her feet to the back of her head, then came to rest her chin atop her closed fists, looking down at him. Tanis took a deep breath, looking longingly into his eyes.

"I'm guessing you need to pee by now," she finally said.

Noah burst out laughing, then nodded.

"Okay. I'll get up," she said. But she didn't. She remained where she was, chin on fists, a faint smile across her pale lips.

He reached up and ran her hair off her forehead with a fingertip, then used both hands to smooth all her hair back, finishing with his hands on her small shoulders. Then he said, "And now, I'm guessing even *you* have to pee."

Tanis frowned. "I only pee once a day. During my morning shower."

Noah broke out laughing again, and had to turn to the side as it turned to a coughing fit. She fell off his right side and onto the couch behind him. The blast of cool this afforded against his sweaty chest was remarkable in its intensity. "Whoa, holy cow, I'm drenched," he said as he swung his legs down to sit up. He needed a good stretching himself. Every muscle in his body was tight from maintaining the position he had slept in for so long under restraint. Tanis sat up behind him and began pulling his shirt up from the waist. He raised his arms to facilitate the process. She reached back and flipped the switch behind the couch that spun the ceiling fan to life. Again, the relief of the cool air was palpable.

He finally stood, stretching his arms above him. His hand went right into the ceiling fan where it slapped at him with a WAP-WAP-WAP! before he could react. "Ow, dammit!" he shouted.

Behind him, Tanis fell over on her side, covering her mouth while she roared with laughter. She was laughing so hard he could see tears fighting their way out from between her squint-closed eyes. Almost as if this were his signal, he spun and dropped to his knees, attacking her sides and the backs of her bare legs with claws that brought the laughter to a point beyond what her voice could maintain. He tickled her until she lay kicking and thrashing like an electrified thing, fighting for breath and howling with what was almost completely unlike laughter.

And suddenly, he could not resist. He planted his lips inside her open mouth and wrapped his hands around the back of her head. The laughter stopped instantly, and she reciprocated with her own hands, pulling herself up to a kind of lounging posture as she returned the kiss full force. Her mouth tasted like salt and butter, stale but not unpleasant in the least, and Noah found himself lapping up her taste. She holding his face, he holding the back of her head. He fell to his rump on his left side, allowing her to sit more upright, and there they kissed for an entire song.

4

Noah allowed himself a much-needed shower even though he had nothing to change into. Tanis had offered to run his clothes through a wash cycle, but he declined, saying it wasn't that big of a deal. He could make it home with the boxers in his pocket, and just wear the jeans. No problem, he had said. Then he had watched as she stood there in the hallway, pink boxers still riding high on her thighs and tank top leaving nothing to his imagination upstairs. Her hair a wreck atop her head, she had stood with her hands at her sides, then raised them as she said, "You're going home?" then dropped them back with a slap.

The ridiculousness of the gesture made him smile. She looked like a little girl complaining that she didn't get to stay up as late as she wanted. Her face still puffy with sleep, he realized he was seeing her as no one else ever did. Sure, there might have been a few, but he was in a small percentile relative to the crowds of music lovers she entertained from the stage above them. And she was perfectly beautiful. So natural, he thought. So ordinary. But in her ordinary state, unmade and unkempt, sticky with sweat and who knew what else, she looked more beautiful than most of the women he saw throughout a normal day – women who *were* made up and presentable. No contest.

"Are you offering me a place to sleep tonight?" he finally asked, after taking her in over a long period of silence in which she simply stared at him. Perhaps she had been taking him in too, he with his shirt off. Or maybe she had simply craved and adored the attention he had been paying her.

Tanis nodded. She did not open her mouth. Did not change the expression on her face. She only nodded. Noah had to smile at her. Then he turned into the bathroom and turned on the shower. At some point during the shower, he saw the door open briefly, then close. He peaked out around the curtain and realized she had taken his clothes after all.

As they lay in bed together, Noah in his freshly cleaned boxers, Tanis in a fresh pair of her own beneath another night shirt, she looked up at him and smiled. Her torso was positioned between his legs, her chin resting on her hands, elbows on the bed beside his hips. Their conversation picked up just about where it had left off earlier in the night. She stayed like that a long time, feet up in the air behind her, swinging and rubbing together, ankles twisting and toes scratching the other foot as she talked, when she did talk. When she was not talking, she was listening. Really *listening*, unlike anyone Noah had ever met. The look on her face reminded him of someone trying to understand a problem they're being presented. Like she was not comprehending what he was saying. But she always did. She would, in fact, sometimes respond with a missing piece to the puzzle he had been putting together with words. It was, he realized, the exact opposite of confusion. Tanis seemed to understand him perfectly.

After several long hours of the conversation, unbroken by kisses or any other foul play, Tanis rolled onto her back and stuck her hand up toward the ceiling as she looked at her fingernails. She reached up with the other and picked something off the corner of one of them. "Noah," she said.

"Mm hmm?"

"I'm not quite ready for the full orchestra," she said.

Noah tilted his head. "I'm not following," he said.

She put her hand on his chest and stared at it. "I just want you to know, I move pretty slow."

Noah nodded. "You want me to sleep on the couch?"

"No, that's not what I mean. I'm going to sleep with you. Probably slammed so tight up against you that you'll finally want to push me off the bed. I'm just not gonna *sleep* with you. At least not yet."

He lifted his chin in understanding. Though he was a little confused, being that they had basically had fully clothed sex earlier, he was not crestfallen about it. Noah had no expectations about their sexuality. "That's totally fine."

Tanis rolled her head to look at him, for her an upside-down picture. "You're okay with that?"

"Of course," he said.

"Good. You know, of course, we can take care of each other when we need to occasionally."

Noah chuckled. "Yeah, you've proven that already. Which was," he said, raising his eyebrows and nodding, "quite a nice surprise."

Tanis reached over and wrapped her hand around his ankle. "You liked that, did ya?"

"Never had an experience quite like it," he replied. And there was nothing but truth in that statement.

That night, she kept her promise. She backed her rump right up against his pelvis and pulled his arm tight around her chest where she kissed his hand, then put it under her lower shoulder. Their legs crossed, tangling together under the covers. He kissed the back of her head. And with the softness of her rear against him, he could not control the response of his body. But he pulled gently away until he was able to cool down and return.

When he did return, he felt her pull his arm tighter against her chest. That spot right above the breast where doctors place their stethoscopes to listen to the heartbeat caged within the ribs beneath. There was nothing overtly sexual about it, just a purely protective arrangement. It obviously gave Tanis a feeling of security, having her man wrapped around her like that, playing the big spoon and shielding her from the world behind her. Noah found himself reading into this deeply. His first impression of Tanis Ransom had been one of a force. A goddess who enthroned herself on the stage, surrounded by talented musicians who lifted her with the music she adorned with her voice. She was powerful. In control of the crowd below her. But here lay a sheep – a tiny, precious being who, stripped of her aura, was no more powerful than a child. The fact that she trusted him – so quickly, no less – to be the shepherd, to lie behind her and wrap his arms round her in a protective embrace… That made him feel powerful himself. He felt like the Chosen One. In a way, he guessed he was. Noah could imagine a great many people being jealous of his position here. Tanis surely had hundreds of fans, if not thousands. Yet it was he who lay here in the darkness of her room, sleeping in her bed, her back against his chest. Her ribs, sheltered beneath his arm, rising and falling slowly, with the rhythm of her breathing.

It was within this blessed, granted authority – this privileged position in which he lay – that he finally drifted off to sleep.

5

Troy kicked off his boots and put his socked feet up on the stone ring of the fire pit as he settled back into his Adirondack chair. "So, you gotta catch us up, dude," he said, popping the top off a beer bottle.

Noah was hunched into his chair, both hands wrapped round his own bottle, which sat almost untouched on his lap. "Well," he started, widening his eyes, and looking for a place to start. It seemed to him that he had lived several months of life in the last two weeks. "We are 'officially' seeing each other." He accented the word with elongated pronunciation.

"Oh, right on," Doug said. He was standing in front of his chair, staring at the fire. Now, he reached over and held his bottle up to Noah.

Noah obliged and clicked the bottle with his own.

"So how is it?" Troy said, looking at him seriously.

"Whoa, hey, you know we don't talk about that," Doug said, pointing the mouth of his bottle in Troy's general direction."

"Knock it off, Rex," Troy said, rolling his eyes. "He knows I'm not asking about that," he added, pointing his own bottle and the forefinger wrapped round it, at Noah.

Noah glanced at Troy and had to stifle a chuckle. Their group did have a pact wherein they promised not to ever divulge intimate information about anyone with whom they were, or had been in, a relationship. In short, they had promised each other not to ever kiss and tell.

"It's all right, man." He took a sip of his beer, thinking he was finished, and then found more. "It's great, in fact. I've learned more about her in the last two days than I've ever known about any other girl I've ever been with."

"Wait, wait, hold up," Troy said. He turned toward Noah now, getting serious. "Is she a cat girl?"

Noah laughed out loud. "Oh, no," he assured.

Troy clapped and looked at Doug. "YES!" he said with authority. "We have a winner, ladies and gentlemen!"

They all clicked their bottles together. "Well, she does have one little black statue of a cat on one of her bookshelves. But no real cats." He took another pull from his beer, then swallowed and added, "No dogs, either, for that matter.

"Well, that's forgivable," Troy said, reaching down to stroke Chief, who lay to the right of his chair. "So," he said, holding a hand of truce up to Noah, "you've spent the night there now."

"Dude," Doug said, turning resignedly toward Troy.

"Just chill out, dude," Troy said, not a little harshly. "I'm not asking about what happened. Just tell us about how it was, spending your first night there."

"Ah, I don't know," Noah said, a little embarrassed. He shifted in his chair and put a foot up on the fire pit, scratched the back of his head. "What do you want me to say? It was magical?" He leaned forward in his chair now, and took a quick pull of beer. "Well, it was. It was freakin' magical. You know why?"

Doug stood still, turned his head toward him. He looked like an attorney poised to object to a piece of evidence the opposing counsel had not yet taken out of the bag.

"You know why?" Noah said again, for effect. "Because we *didn't* have sex." He leaned back in his chair again and finished off his beer. "There. I said it. And I broke the fuckin' rule. Who gives a shit," He said, waving a hand in the air. "It was great because of how we connected. And it was not based on a sexual encounter. We slept with clothes on!"

"Well that's got to be uncomfortable," Doug said, finishing off his own beer. He reached down and took Noah's bottle, then made his way around the back of the pit to drop both into the empty box. He fished them both another from the cooler.

"I think that's swell, man," Troy said. "Really. That's great. That means it's real, right?"

Noah shrugged and took the new bottle from Doug, cracked it open. "I don't know if that's what it means. But I do think it is real. We sat and told each other things about ourselves for like an hour on the couch."

"Told each other things?" Doug said, frowning.

"Yeah. Like get-to-know-each-other chit-chat."

"That's excellent," Troy said. "You know, you should invite her over. See if she likes fire."

Noah and Doug both stared at him incredulously.

"Seriously, guys. What the hell's wrong with that?"

"Dude, what? It was your rule, wasn't it, Roy," Doug said, looking at Noah and holding his hand out, "that said no girls allowed at our fires?"

Troy leaned back making a sour face and swept the comment away with a lazy hand. "Man, we need to loosen up on that shit."

Doug slapped Noah's knee and leaned forward, holding his beer out now, pointing the neck at Troy. "You know, ever since Roy revised his thoughts on ole Tanis's looks the other night, it seems like he can't get enough of her."

"Man, shut the hell up," Troy said, standing to tend to the fire, which did not – as far as Noah could tell – need any kind of tending. "You guys need to get with the century. Women make fires better."

Noah was laughing, shaking his head, covering his mouth as he watched the exchange. The speaker played the cool beats of the Black Pumas at the moment, and the beer was catching up in his bloodstream. He was at that perfect point that only happens once in a night of drinking where he felt truly divine. It was all downhill from here.

Doug threw a bottle cap at Troy and said, "Bitch, you were the one the other night saying girls shouldn't be allowed to win at hide-and-seek!"

Noah said, "It's all right if you have a little crush on her, bro. I can handle it."

"You mother effers need to shut the hell up," Troy said, turning away to relieve himself in the dark.

Noah and Doug laughed again, then Doug leaned in close and put his hand on Noah's arm. "Dude," he whispered quietly, "you should tell her to come. Secret-like. Text her. Let's see what Roy does if she shows up!"

Noah got a sudden rush of excitement at the thought of getting to show her off to his friends. Really show her off. Now that she was actually his girlfriend it would be different than the last time they had seen her at the bar. Well, at least it felt different. He nodded, smirking. "All right."

6

The snow had stopped several days ago but it still sat at the sides of the roads and covered most of the landscape. The heat of the great fire that crackled in the fire pit had pushed back the line between snow and gravel. There were no clouds, and a three-quarter moon hung low in the sky, just above the rooftops. It was cold, and occasionally the guys had to stand up and point their asses toward the fire for several minutes just to keep them from freezing over.

Snow was in the forecast, however, and now the boys sat forward in their chairs talking about the next few days. They were trying to orchestrate a plan, sort the logistics out for a rescue run. Troy was good about giving his guys a few hours off on days when there was ice on the roads. Since everyone who worked at the lift shop he ran drove a four-wheel drive, they all benefited from this grace. They would take an extra couple of hours getting to work in order to assist those who had slid off the roads.

"It's supposed to be bad Tuesday. Like around ten degrees," Doug said.

"I know," Troy said, nodding emphatically. "But we have a couple of rigs in the shop that absolutely have to get fixed. They're these two rich guys' who are running them at MOAB in the spring. So I gotta keep a couple guys in house to get them done."

"How many will that give us then, total?" Noah said. "We'll need all the help we can get."

"Eight?" Troy said, looking at him in the light of the fire.

"You're giving us Blaine, right?" Doug asked.

"I can't, dude. He's the lead on those two rigs. Plus, he rolled his Jeep a couple weeks ago. He's useless to us."

"What the F did he do?" Noah asked. His eyes were wide. Blaine was one of the pros among the group. If anyone knew about off-roading and the technical aspects of everything involved in the rigs that ran them, it was he. He made a lot of money doing what he did, being one of Troy's best salesmen, and so had a really nice Jeep – decked out. He never hesitated to take it on the trails, and never seemed to care too much about the money involved in his investment. But rolling it? God, that hurt. His Jeep had a lot of money in it.

"He went up a four-diamond you're only supposed to go down. Sumbitch slipped down in a crevice and rolled it completely over. About twenty-grand worth of damage," Troy said, rolling his beer bottle between his hands. He was staring at the fire, and thus, did not see her approach from behind his right shoulder. Noah, sitting exactly opposite the fire from where she approached, did.

Noah glanced up and saw peripherally that Doug had noticed her as well. She stepped into farthest reaches of the firelight, just where the gravel began, and found a dog. She squatted to pat him on the head, then stood and made her way to the circle. Troy looked up at her standing at his right shoulder, then visibly flinched, a sort of double-take before shooting a hard look at Noah.

Noah and Doug busted out laughing as soon as Troy noticed her. Tanis put her hand on Troy's shoulder and leaned down to kiss his cheek, saying something in his ear that neither of the other guys could hear. And then she was stepping into the light where Noah could see her, and she took his breath away.

Tanis was wearing tight jeans tucked into brown leather boots, beneath a striped sweater and a red jacket with a thick scarf wrapped round her neck. She had on a dark felt floppy hat that covered her ears, beneath which protruded straight shocks of her purple hair, black in the low light. Her lips were shining in the moonlight, covered with some sort of gloss. John Mayer's *City Girl* came to Noah's mind. This woman did not look like someone who would sit around a fire pit with a bunch of beer-drinking men. She looked too hot to even be seen with any of them. She looked, well, perfect.

She came around the rocks and shook Doug's hand as he stood up. When he got to his feet he pulled her in for a hug, then slid around to his left, offering her his seat with an outspread hand. He took the seat across from Noah, completing the circle. It was then Noah's turn to stand and welcome her, which he did with a hug around her waist and a kiss on her cheek, near her ear.

"God, you look amazing," he said.

She turned her mouth to where it was touching his, and whispered, "Thank you, boy." He could feel the puff of breath against his ear. Then she turned to find her seat. Noah reached over and pulled her seat close to his, so the arms were almost touching. Hey, if he was going to break the rules by inviting her, he was going to break them all the way.

Tanis sat and they found each other's hands atop the armrests of the Adirondacks, then Troy offered her a beer. "You like beer?" he said.

"Yes sir, I do. I've found I like almost anything but tequila."

"Can't drink tequila huh?" Doug asked.

"Oh, I can drink it," she replied. "That's the problem. I can drink it well. But I turn into an alternate-reality version of myself."

They all laughed heartily at that. Troy handed her a bottle of Flag, having already popped the top for her. "Tell us about that," he said.

"Thank you, Troy," said she.

"What, is this a job interview?" Doug said, holding out a hand.

"It's fine," Tanis said, smiling at him. She shook her head and shrugged, her bottle resting on her crossed legs. "I don't know how else to explain it. I do things I wouldn't normally do. Like one time, I played air guitar with my nephew for an entire Dream Theater song. Like down on my knees getting into it like crazy! He played the drums and I nailed the guitar solo. I was on fire! Everyone in the room just sat there watching us. They even clapped when we finished."

The guys were laughing again. "That's awesome. Did anyone get video of it?" Doug asked. The important questions.

She shook her head again. "Not that I know of. Heck, there could be!" she said, spreading her hands as if to bargain. "I have very little recollection of it, you see. Another time I got into ghost-story-telling with a room full of people who laughed at me. But apparently I told a good ghost story. I made one girl look around with wide eyes. And she was rubbing her arms. She had chills!" Tanis was smiling.

"I can't drink it either," Noah said.

"That's why I stick to beer," Troy said, raising his bottle.

They all raised their bottles and did a long-distance toast in the air. "Hear, hear!"

"This is good," Tanis said, looking at her bottle, spinning in her hand. "What is it? Where's the label?" she said, frowning.

"It's home brew," Troy said, as if it should have been obvious.

"Oh!" she said, still looking at the bottle.

"We call this one Pirate Flag," said Doug.

"We?" she said, turning to look at him.

"Yeah. We all get together and brew beer every month. We all take part in naming them. This is our flagship beer. So, hence, we call it Pirate Flag," Doug finished.

"That is so amazing!" Tanis said, turning to look at Noah, a look of true awe on her face. "You never told me that!"

"Never? We've only had, what, two weeks so far?" he replied.

The other guys laughed. She screwed up her mouth and pinched his thigh.

After the laughter had died down, she said, "I would love to sit in on one of those brewing days. I have always been curious about how it's done." Then she held up her bottle as if to look through it at the fire. "That amazes me that you guys know how to do it, and you do it well! This tastes as good as anything I've ever bought in the store!"

"Well, thank you," Troy said. "I think I speak for all of us when I say that means a lot."

"Yeah, we love hearing praise for our beers," Doug said.

"So we hear you make music," Troy said, pointing the mouth of his bottle at Tanis. His other hand was in his pocket. He looked confident in his relaxation. Clearly, Noah thought, Troy was happy that Tanis was here.

"Oh no. That's not correct," Tanis said, running a lock of hair behind her ear with her fingertips. "I create music, sure. But I can't make much of it myself. Not without my band."

"That's very humble," Doug said, smiling at her. Then he looked at Troy. "Yo, Roy." He held his bottle up and raised his eyebrows. Troy reached down and fetched another bottle from the cooler, then they traded them in mid-air by a toss. Each of them caught the tossed bottle and carried on.

"Will you tell us about the band? What are your plans? You guys gonna go big, or what?" Troy asked. He was looking at her with a fair amount of interest.

Tanis was leaning back, legs crossed at the knees, right foot bouncing slightly as she talked. Her right hand clasped Noah's, and her left held the bottle on the left arm of the chair. "Oh, I don't know if we'll get that far. We're all happy with the local scene. I mean, I think if we were ever offered a tour, we'd all take it.

But we would have to have a big band talk first. I mean, I don't know. Like I don't know if Kev would come. He's got a newborn."

"He's the drummer, right?" Doug asked.

"Yeah," said Tanis, glancing at him before continuing. "I don't really think any of us has thought that far ahead. Well, maybe Shannon. He's good enough to go on," she said.

Troy took his seat again and turned in the chair to face her directly. "I think you all could. We've seen you play, right guys?" he looked at the others and continued. "Right? We've seen you and I think you're all good enough. Seriously. You guys are incredible."

Tanis's cheeks raised high with her smile, head tilted. "Thank you, Troy. That's very kind of you to say." She shifted in her seat, as if she were uncomfortable with this much doting, and her smile faded. Then she made a serious face and looked up. She said, "I just don't know how much room there is in the market for our kind of music. It's so eclectic. There just might not be that much of a calling for it."

"Oh, now that's bullshit," Troy said. "No offense," he added, pointing at her again. "I just mean, yours is not the type that waits for an opening. Yours is the type that forces its own hole. Your music will squeeze itself in. The industry will have to make a hole."

Noah found himself nodding. He noticed Doug, across the fire, was doing the same thing. His eyebrows high, he was considering this true as well. Noah turned to look at Tanis. She was staring at the fire, biting her lip. She looked at a loss for words.

She found them though, eventually. "I hope so. I really do."

7.

Later that night, Noah found himself in bed next to Tanis again. She wore one of his t-shirts – all their clothes had to be washed after sitting by the fire. She had not accounted for that in her preparation, but Noah, a veteran by all standards, had it down to a science. In he walked through the garage door, directly into the laundry room where he would strip, grab a towel from the wire rack that stood therein, wrap it round his waist and head directly for the shower.

Tanis lay on her stomach, back arched as she rested her chin on her hands, looking dreamily at her new boyfriend. Noah was on his back, one arm out so he could run his fingers through her hair as they talked. Something had been itching in the back of his mind since earlier in the evening, something she had said at the fire pit. He found himself listening to what she was saying, but with only half his attention. He was, with the busy part of his mind, trying to find that needle in the haystack of the evening's conversations. Something she had said had sparked a question in his mind, but he could not pinpoint it. He wished he would have asked it when it first struck him, but the moment had passed. Now she was saying something about boats.

"I'm sorry," he said, closing his eyes, shaking his head. "I'm trying so hard to listen to what you're saying, but I can't concentrate. I'm trying to remember something you said earlier this evening."

She frowned. "What was it?"

"I don't know, woman! If I knew, I wouldn't be trying to remember."

She slapped his chest playfully. "You don't remember a context?"

"Nope. But something you said made me want to ask you something else. And I just can't place it." After a moment, he waved it away. "Ah, well. Maybe it'll come later."

"I'm sorry," she said, pushing out her bottom lip in an exaggerated pout.

Noah used the hand with which he had been twirling her hair to reach over and pinch that lip. "Are you excited about the show tomorrow night?" he asked, trying actively to forget his pursuit of the elusive question.

"Yes. We're ready as we'll ever be. Kevin was walking around reading the set list tonight, and I felt this, I don't know, just like this peace. This calm feeling just like overcame me."

"Tonight? When was this?"

"I was at rehearsal when you texted me to come to the fire. We had just finished up."

"Does Kevin make all the set lists?"

"Yep," she said, rolling onto her back and blowing a lock of stray hair out of her eyes. "He's got a gift for it. Finding a flow that ties them together in different ways. He also comes up with all the little changes we do in our songs. I call them tricks."

"What does that mean, little changes?" Noah said. He reached over and picked up his beer bottle from the nightstand with two fingers, tipping it expertly to his mouth.

"Like we don't want to play the song the same way every single time we play it. Maybe one time we'll ride out a verse instrumentally for a few bars, dropping the vocals, so I can walk around and talk. Introduce the band or whatever."

"You know, I've never seen you do that," Noah said, "come to think of it."

"I don't, as a rule," Tanis replied. "No one cares what our names our, and these guys don't feel like they need to be named at each show. Not singled out, you know?"

"That's odd," Noah gave. "I mean, I think I would want to be known."

"Well, you're all about the spotlight, aren't you?" Tanis said.

"Oh, hell yeah."

"Sometimes it's just a break somewhere. Like drop the music and let me sing a line solo, just for emphasis. Whatever. Tricks."

"Tricks," Noah repeated.

"Tricks."

"I have a trick to show you," he said. "It's an old Army trick I learned overseas." That bought him a frown. He ignored it and leaned in to kiss her. But instead of kissing her when she parted her lips in expectation, he licked her teeth.

"Ooh!" she cried and broke into giggling. "That is a trick! I got you beat though," she said, holding up her index finger. "I can make this finger disappear."

Noah nodded slowly, skeptically. Then she stuck her finger in his mouth to the knuckle. It did, he noted, not without some pleasure, disappear.

CHAPTER FIVE
concierto

From *Dredge* Magazine

Here Come the Giants:
One Last Orbit Scores Number One Touring Band in the US.
by Steven Jacobi

After ten years together, six of them with a label, rock band *One Last Orbit* takes the number one slot for touring bands in America. This number comes from concert ticket sales, actual seats filled and merchandise sold at those shows. During a brief time-out from their busy schedule, we caught an exclusive interview with frontwoman, Tanis Ransom, backstage at the Pagoda Ballroom in Houston, Texas.

Dredge Magazine: First of all, congratulations on being the number one touring band in North America.

Tanis Ransom: Thank you, Steven. I understand it's not a vote.

DM: Correct. You earned it all the way.

TR: There are no panels of judges to thank. So we owe it all to our fans.

DM: Indeed. Well, this is a huge achievement, no doubt. But I'm guessing nothing has changed for the band.

TR: You're right. Business as usual.

DM: So, any big plans for the fall?

TR: Oh, word, no. I don't ever think that far ahead! We've got about forty days left on the summer tour? I think we're gonna relax for a few months.

DM: Anything new in the studio?

TR: That's funny, in't it? I mean, we've spent two months in the studio since *The Solar Mind.* And we've nothing to show for it yet. [laughs] But no, really, we've been busy. We have a bunch of new material, but it's still raw. In its larval phase, if you will.

DM: Anything you can tell us about that?

TR: No. Sorry. [laughs]

DM: I had to ask. So what's your secret, Tanis, on staying so strong as a band? You've been together almost a dozen years, and we never hear about any drama or strife or anything. What's your secret?

TR: Gosh. I don't know. I mean, it's not really something you think about, right? I mean, if you're not arguing or fighting or anything, then there's no thought of all that. We just get along, I guess. I wish I could tell you there was some secret recipe or something. We do take our work very seriously. And it does probably help that we don't hang out very much.

DM: Can you elaborate on that?

TR: Sure. We don't have a rule or anything. We just have our own lives. Now, a lot of times, we *are* hanging out, because we're in the mode and in the mood. We're writing. Rehearsing. Recording. Whatever. But a lot of the time, we're just living our lives. And we do have separate lives. We certainly don't force it just because we're in a band together.

DM: So it's not awkward or anything.

TR: No. Of course not. Listen. I love these guys. They're like my brothers. And we have a great time together when we're playing. But when we're not making music, we don't try to mandate some sort of relationship. I think that's where a lot of bands get into trouble. They think that since they're making great music together that means they would make great friends off the stage. So they start hanging out. Whatever. We can hang out, and we all love each other. I'm just saying we don't – as a rule – feel like we *have* to.

DM: So there's a rumor out there. Maybe you can put it to rest for me.

TR: Oh no! [laughs]

DM: Word is you have plans to record a fourth album then hang up the saddle. Are you done after four?

TR: Poppy cock.

DM: Poppy cock? So that's a no?

TR: Poppy cock. That's a no. We have no plans to quit this thing we do. I enjoy it too much anyway. It's all I know. If my band wants to be done, I'll go on and do something else. I'll keep singing though. I'll never stop singing.

DM: So, do we see a 75-year-old Tanis Ransom on stage someday, still belting it out?

TR: God, I hope not. Maybe I should have clarified! There will be a retirement. But there will be no reunions or out-of-retirement gigs. Once it's over, it's done. But I'll always sing in my kitchen. And in the shower.

1

It was a packed house. The first band, The Long Lost Love, had just left the stage. And in One Last Orbit fashion, the house lights did not come up as the roadies changed out instruments, amps and cords. Noah had left the billiards as soon as the Love announced their last song. *Stick around for our friends, One Last Orbit!* As if anyone were going anywhere. As if the singer didn't know he had just sung to *their* crowd. It was all good though. Good showmanship, Noah knew. He reckoned the Love were grateful to be opening to such a huge crowd. They were good, but, come on. This was an Orbit crowd, through and through.

Noah saw that Lennie's tribe had strengthened in number tonight. Her usual three to four friends was tonight somewhere closer to a dozen. And he had overheard her saying something about her brother and

Tanis. More than once. He had smiled to himself about that. She was clearly very proud to be the little sister of the singer's boyfriend. *God I love that girl.* Lennie had always treated him like he was the coolest guy in the world, even when he knew he really wasn't. And surely, she had known when he wasn't as well. But maybe tonight, she really believed he was. For, had he not seen the excitement in her sweet hazel eyes when Tanis sneaked up and put her arm over Lennie's shoulder? Lennie knew her music trivia better than most of the people standing in the thick crowd at the Sally West on most nights. Noah had listened as she told people how Graham Nash had left the Hollies to start his new band with Stephen and David after an earth-shattering bout of harmony in Joni Mitchell's apartment one night. He had listened as she had educated friends about how Peter Gabriel had been a founding member of Genesis, and *not* Phil Collins. She knew who had been the original drummer of Nirvana. *Not* Dave Grohl. She knew who Declan Patrick MacManus was. It was, therefore, more than just a little sweet that she had taken such an intense liking to a local band, fantastic as they were. Oh, there was no doubt about it to Noah. His little sister Lennie was starstruck.

Troy found him in the dark as he stared at the stage, bouncing on his heels to U2's *All I want Is You* coming through the house speakers. "Hey, bro," Troy said.

They knocked their fists together, then slapped arms around each other's shoulders. "What's up, man?"

"The whole gang is here tonight."

"Yeah?" Noah asked, lifting his eyebrows. "Who the hell is the gang tonight?"

"Well, Doug brought Alice. Alice brought her sister, her sister brought about five friends." Troy shrugged, looking at Noah.

"What? Why?" Noah said, holding his hands up, beer bottle dangling. "What's the big deal about tonight?"

Troy raised his chin and looked wide-eyed at him. A knowing nod moved his chin up and down. "Tonight it counts. Now it's personal."

Noah shook his head and returned his attention to the stage. What was this? So, what, just because he was seeing the singer, everyone suddenly had a dog in the fight? He didn't even know Alice's sister's name! He had never met her sister's friends! Why did they care? Well, he had to remind himself, Alice cared. Alice cared because Doug did. Doug and Troy were his best friends. If they cared, then their significant others, it followed, would be more interested. More excited. He shrugged to himself. *Cool with me.*

"What are they opening with tonight?" Troy asked, grabbing Noah by the arm.

"How the hell should I know?" Noah said, laughing out loud.

Troy looked at him seriously through the tops of his glasses. He looked like he had just heard a bad joke. A dad joke. "Why wouldn't you know? You're sleeping with her."

Noah held up a finger to object, but Troy made a sour face, shaking his head and waving his beer-free hand in the air. *None of that. You know what I mean.*

"She doesn't tell me stuff like that, bro."

Troy made a lemon-sucked smile and nodded. "It's cool. You don't have to tell me. But just wink if it's *Into the Darkness.*"

Noah laughed again and shook his head. Then decided to play along. If they all thought he had some insider knowledge of what was going to happen tonight, why not let them believe it. It only raised his *Dun & Bradstreet* anyway, didn't it? "Hey man," he said, leaning in to Troy's ear, "if I told you, it would ruin all the fun."

Troy stepped back and looked seriously at Noah again, tongue bulging out his upper lip like he was working through an inner struggle. Then he nodded slowly, seductively. *I got you. I get it.* He smiled that sour smile again, then raised his bottle for a toast. He now thought he was in the inner circle.

As Noah looked back to the stage, he rolled his eyes and chuckled. Lennie and her friends were bouncing and dancing to *Mountain Sound* as the crowd waited for the headline. Noah reflected back on the night he had met Tanis, and found himself full of wonder. *Just a cheesy pickup line. That's all it took to land a rock star.* Well, a rock star, she was not. Not yet, at least. Tanis had said it herself: they had not even gotten that far in their conversations as a band. She didn't even know if all the members would be on board with traveling if they got the deal. But in this little town, in the Sally West, this club – at least for tonight – she was a rock star. *The* rock star. The one all of his friends, and their friends, were here to see. Suddenly, Noah felt very important. Like one of those Instagram influencers. Useless, but popular. People followed them because… because, why? Well, tonight, because he was 'sleeping with' the singer of the main ticket of the night.

Lennie disconnected from her band of gypsy friends and came to Noah, five feet behind her group. He took some comfort in knowing she – and *they* – liked to stay close to him. And in front of him, no less. He knew

Lennie took comfort in that. Being in view of big brother offered her that sense of security. He was proud to provide it. What little he could actually do to provide it.

"You want another beer, bubba?" she asked. She seemed to be a little unsure of her footing just yet. Perhaps in all her excitement, she had started drinking a little bit too early.

Noah leaned in to her ear. "I don't know. Does a one-legged duck swim in circles?"

She lowered her eyebrows and looked at him with great suspicion. "Yes, brother. Yes, it does. I have witnessed this great act many times with mine own eyes." She stepped back and wheeled her hand, the one holding the empty bottle, for emphasis. "I've got you covered."

"Lennie," he said, leaning forward and kissing her on the cheek. "I love you, little sister." Meanwhile, his right hand found her left between them, and slipped a fifty-spot into it. "Buy all your friends a round, too." And tonight, for once, she did not object. She just raised her chin, then pointed the rolled-up bill at him.

"You got it, brother."

When Doug finally came round, Lennie had gotten back with the beers and had pulled Noah into a deep discussion about the Eagles with two of her friends. *Don Henley? Glenn Frye? Joe Walsh?* They had all had solo projects. One of two friends, Noah thought her name was Esther, said "Why can't they just go on without Glenn? Clearly, Don has the better voice!" And this is when Doug had walked up. He looked up at Noah and smiled broadly, knowing where this was about to go. The Fire Tribe had already had this discussion, long ago. And for once, Troy, Doug and

Noah all had agreed on something. He shook his head with a chuckle, knowing he was about to hear it again. Noah winked at him with a look that said, *"Look what this sucker just stepped into."*

"Look," Noah said, holding his hands out as if he were about to play a piano. The beer bottle hung between his thumb and forefinger. "We all know Don Henley is the better musician. Take their solo work. The stuff they did when the Eagles broke up."

"Yes! See?" she said, turning to point at Lennie as if the argument were won. Lennie, smartly, was looking around the place, not wanting to get her feet wet with this old argument. She, like Doug, already knew his feelings on the matter. Lennie didn't have an opinion on the matter. She loved all their music.

"Henley," Noah continued as if she had not spoken, "wrote the better material during their separation." He took a swig of beer, then added. "I mean, look at Glenn's stuff: *The Heat is On*? *Smuggler's Blues*, for God's sake? Compare that to *End of the Innocence, Boys of Summer, Last Worthless Evening*?" He waited for them to reminisce briefly in their own heads, then said, "No contest, right?"

"Absolutely," the other friend said. Noah didn't know her name. She was a short redheaded girl with a spattering of freckles across her nose. She was cute. Esther was nodding emphatically, an *I told you so* look on her face.

"But... Noah said, slipping his free hand into his pocket and pointing the butt of the bottle at them. "Glenn was the voice of the Eagles."

Esther's face contorted. "What?"

Her friend looked at her, unsure what to say.

"I'm telling you. Go back and listen to all the greats. And it's not just that Glenn sings the bulk of them. It's that his voice is what you think of when you think of the Eagles. There's no replacing Glenn. It's over."

Lennie finally had something to say. "Yeah, well, brother, remember, you said the same thing about Alice in Chains when Layne died."

"I did," he said, now aiming the bottle at his sister, raising his eyebrows. "And I stand by it. DuVall is an excellent stand-in. But you can never replace that edge that Layne gave them. Same name, different band."

"Okay," she said, pursing her lips and nodding. She clinked the neck of her bottle against Noah's own. "I can see that. That's fair."

"What do you think would happen if Tanis ever left Orbit?" the redheaded girl asked, to no one in particular.

"There's a symbiotic relationship going on there. They are all talented musicians – every one of them. I think they need her just like she needs them. *Could they* do something beyond her? Yeah, sure. But it wouldn't be the same," Doug answered.

"Well, duh," Esther said. "That's the whole point, yeah? Of course they'd be different."

"I think," Lennie said, taking hold of Esther's arm as she spoke, "what Candice means is a completely different genre." *Candice. That's her damn name.*

"Yeah, for sure. We're not talking Days of the New goes Tantric," Noah said. "They would have to abandon the entire concept of what they're doing. I can't see that ever happening." He saw that Candice was nodding.

"Well, there's your answer," Doug said, then took a pull from his beer. "It'll never happen."

Suddenly, the house music went down. An eerie silence befell the crowd. Noah understood this to be different than a typical band's show, where everyone usually went wild when the lights went down and the music stopped. Here was a crowd of fans who didn't want to miss anything. Clapping and hollering might well cover up some new trick the band was about to unveil. He looked around at the spooky scene. Hundreds of expectant faces stared up at the stage, and he could see them bathed in the purple light emanating from the stage. The source of the light wasn't clearly visible from the floor. It sort of just *was.*

He saw some of them bouncing excitedly but silent on their heels. Some were swaying, anticipatory action. Getting ready to find the mellow and swim into it. Others were standing perfectly still. He saw one man several feet away staring at his phone. A concerned girlfriend tugged on the guy's arm and Noah watched as the man looked down at her, then put the phone in his hip pocket. Nervous laughter erupted somewhere behind him and was quickly silenced by friendly shushes from nearby. He took a slow swallow of beer and watched the stage, wondering what was about to happen. Wondering who would come out first. And then he saw it. Kevin Vig was already behind his drums. Almost invisible. Just a silhouette against the surrounding darkness. And he was sitting perfectly still.

Noah knew he wasn't the only one who had noticed the drummer on his throne, as he began to see people whispering, heads leaning together to tell of the secret. Hushed voices questioned; arms raised pointing. Someone coughed. He could feel the tension in the air. The excitement. The anticipation and wonder. He could smell the sweat of the crowd around him and he had to smile. No one cared. None of that mattered. The only thing that mattered was the show that was about to start. He began to realize just how faithful the following really was. These people were more like a group of worshipers than just fans of a band. This filled him with awe. What a draw these guys had! And yes, he finally had to let a little of it into his own head; he *was* sleeping with the singer. The creator of all this. The true poet and painter behind the sounds they put out.

A very spacey sound began emanating from the speakers, and he could see Benjamin, the keyboardist in low spotlight, nodding his head very slowly. Then the voice appeared at the same time as a spotlight came to life flooding Tanis Ransom in purple starlight. She had been standing in the middle of the stage the whole time! She was impossible to see in the darkness. The electric guitar began its eighth-note rhythm as she sang.

I can't be your star
Your orbit is too far
I'm swallowed by your gravity
Will your ego cause the collapse of me?

Noah was staring at Tanis with a fascination as she was cast aglow in that eerie purple spotlight that made her skin look bright pink. She wore something with sleeves thin as gossamer that ended in some sort of tassels around her hands. Her hair, piled high atop her her in a powerful bun, looked completely black in the matching light. But he could not see her face. Only the nose escaped the shadow created by the light directly over her head.

She was carrying the forlorn tune in a minor key that was haunting as it was beautiful. He felt chills rise on his arms.

Like planets cast away
We fall at night, but we're loved by day

And here, the drummer slammed the kick drum in perfect sync with the rest of the band. One note. One chord, and she was singing without accompaniment.

What will you do when your starlight is gone?

The next single-beat from the band dropped.

When will your orbit swallow your last pawn?

Another beat. They were in perfect time with each other. The beat of the kick was accompanied by the other instruments hitting that chord together. And the chord had changed with each beat between the lyrics.

It can't be long 'til it's truly over

The next beat.

You'll end it all with your own supernova

Then the band all kicked in, full force, about 110 beats per minute, and the crowd was now moving with it. The song had officially begun. The chorus was full band accompaniment with her vocals.

How tall the galactic energy,
 how it makes my trek so small
I'm cast in your dying light – a sickly, stellar pall

When the song had finished, the thunder of applause was incredible. Noah wondered how many in the crowd had been experiencing the song for the first time. He had certainly never heard it. Lennie looked back over her shoulder at him, smiling a sly number as if they shared a secret. He nodded and smiled back at her as he clapped, and watched her return her attention to the stage.

Tanis finally said, "I love you all," into the microphone before she grasped the stand that supported it and closed her eyes, starting the next song with her words.

Noah's heart was racing by the time the song picked up. It was another minor number that had a major-key chorus. The contrast was beautiful, and, again, haunting. He stood amazed by this woman's talent. He had a hard time imagining that one being could write this much greatness into existence. The full array of stage lights were on now, pitching beautiful color onto the other band members. He kept shaking his head in wonder, and found his jaw hanging open more than just once.

The entire set was much the same. It was incredible. A few of the songs they played he recognized from their previous shows, but admitting that he had not been a serious fan of the band, he realized he might have heard a lot more of them and just not known it. His heart was in it now, of course, but this music was more than just attractive to his ears; it was pure excellence. And he found himself wondering how he had not been drawn in before. Had he just not been paying attention? That did not seem likely, as when he went to a concert, he listened to every nuance his ears could pick up. He was, in other words, the perfect concert audience. Noah gave every song his full attention. Was it that he was paying more attention now because he had developed infatuation with the singer? He did not think that very likely either, seeing as how he was the only one in that position. And there was a large ballroom full of fans here who were every bit as invested in the music tonight as he was.

They played for nearly two hours, but Noah could have stayed on his feet for two more. He had not stepped away to relieve himself, nor to get another beer. Troy had slipped out a couple of times to get more bottles for a few of them, but Noah's feet had been glued to his little piece of real estate, about twenty feet back and centered on the stage.

Late in the show, the band had surprised the crowd by playing a very simple tribute with Sheryl Crow's *Strong Enough*. The lights had gone down for over a minute, then that purple spotlight had come on again, shining down on Shannon Kennedy and Tanis Ransom, both on stools. Kennedy had played an acoustic guitar beneath her gorgeous smoky voice. It was a beautiful rendition, and Noah found himself imagining her singing it only to him. *Hell, it could be true, couldn't it? I mean, I am with her now, right?*

It had gone dark again, and when the spot lights came back up, the whole band had rejoined them. The stools were gone, and Tanis was once again holding onto the microphone stand. She said, "I want you all to know how much we appreciate every single last one of you." She accented the last several words by pointing at people, one at a time. "You're the reason we keep doing this. You're the stars in our sky. You're the reason we exist." She waved at the crowd and backed away from the mic as the crowd gave applause, and then the music started. "We have one more. This is called *String Theory*."

Again, the place roared with applause, whistling and shouts of approval. Kevin slammed the snare drum on a beat, joined by a grinding, distorted electric guitar. The tribal beat of the drums filled the air and the lights went out.

In the darkness, Tanis whispered, "We doin' this?"

The lights blasted back on as the band kicked in: a slow, marching beat with tons of distortion and grunge. And Tanis was skipping around the stage. Noah laughed out loud as he realized what was happening – not as if anything were humorous about the event – but with excitement. *This is absolutely wild.* She was literally *skipping* around the stage! She bounced over monitors and cut through guitar stands and over cables strung across the floor. She went behind the drum set and around Mark, the bassist, before rounding back to the front where she crossed the whole stage and went round again. The band was building up to full intensity and her part had obviously not come yet, but he wondered how she would have the breath to sing after such a stunt. The spectacle of watching her skipping around the stage was truly delightful. Noah could not stop smiling. He was also clapping in rhythm with the beat, just like everyone else in the crowd. This was their big hit, he knew. Their upbeat full-force show-stopper. It was a great way to end a show.

When her part finally came around, she had timed it perfectly so that she stopped – literally skidded to a

stop – right in the front middle of the stage. And all in
that instant, the microphone came up to her mouth and
she sang the first words of the song with minimal
accompaniment.

It's gravity bending!
It's dead-mind rending!
I'm always lending…
It's never ending!

And surprisingly, she was not out of breath. Or if
she was, she hid it with perfect magic. Noah reckoned
she did some strenuous breathing exercises to have this
much control after a performance like that. And with
the next part of the verse, the drums and bass kicked
back in and suddenly, the crowd was full of bouncing,
arms in the air – a room full of energy. It was like they
had all just watched *Footloose* and couldn't keep still.

We're sparking hot in this parking lot,
And here you are with your heart in a knot
Can't move forward, can't go back,
Feels so dark like a panic attack…

Pitch darkness befell the place suddenly, and Tanis
whispered,

You got a light?

In the next beat, the lights were back, blinding the
crowd as the chorus drove into them with the force of a
freight train..

I've got this theory!
You wanna hear it?
I'm ever weary...
Won't go near it!

Bleeding sick and dying dry, light my darling soul on fire
Cuts me like a laser blade, it's clear to me your choice is made!

The band dropped off and the guitar followed her words with a heavy strum…

No more forlorn, lost and fearing...
It's string theory

The music blasted back to life, full of double kick from the drummer and some of the heaviest metal Noah had ever heard under this roof. It was shocking, but not unpleasant. It seemed to fit the band's image extremely well. And with the whirs and beeps coming from the synthesizer, the song *sounded* like chaos math. It sounded perfectly, he though, like *string theory*.

All he could do was shake his head as he moved with the rest of the crowd. It was hard not to love the song immediately.

Each chorus had built into it a full musical stop as she sang the hook, and after the words 'string theory' the lights would go dark for a second, then burst back to life in a dazzling array of color where Tanis would be caught skipping around the stage again. It was insane, Noah thought. What a perfect harmony of music with spectacle. And now she had one tiny fist in the air – her left one – pumping it as she skipped to the beat, and he could see the fine lines of the hummingbird blurred by motion as the wrist of her blouse fell away while she made her way around the stage.

After the third and final chorus, this spectacle repeated once again, but this time she clapped on the beat as she skipped, her long turn-taking stride bouncing the back of her hair against her neck – the lot that had not been piled into the bun. She was truly something to behold. How had he stumbled onto someone so magnificent? Noah wondered if he would be able to close his mouth after seeing this. It might just hang slack for the rest of the night.

At the end of the last circuit, Tanis hopped to a stop right as the music ended, and as her feet hit, her fist went up again. And this time Noah could see her chest rising and falling rapidly. She had finally winded herself. But by God she earned it. And she had never missed a note.

The applause was like thunder. Noah felt it in the floor of the Sally West – stomping and shouting and whistling and screaming through hands cupped round mouths. Tanis said, "Thank you so much!" and made a quick bow, dropping the wireless microphone lightly on the floor before turning and walking off the stage, waving at her audience as she left.

2

Once the house lights finally regained their full strength, the crowd began thinning and Noah finally made a visit to the john. When he got back to the bar area, Lennie and Doug were waiting for him. Most of their respective gangs had already excused themselves. *Lightweights.* A few couples were dancing to house music out on the floor, and a sizable crowd was gathered near the door that led to the Green Room. These were the followers, the groupies, the *Comets*, as they had come to call themselves. Those who revolved around the band. They waited excitedly but patiently for their chance to shake hands and hug the musicians.

"Yo, dog," Troy said, coming up behind Noah and putting a hand on his shoulder, "how your girl have that much energy?"

Noah and Doug glanced at each other and Doug smirked. Clearly, he had noticed as well. Troy had maybe had a few more than his usual. When he was this loose and talking hip-hop, one didn't even have to guess. The dichotomy between normal-business Troy and a-few-too-many Troy was vivid night-and-day. Or, as Tanis might say, matter to anti-matter.

"My guess is the two miles she runs every morning before you and I are even up for coffee."

"She's in mad shape, bro," Troy said, holding a hand high for an up-top shake.

Noah slapped his hand, clasped it. "Yeah. The type of woman known to cause sickness in most other women."

Doug smiled at that. He leaned in close to Noah and spoke into his ear. "Hey, man. Any idea where Trixie's been hiding?"

Noah, almost shocked to hear the name, looked around the bar. He spoke out the side of his mouth, "Hadn't even paid attention. Is she even here tonight?"

Doug shrugged. "Haven't seen her in a week."

"Yeah, I don't know, man," Noah said. He watched as more and more people filed out through the front doors into the cold night beyond. He did not envy what they were running into. It was near freezing out there again, with a bitter wind coming in strong from the north at twenty miles per hour. He was not looking forward to sitting in the Jeep while it warmed up. Maybe he could just stay here all night.

He felt a squeeze on his left arm and looked down to see Alice, Doug's girlfriend, had appeared beside him. Noah glanced over her shoulder and noticed her friends had been part of the exodus. She was looking up at Noah with her dark brown eyes full of curious energy. "How the heck did you land that one, my man?"

He chuckled as he took a pull of his beer. "I ask myself that just about every time I see her."

Alice moved in and wrapped her arms around his waist. She was a full fourteen inches shy of his six-foot-one. She hugged him strong then looked up at him and said, "I'm happy for you, Noh. I mean," she said and tilted her head. A pained smile crossed her lips – forced; strained. "Of course I'm – well, you know. I miss her. But I understand. And I'm glad you're happy."

"Thank you, Al," he said kissing the top of her head before she disengaged and twirled away to attach herself to Doug's side. When she got there, she winked at Noah and stuck her tiny thumb up, stuck her tongue out. She was trying to hide it, he knew, but he could tell she was either mad at him or hurt by the break-up. Maybe worse than he was. How had he gotten over Joy so quickly? Noah had scarcely spent any time thinking about her. He'd had plenty to keep his mind full, that was for sure. But was it really to be that easy? Briefly, he thought about what she might be doing right now. Saturday night. Home, alone, doing… doing what? Crying? Sleeping? He felt a pang of guilt and sadness in his chest and wished it could have been different. Well, wished wasn't the right word, was it? He had chosen to leave her. So if that was his choice, he didn't need a wish to keep it from coming true. The part of him that was getting over her was robotic. Noah had allowed himself to dull his emotions and just *robot* himself through it. He knew if he just shut it off and didn't think about it for a long enough time, then by the time he finally did, it will have passed.

And it wasn't without sorrow that he thought of her. As far as things went, she had done literally nothing wrong. And he had dumped her. Stepped over her to get to another girl. To take a *chance* with another girl, he corrected. He had not even been sure what would happen with Tanis when he had ended it with Joy. What kind of a fool was he? But he did have sorrow in his heart for her. Not that it mattered. It wouldn't hold up in court would it? "Yes, your honor, I destroyed a woman's heart. But at least I was *sad* about it. So it's all good."

Everyone, he knew, was probably looking at him like he was the biggest asshole on the planet. And Noah knew he deserved it. He had never killed a perfectly good relationship before. It was unprecedented. Which almost made it worse, didn't it? If he were just known as the guy who couldn't commit, who burgled their hearts and left them at the sides of roads all over town, they would just say, "Oh, well, that's Noah for you. What did you expect?" But that *wasn't* him. So it must look especially cruel and heartless to all his friends. To all Joy's friends, too. And her family. Joy's family had adored Noah.

So yes, he was upset about it in his heart, though no one might ever believe him. They would always question his motives. And they were right to. Because he had no evidence against the accused, had he? If he could blame her for something, they could get their minds around it a little easier. *Oh she did that? Well, it sucks, but I get it. I wouldn't stick around for that either.* But there was none of that. Which left people guessing. He could not truly explain why he had ruined a perfectly good setup. Just that he wanted that "new" feeling back. Because then he would have to call to question his motives with Tanis, would he not? What happens when it's no longer new with her? Isn't that bound to happen? Like time and tide, gravity and shadows – it's an absolute certainty. It will someday fall stale.

Doug had played his devil's advocates on many of their talks about it, saying he was wrong. That it was *not* a guarantee. It did *not* have to fall stale. It could stay fresh and new and exciting forever, if you found the right love. If you kept your eyes on the one you already loved. Not always looking for something new. But Noah wondered if Doug really believed that himself, or if he was just saying what one is supposed to say. "Human beings are monogamous by moral. Not by instinct," Noah had said. "Evolution speaks for itself. We're attracted to newness so we spread more seed. We sew. We reproduce. We recreate. We keep the species thick and healthy."

Doug had looked at him then with a sour face as if Noah had changed the rules in the middle of a poker hand. *Oh, by the way, fours are now the same as aces.* "Dude. That's too easy. That's beneath you," he had said. "Besides, don't you *want* to pursue a morally wholesome engagement?" Ouch.

Noah took a deep breath and tried to clear his mind of all the Joy that had suddenly haunted him. He met eyes with Alice, who was now standing caged within Doug's arms, her back against his stomach as he stood, head turned to the side and talking to a couple at the bar. Alice was, Noah realized, staring at him. She looked, in fact, like she had been looking at him for a few moments. He smiled weakly at her but she didn't smile back. She just mouthed the words 'it will be okay'. He nodded faintly. Had she just read his mind? For as cute as Alice was, as bouncy and happy and full of spice and life, that tiny cowgirl seemed as shallow as a dinner plate on the surface. But Noah knew there was so much more to her than that. He just didn't get to see it as much as Doug probably did. She did not get too serious very often. Alice didn't want to spoil any good times. But, he realized, she was a lot brighter than she came across. She had seen right into Noah's soul as he had been staring off into space, alone in his little world trying to figure out how he had come to do so wrong by Joy.

'Thank you,' he mouthed back and smiled again, a little stronger this time. She winked at him and gave him a reassuring smile.

Noah suddenly heard an elevated excitement coming from the ballroom floor to his left. The band was making their way out. Mark and Kevin were already out, all smiles, hugging fans, signing CDs and albums, posing for selfies with men and women alike. They took their time, Noah noted, and gave each fan the same amount of attention as the last. They were in no rush to run them off. It got a little louder as Shannon appeared through the doorway. He raised his arms in the air and a whole herd of ladies shouted and closed in on him. Noah watched as he put his arms around two of the women for a picture. As he smiled broadly, both women put their hands on his flat belly. Noah rolled his eyes and leaned back against the bar. He put his bottle to his lips and glanced around the bar. Troy had one arm around Lennie, the other hand making animated gestures in front her face. She was good-spirited about it, smiling and staring him in the eyes, letting him tell his story, whatever it was. Noah had to smile. When he looked back at the crowd by the Green Room door, there she was. He felt his heart skip a beat as a memory flashed before his eyes – Tanis on top of him, her chin in the air, her throat against his lips as she came, both of them covered in clothing and sweat – and he had to swallow. She was *his* now. It didn't seem real. She was all smiles and laughs as she waded through the crowd, giving each in turn a chance to say what needed saying, taking whatever pictures they requested. Noah watched with a faint smile on his lips, and noticed as he put the bottle back to his lips, that Alice was looking at him again. She had a mischievous smirk on her own face. A knowing smile. Had his thoughts betrayed him? Had she read these too?

After a few minutes, when she had finally satisfied all the hungry fans, Tanis glanced over and met Noah's eyes. A faint smile played at her lips, and she waved. He raised two fingers at her, elbows resting on the bar behind him. He felt a tap at his elbow and turned to look. Clive tilted his head toward the approaching singer and slid a short glass of cloudy alcohol across to Noah. Noah nodded at him and took the glass. As she stepped into the bar he held it up between his thumb and ring finger. Tanis took it with a warm smile and slipped her arm around Noah's waist as he stepped forward to join her. His right hand reached back and found the near-empty bottle from which he had been drinking had been replaced with a colder, fuller one. He shot a look at Clive, who only gave him a knowing nod. Noah mouthed 'thanks, bro' and turned to see his friends gathering around the couple. Alice, now free of Doug's embrace, wore a great toothy smile and was clapping quietly in front of her chest, her hands making tiny, fast motions. Lennie stepped forward and buried her head against Tanis's chest, embracing her full-on. Noah saw the singer's smile broaden with sweet genuine shine as she hugged his little sister, rocking back and forth with her eyes closed. "Thank you, thank you, thank you!" she was saying quietly. Noah could not hear Lennie's side of the conversation, but didn't need to.

Doug stuck his fist out when Lennie had disengaged, and Tanis bumped it for him, making a tough-guy face and nodding coolly. And then came Troy, not quite stumbling, but close. Noah made a sharp nod in his direction, catching Doug's eyes and Doug spun round to intercept him.

"Hey, bro, slow your roll a little," he said, helping Troy make a more moderate approach.

"Yo, that was a great show, dog!" he said, trying very hard to look sober. He held a hand up and Tanis actually took it, gracefully, and thanked him with a hug and a word in his ear.

They stayed around the bar for a while, had a few more drinks and then, slowly, started to disperse. It was almost two o'clock when Noah finally walked Tanis to her Jeep. Outside, the wind roared and carried with it a stinging dust of sleet. The roads would likely ice over tonight and bring the crew back to rescue work in the morning.

They stood in the horrific wind waiting while each of their Jeeps warmed up, holding hands between the purring engines. "So what now?" Noah asked.

Tanis looked up with him and tilted her head. After a moment, she said, "What do you mean?"

"Where to?"

"Do you want to stay at my place tonight?" she asked him. She did not ask him often. It was, in fact, pretty rare, it seemed to him. It wasn't just an automatic thing, anyway.

"Yes, please. It's cold out here," he said. She slapped her hand against his chest. The soft padding of his coat made a muffled *fump* sound under her gloved hand.

Then she looked longingly into his eyes and said, "Do you remember that time-" but Noah didn't let her finish. He covered her mouth with his own.

3

It snowed all through the night. By morning there had been nine inches of snow accumulated, though that was a math Noah would never understand. As he stood in his boxers and undershirt staring out the window, the steaming coffee creating a patch of fog on the pane in front of him, he could clearly see it covering his entire windshield from the height of his hood. What was that, two feet?

The snow was still falling, too. It drifted lazily down out of a gray winter sky, mingling with the smoke from the chimney across the street to the east. It was six o'clock. He could hear Tanis breathing in the bed behind him. A minute ago, the slow, heavy gait of a thick slumber had hitched and fallen into a shallower rhythm. She would be up any minute. Noah put the mug to his lips and pulled from its warmth. His sock-clad feet stood on bare hardwood by the window. He could feel the downdraft of the cold air from the glass whispering down his legs. He watched as the occasional car crept past, winding up the hill to the north – cautious and methodical. The roads did not look bad. A ton of snow, but no evident ice.

He heard a stirring emanating from the mound of warm bedclothes behind him, blew his coffee, took a sip. "Hey, beautiful," said a smoky voice. He smiled and turned to look at her. Tanis lay half-uncovered, arms stretched across the bed to both sides. Her purple-streaked black hair looked like an inky puddle spilled from her head. The faintest hint of a smile curved her lips, pale and pink from sleep. The dainty nightshirt she wore had gathered round her ribs exposing her belly and he could just see the elastic ruffled waistband of her pajama pants disappearing into the warmth beneath the down comforter.

Noah turned to face her. "Hey, yourself. Want some coffee?"

"Mmmhmm," she hummed and nodded. She was staring at him like a long-lost prize. He went to the bed and sat down beside her, handing her his mug. She leaned up onto an elbow and took a sip. "Will you kiss a morning girl?" she asked, closing her eyes and raising her face to him. Her voice was husky and hoarse.

Without answering, Noah leaned in and kissed her lips, soft and chaste, modestly. She cooed as he broke the kiss, dropping her head back on the pillow. "Perfect," she sighed, eyes still closed.

"Do you always lose your voice after a show?"

She nodded silently and reached up to rub the sleep out of her eyes with two small, white fists. Noah stared at her with something akin to amazement. He wondered how a human with so many attractive features and traits could possibly exist. On a balanced scale – a universe built on equilibrium – would that not mean there was some polar opposite of Tanis Ransom somewhere? He reckoned there must be. *Child predators. Serial killers.*

They exist to justify her existence. They balance the scales of righteousness in a good and fair reality. Something so perfect must surely have an antimatter equivalent. He allowed his eyes to run down her sharp jawline to the fragile neck below, soft and warm. The collarbone, again, sharp and angular, prominent beneath the pale flesh. His eyes traveled down. The lace of her nightshirt betrayed several dark freckles in sweet precious scarcity. Her breasts, only a modest rise above the curve of her ribs – barely lifted the fabric of the soft white cloth that covered them. Her belly had a gentle swell about it, surrounding a deep and perfectly round navel. Her bare hipbones protruded above the band of her pants, contrasting the smooth sweep of her hips. Physically, he observed, there was nothing lacking about her. And so long as he didn't come to find she killed kittens with a fireplace shovel on Wednesday evenings, what could he possibly find wrong with her? Surely, she could not be perfect. That – based on his universal equilibrium – would have to mean there was something out there so ferocious, so indescribably evil that it wouldn't last a day among humans. *Wouldn't it?*

"What's wrong with you, Tanis?" he voiced.

She frowned briefly at him, then touched his arm, dragged her fingernails against his skin. "What do you mean, baby?" she whispered. The use of the pet name startled him. It was the first time she had said it. He reckoned there were a bunch of firsts in his near future. He would have to get used to it.

"I mean," he started, then stopped, frowning. He scratched his chin and shook his head for emphasis. He noticed a coldness fill her eyes. He had scared her with his words. She was worried now. He had to correct this quickly. "I mean, I can't find anything wrong with you.

But I know you can't be perfect. Unless you're not human."

The look softened in her expression, and a smile found her face.

Noah touched her nose. "You are human, right?"

"I must surely be, as both my parents were."

"Then what's wrong with you?" he asked, shaking his head for emphasis.

"You mean besides the fact that I'm built like a boy?" she said, shrugging, wide-eyed.

Noah glanced down at her chest, not much bigger than his, then shook his head. "That doesn't mean much to me." He took a deep breath, then added, "I think you must be perfect then."

Tanis was smiling widely now, and shook her head. "Boy, you might be the sweetest thing to walk the planet."

Noah frowned now. "I think we need to clear something up right quick, my lady." He breathed in sharply and cleared his throat. "I don't *walk* the planet. I don't walk anywhere, in fact. That's why I own a vehicle."

Her smile remained and she rolled her eyes and found the back of his neck with her delicate hand. Pulled him in for another kiss. "I can't believe I got so lucky, meeting you," she said.

"Believe it," he said, taking the mug back from her other hand and stealing a sip. "There's somewhere I want to take you."

A mysterious look flooded her eyes. She twisted her head and looked at him skeptically. "Where is that?"

Noah sat up straight, stretched his back and twisted his neck. It popped loudly. "I think I'm gonna keep the secret a while. Just know that you're going to love it."

4

Tanis had her hands wrapped tightly around the ropes, knuckles white in the moonlight. Noah stood directly behind her, his hands on her hips. He had reached beneath her thick leather coat to put his hands on her. They stood at the precipice of the cliff, toes mere inches from a two-hundred-foot fall to the floor of the canyon. The Devil's Rainbow stretched across the night in front of them.

The weather had improved, and they found themselves in the mid-forties, and all the snow had melted. Noah had not wanted Tanis to have to carry a backpack, so he had all the supplies in his own. It pulled heavily on his shoulders, drawing a tight tension into his neck he knew he would be working out for the next few days. The moon was almost full, and there were no clouds in the sky, to their luck. The rope footpath almost glowed in the radiance of the lunar light.

Tanis looked back at him over her shoulder. "You're sure this is gonna hold me?"

"Babe, if it will hold me, then you have nothing to worry about."

"Okay," she said, and shrugged. "Let's do this." Then she turned and kissed him quickly on the lips. "Just in case, you know?"

Noah smiled at her, then removed his right hand from where it sat atop her own hand, and put it on her shoulder. "You have to give your battle cry as you start across."

She winked at him and shouted, "Andromeda, here we come!" then set off across the rope with a rapidity that scared Noah more than just a little bit.

Noah had to take a deep breath and catch his bearings before he was able to set out himself. He had to remind himself that he had done this before. One foot in front of the other. And with that, raised his chin and shouted, "To ancient times and distant music!" then started across. The hand rails felt hot and sharp against his palms as he rushed an inch at a time across the rope bridge. He was breathing heavily. He knew Tanis was watching him, cheering him on, and he wanted to impress her with his bravery. But he also knew he was facing a fear – maybe a phobia – and had to do it with more care and thought than was allowed for showing off.

About a third of the way across, Noah felt a sharp *twang* come from behind him; a hard vibration had shot through the rope beneath his feet. He did not know what it meant, but it didn't help his already frayed sense of security. Was it someone stepping onto the rope behind him? Was it the rope letting go? Nah. That couldn't be it. This was in national park territory. So they had people who came out and checked the safety of these things, didn't they? This thing was probably as safe as the Golden Gate Bridge. He tried to let it slip from his mind and concentrate on his steps. Why was he having so much more trouble than he had the first time he had made the trek? He suddenly heard her voice cut through the night. "You're doing great, baby!" she shouted. He might have heard her clapping as she said it. So obviously she saw how long it was taking him to cross the bridge relative to her own journey. Now, his fears laid bare in front of him, he had to accept that she was encouraging him because she saw his struggle. She saw his *fear*. And there wasn't the slightest amount of criticism or mockery in that voice. She was *rooting* for him.

Come on, Noah. Man the hell up. You can do this. You've done it! One foot in front of the other. He was taking about one step every few seconds. That wasn't *that* slow, was it? He was doing fine. Had there been two ropes set up, he realized Tanis would have finished with enough time to spare to allow her to travel down his rope and meet at him at the halfway point and walk him back on her shoulders. Maybe this was a bad idea, bringing her here. No doubt, he was showing her his weakness. What kind of man takes longer to cross a rope bridge than a woman? Well, this would show him how she really felt about him. Wouldn't it? He would know where he stood when he reached the far end and – the rope twanged again, harder. Noah stopped, stood perfectly still. He took account of his surroundings. The two rope handles were solid. He had not felt the vibration in those. Only the foot rope.

"What's wrong, Noh?" Tanis called from the darkness some forty feet ahead of him.

"I felt something bad, Tan," he said. "I think the rope is letting go."

He heard her gasp, then the scuff of her boots. "Oh no! Are you sure?" He shook his head, then heard her whispering, "Oh my God, oh my God, oh my God!" over and over and the thought touched Noah's mind how well the sound carried out here. After a long silent moment, she finally called out, "What's happening?" Her words were slightly muffled. *She's covering her mouth with her hands.*

"Not sure. Don't panic. I'll be right there," he said calmly. That set him off. He slid along the bridge as fast as he could manage without a bounce. After a few steps, another twang shot through the rope and Noah imagined he could hear it. He felt it sink a few inches and knew what was happening. It wouldn't be long now. Taking a deep breath, he felt the terror flood his lungs and started moving faster. He was now just sliding his feet forward without putting one in front of the other. He kept his left foot forward and just scooted each along the shivering rope. It now felt very wobbly and sickly with a shake – like a bad stomach full of nausea.

"Baby, be careful!" Tanis said. She sounded much closer now. "Please be careful."

He was breathing loudly through his teeth now, scooting along with a death grip on the hand ropes, ready at any instant to squeeze tight and suspend him like an acrobat above the unknown depths that lay shrouded in absolute darkness. Twenty feet. Noah guessed, though he could not see well enough to confirm. Maybe she could see him though! "Tanis, how far am I?" he shouted. It came out much louder than was necessary.

"About five yards! You're gonna make it. You're doing great!" she reassured.

Faster he scooted, and more and more he felt the rope bouncing beneath his shuffling feet. The rope took a sickening dive, and he caught his breath as it popped completely out from beneath him. Like lighting, his hands contracted on the side ropes. He let out a loud grunt as he felt the entire weight of his body try to rip his shoulders from their sockets. The pain was like scalding water all down his sides, all the way to his waistline. He heard Tanis cry out something like a *No!*

and did not know if she was calling his name or saying 'no'. He only allowed himself to hang for as long as it took to reach the bottom of his fall, then he swung his feet up and hooked them over the arm ropes and let his head hang back, his breath burning in his lungs.

"Oh my God, Noah, what can I do?" she shouted. Very close now. He wondered if she could reach out and touch his boot yet.

It took him a moment to catch his breath, all the while hearing her whispered pleas and moans. She must have been pacing back and forth, too, for he heard constant scuffling from her boots. Then he tried to scoot forward toward her, awkwardly spanning the wide gap between the hand ropes. He hung at the length of his arms with the weight of the heavy backpack feeling like so many safes beneath, but his knees were hitched over the ropes, pulling out what little slack their lateral motion would allow. It was fighting him, wanting to spread his legs wider, which made the scrambling spider-like motion that much more difficult. Had he been going the other way, *pushing* along, toward his head, it would have been worlds easier. For a moment, the thought crossed his mind that maybe that wouldn't be a bad idea. But that would mean abandoning Tanis, which he automatically rejected.

She was still talking to him in a desperate, tear-filled voice, coaxing him on, assuring him he was going to make it, and pleading with him not to give up. To keep coming. He slid, inch by inch, having no idea how far he had left to go, until he finally felt his ankles bang against the wooden posts into which the side ropes were anchored. "Grab my feet and pull!" he cried, filling with excitement and fear. It suddenly felt impossible for him to go any farther, as the backs of his knees had been providing the traction! But Tanis did as he told her and grabbed him by the boots. "Walk backward!" he shouted, almost completely out of breath. She did so, and slowly, slowly, he was able to walk his hands along the ropes – hands that now trembled and felt like little machines made to crank out pain, wholesale. His forearms were burning with it as well. His shoulders were almost numb with the weight of the backpack.

Then he finally reached the posts with his hands and told her she could set his feet down. He had made it. As she did, she leapt forward in the dark, enveloping him with her arms, falling onto him and putting her face against his own. He felt the hot tears smear between her cheek and his. She was still mouthing *Oh my God!* but with a rhythm that followed each breath she exhaled. Noah allowed himself to lean back against the post and rest his arms. They were on fire with the exertion, and his hands were screaming and throbbing, burning like the bites of a billion fire ants simultaneously. He closed his eyes and concentrated on his breathing, trying to slow it down, his heart slamming in his chest.

"I'm so glad you got your feet up!" she whispered in his ear. It was wet with tears. "Thank God you held on. I'm so proud of you. You're so amazing!"

5

When Noah had finally regained enough strength to sit up on his own, Tanis slipped off of him to the side and put her arm around him, rubbing his back softly. He sat shaking his head, catching his breath, and trembling. Then he finally looked at Tanis, whom he could now see almost clearly. Where had that moonlight been before? She was looking quizzically at him, her eyes almost black in the low light of the moon. Her face held an expression that looked as if she had just asked him a serious question. *Will mankind make the stars?* Noah cracked a smile, and when Tanis only straightened her head but kept the same expression on her face, his smile caught and quickly turned to a giggle. She pulled her head back on her neck, her look now turning to something more on the order of *Why did you set a basket full of kittens on my bed?* And then he was chuckling. Suddenly, his chuckle became louder, more solid – more hearty – and he was off laughing.

Noah leaned his head back and howled with laughter. After shrugging off the backpack, he lay back in the dirt and looked up at Tanis, who had now begun laughing too, but a silent laughter; hers had not yet caught. She was still looking at him with something like disbelief. "What in the name of the giraffe are you laughing at, boy?" she said.

This only made him laugh harder. And now he had tears streaming down his cheeks to go with it. His hand found her thigh during the midst of this, and he squeezed it, latched on. He was rocking his head back and forth laughing so hard he couldn't breathe. And finally, Tanis started to giggle. "What in the world is so funny, Noah?" she asked between fits.

He tried to shrug. To hold his hands out as if to say *I have no idea!* but he wasn't sure his shrug was distinguishable from his shuddering. "I… don't… know… but you look…" he started, but only had room for two things at a time. And he was fighting with three: laughing, talking and breathing. "You looked like… you were asking about..." he got out, and almost choked on the spit running down his throat. He turned his head and spat while he laughed, then looked her in the eyes and tried to catch his breath.

When he finally had some control of it, he cleared his face, and looked at her as seriously as he could under the circumstances. "It looked like you were asking me about a basket full of kittens," and lost it completely. This time, so did she. Just having said it brought his hysteria back full force, and now she lay across his stomach dying with laughter herself. Hers was a lot more modest, a lot quieter a laugh, and he realized it was because she was having more trouble catching her breath. He could feel her body wracking with it though.

Noah reached down and pulled her shoulders back, rolling her off of him and grabbed her face with a dirty, rope-burned hand, turning her laughing mouth to his own. They laughed while they kissed. Hers quickly turned to a hard giggle, and suddenly, she was passionately sucking his lips and grabbing his head, pulling him harder into his kiss – as if she couldn't get enough of him at once. His laughter broke off shortly as well, and then he was in a push-up position above her, kissing her fervently. Before he realized what was happening, Tanis was unbuttoning his shirt. She was breathing hard, not wanting to break the kiss, and thus, taking hard gasps through her nose. She followed him as he backed off his hands to remove his shirt. In spite of the cold evening he was still sweating, and felt the sweat go cold as she flung his shirt to the side. He fell back to his previous position, and then Tanis's hands were working on his belt. Noah did not take the time to back off and ask if she was sure, or if she was ready. She knew what she was doing. His one hand was on her jaw, his other supporting his weight as she fiddled with his button, then the zipper. Then she was kicking off his jeans, boxers and all. He had a moment of wonder for what her plan was, then suddenly she was trying to sit up again, removing her own coat. He helped her with the sweater beneath. They used these articles for their blanket. Noah ran his hand along her bra strap down the left side of her rib cage, then paused when his fingers reached the blockage which was where her back met the ground. Tanis opened her eyes and looked deep into him with a mysterious allure. Then she arched her back just enough for his hand to slide under her. A moment later he removed the bra and saw for the first time, by the light of the big moon, what she looked like. He pushed up on his hands and stared at her for a moment, relishing, gazing – leering. His focus shifted between her breasts and her eyes in something like amazement. Tanis lay with her mouth closed, biting her bottom lip, but there was no more of that worry in her eyes like that of someone being judged. Whatever reservations she may have had about her nearly flat chest were apparently gone now. Her face changed from that look of mystery to one of lust and desire, and in that instant, she grabbed Noah by the back of his head, pulling his face to her chest. And then both of her hands were on his head, guiding him – forcing him – to explore. *Stay for a while.*

He felt her shiver as he kissed her with his full mouth, leaving her skin shiny in the pale moonlight. Tanis bucked her hips up and her shoulders came forward, and Noah helped her remove the rest of her restraint. Then her hand was back on his face, and they were kissing again. Her other hand grabbed hard against his rear, and with nothing but a wordless moan, she was pulling him into her. In the distance, he heard a noise that sounded at first like a cry in the night, and then it was spreading. Tanis's eyes went wide with fear, and then exhilaration as it became clear what they were hearing. A magnificent chorus of coyotes was howling from every direction around them. She closed her eyes and leaned her head back, pointing her chin at the sky, then howled her own cry into the night.

They sat huddled under the same blanket, on the same small pallet, naked and staring at the crackling fire. Once it had come roaring to life, Noah had fished out the Thermos of coffee and offered it to Tanis. She sipped from the small tin cup that topped the Thermos while Noah took his own sips from a leather-bound steel flask full of bourbon. Both the hot coffee and the cool bourbon provided about the same inner warmth, he reckoned.

"So how are we gonna get out of here?" Tanis said. They were plenty warm under the heavy wool blanket, but he could still see her breath. Her lips were full and glossy with the wet from the coffee, and Noah thought she looked more beautiful than he had ever seen her, lit by the orange flames.

He leaned in and kissed her, then sat back up and said, "I don't know. I'll call Lennie in the morning and see if she knows another way out of here." He looked around in the blackness, which fell harsh just outside the ring of the fire's glow. He shrugged and said, "Of course, we might not need help. We may be able to see a way out in the morning."

Tanis looked at him, half-amused. "You don't *know* if there's another way back?"

He smiled at her. "Nope. Never been here in the daylight." He took another pull of the whiskey and saw her eyeing the flask. He held it out to her. Tanis took it and swallowed a mouthful of her own. "In fact, this is only my second time here."

Tanis opened her mouth and rolled her eyes. "Oh my God, are you serious?" she shouted through a smile.

Noah couldn't help but smile back at her.

"You bring me out to some place you've only been once, in the dark, and you break the rope – which could be our only way home."

Noah looked at the fire, still smiling as he took the flask back when she offered it. "Yeah, well, you know, there are still two ropes crossing that gully. If worse comes to worst," he said, raising his shoulders in a shrug, but didn't finish the sentence, or the shrug. He could see her peripherally, shaking her head slowly. But he also saw the faintest hint of a smile still remained.

"If you think I'm walking a tight-wire, we need to talk about who you think I am."

Noah's smile widened. "Just saying. We've got options."

She put her hand on his shoulder. "Boy, that was something, wasn't it?"

He looked at her sharply. "What's that?"

"When those coyotes started baying!" she said and took another sip of the coffee, then splashed the rest of it into the fire, presumably because it had cooled too quickly.

"Yeah, that added a nice ambiance to the act, didn't it?" he replied.

Tanis squeezed his shoulder and sat silent for a long moment. Noah met her eyes and they stared at each other. "For our first time to actually do it, I think that made it magical. It was perfect, Noah," she said, smiling.

Noah nodded, reached under the blanket and found her hand, squeezed it. She sat with her knees together in front of her, her chin resting atop them as she looked at him. He finally said, "Can I ask you a question?"

She rolled her chin back and forth on her knees, mimicking a nod.

"How was it so easy for me to get you?"

Tanis frowned at this, but did not say anything. Her question was clear.

"I mean, how was it so easy for me," he said, putting a hand on his chest, fingers spread, "to get you.

I mean, it seems like I picked you up with that first cheesy line. I can't believe that worked."

She grinned, looked at the fire. "I think it worked because of who said it." Tanis reached toward the flask as he took another pull. Noah handed it to her. "And it wasn't just the line. The whole approach was great. I liked you instantly." She looked at him approvingly in the crackling, unsure light, then said, "It doesn't hurt that you're easy to look at, either."

Noah grinned at that. "Yeah, but come on. You probably have guys twice as good looking as me hitting on you constantly."

Tanis pursed her lips and shook her head, her chin still on her knees. "Mm mm."

Noah made a face. "Seriously?"

"Nope. I almost never get hit on. See, guys think a 'pretty woman' just gets hit on all the time. Well," she said, flipping her hand in the air. "Well, maybe they do. I don't know. Actually, yes, I do know. My friend Carrie gets hit on all the time. She's got this gorgeous, curly black hair," she said, shaking her head and rolling her eyes. "But I don't." She picked up the flask she had set between her feet. Took another sip. "I think guys are intimidated by me since I stand on a stage." She handed the flask back to him.

He nodded. "That could make sense. So when do I get to meet this friend of yours?"

She shrugged. "She lives in Ohio. I don't get to see her very often these days. If I ever get rich, I'm buying her a house right next to mine, though."

Noah chuckled. He ran a finger through her hair, pushing it behind her ear. "Well, I don't need a crystal ball to see that in your future."

Tanis frowned and said, "What? Being rich?" When Noah nodded, she giggled, looking at him as if he might be kidding. "Well thank you. I guess we'll just have to see. I might be buying a house for you, too."

"Why? I'm just gonna live with you," Noah responded. She slapped his shoulder. And then they were kissing again.

7.

Lennie kept covering the mouthpiece of the phone – albeit not very effectively, for Noah could still hear everything she was saying – and shouting across the room at whomever she was with. He had asked her if there was another way down the mountain. "What, you're stuck?"

"Yeah. The foot rope broke," he had said.

"Are you joshing me, brother?" said Lennie.

"No. Seriously. I can't think of a good reason to joke about that."

And then she had started shouting at someone else. *The rainbow rope broke! No, it's Noah! Yeah, he's stuck out there!* Then, to Noah, "Are you okay? Are you injured or anything? Oh my God!"

"Yeah, no, we're okay. We're just kind of stuck out here."

"We're? Who's the other part of that 'we'?" Lennie asked. "Noah, my God, how did this happen? I'm so sorry, are you sure you're okay?"

"Yeah. Listen, Len, I just need to know if there's another way down."

"I don't know. Hang on. Jen is checking with Mike and Tonya," she said.

Noah widened his eyes. Shook his head. "Who the hell are they?"

"They showed us the place originally."

"What, you don't know?" Noah asked, incredulous.

"Dude, bro, I've only been there a few times, and it's always been at night. The rope has never broken on me."

He conceded she had a good point. "Okay. Call me back if you hear anything, okay?"

"Wait," Lennie said. "You can't find another way? You're Mister Explorer..."

"It's nothing but dense forest and steep rock every place we can even get to to look," he said. He was beginning to get frustrated.

"You keep saying 'we'," Lennie reminded him.

"Yeah. I'm here with Tanis." It got quiet on the other end of the line. "Hello?"

"Okay, bubba. I'm gonna get help, okay?"

Noah chuckled to himself at that. So since her girl-crush is stuck here with me, she'll get us some help. *Got it.* "I don't need help, sis. I just need guidance."

"Guidance is help, doop shoot. Stay cool. I'll call you back." *Click.*

As they waited, they continued to explore, but it seemed they were on a peaked plateau of some degree, with nothing but steep sides. There was one small chance, Noah thought, on the west side of the hill where the trees seemed to form a sort of path. It looked, come down to it, like they might be able to slide down to the tree level. But navigating back around through the trees did not look hopeful. And the path that led to the side of the rope opposite their hillock was on raised ground as well. Staring out across the two remaining ropes, one could see the ground on the other side dropped away sharply on all three sides. Eventually, he knew, the forest floor would have to rise to meet it. Somewhere. Well, he didn't really *know*, did he? He *thought. Surely it must.*

But if it didn't, they could be lost in the forest. The trees were incredibly dense down there, and with all the undergrowth, they certainly weren't prepared for a trek through them. They had worn their hiking boots and jeans. It was unlikely they would encounter snakes. But bears? That was certainly possible. Noah didn't think it likely though. He thought their biggest adversary was the forest itself. He felt pretty confident in his ability to maintain a direction – but to what end? He simply didn't know *where* to go. The trail from the side of the road where they parked that ran all the way to the rope bridge was a long and winding one. And he had never seen it with the light of anything more than flashlights. In relation to where they were standing now, he had no clue where the vehicle was, or even how far away. It could be fifty yards south, but a two-mile hike if they followed the trail.

Noah dropped his arms and turned to look at Tanis, who stood patiently with her hands in her coat pockets. "Tan, we may have to cross using these hand ropes."

Her eyes got real wide, but she did not speak.

"Have you never done a rope crawl?" he asked her.

Tanis shook her head subtly. "Noah, I've never crossed a rope bridge until last night."

He took a deep breath. Sighed. "Well, it's actually pretty simple. You just sort of hang from it and-"

"NOAH!" she shouted, cutting him off. She pointed at the chasm that separated them from civilization. "Please don't ask me to hang from one of those ropes!"

Noah stopped and looked down between the two hills. It was a ridiculous drop. He thought he could probably do it if his survival depended on it. Thought. Probably. Those were easy words. Now that he looked at what he was saying, he couldn't imagine trying to talk Tanis into the idea. Still, he thought, there didn't seem to be a lot of other options. If it came down to it, what if they *had to?*

He turned back to Tanis and put his hands on her shoulders and repeated the question he had only thought. "What if we have to?"

Tanis swallowed and stared down into the gap, chewing on the inside of her bottom lip. She began shaking her head. He saw the corners of her eyes go glassy. She took a deep breath and let it out slowly, still staring into the awful abyss. "I could try, Noh. If I really had to, I guess I could try. But I'm so scared!" She was shaking her head again. She raised her left hand, and in a flash, it came to him. He remembered her bad hand just as she said it. "I don't think I could count on my fingers!" The tears spilled over, made their way down her pale cheeks.

"Okay. Okay, I forgot about that," he said. He dropped his hands from her shoulders, slid them down her arms and stepped closer, pulling her into a hug. "It's all right, baby. We'll find a way out of here. Don't worry about it. We'll figure this out."

The sun was coming up over the trees to the southeast, foggy and spectral in its weak shimmer. They stood staring at it until Tanis shook her head.

"Now *that's* a Tequila Sunrise if I ever saw one," she said.

Noah looked at her. An idea – a glimmer, a fractal shard of memory – had popped into his head. He tried to dig into it, but it was already slipping away. Tanis looked back at him, concern evident in her eyes.

"What's wrong, baby?" she said, running her hand up and down his forearm.

"Nothing wrong. Just something you said just reminded me of… Oh! Wait. I know!" he almost shouted, and clapped his hands together. Tanis almost flinched. "That night you joined us around the fire pit, you said something that I've been trying to remember ever since. Something you said made me want to ask you a question!"

"Well? What is it?" She stared at him expectantly.

"You said something about playing air guitar with a nephew when you were drunk on tequila or something."

"Yeah," Tanis said, smiling pleasantly at the non-memory. She had said she did not remember the event itself, only of being told about it later.

"So you have a nephew. That means…"

Tanis looked up at him, finishing the thought in her head. "Yeah, I have a brother and a sister. My brother is married. Has two kids." She held her hand out as if offering a truce and added, "There's your nephew."

Noah raised his chin. "How come we've never talked about our families?"

Tanis shrugged. "They're boring. Well, not yours. I love Lennie."

"Yeah, she's great," Noah said and smiled. "What are your sibs' names?" They had turned and were walking away from where their fate lay, at the mouth of the Rainbow.

"Well, my brother is Ren. His wife is Daisy, and their kids are Ryan and Sarah."

"I hope there's not gonna be a quiz on all these names later," Noah said, looking stunned.

Tanis stopped. "What, don't you want to know everything you can about me?" she said, looking at him seriously.

Without missing a beat, he snapped back, "Of course. What's sister's name?"

They turned and began walking again. "Sister is Twyla. She's single. Four years my junior," Tanis said.

"Tanis and Twyla. And, what? Ren?"

Tanis nodded.

"Some pretty exotic names, no?" he said.

She smiled. "I guess so. My mother wanted unique. Remember we had that whole slew of girls named Madison and McKenzie for about ten years? Blggg!" she made a noise that sounded like a gag. "I got so tired of that."

"Yeah, but we were here long before that."

"Noah," Tanis said, stopping him again, a hand on his arm. "Isn't Troy single?"

"Yeah," he said, frowning. "Why?"

"I should introduce him to Twy."

"Twy?" Noah said, making a sour face. "Like Twyla is just too long to get it all out in one breath?"

Tanis slapped his shoulder playfully. "He's so her type. Kind of dorky; real smart; driven."

Noah nodded, pursing his lips, raising his eyebrows. "Yeah, he's definitely all those things."

Tanis tilted her head. "Is he a good guy? Like you?" she said, rubbing his arm again.

"Yeah. He's good as they come. Just a little neurotic sometimes."

8

A half-hour later, Noah's phone – almost dead by now – buzzed its chirruping call into the crisp morning air. He and Tanis had built the fire back up while they waited, though they had no breakfast to heat over its flames. Noah pulled his phone from his shirt pocket and answered it.

"Lennie. Talk to me, baby."

"Okay, so here's what we're gonna do. We're going to come out there and try to figure out a way to get you across."

Noah rolled his eyes and pulled the phone away from his ear as he looked at Tanis, shaking his head. *She has no idea either*, he mouthed. Putting the phone back to his ear, he heard her asking if he was still there. "Yeah, sis. I'm here. I was just hoping you knew another way out of here already. I'm not sure how you're going to be able to help."

"Hmm," she said, the equivalent of a verbal shrug. "We'll figure something out. Anyway, we're on our way. Should be there in a couple of hours."

Noah sighed. "Okay, well, we'll be here."

"Hey, Noh?"

"Yeah?"

"Take care of that girl."

The sun was warm on their faces but the morning air was still chilly. Lennie had texted Noah some fifteen minutes ago, letting him know they had parked. They were on their way up the trail now, with a series of tools and rigging to assist the stranded. Noah wasn't sure he liked the idea of the word *rigging* but said nothing, and did not mention it to Tanis. Whatever would be, would be.

When they finally started hearing the voices of their rescuers coming up the trail some hundred feet away, Tanis stood up and faced the ravine, bouncing on the balls of her feet – more in anticipation than excitement, Noah guessed. Then Lennie's face was visible, between two of her male friends, coming up the hill to a stop between the rope anchors. They were less than seventy feet away, but had to shout to be heard.

"Are you guys okay?" Lennie shouted.

Noah gave her a thumbs-up.

Tanis shouted back, "Thank you guys for coming!"

Lennie smiled broadly, then waved. One of the men shrugged off a backpack. The other dropped a large duffel bag and squatted to unzip it. Tanis turned away and looked at Noah.

"I'm going to have to rope crawl after all, aren't I?"

Noah took her by the hands and pulled her close. "I don't know what they're planning, but you'll get through it. I'll be right there with you."

"Noah!" one of the guys shouted. Noah broke away and stepped to the edge. "Try to catch this!" he said, then held up a baseball. One end of a stretch of 550 para-cord was duct-taped to the ball. Noah held up his hands. The guy reared back then flung his arm forward. The ball sailed across the chasm, a perfect lob and Noah caught it with a snap. The guy – Noah was sad he didn't even know the man's name – gave him two quick thumbs up, then turned back to dig in the duffel bag at his feet. Lennie was standing there talking to him, the other end of the para-cord in her gloved hands. The cord dangled between Noah and his sister, connecting them. Noah could not hear what they were talking about, but being that he and Tanis had not been briefed on what the plan was, he guessed the group across the gap had it all figured out.

When the man pulled a shining chrome bar with black rubber handles from the bag, Tanis moaned in agony and had to turn away. It looked like something out of a weight room – wide, with the handles cocked down at an angle and a hook in the middle. Then the other guy pulled a pulley out of the bag and clipped it to the bottom of the handle apparatus. Noah could hear Tanis stifling a sob from behind him. But she did not speak up. He was about to shout to the other side that anything involving her holding onto a handle was out, but suddenly saw what the plan was. It all snapped into place when the first guy brought out what looked like a SCUBA diver's vest covered with rigging straps and a large steel hook on the front. This got snapped to the loop in the handle as well, then the whole thing was attached to one of the hand ropes that ran across the chasm. Lennie handed off the para-cord and the man tied it to the vest's belly hook.

Then the man stood straight and put his hands around his mouth. "Okay, pull it to you, Noah!" and Noah did as he was told. "Buckle Tanis in first so you can make sure she's in tight!"

Noah pulled the cord, bringing the vest and its attached apparatus closer and closer. He noticed his hands were trembling. He also noticed Tanis was breathing very heavily now, and turned to look at her as he tugged. "You're gonna do fine, baby. I promise. It'll all be over soon," he said, then realized that was not the most eloquent selection of words to use in this case. It held a certain absolute that could not be denied, chilling in its finality. "I mean, you'll be over there in Lennie's arms before you know it. And then in mine shortly after."

Tanis nodded, looking like a little girl trying to hold back her tears. Trying to be a big girl. He wanted to hold her. But now was not the time. He needed her to be strong.

As the vest came to the end of the hand rope, he grabbed it and disconnected it from the weight-room handle, then noticed the length of para-cord hung toward the abyss below, about seventy feet down. He nodded as that, too, fell into place. He fished up a few feet of it and handed it to Tanis, then said, "Can you pull this up until you reach the end?" Another length of cord still hung across the gap where one of the men had tied it to the post on the other side.

She nodded and stepped forward, bravely. Noah was impressed with her ability to fight through what must be incredible anticipation and stress. She was facing absolute terror, but had not said a single word in complaint. The tears were easily forgiven. Hell, he thought, he might shed a few himself before this was all over.

When Tanis finished retrieving the dangling para-cord, Noah wrapped the end of it around the post and tied a quick knot. Looking up, he saw the men standing there with their arms crossed, nodding. The ball-thrower gave him another thumbs-up and a smile. Noah returned the gesture, then held up the vest to Tanis. She took a deep breath and stepped forward, turning her back to him as she did so. He helped her put her arms through the holes, then spun her back around, pulling the rigging straps tight and buckling them across her chest and abdomen. Two straps dangled between her legs. He squatted and pushed the ends through her legs and brought them up to buckle in the back.

"Tighten those as tight as you feel comfortable around your thighs. They're going to pull tight, but they'll keep you from slipping out the bottom of this thing," Noah said. Tanis sucked in a breath at the thought of that but nodded and actually got out the word *okay*.

Then he stood up again, and tugged on the straps across her front, making sure they were all snug. "Okay, I think you're ready."

Tanis grabbed the opening of the vest near her neck with both hands and stepped forward into Noah's arms. He gave her a tight hug and whispered in her ear, "Right behind you, babe. You're going to do great." He felt her nod against his collar bone, then put his hands on her shoulders, stepping back a foot. Noah stared into her eyes for a moment and then gave her a long but chaste kiss on her frightened and trembling mouth.

Looking at the apparatus that still hung from the rope, Noah could see an extra strap with a D-ring sewn into it with extremely heavy stitching, dangling from the top. He unbuckled the whole thing and clipped the ring at the bottom of this strap to the rigging clip on Tanis's vest. Then he hooked the D-ring back to the rigging clip on the rope, easing her forward as he did so. Now she was attached to the rope. He stood behind her, hands on her shoulders, and knelt where she squatted.

Across the gap, Lennie yelled, "You ready, sweets?"

Tanis nodded feebly.

Noah said quietly, "Whenever you're ready. But I wouldn't wait too long or-" but they started pulling from the other side, and suddenly, she was out over the gulf, legs akimbo, dangling like a bungee jumper at the end of her tether. He could see the straps of the vest tented up toward the rope, separated from her by sixteen inches of nylon strap. The weight-room handlebar still hung connected to that same upper D-ring, suspended above her. Noah reckoned its only purpose was for resting one's arms. "Grab onto that handlebar, sweetie," he said, before she got too far out. "It might make you more comfortable." She did so, and as she spun hither and tither on her long frightening journey, Noah saw that she was completely relaxed, head hanging back limply, and eyes closed against the terror. He let the para-cord slip through his hands as she slowly, inch by inch, grew farther from him and closer to home.

"You're doing great, girl," one of the guys shouted, adding a few claps to the encouragement. "Hang on tight!"

When Tanis had gone twenty or so feet, Lennie called across, "Tanis! Give us your battle cry!"

And Tanis, without missing a beat, screamed out in a perfectly firm voice, "Back from the black hole!"

Lennie shouted, "Yay!" and raised her fists in the air. The guys on the other side clapped. Noah huffed, smiling in spite of his apprehension. The stress had been almost palpable. She was going to make it after all. Now whether or not she would forgive him for bringing her out here only to get stranded, he would just have to wait and see.

Shortly after her triumphant shout, they had her by the feet and were pulling her upright. Noah let out a long-held breath and found himself clapping with the rest of the team who did not have their hands on Tanis's safety. When she was unstrapped, she and

Lennie embraced and Noah could see the tears on Tanis's cheeks, but she was smiling. Once they had reattached the vest to the pulley, Noah pulled it back across using his end of the para-cord. In under a minute, he had it back in his hands, and began strapping himself in. He looked across and saw Tanis standing there staring at him, her hands clasped as if in prayer just below her chin. She was smiling at him. She had achieved greatness. He only hoped he could do the same now that the chips were down. Lennie stood with her arm around Tanis, her head leaning on the taller woman's shoulder. Noah liked seeing them together. If his sister loved someone, that person *knew* she was loved.

Once he had himself strapped in, he made the awkward advance to the hand rope and clipped himself to the rolling pulley and tugged on it a few times. One of the guys across the way shouted, "Make sure you cut your cord loose over there!" Oh yeah. Noah looked back and saw that the para-cord he had used to retrieve the vest was still tied to the post. He slipped his knife out of his front pocket and flipped it open, slashing at the thin rope. It sliced neatly through it. Then he watched as all seventy-something feet of it slithered off the edge of the cliff to dangle straight down from where he hung.

"All right, let's do it!" Noah said, trying to sound confident. And they began to pull him across. At first it wasn't as bad as he had imagined. The constant back and forth semi-twist got annoying pretty quickly, but he found he could almost control it using the handlebar arrangement above him. After twenty or so feet, he allowed himself a look down, and saw the fog had closed in beneath him. It reminded him of a scene from *The Lost Boys* where they all dropped from the bridge into a thick fog. He could not see anything but the eerie cloud beneath him, and wasn't sure if that should have been comforting or spooky. When he looked back up, he saw Lennie looking at him expectantly, so he shouted, "Here come the pirates!"

They all shouted, some of them clapping. Lennie and Tanis stomped around hollering back at him, almost dancing in circles. Noah felt the tension drop away and found himself almost enjoying the suspension. He hung onto the handlebars, and shortly, felt his feet his something solid. And then they were pulling him off, celebrating, clapping him on the back while they unbuckled him. Lennie buried her head in his chest. He wrapped his arms round her and kissed the top of her head. He looked up and saw Tanis smiling at him. She winked and stepped up as he raised one arm. Noah hugged them both together.

Back in Noah's Jeep, he sat gripping the steering wheel tightly, staring straight out the windshield. The silence was remarkable. After spending the last fourteen hours atop the mountain, the quiet had taken on a different definition. Here, inside the insulated cab of his vehicle, there was no gentle breeze in the trees, no birds calling, the night sound of the cicadas and crickets – just still. It made his ears ring. He felt the security – the solid connection to stability here. After a sleepless night of wondering what would happen, the intensity of the wait, the anticipation of the coming morning, of having to face their dilemma, he finally felt the buzz draining from his blood. The buzzing, electric vibration that he had fought to keep beneath the surface while he handled the situation – it was finally turning to smoke. Tanis had asked him sometime in the night what would happen if they were attacked by animals or something. They had made no emergency preparations. He had stroked her hair and told her not to worry, the fire would keep the predators away. And he had been right. But it had been a stroke of luck. Noah had not wanted to call Lennie and try to start figuring out their escape in the dark of the night. He wanted to scout the land, see if there were any other paths back to safety before he called for help. He now could not imagine the rescue they had undergone taking place under the moon.

Tanis put her hand on his thigh. He could feel her looking at him. He turned to face her. "I am so sorry I got you into that."

She frowned, wincing against the statement. "What, are you kidding? That was a life experience, Noah!" She smiled broadly. Genuinely. The fear and anxiety had completely left her, he could see. She looked completely relaxed – fresh.

Noah pursed his lips, raised his eyebrows, nodded. "Yeah, I guess you're right. I just feel like a fool for bringing you out here to show off this place only to get stuck out there," he said, waving his hand toward the trail.

Tanis shook her head. "Nay, cowboy, don't talk like that. I wouldn't change a thing. And now I have a story to tell."

"Or a song to write," Noah suggested, the hint of a smile touching the corner of his mouth.

"Or a song to write. I think that's a heck of a great idea," she agreed. Tanis looked around, flipped her hair back, then added, "That might be the most exciting thing that's ever happened to me."

Noah just nodded, pensive and staring at the dash. The heater was finally starting to blow warm air. He held his hands up to the vents on the dash, made fists and relaxed them.

"You know, I think we owe Lennie a huge thank-you," Tanis said, poking his thigh with her finger. "Her and her friends. That was super cool of them."

"You boys ready for next weekend?" Troy asked. The Fire Tribe was back at the pit behind Troy's house, feet up on the stones, cold beers in hand. Noah had told them all about the near failure of his excursion to the Rainbow with Tanis. Troy and Doug had had a good laugh about it. And as they had laughed, Noah had realized it *was* funny, and had found himself laughing with them. The stress of the moment, however, had not been funny at all. Not in the moment, at least. He took a good ribbing for trying to show off to a girl and getting stuck.

"Is this a bring-your-girl trip?" Noah asked, taking a pull from his beer.

Troy sat back and shrugged and looked back at him. "Fine with me," he said, then looked at Noah. "Is your girl free next weekend?"

Noah shrugged as well, and made a face. "No idea, bro. I can find out though. She might be rehearsing."

"Who you gonna bring?" Doug asked, looking at Troy.

"Please tell me you're not bringing Trix," Noah said, pointing his bottle at Troy. Doug shot him a glance, a smirk on his face.

"Why?" Troy said, holding his hands up. "What's wrong with Trixie? She was fun!"

Noah sat back, shaking his head. "She's just got..." he started, then couldn't figure out how to finish. He didn't want to hurt Troy's feelings by letting him know Trixie had only come to get close to Noah. And it might sound like bragging if he didn't tell him the *whole* story.

Doug was leaning forward, elbows on his knees, bottle danging between his fingers. He was staring at Noah, and was ready to take over. "She's got too much energy, bro. I think we should get you someone a little duller."

"Duller?" Troy said, eyebrows raised. "What the hell's wrong with you two? You know I don't get girls as easy as you guys. I finally score a date with who I think," he said, putting a hand over his chest, "is actually hot as hell, and she's got too much energy?" He shook his head. Took a sip of his beer. "I can't win for losing."

"Dude, Roy," Doug said, "I'm sorry man, you're right. Bring whoever you want."

"Huh." Troy shook his head. "That easy?" He turned to look at Noah.

"Whoa! NO!" Noah said, sitting forward so fast that some beer shot out of the bottle and onto his sleeve. They both looked at him. "Dude! I completely forgot!"

"What the hell did you forget?" Troy asked, holding a hand up.

"Tanis has a sister she wants to introduce you to!"

"Tanis has a sister?" Troy said, turning toward Noah. His body language suggested a serious interest.

Noah grinned. Doug piped up, saying, "Yeah, dude, when were you going to let us know this shit?"

Noah looked at him. "Well I didn't find out myself until the other morning when we were stuck on that hill!"

"How the hell do you not know someone has a sister for that long?"

Noah shrugged. "It just didn't come up. I don't know. Anyway, her name is Twyla."

Troy licked his lips. "What's she look like? I mean," he said, closing his eyes. He shook his head. "I mean, what's she like?"

"Haven't met her," Noah said, putting a hand in his pocket. With the other, he took a sip of his beer.

"Well," Doug said, "that might get awkward having to share a tent with a dude she just met."

"No, dumb ass. The girls have their own tent," Troy said.

They both looked at Troy now. Noah was nodding. "Yeah, man. That could work."

10

The next weekend, the men sat around the fire awaiting the women's arrival. They had planned it so the women could all ride together. Tanis, Twyla and Alice would be stopping to get a drink or three at the Doubloon, a tavern on the edge of town within crawling distance of the campgrounds. Meanwhile, the boys got camp set up. Noah liked the idea, because it gave the gals time to get to know each other a little bit, and plenty of time for Alice to tell Twyla all about Troy. *Son of a bitch*, Noah thought. *That's a lot of Ts to keep up with. Twyla, Tanis, Troy…*

Noah and the guys had setup two large tents on opposing sides of the fire. When they had finished, Troy had tossed an armload of blankets into the women's tent on top of the three sleeping bags that lay atop the three cots. They would sleep in luxury tonight.

Troy was full of nervous energy even though they had all smoked a bowl a half-hour before just to try to calm him down. A blind date was one thing. But on a camping trip where they would be somewhat stuck together for the duration of the weekend might be another. On the other hand, Doug had reasoned with him, it wouldn't be so bad as a typical first date, since there was no real pressure, and plenty of other people to hang out with if they didn't hit it off. Still, the anticipation was clearly getting to Troy. He was sitting with his palms together, sandwiched between his knees, his legs bouncing up and down on his toes.

"You've never seen a picture of her?" Troy asked.

Noah laughed. They had been over all this already. "No. No pictures dude. She didn't even describe her to me. I asked her siblings' names, she told me, then she said you were just Twyla's type."

"She said that?"

"Yes, dude!"

Doug added, "Come on man, stop worrying about it. You've seen Tanis. If they came from the same mom, then she can't be bad looking."

Noah tilted his head thoughtfully. *There is that.* "Yeah. Same mom. That's why she said they all have those slick ass names. Mom wanted something unique."

"Twyla and Troy. Kind of has a ring to it, no?" Troy said.

"Yeah, man," Doug said, holding his bottle out for a clink. Troy clinked it.

They had been sitting there for about an hour when they finally saw headlights round the bend through the trees. Troy sat up straight, swallowed. Cracked his neck.

"Dude, you're good," Noah said, holding his fist out for a bump. Troy nodded as he knocked his fist against Noah's.

"Yeah. Good. I hope I live up to her expectations."

"Stop that shit, dude! Of course you do! You're money, bro," Doug said.

As Alice's pickup rambled up to the railroad tie that served as a parking block for the campsite, the lights and engine cut off simultaneously. Then the doors squeaked open and the three women came into the light of the fire.

"Howdy, boys!" Alice said, taking off her cowboy hat and holding it over her head in a pose. All three men stood up. Tanis then came out from behind Alice with her sister, her arm tucked through Twyla's as if she were trying to keep her from dashing forward.

"Hey, guys!" she said. "This is my little sister, Twyla." Twyla raised a hand in a wave and smiled broadly.

The guys waved back at her and Doug, the closest to them, stepped forward. "Hey, Twyla. I'm Doug. This is my boy, Troy. And that's Noah over there."

"Hi!" Twyla said. She did not look the least bit shy. As Troy walked up to shake her hand, she leaned forward seductively and offered her cheek for a kiss. Noah thought she might have soaked up those drinks. They shook hands and Troy did kiss her cheek. Then she stepped back and looked him over. Noah and Doug exchanged a quick glance while their respective girlfriends made their way to their sides.

Noah smiled at Tanis and put an arm around her. Then Twyla came closer and he was finally able to get a good look at her. She did not look like Tanis. That much was clear. She had large, dark eyes, and short black hair that sprouted out from beneath her bowler's hat down to her jawline. She looked to be about the same height as Tanis, but maybe a little thicker. Tanis was thin as paper though. As Twyla shook Noah's hand, she smiled, showing lots of big white teeth. *My God, she's drop-dead gorgeous.*

"What are you guys drinking?" she asked as she shook Doug's hand.

Doug offered her his bottle. "It's home brew. We call it Pirate Flag."

She took the bottle from him and took a thoughtful swig. "Arrrr!" she cried, making a face and a fist. "That's good!"

Everyone had a chuckle at her sudden pirate outburst.

When they had all settled into their own collapsible chairs, Noah could see that Troy was enthralled with the girl. He hoped Troy wouldn't run her off with his exuberance. But Twyla seemed to be every bit as excited as he. Noah exchanged another glance with Doug. Doug raised an eyebrow and Noah nodded subtly.

"So how was the Doubloon?" Noah asked Tanis.

"That place is cool," she said, putting her hands out as if she were about to play a piano. "I'm serious. It reminded me of one of those old jazz caverns on Beale Street. Smoky like a dive. They had good music on too."

Noah nodded. "We'll have to stop in there sometime and check it out."

Troy's and Twyla's chairs were pretty close to each other, and they looked like they were getting on swimmingly. "So you run the Lift Shop?" she asked him, looking curiously at him as he spoke.

"Yep. Opened it three years ago," he replied.

"How come you guys don't work there?" Twyla asked, turning to look at Noah and Doug.

Doug smiled. Noah chuckled. "Because we have real jobs, sweetie," Doug said. "Not everyone gets to play with toys all day."

Troy flipped them both off at the same time.

"Nah, the truth is, we have to have jobs," Doug said. "He gets to play with toys all day."

"You mean I have to babysit while all my employees get to play with toys all day," Troy corrected.

"So what do you do, Noah?" Twyla asked. She was sipping on her own bottle now.

"I'm a web designer." She nodded, pursing her lips. "And you?" he asked her.

"Well, by day, I'm what you call a 'waitress'," Twyla said, making quotes with her fingers.

"Oh yeah?" Doug asked, cracking another bottle open. Alice was leaning her head on his shoulder and staring at Twyla and Troy with a smile of approval. "Where do you wait?"

Twyla was adjusting her bowler's hat, taking a sip of beer at the same time. "It's a steakhouse. Called Paul Alan's."

Noah's heart stopped. His breath stopped in his throat and he made eye contact with Alice and Doug almost simultaneously. He swallowed hard then looked cautiously at Troy. Troy was chewing his lip and dusting off something that didn't entirely exist on his shirt. Avoiding eye contact. Noah knew Troy didn't have the best poker face.

"How long uh," Doug started, then waved his hand, stirring the air, "how uh, how long you worked there?"

Twyla, no dummy, shot him a look as he fumbled his words, and held the look for a long while, then finally said, "Well..." She sat back and wiped her lips. "It will be four years in the spring. I started right after college."

Doug raised his chin and held it up. "After college? How old are you, young lady? You don't look old enough for that many years of stuff."

"Ha!" she said, pointing at him, a big smile on her face. "I went to community college. I was done in two years." Then her face got serious. "If you have a ten-spot in your wallet, it's worth more than my degree."

Noah still had not recovered from the shock. If she had worked there for four years, then Twyla certainly knew Joy. And *almost* certainly, would have probably known she had gotten dumped by someone. Well, he thought, maybe not. Because Noah isn't a real common name. She would surely have made *that* connection by now. So maybe she wasn't close enough to Joy to know by *whom* she had gotten dumped. And, he thought, maybe Joy had not spread that around like a virus. She was a very private person, after all. But God was this too close for comfort! This gal definitely worked with his ex.

"Hey, an associate's degree is better than what I've got," Alice said.

Twyla waved the comment away. "Oh I don't worry about it," she said. "What was it our daddy always used to say?" she asked Tanis, looking at her in the orange light of the fire. "A degree is only..."

"Worth the person it's printed on," they both finished together.

"That's why I spend half my time on music," said Tanis.

"So you skipped the college thing altogether, then?" Doug asked. He looked at Noah again. That look said so many things in it. Primarily, we will need to keep a close eye on this situation, bro.

"No," Tanis said. She was leaning forward in her chair, wagging her empty bottle around on her fingertip between her knees. "No, I didn't quite skip it," she said.

Twyla almost shouted, "Oh, bullshit, Tanny. You're being modest," she said, making daggers at her sister with her eyes. Then, to Doug, "She's being modest, guys."

Tanis was shaking her head, screwing her mouth up. "Yeah, okay, sis. I went to college."

"Well! This is too interesting!" Troy said, clapping his hands together. "What did you study?"

Tanis took a deep breath and returned the daggers to her sister. Thanks, that look said. "I majored in physics."

"Christ," Doug said, shaking his head. He was staring at the fire, wide-eyed.

"That's pretty impressive," Troy said. "Did you know this, Noh?" he asked, pointing his bottle at Noah.

Noah shook his head. Made a face.

Twyla was shaking her head and rolling her eyes. The bottle dangled from her hand now as well. "Come on, Tanny. You're still being modest."

"What the flip else you want me to say?"

"Duh!" Twyla said, making an expectant face at her sister now, "You didn't *went to college*, sister!"

"What? What does that mean?" Doug asked. Noah was still too stunned to talk. He wondered how much of this he would remember in the morning. Would he forget it all because of the adrenaline high he was on from being blasted with the information that his girlfriend's sister might know his ex?

"I have a bachelor's degree. Big deal. Come on, Twy, let's stop this!" Tanis said. She looked truly humiliated now. Noah turned to look at her in the chair beside him, frowning at her.

"You have a degree?"

She looked back at him and gave him a thin smile. Nodded. That smile said, *Yeah, but let's please drop this hot potato.*

"Still being modest, actually," Twyla said, shaking her head and taking a swallow of her beer.

"Spit it out, Ransom!" Doug said. A few others laughed. Not Noah. And not Tanis.

"She's still going to school, guys," Twyla said, nodding her head proudly.

"Oh. Well, that's great! What's the big deal about that?" Doug said.

"Why is this a big deal, guys? I really don't feel comfortable talking about this!" Tanis said.

Noah squeezed her hand. She looked at him, then back at her sister, who was shaking her head with a smirk on her face.

Twyla looked directly at Doug and said, "Tanis is on a PhD track."

"Whoa! That's amazing!" Troy said, clapping. Doug was nodding dramatically.

"That is great! What are you studying?" Noah asked, leaning back to get a better angle on her face.

She turned to look at him and took a deep breath. "I'm in a PhD program for Astrophysics."

This was met with hollers and gales of laughter and cheering.

Tanis, though, was shaking her head.

"Why are you so ashamed of your success?" Troy tried.

Tanis looked at him, a pleading look – almost as if she had been hoping he would be the one to stay out of it. "I'm not ashamed in the least, Troy. I just don't like being thought of like that. I would much rather be thought of as a performer. An artist. Not a scholar."

Troy sat back in his chair. Doug, still shaking his head, found his chair as well. "I guess that makes sense," Doug said.

"Thank you," Tanis said.

"This is fascinating. I had zero idea," Noah said, holding out a hand at her. Troy stood and grabbed another couple of logs to drop on the dying fire.

"Anyone need a beer?" Troy asked.

Doug held up a finger.

"Yeah, sure," Noah said, handing him his empty.

"That was the point, Noah," Tanis said.

"Ouch," Noah said.

"Sorry. Nothing personal," said Tanis.

And Noah realized she was right. This was not about him. She was modest.

But where had all this taken place? He had never seen a school book in her apartment. A book bag in the backseat of Mally. Would this not be consuming large amounts of her free time? How did she have room for the music? The rehearsals and writing sessions and gigs… All the rest?

These were questions he would definitely be wanting to get to when they had more time alone together. And, well, maybe when they knew each other better. Clearly, it had been something she had kept private from him for a reason.

Alice, obviously seeing that Tanis was uncomfortable, offered, "Well I did skip college altogether."

"Is that so?" Twyla asked, raising her eyebrows. "What do you do?"

Alice wiggled her hips back and forth in the chair and snapped her fingers. "I just dance for my man. He pays for everything." Everyone had a laugh at that.

"Really? You don't work at all?"

"Nope," she said, popping the P and pursing her lips. She looked proud of her non-productivity.

"Well, that must be nice," Tanis said, smiling. She looked relieved to be off the hook.

After a comfortable amount of time had passed where everyone got to know each other, Tanis suggested they take turns telling stories – two a-piece: on false and one true – and see if anyone could guess which one was the true one. It did not last long, though, as it devolved into jokes and laughter; everyone was getting quite cozy with the copious amount of beer they were imbibing. At half-past-two, Doug said he was retiring to the tent, which spurred the question from Tanis – what were the sleeping arrangements? She had looked pointedly at the two tents and it was quite obvious what the arrangement was meant to be, but she looked as if she might not approve.

Doug turned, both hands in his pockets and looked at her over the dying fire. "Well, we figured the girls could crash in that one," he said pointing over her shoulder, "and we'll be over there." He threw a thumb over his shoulder.

"Oh," Tanis said. "No men to protect us in our tent, then?" she asked. She put a fingertip on her bottom lip as she said this and Doug might have blushed.

Troy, ever the pragmatist, replied immediately, "You're close enough for us to hear anything that happens. And we're well armed."

Tanis looked over at him casually. Security was clearly not her concern. Her gaze returned to Doug, as if in search of a better answer. He finally removed a hand from his pocket and held it out, palm up. "Do you have a better idea?"

She looked over at Troy again, sitting back in his chair and staring at the fire. Twyla was doing the same. Their hands had interlocked at some point during the last hour, and she was sitting as close to him as the arms of the chairs would allow. "Well, I was just thinking that these two might like to spend some time together."

"Oh, we're good," Troy said, glancing at her. "I've got extra sleeping bags and blankets and whatnot. We'll make do by the fire."

A smirk found its way onto Tanis's face as she stared at her sister. Twyla finally met her eyes and Tanis raised an eyebrow. Twyla nodded almost imperceptibly. Then Tanis looked back at Doug and smiled again. "Then I think that's settled. You and Alice can have that tent," she said, pointing at the one behind Doug, "and Noah and I will sleep there," she said, thumb over her own shoulder.

11

The fire flickered, creating queer shadows that lurched and danced a galliard on the walls of the tent. Noah lay on top of Tanis, staring into her dark eyes as they breathed together. There was no sound except for the occasional crisp pop of the flames outside. After Doug and Alice had zipped their tent closed, there had been not a peep out of anyone. Noah had wondered briefly how Troy and Twyla were fairing on their sleeping bags by the fire pit.

Tanis was looking at him through half-cocked eyes, chewing her bottom lip as she stared up at him, taking deep, heavy breaths through her nose. He felt her toes against the inside of his ankles as she continually pointed and then relaxed them. Noah was completely still. Every once in a while, he would push forward and watch her eyes close, feel her fingernails tighten against his triceps, watch her chin lift as she rolled her head back on the sleeping bag. And then he would hold his position again, staring into her eyes. Tanis would squint and take another deep breath, then slowly relax her grip on his arms, regain her posture. Tiny beads of sweat stood out on her bare chest. In the darkness of the tent, the odd fabric turned the firelight a sickly green, and caused her nipples to look dark against her pale chest. Noah would occasionally bend his neck and lick the sweat from her chest, her breasts, her neck. When she lifted her arm above her head to pull her hair up and get it out of the way, he licked her rib cage, her armpit, kissed her cheek. She was studying him as he lay on top of her, as if to wonder what he would do next.

Noah leaned in to whisper in her ear, "What are you thinking?" and allowed himself to slip forward, easing his way into her.

Another clawing sensation as her fingernails tightened on his arms – and he realized it must be subconscious; she had no real waking idea that she was squeezing him, tearing into his flesh. She was still biting her lip when she opened her eyes, now breathing so heavily that her chin rose and fell with her chest as she heaved, her pelvis now taking a life of its own against his hips. The intensity in her eyes could have set light to candles.

"I'm thinking I may be in love with you, Noah Wright," she said breathily.

Noah's heart skipped a beat and he felt his wrists tremble. Retracted. Watched her let him go. Watched her anticipating the next push – the next internal shock. Her lips were pursed as she watched him. Tanis was completely under his control, allowing him full authority here in this tent, warmed only by their body heat. After several fast breaths, she licked her lips and said, "What are you thinking?" Her fingertips stroked the backs of his arms.

Noah leaned in close again and licked her lips, then said, "I'm thinking this is where I was born to be."

"Oh, God!" she said, closing her eyes again. He felt her contract around him. Then they were kissing heavily, and there were no more stops to pull. He was moving. His rhythm picked up and he felt her matching his gait, a mirror image from beneath him, still staring right into his eyes. He saw glassy spots at the corners of her eyes and kissed them away.

Tanis was now looking at him as if she were the saddest creature ever created – a pleading from her soul. "Noah!" she cried softly.

Noah put his mouth to her ear and whispered, "So it wasn't your father who was the thief."

Tanis laughed a breathy, quiet gasp as she came.

12

The next morning, the guys were up early and out on the road. Still calling the campsite their home base, they had a little rescue work ahead of them. It had snowed through the night and a lot of it stuck. Everyone but Tanis had come out this morning. She had early band rehearsal, so Noah was the only one in the crew with an empty passenger seat. He stood with his hands in his pockets, shivering to the bone. He watched Troy pull into the parking spot just in front of him, talking to Twyla, who was smiling brightly in the passenger seat. She was bundled up in a thick parka and a scarf, and waved at Noah with a bright pink mitten. After a moment of conversation, Troy popped the door and hopped down, rounding the front of the Jeep to where Noah stood.

"What, no coffee?" Troy said, spreading his hands.

"If I drink one more drop of coffee, I'm gonna be pissing every ten minutes."

"Where's Doug?"

Noah hiked his chin toward the diesel filling bays in front of the truck stop. Troy looked back over his shoulder, his breath a cloud in the frigid air. The snow was still coming down like an avalanche from a thick gray sky that made it hard to determine if it was morning or evening. It reached almost to the tops of their boots.

"Twy gonna help you rope some fish?" Noah said, lifting his chin toward Troy's passenger seat.

Troy shrugged and made a face, pursed his lips. "She wants to see how this shit works. You know how it is."

Noah nodded. "Tanis wanted to come but she had band camp."

Troy shrugged again. "Lucky her. It's too damn cold out here." He pointed a gloved finger at Noah and said, "Better hope it ain't her needing a rescue next time."

"Please. Mally can get her out of anything," Noah replied.

"Yeah, but can she drive it?" he said, smirking. After a moment he said, "Once she quits that band business, she can start helping us out here."

Noah shook his head. "She doesn't even have a winch. We gonna stand here and talk all morning, or are we going fishing?"

"I thought we were waiting on the Double Ds over there," Troy said, pointing a thumb over his shoulder.

"They'll catch up."

They cruised up and down the highways in and out of the island, riding the radio, as they called it. The four Jeeps stayed in their own zones, waiting for a call from one of the others saying they had found a fish – a vehicle that had slid off the road into a ditch. Noah was smoking a cigar as he drove, letting the smoke get sucked out the driver's window, which he kept cracked. He found himself thinking of Twyla, and how quickly she and Troy had clicked. It had literally almost been instant. They had slept in the same sleeping bag together the first night they had met.

Of course, Noah and Tanis had not been slow to start, themselves. Some might have called their relationship expedient, in fact. Was it just that way with the Ransom girls, or had Troy and Noah just gotten lucky? He thought about how Twyla always wore hats. He realized he loved a woman in a hat. She wore them well, too. She was absolutely adorable. Where Tanis was more of a structured beauty – a classical sexy facial structure, Twyla was baby-faced and cute. They had two totally different looks, though both were very pretty. But why, Noah wondered, was Twyla even on his mind? Was he jealous? He knew he was not just out for the next big thing.

His mind went back to Tanis, then, and he smiled to himself as he turned onto 102, which would take him to the northern bridge off the island. She really was a find. Especially for a guy like him. Noah had never had any trouble with the ladies, but this one… *This one*… She was way out of his league, he thought. Tall and slender with dark, mysterious eyes and a mouth that always seemed to be smiling. Her upper lip, harp-shaped and full, always seemed to be pushed out just the slightest bit, so she could show her perfect white teeth with just a tilt of her head.

Noah checked his mirror and put on his blinker, gathering a little speed for the highway. The snow was coming in like a blizzard. If there was anyone in the ditch, he was going to have to pay close attention to even be able to see them. Everything off the sides of the roads was pure, blinding white.

He thought back to her last show the other night. She had stood in with a band called Dusty. That seemed to be a pretty popular gig for all the local bands. To have Tanis Ransom come up on stage and sing a song or two with them. It was always surprising to the crowds, but it seemed to happen often enough, at least in Noah's estimation, that no one could truly be that surprised. Every couple of weeks she was walking into the spotlight from a dark corner of the stage and smiling to thunderous applause.

The evening she had joined Dusty on stage, they had played *Lady* by Little River Band, one that always got Noah singing – a favorite from the seventies. During the second verse, when the bass line went to that up-and-down pop, she had marched in place on the stage, lifting her feet a few inches as she swayed her hips back and forth. Left, right, left, right… It was mesmerizing. She swayed side to side on those silently marching feet, her shoulders rolling forward and back as she sang with her eyes closed and it was perfect. Noah thought maybe the Little River Band had written that song with her marching in mind. If he had not already been in love with her at that point, he thought that attractive march might have done him in. And she sang *Lady!* She did not change the words to suit the opposite sex. She sang it just like they had written it, as if she were looking at another woman. Noah had stood in the audience just shaking his head. He was truly in awe.

Up ahead, he saw brake lights whip across his vision and take a sickening jump into the air, then down into the ravine beside the highway. A blast of snow and smoke went up and he grabbed his handset. "Yo, Fire Tribe, we have an active at Main and Fire Road, northbound." He heard the radio crackle with responses from the rest of the crew, and pulled up behind where the car had gone into the ditch. It took Noah a moment to register that it was a black Mazda. And when he did register, it still didn't click with him. He hopped out of the Jeep, leaving it running and jogged down into the ditch to the driver's window. There was red fluid seeping out from beneath the front end of the car. Something had punctured the radiator. He knocked on the window and realized for the first time the stereo inside the car was blasting. It was shaking the windows. He knocked, but saw no movement inside. The song played on. Maybe the driver couldn't hear him knocking. He made a tunnel around his face with his hands and put them up against the glass. There she was. Unconscious, at the very least, leaning against the steering wheel, blood running freely from her open mouth. It was Joy.

Noah banged on the window. It only vibrated back at him. He could tell the song, but could not place the name of it. It was one that he and Joy had listened to together many times though. He heard skidding tires behind him and turned to see Troy jumping down from his own Jeep and jogging down to the passenger window. "What the hell? Is it Joy?" he shouted over the car as he came close.

Noah stood up straight and looked at his friend over the top of the vehicle. "Yeah. Yeah, it's her." He swallowed, suddenly very scared. "She's out!"

Troy looked back at him then bent to look through the opposite window. He stood up again and turned to look back at his Jeep. He made a motion and Twyla rolled down the window and stuck her head out. "Call 911!" he shouted. She nodded quickly and rolled the window back up. Then he tried the door. "Is your side open?" he asked Noah.

Noah was in too much shock to think about it on his own. He tried the handle. It was locked. Troy came racing around the front of the car, only briefly glancing at the red fluid that now stained a gigantic portion of the ground. Suddenly he was pushing Noah out of the way, and drawing his knife from his front pocket. He gripped it backward and brought the back end down against the driver's side window. The small pointed protrusion there was a glass-breaker, and it worked on first contact. The entire window splintered and broke into so many thousands of tiny shards. The music from inside the car was suddenly very loud – it filled the thick morning air with an eerie presence of its own.

Then Doug was there, grabbing Noah by the arm. "You okay, bro?" he was asking, pulling Noah back away from the door. Noah couldn't answer. He just stood and watched as Troy yanked his glove off and reached through the window, putting his bare fingers against Joy's neck.

"Oh, Christ," he said, standing up straight.

"What? What is it?" Doug asked. He still had hold of Noah's arm, and Noah was suddenly thankful for that, as his level of fright seemed to be multiplying by the second.

"Dude, I think her neck is broken. She has no pulse!" Troy shouted, and he was running up the hill to the passenger side of his Jeep where Twyla opened her door and handed him her phone. She seemed to be reading his mind.

Noah stood in shock, staring at the former love of his life, wondering what exactly he was seeing. He heard Doug pulling him back verbally, saying it was going to be okay, just to take it easy, to back up. Noah could also hear Troy in the background, foggy, somewhere seemingly miles away, saying something about paramedics and a possible broken neck. No pulse.

Noah broke free and walked forward, then reached in and pulled the door open, despite Doug's protests. He knelt in the snow beside the car and put his left arm over her thighs and touched her shoulder with his right hand. His face was even with hers. She seemed to be looking at him, though her eyes were almost entirely closed. He was trying not to move her, but wanted to *accidentally* shake her – to do something to elicit some sort of response. But he could see no fog emanating from her mouth like the rest of them. Everyone was making his own clouds this morning. But not Joy.

"Joy!" he was shouting. "Joy! Are you okay? Are you with me?" When Doug finally got his hands on Noah's shoulders, he realized he *was* shaking her.

"Dude, come on, bud. You're going to make her worse. You need to step back and let the pros take care of her."

"What pros?!" Noah shouted, turning to look at Doug. He was suddenly angry on top of scared. "Where the fuck are they?" he said, holding a hand out to illustrate the sheer lack of emergency rescue vehicles.

Doug was standing in front of him now, holding Noah by the shoulders. "It's okay, brother. Calm. They're on their way."

Dennis came walking up behind Doug, hands in his pockets, his pretty smile on display. Noah wanted to knock the smile off his perfect face. Doug brought him back. "Dude. Noah. She's okay, bro. I need you to calm down for me, okay?"

Noah was shaking his head and trying to break free of Doug's strong hands – trying to get back to the car. Back to Joy. Then Troy was in front of him, another face in the confusion. The music was still terribly loud. It finally clicked for Noah and he realized what the song was: it was one they had shared intimately. Haunting.

She had been listening to this when she died, he thought. He could not help it. The thoughts were jamming into his head like knives as his lungs burned from the cold air he was sucking in between gasps and cries for Joy. Noah could hear sirens on the horizon. But she wasn't breathing. He tried to point, and tears poured forth. Everything blurred and there were many of her. Like seeing her through a fly's eyes, there were tens of her in front of him and he couldn't tell which one was real. Were any of them?

"She's not breathing, you fuck! Look!" he shouted, trying still to break away. But now Troy and Doug both had him, and they were pulling him back away from the car – away from the cacophony of music that blasted from her high-dollar stereo system. "Joy! Say something!"

They were talking calming words into his ears, but he couldn't hear them. The music was too damned loud. And the scene was too confusing. On the edge of his conscious mind, Noah realized Dennis was not smiling to be smiling. He was trying to be calming. He now had his hand on Noah's shoulder as well. Blurs of yellow and gray rushed in front of his eyes as the paramedics arrived and took over the scene. Someone hit the unlock button on the door, then someone else opened the passenger door and reached in, turning off the key. Suddenly it was silent. And he could hear Doug in his ear. "It's okay, bro. Everything's gonna be okay."

Noah pulled back from him and frowned hard at his best friend. "What the hell? She's dead!" he shouted, pointing at Joy's lifeless body. And then a new face appeared. It was Twyla. There were tears in her eyes. She stepped forward with her arms out and embraced Noah. She wrapped her arms around him and put one hand on the back of his head. He could feel her fingers through the cloth of the mitten, rubbing his hair under the toboggan he wore. And before he realized what was happening, he was sobbing against her shoulder as Twyla stood rocking back and forth gently on her feet.

He watched through wet eyes as they hauled the stretcher up the side of the hill to the road where the ambulance waited, lights silently splitting the morning air with red slashes. Noah tried to sit, but his friends would not let him. "Nah, bro, you'll want to get off this snow. Come on, let's go up," someone said. They led him back up to the line of idling Jeeps.

Noah felt numb, and his ears felt hot; he could feel the blood pumping through his head as he tried to wrap his mind around what had just happened. "Is she okay?" he asked feebly. He knew the answer, for he had seen them trying chest compressions on her. He had seen them searching for a pulse, an ear just above Joy's open mouth trying to feel or hear a breath. He had seen the look of despair in the paramedic's eyes when she had looked up at her partner, pleading for help he could not give. And the most damning of all, he had seen the way they covered Joy's face with the sheet just before hoisting the gurney to carry it up the hill. They just don't do that to living people.

CHAPTER SIX
Recovery

From *Front Row Magazine*

And Then There Were Others
by Jason Dormir

According to the old cliché, imitation is the greatest form of flattery. Well, if the adage is true, then One Last Orbit should be over the moon. Shannon Kennedy, lead guitarist for the band, says he is not only humbled by the gesture, but impressed. There are – as far as we know – four bands that exclusively cover One Last Orbit material. And Shannon has been to see all four of them live.

While he did not make his presence known at all four shows, he did at the last one, where the tribute band StarStreak was playing the Tea Room in Jersey City. After what Kennedy describes as "a phenomenal show" he surprised the band backstage in the green room where they took pictures and traded autographs.

"I was really impressed. It's one thing to hear someone cover a song of yours, but when someone is so passionate about your music that they play nothing but your music, it's overwhelming," Kennedy says. "I heard these guys cover so many of our songs, and was like, wow! You know? It was definitely a humbling experience."

It takes more than one person to put on the show though. One Last Orbit is a five-piece ensemble. Three of the four cover bands have as many. StarStreak does it with four. Lead singer, Kimberly Bernard also plays the bass. We asked Kennedy what he thought of her vocals compared to Tanis Ransom's, who sings for his own band.

"She was fabulous. Just fabulous. You know, there are a lot of people out there who can do what we do. And a lot of times in music, it's not about who does it best – but who does it first. You try to write music no one else has ever thought of. And come up with chord progressions and riffs no one has ever thought of. Well, that's getting tougher and tougher these days. So we're left with making unique sounds and exploring different thematic endeavors. It's very cool to go see a band playing your songs – you know, to see what parts they really concentrated on; to see where they emphasize the little nuances you thought no one would ever notice about your own music."

One Last Orbit are famous for those little nuances. They make sound where others leave silence. They accentuate notes and beats that others pay no mind. It's likely these tiny emblems of delicate attention to detail are not unique to this band. But it is also safe to say this band has capitalized on them. This band does it more than the others. How flattered were you, Shannon?

"It was overall very flattering. I got to hang out with these guys after the show and answer questions. I had questions of my own as well, though. I was interested in why they chose us. When you see a talented bunch of musicians who have dedicated their entire repertoire to your music, it's awe-inspiring. It kind of shocks you, you know? You wonder what it is about your music that made them want to do what they do. Very flattering."

1

Noah stood on the long lawn behind his house, staring down at the creek twenty feet below his boots. It was barely a trickle but it created a nice sonic background for his jumbled thoughts. The smoke from his cigar clung to his coat as if for protection as it climbed slowly to join the racing wind above his shoulders. He chewed his lip, lost in thought, tears stinging the corners of his eyes. But these were not tears of sadness, just a natural reaction to the cold winter wind in his face. He had shed plenty of the other kind of late. This respite – however brief it should come to be – was a welcome break from the other kind, almost worth relishing. And the intervals of waking wherein his eyes were dry had become so rare – so *foreign* – that he almost wondered if something were wrong when they paid their short visits.

He had eschewed his responsibilities at work. Having enough in his savings to hold him over for a few months made the indulgence that much easier to swallow. Thoughts of every loss Noah had ever faced had resurfaced in the last two weeks. The loss of his grandfather had tainted his dreams on the first night after Joy's funeral. That was dreams of the cool one who showed him how to take his handgun apart and clean it; the one who spent hours alone with him in his room making secret plans to take over the world – which typically only really involved sorting baseball cards or drawing floor plans for the best missile silo bunker – and teaching him how to appreciate the small things in life. His dog, the big fluffy asshole who weighed close to a hundred pounds and had no idea, that would jump up on Noah, often knocking him down. Cowboy was his name, and Noah had loved that dog more than anything else in life from his mid-teens until the dog's sudden death when Noah was twenty-two. He had come home from work at lunch during an ice storm to check on the pipes and found Cowboy at the bottom of the pool. He had walked out on the ice that had formed atop the water and fallen through. And now he was a frequent visitor to Noah's dreams again. Why now?

More than the personal pain he suffered over that one was watching his little sister come running to the edge of the pool and slam herself down on her knees, open hands covering her face, openly weeping as she cried the dog's name over and over. That had taken Noah to another dimension of grief. Lennie suddenly became the most important thing in the galaxy to him. He knew she was forever his to take care of. The pure anguish in her voice was so heart-wrenching that he almost forgot he was stricken by the sadness as well.

He had also been visited by his old friend Arnold lately. Arnold and he were thick as thieves at eleven, twelve years old – right at that sweet age just before the discovery of girls but right after baseball starts making sense – and they spent every waking moment together. Arnold was red-headed and covered with freckles, which bought him his fair share of bullying at school, but Noah had loved the boy and had befriended him the first day he showed up to sixth grade – the new kid in class.

These dreams – these ridiculous animations in the deep hours of the night – that came so realistically back to the movie screen of his mind had been haunting not only in their eerie familiarity but their clarity as well. He would wake up panting and sweating, thinking he was back in the days of the actual event – a contemporary to the lovely madness. Sometimes he would already be crying; other times it took a few seconds to get started, but it always came – reminding him how bad this one or that one had ripped his heart out.

Arnold had been the weird kid in class – not sure how to act, because of the scorn and chastisement he faced at home – and often times came to school looking lost and forlorn. Arnold was severely abused. And one day he just didn't come to school. It took weeks for the news to finally reach Noah, that Arnold's father had beaten him to death with a piece of lumber. Now, here he was again, dying over and over in Noah's dreams, along with Cowboy and William Wright and Joy Kennebell and all the others who didn't quite resolve in the eye of his dream – those with blurry faces. Being awake was only a relief inasmuch as it freed him from dreams he could not control. But being awake was no vacation from the misery of the nightmares. It had its own ghosts.

Was it better to face this alone? To endure the trauma of the haunts without feeling like he was burdening someone else? Or was it better to have a shoulder? Every time he tried to weigh the benefits of one against the other, he would crumble up in tears again. If there were any other subject matter in the universe, Noah reckoned, then his mind might have been made up for him automatically. But that it was Joy Kennebell and her untimely death, and the fact that it was Tanis Ransom who would be providing that shoulder, well, that took a lot of the decision-making right out of his hands, didn't it? She had, herself, been respectfully absent for most of the seconds – those long-winded things that looked a lot like years to Noah's tear-stained eyes – that filled his days. As he spent time reflecting on the why of it all, Doug had reminded him several times, that it was a very uncomfortable position for Tanis to be in, and she was doing nothing more than just being absolutely classy.

Were she to sit in with Noah and tell him he was better off now, or that everything would be okay, or that these things happened – he might well hold it against her in the future. Maybe she wouldn't say enough. Or maybe she would say too much. It was just not a hole anyone wanted to find herself having to fill. And Tanis's being politely away was just the perfect answer to such a conundrum. But it still had the ring of selfishness – of coldness – about it… An audience unfit to participate in the telling of the worst story he had ever had to tell. Sure, they still talked. But the conversations were very surface-level engagements – palaver of the most basic and banal substance. He wanted so badly to rip through the membrane that was keeping him from her right now and grab her by the shoulders – to say, "Hey! It doesn't matter that it was Joy! It doesn't matter that we were a *thing*! Yes, it hurts, but not because I'm still in love with her! Not because she's still alive in my heart!"

But somehow, Noah believed – and possibly without ever truly acknowledging anything more than the concept of it – that Tanis would be there for him when he was done with his grief cycle. And maybe before he had completed the required five stages. She was only giving him space for his own benefit. Not only classy was this arrangement, but smart. That subconscious part of him that reminded him daily that he would finally come through this also reminded him to thank Tanis Ransom for her superior judgment.

Noah felt rather than heard the tromp of boots on the dead grass behind him, and held his cigar up to examine the ash. He was down to the third third of the smoke, the point at which he usually let it burn itself out on the saddle of a thick ashtray. Good as done. The third third was packed with nicotine, but bereft of the wonderful flavor that kept consumers spending their money on something they would only set fire to in the end. He flicked it out into the wind where it sparked wildly and dropped into the cold water of the barely-flowing stream.

"Hey, gorgeous," said a sweet twang from behind.

Noah smirked as he recognized the voice that had addressed him, against the strong wind that once again caused him to raise a sleeve to his eyes and wipe away the wetness. "Hey, Alice." He turned to look at the silhouette that strode slowly toward him from somewhere nonexistent. From the shape of her, Noah could tell she wore a coat over her dress and her hands were in the pockets of the coat, creating perfect triangles with her arms against the dying light of a weak winter sun. The cowboy hat atop her head looked like a giant oval of black against the red-orange background.

He could still not see her face, but knew she was smiling. Despite the pall that hung perceptibly in the air around his shoulders, she was smiling. Alice walked right up to him and took her hat off, then buried her face in his chest, wrapping her arms around him. Noah squeezed her right back, resting his chin on the top of her head. "Hey, Alice," he said again. "Alice, Alice, Alice," he rattled off, mindlessly.

She looked up at him in the ember-colored evening, eyes squinted in a defensive posture against a possible savage gust of the wind, or perhaps anticipating a tear from the face that loomed above hers. But still she smiled. "How are you holding up, my guy?"

Noah shook his head. "Why does that need to be asked?"

Alice pursed her lips and frowned hard at him – an obvious exaggeration of confusion – perhaps trying to hide a hurt this time. "Not sure I follow you, brother," she said, still through pursed lips. She was hurt, and Noah knew it, though he didn't quite know why.

"I don't mean that against your question, Al. I'm just saying, why am I feeling like this at all? We broke up! I'm with someone else now!"

Now Alice's false frown turned to something a little more real as understanding flooded her countenance.

"Dude, fuck off with that shit! She was a big, big part of Noah Wright's life for a long, long time!" This last she said while jabbing his chest with the nail of her pointer finger. "I don't care if she wasn't the one anymore, Noah! She *was* the one for a time in your life. And she's still someone you knew and loved! I loved her too, as a human. A friend."

Alice stared straight into his eyes, almost defiantly. Challenging him to object to these truths. Noah breathed in deeply and wiped his eyes with his sleeve.

"Dude, it's a loss. No matter if she was tied to anyone or not. Big loss."

He found himself nodding. "Yeah," he gasped. "Big loss. For sure."

Alice reached up and wiped the tear from the corner of his eye with her thumb. She crossed her arms, then stared at him for a long time through serious eyes. Finally she screwed up her mouth and said, "Noah, come with me."

He took her hand and followed her up to the house. At the back screen, she turned and took his hand in both of her own. "Noah, they brought your car back."

Noah frowned. "My car? What car?"

"The Mazda." She closed her eyes as she explained, "It was in your name. You bought it for her. Remember?"

He was shaking his head, even though it was indeed coming back to him. The registration renewal did in fact come to him every year. It was one of those bills he pencil-whipped, scarcely paying attention to it. Check the boxes, send the check back, then slap the sticker on when it comes back…

"Is that why you came here?" he asked her.

Alice smirked and nodded. "Yeah. Drew called me and asked if you were ready for it."

Before Noah could even mouth the name, Alice was nodding and shaking her head at the same time. "Yes, Drew. He's a friend of mine. Works for the wrecker who picked up the car at the scene."

"Why the hell is it just now getting here?" Noah asked. This situation was starting to make him feel like he was swimming in Jello.

Alice looked away and shrugged, keeping her shoulders high while she looked back at him. "I don't know. Insurance? Cops? I don't know. But it's here now." She took a deep breath and magically produced the keys, dropping them into his hand with precise fingers.

Noah looked down at them and felt a crisp twinge of regret surge through his bones. The reemergence of his questioning logic – the parts of his mind that tried to fit those puzzle pieces together – reminded him that she would perhaps still be alive if only he would have stayed with her. He closed his eyes momentarily and shook his head. "Alice," he started.

"Hey, dude," she said, grabbing his chin with the tiny fingers of her left hand, "You've got to buck up, bro. This is a car. And it's yours." Then she looked down at his hands. She wrapped her hands around his, closing his fingers around the keys she had placed there. She looked back up at him then, and added, "It's your car, bro. It's just a car. Deal with it." Then she gave him a half-cocked smile that might have been entirely faked and turned away. Her silhouette quickly mingled with those of the trees behind her, becoming one with the blackness.

2

Noah stood staring at the car, the black Mazda, the keys sitting in his open palm like a scorpion. What would he find inside? Had they cleaned out the gore of the accident – the physical bits of trauma that were now the only remnants of a human life lost to tragedy? Had they even thought of that? Had they cared? Who were *they*? If the they he had in mind were made up of friends, allies in this catastrophe, then surely they would have known he would rather have seen the car burned than to find in it bits of his ex-girlfriend. And according to Alice, at least Drew had been on that team. Maybe Drew knew what Noah was going through.

He raised his chin and stepped forward. Regardless of what was going on inside the car, he would have to handle this. Sell it or scrap it, he would have to be the one to do it. And he knew that involved getting into it at least once. All her personal belongings were still presumably inside it – at least the ones with which she was traveling at the time of her wreck. He made it a few steps before he had to stop and let the spook pass him – enemies in a hall, turning shoulders to avoid bumping against each other. Noah steeled himself and took another step forward, then his hand was on the door handle.

With a deep breath and a small wordless prayer, the handle gave way to little exertion. The door popped open with a familiar clunk like it always had before –

like nothing had ever happened – just like normal. He pulled it until it stopped on its detent, hanging wide enough to allow entry. Another few deep breaths brought him the courage it would take to finally overcome this beast that stood face-to-face with him.

And suddenly he was in the seat, cold and observant, head swiveling slowly as if on an oiled gear, taking it all in. *This is it. This is where it ended for Joy Kennebell. This is where a human lost her life.*

After the shock of the situation cooled itself through chills up his spine and down his arms, he began to actually take in his surroundings. A Styrofoam cup from Tilly's Tacos stood in the front cup holder, lipstick on the straw. That elicited a chest heave from Noah. An almost-smirk tried to fight its way onto his face. He shook his head and touched the angry red lipstick with his finger and thumb. Her padded cloth wallet was in the forward console beneath the stereo. A paisley pattern sewn into a zipper pouch. He pulled the zipper across the teeth with a deliberate slowness until its innards revealed themselves in a shamble of organized chaos. The hard edges of credit cards sandwiched between the thin white paper of receipts and scrawled notes, a few pennies and tiny rubber bands that might once have been used to hold a pony tail in place.

Noah leaned his head back against the headrest and tossed the wallet back into the console. With his head against the headrest, his eyes came to rest on the sun visor. He reached up absently and flipped it down, and was startled by a card that fell to his lap. His eyes focused on the blue scrawl on the front cover of the envelope and he realized he was staring at his own name.

He ran his thumb over it before sliding a finger beneath the flap on the backside. As he slid the card out of the envelope, he found his mind was racing. When had she written him a card, and why? He flipped it open and looked at the contents – a black-and-white glossy printout tucked inside the fold of the cardboard, and a small wallet-sized photograph of Noah and Joy. The photo was from when they had visited the State Fair a few years prior. The half-smirk on her face reminded him of her mischievous nature – she almost always had something going on beneath the smile in her pictures. There was always a story.

The blue ink stood out on the white paper of the card, written in the familiar hand of his ex-lover, comfortable as a plate of pancakes from grandmother's kitchen. *Polka Dots and Moonbeams* fluttered into Noah's mind and he had to look up before he began reading. A pickup truck ambled by, diesel engine growling and vibrating the floor upon which his feet now rested. He shook his head and looked back at the card, reading the love note written within. A love note was not precisely what it was, but it was indeed a note from his lost love. So, he felt, it was in the same realm. It spoke of love lost and sorrow, regrets and wishes, apologies and pleas, but not in the voice of someone asking for another chance. It was acceptance and forgiveness, and possibly a request for something in the realm of friendship. And as he read to the end of the brief letter, his understanding began to blossom. The glossy paper he now held against the back of the card with the fingertips of his right hand began to reassert itself. It began to feel more urgent, as if wanting him to bring it forward again. Like it might be begging him to give it another chance to be heard. So he did.

And this time it clicked.

It was a sonogram.

3

Well, that changed things, didn't it? Noah sucked in a sharp breath and stared out the windshield. His heart was suddenly slamming in his chest. He shook his head with the weight of this new information. *Oh my God.* He had to think back to the last time they had lain together. It had been, what – months ago? But he didn't know when she had written the card. He looked at the date on the sonogram and realized it had been taken about four weeks ago. *She had forgotten to give it to me.* Or maybe not. Maybe she had been fighting with herself about whether or not she wanted to. *Decorum.* Maybe she had been trying to spare his feelings. But obviously, he would have found out sooner or later. She would eventually start showing. Or further down the line, actually have the baby. Joy had surely known she couldn't – nor *wouldn't* – be able to keep it a secret forever. Or…

His mind went south, thinking about the accident. The *accident*. The one that had taken her life. No. He shook his head again. No way. It was an accident. It had been sheer stupid coincidence that he had been the one closing the distance on her that morning. He pushed the thought from his mind.

And another thing. He had not heard from anyone else about this. So obviously, she had not told anyone. Because someone – his friends – would have said something to him about it. A congratulations or a *hey, what do you think of that?* Noah knew his friends were closer to him than to Joy. They were his friends first. So maybe she had no one to tell. That meant that the secret had died with her. He looked back down at the glossy sonogram in his hand, rubbed his thumb over the tiny bulbous head in the picture, and then crumpled the paper up into a ball.

No. It would *not* change things. It couldn't. There was positively nothing he could do about it now. There was obviously some fair amount of grief he would be treading through in the near future. But at least it had gotten no further. How terrible it *could have been* had she carried to term. A car seat in the back. He breathed in and put his hand on his forehead, squeezing his temples, and let out a growl that escalated in volume to a full yell. Then he stood up and slammed the door to the car. He would bury this balled-up paper in the bottom of his kitchen trash bin.

As Noah came out of the kitchen, he clicked on the streaming stereo. Started a playlist. A little *Hysteria* to get things going. He stared out the back window for a time, the whiskey already warming him from the inside, and watched the sun set. He had been thinking about what Alice had said. *You've got to buck up, bro.* She was right, of course. He couldn't just crawl into a hole and put his life on hold. Besides, he had people waiting on him. People who might not wait for too long. Two weeks was all he was willing to allow himself.

Over those last two weeks, before Alice had come to announce the arrival of Joy's car, Noah had spent several hours gathering all of Joy's things and boxing them up. Most of it had been clothing, and the rest had only filled one box. Since they had not lived together, there were only a few things. A watch, a couple of purses, her toiletries and some trinkets she had set on shelves around the house. A picture frame here, a candle there. Almost nothing that would indicate ownership to anyone who didn't know it was hers. Her mother had come by and sat with Noah for a long time on the couch, hands folded between her knees, perfect posture, asking him if Joy had been happy. Had she been happy during the last days of her life? The thought of trying to find a way to answer this honestly had evaded Noah. What the hell could he say? So obviously she had not told her family that they had broken up. Mom had come by, thinking she would catch some last glimpse of Joy in her old joyful self. Noah felt terrible for her, but wasn't able to give her anything more than minimal hope. He told her that yes, she had been happy, as far as he knew. He tried to skirt the edge of the truth, not quite committing to anything like that she had stayed with him in the house or not. In case someone finally presented the truth to them, he didn't want to be caught in a lie. Though there was likely no reason he would ever see them again in anything more than coincidental passing on the street, he didn't want to paint a false reality. So the picture he developed for her had been full of dark spots, where there was just nothing to say.

His heart went out to her as she sat there smiling through her tears, trying so hard to swallow that her young daughter had died out of order. A parent should never have to bury her child. And, of course, he had completely buried the truth of what he knew about the sonogram. On that, at least he would have plausible deniability. There was no evidence of it in his possession. If medical records revealed anything down the road, he had no control of that.

Noah ended up giving the box of Joy's personal belongings to Lennie, as she would be able to separate more easily what should be kept or given back to the family. There were no heirlooms. But he did not want to make those choices. And if Lennie decided to keep it all, he reckoned that would be all right as well, as he didn't usually spend much time at her place anyway. Now there were a few spots on the mantle and various other surfaces throughout his house that stood empty. Small spaces waiting to be filled in with life continued. Like pulling one's finger out of a glass of water, the dent disappeared quickly. The cycle of life had to continue. Slowly but surely, those spots Joy used to fill would be replaced with other things. Other people. Other memories. And eventually she would fade to obscurity.

Sighing, he turned to the counter and picked up his phone and called Tanis. She would be happy to hear from him. His blood felt warmer already, just thinking about her.

No answer.

He sighed and put the phone in his pocket. Suddenly, it buzzed. Noah pulled it out and swiped it unlocked. There was a text from Tanis.

> *Sorry, can't talk. Riding with Shannon.*
> *Loud in car. I don't want you to rush,*
> *okay? Get better, but take your time.*

He looked up at the back window again, phone
frozen in his hands. Was he ready for that? It seemed
like she was fine either way. She was ready to be back
with him, or ready to wait longer. His choice. But that
was kind of a gentle ultimatum, was it not? Don't rush
this and come back still bawling over Joy. Either come
back well over her, or take more time. He nodded.
Yeah. Good call. Noah had the sudden feeling that the
quickest way to get over this funk was to surround
himself with people who weren't going to put up with
the bullshit. Of course all his friends would be
mourning Joy in their own ways. But none of them had
been as close to her as he had. And they wouldn't be
walking around sulking about her. So he just needed to
suck it up. To *buck up*. He nodded again. Then he sent
a text back to Tanis.

I'm ready, Tan. I miss you.

Noah felt good about that. If anyone could help him
get over this, it would be she. She with the eyes that
looked into his very soul. He still got those damned
ridiculous butterflies when he looked at her. And it did
more to him than he would admit to feel her full lips
against his own. He felt the buzz in his pocket again.

*Oh, I'm so happy, Noh! I'm going to
come pick you up in the morning at 7. I
have a surprise for you. Be ready!*

Seven? What the hell could she possibly have to surprise him with at seven on a Sunday morning? He shrugged and slipped the phone back into his pocket, then started the shower. He would knock the cigar smoke off, then crawl into bed a little early tonight. It would be nice to go to bed not completely sloshed for once.

4

It was close to seven o'clock and Noah was pacing nervously, sipping coffee and watching out the front windows for evidence of a vehicle entering his driveway. He scooted across the hardwood in his socked feet, checking his phone every few minutes. Why he should be so nervous was anyone's guess. He guessed it had to do with seeing Tanis again for the first time in a fortnight. Would he say something stupid? Would he push her away? Exile her by accidentally shedding a tear over Joy? Strangely, he felt like he didn't know how to act. Like high school all over again.

His hands were trembling from the caffeine. Noah dropped the mug in the sink then went to splash water on his face and brush his teeth. When he came out of the bathroom, he glanced out the front window and saw a different pattern of light. He pulled the front door open and started when he saw Tanis standing there. He had not heard her knock or ring the bell.

She raised a gloved hand and smiled at him. All Noah could do for a long moment was stare in shock at her. She wore a beanie cap that came down over her ears, framing in her red cheeks and nose, her thick lips and her dark eyes. She stood still, smiling, and waiting for him to make a move of some sort. He finally shook his head and stepped forward, taking her in his arms. "God, you look fantastic."

"Thank you, Noah," she said, wrapping her arms around his neck and standing on her toes to put her face against his neck. They stood there rocking back and forth.

"Seriously. I think the absence made you more beautiful than ever."

She pulled away from him, keeping her hands on the back of his neck and smiled pleasantly at him. "How'd you get to be so sweet, boy?"

Noah's heart fluttered. *God, I love it when she calls me that.* Nothing about the man standing there liked to be thought of as anything other than a man. But somehow when she said it, it was okay. He knew her heart.

"Are you ready?" she finally said. Noah saw the look in her eyes and understood that she was asking him two questions at once. When they walked off this porch, he was walking into the next chapter of his life with her. The one without Joy. There would be no more shedding of tears for her. He took a deep breath and smiled at her, then leaned forward and answered with a kiss.

Noah had to use the handhold to hitch himself up into her Jeep. His pride divided evenly between the half that loved that he had a girlfriend whose Jeep stood higher than his own. The other half, well, that half was just jealousy. The leather seat was warm. His Jeep didn't have leather seats. Another point in her favor. The darkness outside was just beginning to be broken, but it was still dark inside the interior of the vehicle. He immediately noticed the ambiance she had added. Purple LED lights under the dash shone down on the floorboards, illuminating the foot spaces. Her stereo also had some wild purple lighting behind the buttons. He could tell immediately that her sound system was better than his own as well. He could feel the bass beneath him, even though it was currently at a very low volume. "Nice," he said, pointing at her stereo.

Tanis looked at him and turned the knob a few notches toward the passenger side.

"Good God! How much did you spend on this system?" he shouted over the music.

Tanis rolled her eyes and smiled, showing lots of teeth. Then she shrugged her shoulders. "I can't live without music. It has to sound good."

After a few minutes, he finally asked, "So are you going to tell me where we're going?"

She looked at him again with a mischievous smile in her eyes. "You haven't figured it out yet?"

"No. If I had to guess, I would say band rehearsal though," Noah said.

Tanis closed her eyes and shook her head proudly as she pulled on to the Interstate. Then she reached over and squeezed his thigh. "You're gonna love it though."

Noah had to admit in a deeper part of his mind than he could actually access, he was happy with the way Tanis was handling his grief. She was leaving it to him.

His business. Since it was based upon the loss of a former girlfriend, it was none of hers. Were it a family member, he reckoned she would have been there through the whole thing with him. But this could get awkward if someone didn't know how to act. Or how to respond. He actually quite admired that she had not asked him flat out how he was doing. It was almost as if she were just expecting him to be over it. While that felt a little harsh, he saw the reasoning in it. She didn't want to participate in any grieving over someone she would now never even meet. Noah could see that this was the best way forward. And obviously, so could Tanis. Acting like it hadn't happened would remove any unnecessary awkwardness, unless he decided to bring it up himself. Which, now, of course, he wouldn't.

5

After a half-hour of driving, she put on her blinker and exited the highway. Noah noticed the subtle change in the volume of the tires on the road. The hard top of her Jeep provided more insulation from the loudness outside than did his soft top. Mally was definitely more luxurious than his rugged rig. This made him smile. Yeah, he was proud of it. His girlfriend was hot.

They pulled into a parking lot behind an unmarked building and she put it in park. She looked over at him and took his wrist, staring at him seriously. "Are you ready to be over the moon, Noh?"

He shook his head. "I have no fuckin' clue what you're about to get me into. But yes, I guess I am."

"Good!" she said, patting his arm and popping the door open. He followed suit, hopping down from the lifted ride and closing the door. He pulled up his jeans and looked up at the building, trying to find some kind of clue as to what they were about to do.

When they rounded the front of the structure, Tanis pushed a button on an intercom, then pulled Noah close and leaned her head on his shoulder, taking his left hand in her right. In a few seconds a buzz rang through the intercom and the door latch clicked. She pulled it open and they stepped into a nominally lit waiting area. Tanis led the way through the room, where she then turned the latch on another door leading them into a hallway. This had the eerie feel of a doctor's office, but that would not put him over the moon. So he abandoned that thought. They went a ways down the hall and she knocked on then immediately opened a door that looked like all the rest.

They stepped into a tiny room with walls that turned to glass at waist-height. It was dark in here, but through the glass, the rest of the area was dimly lit. It took Noah a minute to figure it out, but he finally did catch on. Tanis was looking at him expectantly, a childish smile on her face. She slung her purse off her shoulder and dropped it onto a chair in the corner of the small room. There was one other chair. And directly in the middle was a microphone on a stand.

Through the windows, he saw the other band members standing around, guitars slung round their necks, staring back toward the front of the building. On that wall was a large rectangular window where the producer sat, headphones on his head behind a giant block that Noah couldn't see, but knew instinctively was a mixing board.

Shannon, the guitarist, was talking to the man in the control room, twirling his hand in the air and bouncing on the balls of his feet. The bass player stood silently behind Shannon with his hands resting on the top of the bass, just watching. Noah looked down at Tanis's smiling face, still looking back up at him awaiting a reaction. So far he had been too stunned to say anything.

"We're in a studio. What the hell?" he said, eyes wide. "This is fuckin' amazing, Tan!" He took her by the shoulders and shook her lightly, then kissed her on the lips. "What are we doing here?"

"We're recording a record, goof ball!" she said, slapping his shoulder. "Okay, check this out," she said, pulling him by the shirt sleeve to turn and follow her finger as she pointed through the glass. Straight across from them, across the big room where the two guitarists stood, was another glass window through which he could see the drummer sitting behind a large kit. The drummer was playing, swinging sticks and crashing cymbals, but Noah could not hear them. "That's Kevin over there. The drummer," said Tanis. Then she swung to the left, at the end of the room opposite the control booth and Noah finally noticed the man standing behind a keyboard, headphones covering his ears, typing something on his phone. "That's Ben Redding on the keys."

Noah nodded. This was a little overwhelming. The industrial feel of the place was made beautiful by the blue and red lights that illuminated the main room. It wasn't bright, but nor was it too dark to see. Just a comfortable ambiance.

"Of course, you know Shannon, there, on guitar," Tanis said pointing, "and that's Mark on the bass."

"This is crazy cool, Tanis. I never thought I would see the inside of a studio."

"Pretty cool, huh?" she said, genuinely excited to be sharing it with him. "Notice how none of the walls are actually parallel? Sound has no chance to echo and bounce."

Noah nodded with understanding. "Ah," he said. The floor in the main room was covered with snaking cables running over and around the large rugs. Equipment and guitars were also spread about the room, seemingly at random. There was one stand in front of the drum room window, just to Shannon's left, that held four guitars on it. Noah was astounded. Why would anyone need so many guitars?

"So, you can put these cans on and hear what everyone is saying, but you'll have to stay quiet, okay?" Tanis said, handing him a set of the studio headphones. They ran into a box that had buttons and potentiometers on it. "If you want to hear everything at once, press this button," she said. "The others single out what you can hear individually."

Tanis put on her own cans and adjusted them on her head. "Notice how you can't hear the drums? They've been cut from the main feed by the producer in the control room. His name is James, by the way." Tanis turned to the pod in front of her and flipped a switch, then said, into the mic, "Hi guys."

Most of the guys in the other rooms looked over through her glass now, and Mark waved. She turned back toward the door and slid a switch up, bringing a little blue light into the room from above. "Hey, Tan," said Shannon into his microphone. Noah stood behind her with his arms crossed, just taking this all in.

"I have my boyfriend with me today. He promises he'll be good," she said.

"Tell him to get out then," said a voice. Noah hadn't seen who said it. "We don't like goody-goods in this bitch."

They all laughed. After a minute, the same voice said, "Just kiddin'. Welcome, man." Noah caught a glimpse of the drummer raising a stick and waving from across the large room.

"Tell him he can come into the control room if he wants," said James.

"He's hooked up. He's hearing you."

Noah waved. He felt a surge of pure adrenaline flood his veins. The excitement was almost palpable. He felt as though he were standing on the edge of a precipice looking down over nothing but awesome. He could not touch it. Couldn't actually participate, but the world was his to explore. *Unreal.*

"So what are we workin' on?" said Tanis, pulling up on her sweat pants. They were pink, and without the usual cuffs at the bottom, so they flowed around her feet. She had removed her jacket and now stood in a tank top that could have been blue, but Noah figured it was probably white. The light was playing tricks on his eyes. He did notice, however, that she was sans the bra. Would she not get cold in here? He was still wearing his jacket and knew he would not be able to take it off anytime soon.

Shannon turned toward the iso booth in which he and Tanis stood, and spoke directly to her. "It's the B minor progression you gave me last week. What did you call it?"

A big smile crossed her face, Noah could see from profile. "Yay! Goody! *Cosmic Chasm.*"

Shannon pointed at her with a pick in his fingers. "Yeah. Wanna hear what we've got so far?"

She sent back two thumbs up.

Shannon turned back to the producer's window and put his hands atop the body of the guitar. Mark unslung his bass and dropped it onto a stand, then approached the window and leaned his forehead against it, sticking his tongue out at Tanis. She put her palm up against his face and stuck her own tongue out. Noah instantly loved the camaraderie they shared. Mark looked over at Noah and gave him a thumbs-up. Noah sent back the gesture, grinning like an idiot.

Shortly, the music started playing. It took a moment for Noah to realize no one was actually playing. They were listening to what had already been recorded. It was a piano-rich melody with some high-hat syncopation in the background. After a minute the bass kicked in, then a screaming slide down the neck of the guitar that fell into a ribbing rhythm. Tanis leaned back, clapping and smiling wide – that smile that showed all her teeth and looked like she was laughing. "Yeah!" she shouted, wrinkling her nose with the smile. She started clapping lightly as they all listened. The drumbeat fell into a slow but powerful rumble that reminded Noah of something off a Phil Collins record. Chilling. It was a song full of darkness, though it was rich and beautiful.

And just as quickly, it all stopped, instruments fizzling out one by one.

"That's all we've got so far. I wasn't sure if you wanted something more bass-driven or something more sirenish," Shannon said, turning to face the iso booth again. Noah could tell Shannon was the leader of the band. His presence and command were without question. It was a subtle pack-mentality feeling that Noah caught onto almost instantly, though there was nothing overtly aggressive or forward in the man's actions. Though just as obviously, he took his orders from Tanis herself. This lithe being standing here a few feet away from Noah, who looked like she barely weighed a buck-twenty, bouncing in her sweats and tank top, fists smaller than a tennis ball, had more power in her than any of them. For she was the queen.

6

After they had spent a couple of hours adding layers to the take, they were ready for a vocal track from Tanis. She had taken off her cans and Noah had followed suit. He had asked her, "Are you not freezing your titties off in here?"

She had looked down and covered them with the fingers of each hand, then looked back up at him, grinning. "Nothing to freeze off, baby!" Noah shook his head and rolled his eyes. "No, I get really hot when I start singing. I'll be sweating in a minute. You watch," she said, holding a finger up at him.

He had to shake his head again. *How had he gotten so lucky?*

"Okay, Nono. Here's how it works," Tanis said, spreading her hands in front of her, "anything you say or do in here will show up on our record. So you have to be really quiet, okay?"

Noah nodded. "Yeah. No problem here," he said, zipping his lips.

"Okay. We'll have to do another take if there's any noise," she said. She was now standing with her hands on her hips. "But I'll screw up at least a dozen times. So it's not that big a deal, really." With this she rolled her eyes. "And one other thing. Just make sure you keep the cans on your ears. Otherwise you'll only hear my singing isolated. That ruins the illusion that I'm a perfect vocalist."

Out of the corner of his eye, Noah saw Mark laughing out loud in the studio, bending over and grabbing his knees. Noah realized her mic was still hot and had to giggle himself. He was having too much fun. Tanis stepped forward and lifted her chin at him, raising her eyebrows and pursing her lips. She was asking for a kiss. Noah complied, then watched as she donned her studio ears. He did the same, then backed into the corner and got still and quiet.

"From the top, James," Shannon said. "Keep me live on a new track, though, okay? I'm gonna mess around with some shit."

James looked down at the board in the control room, flashed a thumbs-up at Shannon. Mark was now sitting in a chair against the back wall by Ben, the keyboardist. They each had a beer bottle in their hand. *Holy shit, these guys start early.*

And then there was music.

Noah's head was flooded with the spacey music he had heard before, but more complete this time. It almost sounded good enough to be called finished, at least to his untrained ears. Tanis stepped up to the mic and clasped her hands in front of her chest, swaying back and forth as she waited for her part to come. As far as Noah could tell, she wasn't looking at any particular band mate. It appeared Tanis was staring at her reflection in the glass in front of her, until he finally focused on that reflection himself. Then he saw that her eyes were closed. She was in a zone.

A thought flashed through Noah's mind: if this ever went anywhere – like the radio, for instance – he would have the memory of having been in the studio, standing a few feet from her while she recorded it. That was pretty damned cool.

The music had a dark and eerie feel to it that went well with the thematic wonderland Tanis Ransom was known for creating. One could almost imagine she was trapped in a space ship. Lost in space. Eyes on quasars and black holes and clusters of new stars, cold and alone, never coming home. And this was all felt before she even opened her mouth for the first vocal note.

As the moment approached, he could tell that her time was near. The music dropped out and left her with a drawn-out bass line and she drew in a deep breath, then held her hands up in front of her and broke out laughing. Noah could see James from the control booth look up, shocked, and the music stopped shortly. He could hear laughter coming from the guys in the main room as well, distant and airy as they were not close to the microphone.

"Sorry," she said. "I just had a funny thought is all."

"Well how about saving that shit for another time?" Kevin said from the drum booth.

Tanis flipped him off through the windows, both slender middle fingers lifted high above her shoulders. She was wrinkling her face and smiling in shame. "Okay. I'm ready. Give me one bar, James."

"One bar, coming up."

The music started again just a few seconds from where she would start. This time, she filled her chest with the same deep breath, lifted her hands again, and belted out a siren's cry. Hell of a way to start a song, Noah thought. It fit perfectly though, and he felt chills rise on his arms. Then her vocal melody dropped through a series of notes into a detectable pattern as she started singing the actual lyrics.

Out here all alone, hanging by a thread
It's been a hundred years, all my loved are dead
I can hardly see the light
from the once fulfilling sun
That warmed our skin together
before my starry run

I hang here on my tether lest I float away
But long since has the other end
been severed of the sleigh
Rescue me
Won't someone come… and rescue me?

A killer stellar shower sparkles

distant 'cross the void
T'would be nice to 've shared this walk
I think you'd have enjoyed
Adrift I've fallen, lost at sea,
my anchor frayed to bare
And stranded here apart from you
with no more words to share

I hang here on my tether lest I float away
But long since has the other end
been severed of the sleigh
Rescue me
Oh God, won't someone come… and rescue me?

At this point, Tanis stopped and stood up straight, then said into the mic, "You can stop, James. I need to roll around on this a little." Then she took off her cans and hung them on the stand. She stretched her arms above her head and turned to Noah, who stood speechless, tears in the corners of his eyes.

"Whoa!" she said, stepping forward and embracing him, burying her face in his chest. He removed his own headphones and set them on the chair behind him. "Don't cry, sugar sweet!"

"I'm not crying. Someone slipped in here and cut some onions. You must have just missed 'em."

Tanis pulled back to look him in the eyes. She was smiling. "I'm glad it moved you a little. Know what it's about?"

Noah breathed in and shrugged. Put his hands in his pockets. "Trapped in space, I guess. Floating on a tether that's not connected to the ship at the other end anymore?"

She nodded and shrugged, bouncing her head around. "Yeah, well, literally that's what I'm saying, sure. But it's metaphor for something else."

Noah stared at her for a long moment. Then it came to him. "Oh. Oh, wow! Holy fuck. You wrote that?" he asked dumbly.

She laughed out loud. "Yes, silly boy. That's what I do."

He was shaking his head. "Now I'll have to go back and read the lyrics and see if I can catch all the analogs."

"Only difference is in the song we're on opposite sides of the chasm."

Noah nodded. "Nice. Very nice. I love it. I felt like a complete tool for taking you out there and getting us stranded, but now it looks like it's turned into something lovely."

"Thank you, sweet boy. You know how to make my heart smile," she said, putting her hands on his face and drawing him in for a kiss.

"What's it called?"

"*Just Another Star*," said Tanis.

7.

Noah's trip to the studio had awakened in him a desire to know more about the rest of the band. Seeing them interact and be people instead of rock stars had been very sobering. Only having ever seen the guys on the stage, and coming off the stage, he associated them with stardom. Though they were all wildly talented, he didn't know if they would make it. Most bands didn't. Most bands don't. Tanis had told him it takes the right person being at the right place on the right night hearing them play, then talking to the right person about them. That magical formula was obviously not rare. There were thousands of bands on the radio. Whether all were worthy of being there might be up for debate, but that 'magic moment' – that *perfect storm –* was not a unicorn. It did, in fact, happen. The question for every band, therefore, was, 'will it happen to *us*?' And naturally, in Noah's mind, *will it happen to Tanis? To One Last Orbit?* He loved the thought of it. But Troy had rained on the parade a little bit when he had told Noah not to get his hopes up too much.

"Millions of bands *don't* make it. For every band you hear on the radio, there's a hundred thousand playing in garages somewhere that don't make it. And some of them deserve to. Some are fucking amazing," Troy had said. And Noah had known it was the truth. The likelihood of OLO actually making it big was pretty remote. Not for a lack of talent. But for their music. Theirs was such a niche genre. Not even a real genre. Sci-fi Pop? Space Opera Rock? There just wasn't a big calling for it, Coheed and Cambria notwithstanding.

It wasn't like Noah had a dog in the fight anyway. Being the boyfriend of a lead singer was cool. It was kick-ass, in fact. It had its perks, for sure. But whether they ever got signed didn't directly affect him. If he were with her, married, or otherwise tied-in with her, then he might see some benefit, but what benefit would that be? Riding shotgun on the tour bus? Spending his life in hotel rooms with her instead of at home, looking at the lake? He knew the life of a rock star wasn't necessarily something to be coveted. But the point, at least to him, was that there wasn't much point. There wasn't much point in his thinking about whether they would make it or not. Because not much would actually change for him. Put bluntly, he didn't really care if they made it or not. But he did have to admit, he was a little starstruck by the whole experience. Seeing those guys – and Tanis – in the studio had shown him a side to them he had not previously been exposed to. It was really cool. The worry Tanis had spoken of at first, about a rehearsal ruining the magic of the show – well, that just didn't come into play. This had not been a rehearsal, obviously. But it was a vision of *the work in progress* – the rare glimpse at the behind-the-scenes footage in the making, watching it all come to life. It had, in fact, had the opposite effect on him. It had made him appreciate the live sound even more, having seen how it got recorded. They had worked on two songs that day. *Cosmic Chasm*, and *Just Another Star*. Noah had heard that one live at one of the last shows he had attended, so the intensity that came with seeing it being recorded was even more profound.

Noah asked Tanis why she never hung out with any of the guys from the band. Noah thought he might be able to invite them to fires, or just meet for a beer or something. He just wanted to see more of them. Tanis had told him that none of them really hung out that much outside of rehearsals and concerts. They had their own lives.

"We really only make music together. None of us sees much point in forcing a friendship where there isn't anything there," she had said.

"Seriously?" replied Noah.

"Yeah. How fun would parties be? Alls we could talk about would be music," she had replied. "Everyone else would get bored of it pretty quick."

"All you could talk about would be music, *because* you haven't hung out enough yet!" he had said. But his point was lost to the general apathy that had defined the band's unspoken policy on the matter. Simply, no one had tried to push a friendship, so therefore, no one tried. They all had their own lives and interests outside of the music. And that included their own friends. She had shrugged, and the conversation had just fizzled out.

But one night, several weeks later, he had finally talked Tanis into asking Shannon to join them for a drink. Shannon was by far the one Noah would most like to get to know. He kind of ran the band, Noah had noticed. He commanded respect. His talent on the guitar was something else. But he was also just attractive by nature. Noah was attracted to the power and presence this guy commanded, and just wanted to be around him.

They were sitting at the WhiskeyNote, a little hole-in-the-wall stage with a bar, squeezed between two buildings on Long & Winding Road. A three-piece ensemble was on the stage playing some pretty good

Simon and Garfunkel covers while Noah and Tanis sat against a wall in a two-spot having whiskey sours. The place brought in a fair amount of traffic. It was one of the local dives that locals called home during the tourist season, because the tourists almost never found it. Plus, they could fill it up before the tourists even got out of bed. You take every seat at every table, and leave no room for the tourists.

Noah said, "Hey, will you indulge me just this once? I would love to have Shannon come up and have a drink with us."

Tanis had widened her eyes like she was about to lose her mind and said, "Noah! Gosh!"

"Pretty please?" he had said, putting his hand on hers on the table. But her other hand was already fishing the phone out of her purse.

"I guess I'm just not enough for you," she said, swiping the screen. Before he could respond, the phone was up to her ear, and she was chewing on her thumbnail. That had been one of the first things Noah had learned about Tanis, once upon a time, sitting on a couch and tossing popcorn into each other's mouths: '*I chew on my nails when I get nervous. I don't bite them, though.*' But why would she be nervous?

"Hey, Shan. What are you doing right this very minute?" Tanis said. Only being able to hear her side of the conversation was interesting. And Noah had to squint to hear that much. The jazz trio on stage was quite loud. "Uh huh. No, I was wondering if you would be so kind as to come have a drink with me and my boyfriend."

Noah had only heard her use the term one other time. And it still had an effect on him. His heart skipped a beat. It was neat. Here he sat with the woman of many men's dreams – a gorgeous woman who led a band, turned heads everywhere she went, and was on a PhD track in Astrophysics – and she was calling him her boyfriend. Fucking awesome.

"No, not really. He just wants to pick your brain or something. Uh huh. We're at the Note. Okay. Cool," she said. Then she hung up. She slipped the phone back into her purse and took a sip of her sour, then looked at Noah with a mischievous grin. "Looks like you'll get your wish, sweet boy."

Noah's chest filled with excitement. "Thank you, Tanis. I am forever grateful," he said, putting a hand on his chest.

She rolled her eyes.

Shannon came oiling into the tavern about thirty minutes later, wearing a pea coat and a fancy scarf. His dark brown hair hung around his face, even covering part of his glasses. He immediately spotted Tanis and smiled, then stopped at the bar and picked up a drink before joining them at the two-seater table. He pulled an unused chair up from a nearby table, then shook

Noah's hand as he held back his scarf with the other hand.

"What's up, guys?" Shannon asked.

Tanis was holding her whiskey between the thumbs and index fingers of both hands, the rest of her fingers sticking out like she was handling the Hope Diamond. "Nothing much. We were just enjoying a quiet little date together, alone, until you showed up."

Shannon laughed with no sound, then took a drink of his own orange liquid. He looked at Noah. "How you doin' man? Did you have fun at the studio the other day?"

Noah nodded. "Yeah, man. It was a cool experience. I think everyone should experience that at least once in life. For someone who appreciates music as much as I do, it's important to see how it's made."

Shannon nodded, his head sliding back and forth. *Groovy, man.* "Yeah. For some people though, it ruins the magic to see behind the curtain."

"See, that's what I told him about rehearsals," Tanis said, looking at him without turning her head.

"Do you play anything yourself?" Shannon asked Noah.

"Just records. Never picked up an instrument." Noah shrugged. "Some people, like you," he said, holding his hand out toward Shannon, "are born to make music. Right? And you, Tan," he added. "Some are just born to listen. I'm in the latter."

Shannon shrugged, taking another drink then setting the glass down and putting his hands on his thighs. "I guess that's one way to look at it."

Noah, feeling confident, said, "Without an audience, it doesn't make much sense to play it, right?"

Shannon held up a finger. "Ah, now that's where you're wrong. The experience of making music is more than just about showing it off. I love creating. And playing. Even if we're playing to an empty room. The magic is still there."

Noah pursed his lips. Nodded. "Yeah, I hadn't considered that. But then, I've never made music."

Shannon wagged his finger in agreement.

After a few minutes of Shannon and Tanis catching up, Shannon suddenly turned to Noah and surprised him with, "So who's your favorite band of all time?"

Noah leaned back, hands on his thighs and smirked. "Man, that's always so hard to answer. First instinct, first thing to mind, The Rolling Stones," Noah said. "Hands down." He gave Shannon time to nod. It was a nod, he noticed that was non-committal. He neither agreed nor disagreed. "But you give me time to think about it, to really dig in, there are others that float up."

"Okay. Ronnie or Mick?"

Noah raised his eyebrows. "Ah, fuck, man. Great question. The way Mick and Keith played off each other's strengths was phenomenal. But I like Ronnie. He's a great, reliable guitarist."

"Isn't that a little bit like Sammy or David?" Tanis interjected.

Shannon looked at her. "Not really. Roth did a lot of the writing, and so those songs were so different than the ones Sammy sang. It's hard to compare. Song for song, pound for pound, David Lee Roth sang the David Lee Roth songs better. And Sammy sang Sammy's better. I know," he said, raising his hands. "It sounds like a give-up answer. But it's true. You listen to some songs on 'Balance' where Sammy was top of his game, it's just incredible what he could do with his voice. But 'Diver Down' and '1984' were retardedly good because of Dave. You can't compare."

Tanis was staring at her drink, still holding it in front of her face. She seemed bored with the music trivia portion of tonight's chatter.

"So I don't need to ask you Beatles or Stones, right?" asked Noah.

"Who. All the way, give me the Who," Shannon said. After a moment, he could see from Noah's smirk he wasn't getting off that easy. "Okay, shoot man. Beatles. But only because I'm such a fan of George Harrison's guitarism. Especially his solo shit."

"I can get on board with that," Noah said. "Okay, so back at ya. Best band of all time."

"Felix Hebrew and the Arabian Nightmares," Shannon said without missing a beat.

Tanis did a spit take, blowing whiskey all over the table in front of her, then dissolving into belly laughter. Noah was laughing out loud too, but was pretty sure he was being trolled. Shannon looked at Tanis, then back at Noah, shaking his head.

"Seriously?" Noah asked. "Is that a thing?"

"Yeah. Hell yeah. They were a local band from Charleston, where I grew up. Phenomenal band."

"Okay, fair enough. I don't guess I would have ever heard anything by them," Noah said, taking a sip of his whiskey. Tanis was still giggling.

"You okay over there, hon?" Shannon said. She ignored him. He looked back at Noah. "Nah. They released one indie record. Sold the CD at their shows. It was really good though. Best song on the album was called *Gassy Burrito.*" And Tanis was off laughing again. She had to stand up this time, knocking the chair back a foot with the backs of her knees.

Just watching her made Noah laugh out loud himself. She stood with her hand over her mouth, eyes closed, and gasping. Her other hand was waving in the air in front of her. Shannon was now leaning back against his seat with his own hands on his hips again. Noah had mind to wonder if men subconsciously mimicked the way the others were sitting in their groups. Shannon held up a hand and looked at Noah. "What's wrong with your chick, bro?"

Noah giggled at that. He liked that someone as important as Shannon was calling her his chick though. If Shannon accepted and acknowledged it, that meant it was for real, right?

"Gassy burrito, huh?" Noah said. Tanis had turned and excused herself to the restroom. She was still shaking with laughter as she walked away.

"Yeah. The names were funny like that but they were really good. Not like Frank Zappa. Like, Zappa had this ridiculous talent; I don't mean he was bad. But most of his shit was jokey like that, you know? *Titties and Beer? Stick it Out?* Come on. You can't sing that shit seriously, right?"

Noah nodded at that, recalling the words to *Stick it Out*. It definitely wouldn't make mainstream radio.

"But these guys had some songs with names like that. Like *Snot on Your Mustache*. But it wasn't a funny song at all. In fact, it was an instrumental. But it was so rich," he said, shaking his head.

"A la *Peaches in Regalia...*" Noah said, holding out a hand.

"Yes, exactly. One of Zappa's best instrumentals."

"Where do they come up with the names, though?"

"Who knows?" Shannon said, shrugging. "Good shit, though. But to answer fairly, I'd have to say Dream Theater. Back when they had Portnoy on drums, especially. That band is tighter than a-" he started, but was cut off suddenly by the slamming down of three shot glasses onto the table. Both the guys sat back instinctively, reflexively, as whiskey sloshed from the short glasses.

"Drink up, boys. To big music," said Tanis. They all picked up their shots and slung them back.

Shannon made a face. "God, Tan, fuckin' Fireball? You could'a warned a brother."

"Aww, what's a matter, does it burn woo widdle cheeks?" Tanis said, sticking her bottom lip out and pinching Shannons's cheeks from behind him as she stood leaning over him. From her vantage, she did not get to see how he rolled his eyes at that. That look said he was used to her goofing off like this. Noah was quite enjoying seeing her in her element. She was obviously completely comfortable around Shannon, even though they supposedly never really hung out together outside of the music.

"Come on, guys. Let's go get some fresh air," Tanis said, her hands tapping out a drumbeat on Shannon's shoulders.

He looked halfway over his shoulder, but not far enough to actually see her. "Seriously? I just got here!"

"It's getting stuffy in here," she said. "I paid the tab already." Then she turned and headed for the door.

Noah and Shannon exchanged a look, then downed the rest of the whiskey in their old-fashioned glasses. "Okay, I guess we go," Shannon said.

They walked down the sidewalk toward the parking lot. A light mist fell from the sky. It wasn't enough to immediately make its impression, but if one were to stand still in it for five minutes, one would be soaked. Shannon walked with his hands in his coat pockets while Tanis and Noah held hands, walking slightly in front of him.

"Who's playing the Alexandria?" Shannon asked as they approached the little bar. Another hidden treasure in the Bar Harbor downtown strip that mostly lay dormant during the winter, The Alexandria was tucked between two unassuming office fronts. Most of the bars shut down during the off season, so the locals flocked to the watering holes that did remain open. They each had their own regulars, too. Noah had only been there a few times, as he typically ended up at the Sally. But Tanis apparently came here often.

As they drew closer, Noah could hear the loud brass of the cymbals from an unmiked drum set, and some alcohol-soaked vocals ringing out. Shannon pulled the thick door open and the sound of the crowd blasted out at them along with a wave of heat that Noah was ready to welcome, as his hair had picked up a layer of wet from the drizzle.

A man stood on the stage with an acoustic guitar, shouting the verses of an Irish folk song into the mic while the audience clapped loudly on the one and the three. And he noticed quickly, it was all-inclusive. Everyone was clapping. These people knew how to have a good time. He was instantly engaged.

Just inside the door, Shannon twisted sideways and slipped through the crowd to the bar at the side of the small room. Tanis and Noah squeezed in away from the door, and she immediately began clapping along and bouncing with the beat. A huge smile split her face. After a quick minute, Shannon returned with an armful of pints, handing them off to the others. Noah took his, then they raised them and knocked them together. He took a long draw of the Irish Red. He noticed the other two doing the same thing. He was actually quite impressed to see that when Tanis pulled the glass away from her mouth, it was only half-full. She looked up at him with a wicked little smile, then stood tall and kissed him on his lips.

The three of them bounced and clapped and shouted, singing along to the songs they knew and drinking beer well into the evening. When they had finally had enough, and the Irish folk band had said their goodnights, Noah, Shannon and Tanis made their way toward the front of the tavern. As they neared the door, Noah saw a man standing just inside it stretching his neck to see over the crowd, as if he were looking for someone. A large white square attracted Noah's eyes, so he looked down and noticed it was a press pass hanging from the man's neck on a lanyard. The other two had already made it through the door. Noah reached out and touched the string holding the pass and said to the man, "You need a press pass to get in here?" He had been half-joking and didn't expect a response.

"Ha! No, I just came from an event. Hadn't taken it off yet, mate," the man said, leaning in to be heard over the crowd.

"You write for the paper?" Noah asked. He was shoulder-to-shoulder now, about to go through the door himself. Tanis was standing a few feet outside the door looking at him with a passive smile.

"Nah, I review bands for WhiskeyNeat Magazine," said the man.

Noah stopped in his tracks. The name sounded familiar. He had seen WhiskeyNeat on the news stands, of course, but something felt funny. He was making a face the man must have recognized, because the man added, "I know. Not to be confused with the WhiskeyNote, down the street." He was smiling a wide one. It was contagious. Noah had to smile too.

"Fair enough. You review bands though, yeah?" Noah asked.

"I do. I'm Ken. What's your name?" the man said, holding a hand high but close to his chest. The crowd made everything close-tolerance.

"I'm Noah, but I'm not the one who matters. I think you should come review this band," he said, pointing at the two waiting expectantly outside the door. Ken turned to look at them.

"Oh yeah? And what band is that?"

Noah put his hand on the man's shoulder. "Come outside for a spot. Tanis, Shannon, this is Ken. He writes for WhiskeyNeat Magazine."

Tanis's eyes widened at this and she stepped forward offering her hand. The man came outside and shook it. "You guys are a band?"

"Well, we're forty percent of a band," Shannon said. "Tanis is the vocalist. I'm the guitarist. We play for One Last Orbit. Heard of 'em?"

"Can't say that I have, mate," the man said, then added, "Sorry!"

"See, that's the thing. You need to," said Noah, returning his hand to the man's shoulder. "When's the next gig, Tan?"

She had her hands in her pockets now, looking reluctantly hopeful. "Friday, week," she said.

"There you go," said Noah, turning back to Ken. He rubbed his hands together. "Eight days from now. Be at the Sally West. Know where that is?"

"Oh, sure," said Ken. "I've been there a few times."

"Cool. So will you come? If nothing else, I'll buy you a drink."

The man was nodding. "You're not shitting," he said, looking at Noah. Then he turned to look at Tanis and Shannon. "You guys are good?"

Tanis closed her eyes and nodded modestly. "We draw a nice crowd sometimes."

10

"Holy shit, Noah!" Tanis screamed. This was not the first time the phrase had been uttered since they had climbed into Noah's jeep, either. The streetlights swept through the cab in slow-motion, as the rain was coming down hard and heavy now. They had been on the highway for almost half an hour and had barely made any progress. Noah guessed there was a wreck up ahead. It wasn't cold enough to have frozen yet, but people still drove like they were on an ice rink even when it was just rain.

She was sitting sideways in the seat, which caused her to continuously have to adjust the seat belt across her chest. She had been talking with her hands a lot, shouting and leaning over to kiss him on the cheek, hugging him and clapping frequently. Overall, Noah didn't think he had ever seen her so animated or excited about something. Tanis was usually a pretty reserved gal. Tonight, she was bouncing around like an electrified goldfish.

"I can't believe we're going to have a magazine at our effing show, Noah!"

Noah laughed out loud at her seemingly random courtship with profanity. It didn't seem there was any pattern to it. Maybe she only allowed herself so many words per day.

"Yeah, and WhiskeyNeat, at that. That's a big one."

"Yes! Oh my God. I can't believe it," she said. She had been holding onto his stick shift with her right hand but now she put her hands in her hair, messing it up in what seemed a deliberate fashion. "How did you know that guy? Oh my God," she said again. Then she screamed a high-pitch squeal and turned to face the front. "Oh my God, you're so getting laid tonight, boy."

Noah laughed out loud again. "Wow. I have never seen you this excited. How has no one ever reviewed you guys before?"

She made a face and shrugged. "I have no idea, Noah!" she said, almost sounding like an accusation. "I would have no idea how to get someone to come listen. Or who to call."

"Well, yeah. No. I mean, he said he has been to the Sally before, several times. So he just hasn't shown up when you've been there."

"Yeah. Noah, that's Ken Drutch. He chases Dreadwire. He has written about them a bunch of times. And I know they play the Sally a lot."

"Ah. So you're saying he doesn't just show up there at random to check out the act of the night," said Noah.

"Hell no. Not at the Sally. Do you read WhiskeyNeat?"

Noah shrugged. "Not like faithfully. I pick up a copy every once in a while when there's a band on it that I like."

Tanis suddenly got real still and then put her hands in her hair again. "Noah, what if he writes about us? What if we like make it into the magazine?"

"Then I'll buy a copy," Noah said, looking over at her.

She turned to look at him seriously, then leaned in and kissed him hard on the mouth. Noah was endeared to her seeming vacancy of thought about the fact that he was operating a motor vehicle. Much like a child or a dog that has no idea it weighs anything, and just knows you can hold it. She just seemed to know there was nothing she could do that would put that control in jeopardy. It was affirming in its own way.

"You better buy a case of 'em!"

Noah shouted, "A case?! I ain't buying a case unless you make the fuckin' cover!"

"Oh my God!" she cried. "The cover? What if, Noah?" And then she was dancing in her seat, shaking her tiny fists in front of her closed eyes. He had to laugh again. Her excitement was contagious.

"Hey, I guess it's possible. You're hot enough, babe," he said. And he meant it. She knew he did.

She rolled her eyes though, staring half-cocked at him. "Yeah, well, they only put labeled bands on the cover. But it's fun to think about. Man. Maybe someday though."

Noah looked over at her again. They were approaching the red and blue lights that twirled up ahead. They would be past the wreck in a few minutes, and could get on with their lives. "Maybe someday," he agreed.

"Maybe someday."

11

Back at the house, Tanis kept her promise. They showered together, then sat up in bed, Noah leaning against the headboard and she sitting cross-legged and facing him, talking about the ins and outs of being on stage. She told him about how they setup for each show, and tried to make them all unique experiences, and how it's more difficult to do with fewer songs. They were working with about twenty-five original songs at this point, and had a pretty good catalog of covers they could pull from, but Shannon and she only ever liked to play one cover per night. There were times they had done a second one, but it was exceedingly rare. And the covers they did play had to be something she believed in. Something she could feel. Something she could make her own.

Shannon was such a great guitarist, she had said, because not only could he play the licks, but he could seemingly read her mind. When she was going for a particular feel or image in the music, he was always able to come up with it. "It's like he's able to divine it from the umbra," she said, holding her fingers up like she were examining an invisible crystal ball. This translated to good cover songs, because she was always looking for a unique take on them. She would not just cover a song exactly the way one was used to hearing it. No one wanted to see that. "No one bought Ryan Adams's 1989 record to hear Taylor Swift. They bought it to hear Ryan playing her songs like he heard them."

"I get that," Noah said. "What are some of your covers?"

"Oh, we've done a bunch. You want to know what one of my favorites is though?" she said, putting a hand on his knee.

"Of course," he said. He sat against the pillows with his hands clasped behind his head, just staring at her as she spoke. The shape of her lips when she made the long-O sound, the way her bottom lip would pull to one side when she emphasized a particular word, the way her left eyebrow would rise a little when she was saying something she thought was really important – he caught all of these little nuances that made Tanis who she was. And he loved and adored every single bit of it. She was absolutely fascinating to him.

"We covered *Timshel* by Mumford and Sons. And what's funny is that I'm not typically a big fan of them.

I mean, I could take 'em or leave 'em," Tanis said, looking off into the distance in the wall behind Noah. She was seeing what she was saying. Her eyes were full of mystery. "But I was on the way home from a carnival one night. A carnival, of all things. And this damn song came on. I was streaming a playlist built off of something or other. I can't remember what. And that song came on. I looked at the stereo and just froze. I was like, 'Mumford wrote this?'" she said, shaking her head. "I was like, holy hell that's good. And I knew I had to cover it."

"I would love to hear you guys do that one," Noah said.

"Well, we only did it a couple of times. I'm not even sure I would remember it now. But yeah, it was pretty good. It was just me and Ben."

"He's the keyboardist, right?" Noah asked.

She nodded, pursing her lips.

"I think my favorite remake of a song, and hear me, I'm not saying my favorite cover – I'm saying remake – was Joy Williams covering *Ordinary World*," Noah said. "I can't listen to that without crying. It literally gives me chills all over and makes me cry. Every time."

"That's by Duran Duran, yeah?" said Tanis.

Noah Nodded. "Talk about making something her own. It sounded nothing like the original. But I'm betting Simon LeBon called her and said, 'You got that one right, baby.' Because she fuckin' mastered that song."

"Well, I'm going to have to check that out. I love that song. I didn't know anyone covered it. I guess I don't even know who Joy Williams is."

"You'll love it."

Tanis breathed in deeply, then looked at him through squinted eyes. "Noah, I want to do something for you."

Noah pulled his head back. He pulled his hands out from behind his head and stretched his fingers in front of him, before clasping his hands on his chest. "Yeah? What's that?"

"I want you to choose a song that you want us to cover."

"Really?" he said. He suddenly felt very important. "Holy shit. You're serious?"

She was nodding. "Yup. Anything you want. Your musical acumen is remarkable. And I trust you."

Noah widened his eyes, nodding. "Wow." He was speechless beyond the one word. "Wow."

Noah knew he couldn't take this lightly. Choosing a song for them to cover was a huge job, considering all the angles it affected. Potentially many people would be hearing it, for one. And if the band really liked the song, and really liked their own cover of it beyond that, then they might take to playing it at many shows. It might be their signature cover. Like Dave Matthews Band did with *All Along the Watchtower.* DMB played that song at just about every live show. And furthermore, the crowd actually *wanted* to hear it. They would ask for it. If Noah picked the right song, then he could be starting something really big with this. And it had to be something they had not thought to do themselves.

He would know pretty quickly if he chose the *wrong* song. It would go over like a lead balloon. Either they wouldn't get around to arranging it, or they just wouldn't play it. That would probably be better, somehow, than their playing a song no one in the band liked, just because Tanis had made a promise. Talk about a lead balloon. That could be bad all around. So Noah knew he would have to spend some real time thinking about his task. Because, he had to admit, he really *wanted* to give them a good song to cover. He was honored and excited by the trust she put in him to do so.

CHAPTER SEVEN
live

From *Front Row Magazine*

A Walk Among Stars
by Rod Agnew

I had a rare and great opportunity to hang out with one of music's best keyboardists last month. Ben Redding of One Last Orbit invited me to his house in Gallatin Valley, just outside of Bozeman, Montana. And it took no time at all to realize I was in the presence of real, genuine hospitality.

Benjamin's house sits in a sort of bowl, surrounded by mountains. The land itself looks untouched by man, but for the three homes on it. The singer and the drummer, Tanis and Kevin, live nearby on the same stretch—each house about a hundred yards from the others. This arrangement came to be when the band uprooted itself from Bar Harbor, Maine a few years ago. It is a stunning view. Mountains and trees everywhere you look.

I asked him how he keeps a humble disposition when surrounded by such a view.

Redding said, "Are you kidding? If there's anywhere a man can be reminded how small he is, it's here. Right here surrounded by mountains." Well spoken, Ben.

The remaining members, Shannon Kennedy, guitarist and Layne Billings, bassist, live in Bozeman, just a short drive from the land.

After the band's recent touring success, they have all taken a hiatus to rest, recuperate and get back in touch with themselves. But they're serious about taking a year off. Staring out at the mountains, I see Ben Redding's point. This place has the effect of making one feel small.

I spoke to him about the future plans of the band, and he shared with me that they do have plans. He won't tell me what they are, but he said Tanis has not stopped writing. Maybe another album is on the horizon? He winked when I asked him about it. "It's already written, my friend. We just have yet to hear it."

1

It was Friday night and the rain was coming down in torrents. Noah was especially nonplussed by this, as he knew turnout for shows dramatically decreased when people had to fight the weather. It was easier just to stay in. Stay dry. It was easier to go out another time when it was a little drier. He had stationed himself on the deck of the Sally West, leaning on the wooden railing, looking out over the water below. Fortunately, the rain was coming in from the other end of the building, so he was mostly dry. An occasional gust would whip up and pepper him with a face-full of cold mist. But it was bearable. And he didn't want to chance missing Ken Drutch.

Doug had shown up a few minutes before and headed directly inside to get drinks. Trixie, it seemed, was not working tonight, which was a not only a huge surprise to Noah, but a relief. Thinking back, he couldn't remember the last time he had actually seen her. Noah stood looking down at the water crashing on the rocks below, wondering whether the rain was too much for someone who wrote for a magazine. They had not exchanged phone numbers or anything. The guy had acted interested in coming to see the band, and Noah, had, of course, taken him at his word. But when it came down to it, he might have just been being polite. Coming to see a band perform strictly on the word of a few strangers was a big step. The one saving grace Noah could think of was that the Sally West was not a small venue. And Ken had said that he'd been there a few times. Tanis had even confirmed she knew the guy's work, and that he had reviewed Dreadwire. And had furthermore chased them. So he knew the venue. Simply put, shitty bands didn't play the Sally. The door was too big. If a band couldn't draw several hundred people, it just wouldn't be worth it for the venue to book them. So maybe Ken would make the connection that if they were playing the Sally West, it followed they must at least be somewhat decent. If they *did* draw that many people, then they must be at least worth listening to. So maybe he would make the effort to come and see them. Even in the rain.

Noah felt a slap on his shoulder, and turned around smiling. He was almost disappointed to see Troy standing there, large droplets of water standing on the shoulders of his waterproof Members Only jacket. He turned and clasped Troy's hand, then pulled him in for a bro-hug. "Hey man. Good to see you."

"Yeah man. Why you hangin' out here?" Troy said, putting his hands in his pockets. Twyla stood behind him, leaning in and putting her chin on his shoulder and smiling at Noah. Noah hiked his chin at her and smiled.

"Sup, Twy? I'm waiting for someone." Noah suddenly realized he hadn't seen Troy in a few days, and that had just been briefly. He had not gotten the chance to tell them about Ken. Then it occurred to him that maybe Tanis hadn't told her sister, either. "You guys know who Ken Drutch is?"

Twyla pursed her lips and shook her head, never removing her chin from Troy's shoulder. Troy frowned. "No. Should I?"

Noah shrugged. "He writes for Neat. He's coming – well, hopefully, he's coming tonight."

"Oh, fuckin' A. That's bad ass," said Troy. Then he frowned again. "Wait. You know him?"

"We ran into him the other night at the Alexandria. I told him about Orbit and he said he'd come out tonight to have a listen."

Troy made a serious face, raising his eyebrows. "Whoa. That could be huge, bro." Twyla pulled back from Troy's shoulder and actually clapped, smiling widely.

"Yeah. I really hope he shows up. The weather sucks."

Troy furled his mouth then held up his hands. "What are ya gonna do?" he said, shrugging.

"Yeah. But if he doesn't show, I have no way of finding him again."

"Did you tell him the name of the band?" Twyla asked.

Noah nodded, looking over her shoulder as a lone wolf came stomping up the stairs hunching his shoulders against the cold rain.

"Then he'll find them later if he doesn't show tonight. You've probably piqued his interest," she said. Noah hadn't thought about that. But it was actually a good point. A band with the name One Last Orbit sounded pretty mysterious. He knew *he* would want to check them out just on the strength of their name alone. "Well, I'm going inside." She kissed Troy on the cheek, hugging him from behind. "Don't stay out here too long, babe," she said, then turned and bounced away.

Noah nodded knowingly at Troy. "I guess that's going well," he said, once she had made it through the heavy double-doors of the bar.

Troy shook his head, raising his eyebrows. "Bro, she is so amazing. I can't even believe it. I have no idea what the hell she sees in me."

"Ah, man, you're exactly what she looks for. Just accept it."

"Man, a girl like that should be with some thick ass guy," said Troy, shaking his head again.

"Stop that shit," Noah said, clapping his shoulder. "If you start looking too hard for a reason, she may find one."

"What do you mean?" Troy asked. He looked around Noah to see the water behind him.

"You'll start seeming insecure. Which you are," Noah said, holding a hand out as if to weigh options. "You don't need to advertise that shit. See, once a girl starts seeing how insecure you are, or that you can't just accept that she likes you, she starts questioning why she *does* like you. Like maybe you know something you're not telling her and she needs to look a little closer. Like you're hiding something from her. She'll start wondering if you're right. You don't want that shit."

"I guess that makes sense," Troy said, nodding.

"Fuckin' A it does. You need to be acting like you're the most confident son of a bitch on the planet. Turn that shit the other way, you know? Make her think you know something you're not telling her. About how bad ass you are. Like you always have some shit up your sleeve," Noah said. He put his hands in his pockets to warm them. Another loner made his way up the walk and made eye-contact with Noah. Still no Ken.

"If you make her believe you're not showing her *all* of your bad-assery, she'll keep wanting to see more. She'll be overwhelmed with intrigue. Confidence is a man's best friend, bro."

Troy was staring at the trees behind Noah, nodding slowly. "Yeah. Okay. Like letting her know she made the right choice."

"There you go," Noah said. Then he looked around the parking lot. The sun had gone down without his even realizing it. The clouds had been too heavy all day to let much light through, so it had been a subtle change. Now the street lights in the parking lot had taken over the duty of providing the light. "Man, let's go in. Fuck this shit. He ain't coming."

Troy shrugged and turned toward the door. As they were going in, they ran into Doug, who had a drink in each hand. "Hey, bitches. You're coming in?"

As they settled into their spot, Noah glanced around the floor. He might have recognized a few of the faces. Of course, Noah couldn't remember all these faces, but he didn't *not* remember them, either. As he saw them, they became familiar. These were Orbit fans. *Comets.*

Cool Change by the Little River Band graced the house speakers. Noah nodded at the familiar piano. Troy, looking about the near area himself, said to Noah, "Sorry your guy stood you up, man."

Noah shrugged and took a sip of his whiskey. "What are ya gonna do?" After a minute, he said, "Didn't really stand me up, anyway. It's Tanis who suffers for it. She was so damned excited, bro. That's what sucks so bad. You should have seen how happy it made her. She was up all night talking about the what-ifs."

Troy shook his head, took a drink of his beer. Twyla was behind him, bouncing to the beat, her lips pursed in approval as she stared at her phone, thumbs dancing across the screen. Noah was happy for him. He deserved someone like her. And she seemed so comfortable with him. Like maybe all that shit Noah had told him earlier had been for nil. Maybe none of it was even necessary. Maybe Troy didn't need to overthink it. Didn't need to act at all, any certain way. Just be himself. She seemed completely taken by him. That was wonderful to Noah, who had seen his best friend hurt too many times. Noah felt the sudden urge to toast his buddy, and raised his glass. Troy frowned, then caught Noah's eyes and nodded. Then he raised his beer glass and clinked it to Noah's whiskey glass. Troy smirked. It seemed he knew exactly what Noah was thinking.

After a few minutes of standing there listening to the house music and shooting the shit, catching up on the last week, Noah was almost knocked off balance by someone on his left, who suddenly rammed into him from the side, then put her arms around him. Before he had a chance to react, he realized who it was and put his arm around her shoulder. She was leaning hard into him. He felt important every time Tanis hung on him like this in public. Because he was an exclusive group of one member. The one single person in the entire bar she was wrapping her arms around and putting her head against his chest. When he got down to it, it was more than just the entire bar. The entire *universe.* There was only one of her. And she was with him. Important was an understatement.

As the song ended, the place was overwhelmed with the low-fi bass of Billie Eilish's *Bad Guy* and suddenly all the women were dancing. There was hip-shaking and snapping, and a whole lot of getting close to each other. Tanis and Twyla were dancing like preteens, jumping up and down, flailing their arms about and banging their heads. They looked like one woman in a mirror. Noah and Troy stood staring at them, sipping their drinks and smirking. After a minute, Troy looked back at Noah and nodded, a sly smile on his face. He held his beer bottle up and Noah clinked it with his glass. *Lucky guys.*

Twyla kept trying to get Troy to join her but he would only shake his head. Troy wasn't much of a dancer. Nor was he one for being the center of attention. And now these two women were getting some attention. People were starting to realize who was out here dancing. There was some pointing and talking behind hands as people recognized the singer.

After an undetermined amount of time, Tanis suddenly leaned in and kissed her sister on the cheek and said something in her ear. It was so sudden that it took Noah seeing her smile to realize nothing was wrong. *She must have a killer internal clock.* She then turned and spoke to Noah. "Gotta go. Holler for me," she said, then kissed him on the lips. Noah smiled and nodded.

2

The house went dark. The crowd got loud. The house music stopped. Whistles and stomping, clapping and hollering. Only a single purple spotlight remained on, and a vibrating note that sounded like a warbling bass guitar played through distortion. It had seemingly come out of nowhere. Tonight was a big night for One Last Orbit. They were playing a double-set. Tanis had called it opening up for themselves. They would play a sixty-minute set followed by a break, then a ninety-minute set.

When Tanis had told him about it, Noah had asked if they even had that much music. She had looked at him seriously. "You realize you can make one song last ten or fifteen minutes, right?"

Noah had rolled his eyes, then she had said, "You can literally stretch the songs to make them as long as you need to. We could, therefore, play all night," she had said, jabbing a finger at his chest to emphasize the last three words.

Then she had stared blankly at him for a time. "But yes. We have enough material for two-and-a-half hours."

Noah loved these times when the band was about to take the stage: watching the faces of the expectant and excited crowd. The nervous bounces and smiles at the stage as people anticipated who would come out first, and when. He looked up at the stage just in time to see Mark appear out of the darkness. He was the cause of that crazy prolonged bass note. As he appeared, he looked out over the crowd, nodding his head, pursing his lips. He reminded Noah of Mark Tremonti in that instant. The man in charge of the crowd, if only for a moment. He walked right up to the edge of the stage and put a foot up on the monitor, still nodding his head as he finger-picked the bass notes.

The intensity of the rumbling bass line finally dwindled and he began to pick a melody on the strings.

The crowd recognized it and started applauding. The applause turned to claps on the beat. After a few bars of this, another spotlight switched on, and suddenly, Shannon was joining him on stage. Shannon was finger-picking an acoustic guitar, a perfect harmony with the bass line. The clapping intensified.

Noah was rocking back and forth on his feet. He didn't recognize the song, and found some interest in that. He thought by now he had heard all of their music. How many songs had Tanis said were in their repertoire? Twenty-five? Thirty? Surely he had heard that many by now. Surprises never ceased. And then there was the drumbeat. A third spotlight broke through the darkness and Kevin was playing a solid but simple supporting beat to the stringed melody.

Twyla, Noah noticed, wasn't even looking at the stage. She was swaying back and forth with her eyes closed, snapping her fingers as her long arms swung out to her sides. Clearly, she knew the music. Noah wondered how many shows she came to, and wondered how many times he had been close to her in the crowd before they met.

When Tanis finally came to the stage, the band had been playing supporting music for nearly five minutes, and Noah could see what she meant about how easy it was to make it stretch. Tanis walked into the spotlight with a confidence and presence that he didn't quite understand. He knew her to be an outgoing, gregarious woman. But this seemed beyond even that. She looked nothing short of professional. And it was instant. The instant she made the light, she was in charge. There wasn't a second of hesitation or unsure. As her hands grasped the microphone, he could see very clearly that she was not trembling. And he couldn't help but smile widely. The pride he felt inside was almost as intense as the music.

And then she began to sing. His pride turned to goosebumps. His smile turned to amazement. His eyes went glassy.

You're moving like a superstar
 and burning up the land
What's with the smile?
You've got stardust in your hair
 and sun drops in your hand
I can feel your heat for miles.

You've knocked me out of orbit
 and set my trail on fire
How did you know?
I can sense in you a carnage
 that leaves little for desire
It's time to show

It's time to show you my corona!
I can burn hotter than she ever did
Just watch for my corona!
Don't forget who rescued you before this fire
became your id.

At this last word, Tanis grabbed the mic off its stand, lifting it swiftly into the air as she turned and threw her other fist at the sky, stepping back and closing her eyes. She stood in the middle of the stage, just out of the spotlight as Shannon wailed on a guitar solo – eerie and forlorn, putting everyone in the crowd right out there with her – lost in lonely space.

Noah wondered how many shows he would have to attend to stop being surprised by his girlfriend's talent and presence on the stage. A lot of it was created off-stage, he knew. The writing, the rehearsal, the creative process. But it seemed new to him each time he witnessed it. She always took his breath away. Always gave him the chills at the right moments, the tears, the laughter when something seriously cool happened – he had not yet gotten used to it. It was still new. Still fresh. Would that ever wear off? Would it lose its luster like a relationship tended to do? Become *routine*? Would he ever attend a One Last Orbit show that was *just another concert*? It sure was hard to see that as a possibility at this point. And he supposed that as long as they kept writing new material, there would be no reason to think it couldn't stay amazing every time he saw them play.

When the show finished, they all came to the center of the stage and bowed. The crowd was so loud Noah almost had to cover his ears. He thought it might be the loudest he had ever heard a crowd at the Sally West. For any band he had seen there. He scanned the crowd again, looking for Ken Drutch, wondering if the man had slipped in at some point without Noah's seeing him. It was more than just possible. And with the realization of how loud the crowd actually was, Noah took inventory of how many people were there. If the shitty weather held anyone back, those who didn't come were strongly in the minority. This was a packed house.

Doug brought him back from his thoughts with a clap on the back. "I think that was their best show yet," he said in Noah's ear.

Noah nodded, then pointed to the high-top tables that stood at the edge of the concert area. Doug affirmed with his own nod and grabbed Troy by the arm, pointing. Troy gave him a thumbs-up. They all made their way to the tables. Noah slid up to one and swished back the rest of his whiskey. He had been nursing the glass for the last half-hour, not wanting to miss the show for a refill. He found he was almost out of breath with excitement.

As Troy sidled up to the table, he held his fist up and Noah knocked it with his own. "Dude, bro," was all Troy said.

"I know, right? I still can't get over it."

"Feel so sorry for deaf people," said Doug.

Noah frowned and looked at him. "What the hell brought that up?"

He shrugged, looking around the area. "I don't know. I mean, you can pretty much describe everything to them. But they'll never get how awesome certain pieces of music actually are."

"I don't know, man. Beethoven wrote almost half of his piano sonatas after he went deaf."

"Yeah, but he knew what music sounded like," said Doug. "He wasn't born deaf."

"But he never got to hear his last ones. Which are, arguably, some of the best pieces of music ever made. Have you ever heard Sonata number 28?" Noah said, leaning in.

Doug shrugged again. "Maybe. I'm sure I have. Why?"

"Dude, if that shit doesn't give you chills – fourth movement, E major climb up about seventy keys… Fuckin' beautiful. And he never got to hear it."

"Yeah, see, you're making my point for me," Doug said, holding out a hand. "I think. What *is* your point, Wright?"

Noah pointed at him and said, "You said you felt sorry for them because they would never get to experience how awesome certain music was. And I'm certain he understood very well."

Troy pitched in and said, "I think he could feel vibrations through the keys. That's how he knew if it sounded right or not."

"Well, that among other things. I think by that point he had a pretty good grip on what he was doing," said Noah. They all laughed.

"True," said Doug. "I don't know. I just mean, well, take that shit, for instance," he said, turning and holding his hand out toward the stage. "How would you describe that show to someone who can't hear?"

Noah was nodding. "Yeah. I have no idea. Which is why," he said, getting suddenly louder, "I was hoping fucking Ken Drutch would be here! So he *could* describe it in an article."

"Well, just because he shows up doesn't mean he's going to write about them," Troy said. "I'm getting refills. You guys in?"

"Do bears wear funny hats?" asked Noah.

Doug said, "If that mother fucker heard *that* show, and *didn't* write about it? I would suggest he's a fuckin' idiot."

"Your point," Noah said, raising his empty glass to clink it against Doug's presumably empty bottle.

3

It was almost a half-hour later that Tanis finally emerged from the crowd and joined them at the table. The clusters, as she called them, had been teeming with new faces tonight. She had signed a hundred t-shirts and taken at least as many selfies with the fans. She had told Noah, in the privacy of a bedroom – away from overhearing fans – that she knew she would have to set limits at some point. Or stop altogether. It didn't scale very well. If it kept growing the way it had been, she would never get out of the club. But for now, she had a hard time saying no to anyone. And what if she put a numerical limit on it, and the signing or selfie-taking ended right before some honest fan? How shitty would that be? There was no easy answer. So for now, she just indulged them all.

Noah had told her that perhaps the best way to handle it when she was ready, was to just escape out the back. Make milling through the crowds a thing of the past. That's how the national acts did it. They slid out the back and right onto their tour buses. Problem solved.

Now she stood here with a vodka tonic, sucking through a tiny stirring straw and beaming at her new friends. Twyla was standing beside her, being clingy in a sisterly way. Troy was across the table from them, happy to give Twyla the space. The crowd had mostly cleared out. The rest were the non-fans and the die-hards who always stayed around for pool and darts after a show. The bar side of the house was still hopping.

"So has anyone seen Trixie lately?" Doug asked suddenly.

Noah almost rolled his eyes, but had peripherally seen Tanis looking at him. He wondered what that was about, but knew he had no way to ask. *Why the fuck did he have to bring her up?* He shook his head, pursing his lips, looking uninterested. In fact, it wasn't an act. He wasn't interested. He was more interested in the longevity of the pointed absence than any reemergence she might effect.

"Good question," Troy said, looking about the bar as if he had just not noticed her tonight. "When was the last time any of you even saw her?"

Doug said, "A few weeks, I think. Hell, it could have been longer though."

Noah yawned, again effecting a disinterest. He shook his head when the guys looked at him. He knew Doug hadn't brought her up to try to get him talking about her in front of Tanis. Doug knew what Trixie was. He had been genuinely curious. As Noah should have been. And if he were innocent of all charges, he would be curious, would he not? Perhaps disinterest wasn't the right posture here. It might make him appear to be hiding something. Like knowledge. Not just feelings.

"You know," he finally said, "it's interesting you bring that up. Because I hadn't even noticed she wasn't around." Doug tightened his mouth at this, but kept quiet. "Now that I think of it though, I guess it was the last time you and I saw her here," he said, looking at Tanis. "The night she asked about Joy and all that."

"The night of our first kiss, in other words?" Tanis said, raising an eyebrow.

Noah smirked. "Yeah. That."

Troy finally, blessedly, changed the subject, when he said, "Well, Tanis, the show tonight was superior."

"Thank you, doll," she said, smiling and tilting her head at him.

"Yes, Tanny. You sounded better than ever up there," her sister agreed.

Tanis smiled and hugged her, leaning her head against Twyla's and squeezing her around the shoulders.

Noah was nodding. "So what's next? When's the next gig. You guys gonna play anywhere else?"

Tanis was sipping from the straw again, looking at him. "Well, there's no other venue in town big enough, unfortunately."

They all laughed at that.

"You guys know what I mean. I'm not trying to brag. But our normal crowd is now in the four-to-five hundred range."

"That's seriously cool," Troy said, shaking his head and staring at his beer bottle as if in concentration. Doing the numbers in his head.

"Where do the other guys go after the shows?" asked Doug.

"They all like to sneak out. Take right off. Get home to wives and girlfriends. All that. They're not real big on the schmoozing," said Tanis. "Our next show though, to answer your question, Noah, is next month. The fifteenth. It's a Saturday night. Land Never Claimed will be opening that night."

"Kick ass," Troy said, taking a drink of his beer. "That'll be a sellout show."

"They all are," Twyla said, then clapped a hand over her mouth, eyes wide as saucers. Tanis was giving her a scornful mother look. She was obviously sharing trade secrets.

Noah chuckled. "If you guys can sell out on a rainy night like this, then I don't doubt it."

Troy was suddenly looking over Noah's shoulder. Noah's whiskey glass stopped halfway to his mouth. He was about to ask what the hell Troy was looking at, when a man appeared at his left shoulder. He was tall. He stood a good five inches taller than Noah, who wasn't short.

"Hey guys. Excuse me. I wanted to introduce myself," the man said. Noah's first thought was going to be *well good for you. But who the fuck cares what you wanted?* But then the man extended his hand to Tanis. And he added, "I'm Rod Agnew. I write for *Front Row Magazine*." And then Noah noticed there was a business card between his fingertips.

Tanis took the card, with a mischievous little smile touching her lips. "Well, hello there," she said. "Tanis Ransom."

"Yeah. I know. Great show tonight," he said. "I just wanted to let you know I'll be doing a piece on you guys."

Tanis's mouth dropped open. She was staring at the business card, then she looked back up the man and put her hand to her chest. "Did Ken send you?"

Noah pulled his head back on his neck. *What the hell?*

The man nodded, grinning. "Yeah. He asked if I was interested in catching your show tonight. You guys don't really play the kind of music they write about."

"You mean," Tanis said, "they don't really write about the kind of music we play."

"Yes, that," said Rod, pointing two fingers at her. Noah noticed they had an instant connection. Then he remembered that Tanis could be that way with anyone. She could easily switch personalities and talk shop in any fashion presented.

"Well, I appreciate your coming, Rod. Thank you for introducing yourself. I'm glad you liked the show," said Tanis.

"Well, on a personal note, you could call me a fan." Rod had put his hand over his heart as he said this. "I came to observe, but found more than I had expected." Then he stood there nodding slowly for a moment. Like he was mesmerized by her. Noah adjusted next to the man. Took a sip of his whiskey. He wasn't sure how to feel about this, all of a sudden. It was sure looking like he might be flirting with Tanis. But then he remembered how excited he had been about the prospect of having Ken show up. He had offered to buy that man a drink.

Fuck it. Why not? "Can I buy you a drink?" Noah asked him.

Rod glanced at Noah briefly, then returned his gaze to Tanis. "No, thank you very much. I don't drink. I'm gonna get out of here and leave you all alone," he said, making eye contact with each of them at the table. "I just wanted to let you know." And then he nodded again and waved, then ducked out.

Tanis stood staring at Noah, head shaking subtly. When the man was far enough away, she said, "Holy effing cow."

"What the hell was that, Tanny?" said Twyla. Tanis looked at her.

"I don't know. Noah, was he hitting on me?"

Noah breathed in deeply. "I don't know. Couldn't tell."

"Hey guys, why don't we celebrate what just happened here?" said Doug, leaning in and holding his bottle above the table. "Let's not get hung up on what didn't happen. No conspiracy theories here, okay?"

Tanis looked at him for a moment, then nodded. "Yeah. Good call." Then she put her glass in. The rest joined her and they all clinked glass together.

4

On the drive home, Noah was silent. Tanis wasn't saying much either. She had tried starting conversation a couple of times, but Noah's short non-responses weren't making it easy, so she stopped. And now they rode in silence. The street lights swept through the car lighting up their faces in an unsteady rhythm. Noah was rethinking the awkward conversation the magazine writer had brought about, and wondering why they weren't all excited. He wondered if that was normal: for a man to approach a table for the purpose he had proposed, and *not* shake hands with every man or woman at the table. Was that normal? Or rather, was it weird? Obviously, a magazine writer would have no interest in any of her friends. So maybe he just didn't want to waste anybody's time. Put forth no false pretenses. No need to lead anyone on. What's the point of introductions if you have no interest in the acquaintance? It made sense on a rational level, but Noah couldn't get it to wash. It wasn't that it had seemed rude, at all. It had seemed perfectly business-like. But that long stare the man had given Tanis had changed everything. It was why he was questioning the whole encounter right now instead of talking to Tanis. And she was feeling it.

"I'm sorry if you're upset with me," she said, almost as if reading his mind.

"Why would I be upset with you?" he responded, looking over at her in the darkness of the car interior. The streetlight whipped through and he saw her face.

"Well, you sure seem like it. I don't know what I did, but you seem distant."

"I'm sitting here thinking about what happened," he finally said. "It's not you. It's that fucking writer. He made that shit so awkward."

"Yeah," Tanis agreed. She reached over and put her hand atop Noah's on the knob of the stick shift. "But it's really not my fault is it?"

"Of course not, babe," Noah said. "It just got me to thinking. Other men are going to be interested in you. They're going to hit on you. They'll be at every show. You could literally walk out and pick out almost any dude in the crowd. And guaranteed, he will want you."

Tanis was shaking her head. She put her hand up to her mouth, covering it with the side of her finger. "Noah, do you know how crazy that sounds?"

"It's not, Tan. Seriously. I'm not wrong."

She shook her head harder. "No. I'm not arguing that. But for you to get upset about it, or think it means anything is just a little beneath you."

"You think?" he said. "You know, if this ever gets 'routine' between us – if we ever lose that 'newness' – then there will always be a hundred guys waiting there to bring back that excitement."

"Noah, I don't want those other guys. I don't look at every man as a sex object. Even if he's good looking. None of that matters. What matters is what we have. You approached me and had something to say. We had great conversation from the beginning. I fell in love with that. Don't you see that?"

Noah did see it. But he still had an ounce of worry in him. What about all the shows he couldn't make it to? What if the band did get picked up, and they started playing a national stage? Stages all over the country? The world? She could then have any man in the world. "If you get your pick, you'll surely find the one you're with isn't quite the best one you could have."

"Noah, stop!" she said, raising her voice. "You're upsetting me now. That's not how it works. Number one, I don't talk to every guy at every show. And I don't talk to them long enough for anything to happen."

"Ah," he said, holding a finger up, "so you're saying that if they had a little more time to spend, they could effectively make something happen."

"Oh my God! I'm not doing this. I can't, Noah," she said. She turned to look out the passenger window. Noah turned onto his road. There were no streetlights on this road, so the car returned to full darkness. "You're really hurting me right now, Noah."

"Sorry. I'm just telling you how I feel, Tan."

"Well I wish you would trust me a little. You realize for something to happen, it would have to come from both directions, right?"

"What the hell does that mean?"

"It means someone would have to hit on me, wanting me, and I would have to want it to happen, too. It's a two-way street, is what I mean."

As they pulled into his driveway, she unbuckled her seat belt. She popped the door open before he even came to a stop. And as he pulled the brake handle and turned off the key, Tanis was climbing up into her own Jeep. All Noah could do was sit and stare at her as she started it, then turned to look at him, her face almost invisible, lit only dimly by the instrument cluster two feet in front of her. She shook her head. Then she was backing out of the driveway.

Noah wasn't scared. He wasn't even angry. What he felt was… numb. Numb was the best word he could think of. He would be sleeping alone tonight. Alone for the first night in months. And all he could feel was *nothing*. He was sure that by four o'clock, his eyes – if they had been able to close to begin with – would pop open and he would see with great clarity what a fool he had been. But right now, thinking back about the whole exchange, he didn't see why she had even left. Was his reasoning not legitimate? Whether or not she ever did take interest in a fan, or a magazine writer for that matter, the fact was, it *could* happen. Right? He was just bringing that topic to light. Just thinking out loud. He had not meant to start a fight. Perhaps it was just that Noah was finally realizing how precious a thing she was to him. Something worth treasuring. Worth reveling in. And like any jewel, any valuable thing, it begged consideration. That's all he had been doing: considering. *What if?* That's all it was. A small series of what-ifs that could possibly present themselves down the road. And all he had meant to do was think about how he would handle them when they happened. His best bet might have been not to voice them to her, but he was trying to maintain that transparency they had developed. To not keep anything from her. He was, simply put, baring his heart to her. Noah worried that she would meet someone at a show sometime down the road. Someone who was better looking. Had a better pickup line. Had more to offer. Had something better to say. Whatever the case, if she met that someone and there was a spark – just the *hint* of a spark, it could fire. And if that happened she could realize that Noah wasn't that great after all. Or maybe not that he wasn't that great, but that this newcomer was just a little greater. A little better. A little nicer. Whatever. Was that not a possibility that at least deserved some consideration? It didn't sound dumb to him.

Noah sat in the Jeep for a long time, just listening to the rain patter on the sail cloth of the soft top. The rain had not stopped in almost twenty-four hours now, and showed no signs of slowing. What finally got him to pop his own door open and brave the rainy walk to the house was his damned bladder. He had not used the men's room at the club, and had to think to remember the last time he had gone. Either way, he had to go now, and that ruined his solace. He climbed out of the Jeep and walked – in no real hurry – the sidewalk to the front door. He let himself in and walked straight across the carpet to the bar to pour himself another glass of whiskey. Then he made his way to the bathroom to relieve the pressure.

5

Noah woke with a start. His bedside lamp was on. He didn't remember turning it on before he went to bed. But then, he didn't remember anything about coming to bed. What he did remember was standing in his living room, cranking up his stereo and spinning Chicago's Greatest Hits on the turntable. He had slung back at least three short glasses of bourbon to that record. He thought there might have been another one after that as well. Maybe Gerry Rafferty. It was all speculation at this point. As of now, the sunlight was too blue – too weak – to represent true sleeping-in. *Must be six o'clock.* As of now, all he truly knew was that his head was a wreck and the far side of his bed was still made. He flung his arm across to the cold side of the bed and made a half-armed snow angel with it, as if to confirm its true state of emptiness. That was another thing he had no trouble remembering. Tanis had not come to bed with him. He had not stood in the living room dancing toe-to-toe with her while he spun records, glasses hanging from their left hands, occasionally kissing while they shifted their weight from foot to foot, enjoying the music. And the company. He remembered that very clearly.

He slapped his hand over his eyes. "God. What the hell have I done?"

When he finally managed the strength to spin his legs off the edge of the bed and sit up, the headache came plowing in full strength. Another morning after. All too common these days. He stood up and wandered into the bathroom, started the shower and leaned against the basin. Noah instinctively knew he would be spending the day thinking about what he had done wrong last night. He couldn't think about it at the moment, though. He swallowed four aspirin tablets and tossed back a mouthful of mouthwash, then stepped into the shower to soak away the pain.

At some point during the wee hours of the night, it had finally stopped raining. Noah sat at the table in his nook, drinking coffee and staring out at the back yard. Doug had spent the night with Alice, so Noah had the place to himself this morning. Since Alice hadn't made the show last night, Doug had headed straight there to get some time in with her before she had to work today. Her shift would start at eight, so Doug would likely be walking through the door any minute. When he pulled into the driveway and saw that Mally wasn't there, he would naturally be inclined to ask Noah where Tanis was.

Noah considered what his answer might be. What *should* his answer be? He didn't really know how to answer that. Tanis had not texted him when she got home last night. No further thoughts on the argument. No last words. No by-the-ways. Just radio silence. What did that mean? Did that mean she had broken up with him? Noah didn't think that was the answer. Though it could get there pretty quickly if he didn't figure out how to recover it, he reckoned. His mind went back to that last thought for a moment. Why *hadn't* she texted him? She must have been truly upset with him. For good measure, he picked up his phone and unlocked it, looking for the umpteenth time to see if there were any missed calls. Sure enough, there was a text he had somehow missed. His heart skipped a beat with fear and excitement as he opened the text.

It was Doug. *Hey man, heading home. If you and Tanis are on the couch you might want to cover up.* He sighed and dropped the phone on the table. It had not been the text he was hoping for, but he did feel relieved all the same. It could have been a breakup text. Though he knew Tanis to have more class than to end a relationship over SMS, he was on edge right now. Out in the edge of some dark, lonely galaxy she had created, no stars in sight. A place where physics was a myth. Anything was possible.

He heard the key turning in the front door. *Here we go.* Noah stood up and dragged back into the kitchen to refill his coffee mug. His headache had taken a back burner. It was by no means gone. It sat on the edge of his thoughts, reminding him that it could pop back in at any time, if it were so inclined. And it would do him well to remember that. *Oh, Evan Williams, how you mock me.*

Doug came into the kitchen, dropping his keys in the bowl on the bar. "What's up man?" he said. Then he frowned. "Damn, dude, you look like shit. Late night?"

Noah shrugged. "I guess you could say that. Before you ask, we had an argument. She left before she even came in. I don't want to talk about it yet. Just give me a bit."

Doug raised his chin, then slowly dropped it, pursing his lips. "All yours, brother." He put his elbows on the bar and ran his fingers through his growing stubble. "Got anymore of that breakfast fuel, chief?"

Noah slipped another mug off a hook and filled it for him. Slid it across the bar. "How's the small Frye?" he asked.

"Small Frye is good as ever. She said to tell you sorry she missed the show last night." Doug frowned. Tilted his head. "Well, she said, 'tell *them* sorry'. So perhaps she meant Tanis. Either way, she's good. Working all day on a shitty Saturday when we should all be in bed."

"Amen, brother, preach that shit," said Noah. "Well, it was a killer performance last night."

Doug nodded. "Yeah, man. And this writer… How cool is that?"

Noah looked up and made eyes with his friend. Then he sighed. "Did you see the awkward stare?"

Doug nodded again. "Yeah. We all did. Guess that's what this is about."

Noah nodded this time. "So tell me if I was wrong, bringing it up. The thought that she'll have loads of dudes looking at her. Flirting with her, hitting on her, trying to score with her – everywhere she ever goes. Am I wrong to bring up that fact? Like that it could put us in danger? I mean, maybe it won't. She says she's in love with me. I'm special. But I mean, like the possibility of it. Being exposed to it all the time, if it ever gets routine between us, won't that allow a spark to fire? Am I wrong for asking that shit, Rex?"

Doug didn't hesitate. "Yes."

Noah stared at him for a long moment. Then made a face. "Well?"

"Well, nothing, bro. You want to hear it?"

"Yes. Yes, Doug, of course I do."

"Okay," he said, making a *here-we-go* face. "You asked for it. You need to fuck off with that shit. If she said she's in love with you, then you need to latch onto that with every part of you. If you love her too, that is."

"Of course I do. She's the best thing ever happened to me, man."

Doug held out a hand over the bar, as if offering something. "Well, there you go. So forget that *if it gets routine* shit. You may be the only one who even thinks about that. You're certainly the only guy I've ever known who talks about it." Noah tried to say something but Doug looked away and held his hand up. Noah shut up. "You asked for it. Let me finish."

He swallowed a gulp of coffee, then continued. "You're the only one who talks about wanting shit to keep that new car smell. It doesn't, bro. Shit gets old. It gets routine. Relationships get boring. Don't you think I've gone through that shit with Alice? She's four-foot-eleven. Ninety-five pounds. She has no titties. Don't you think I've looked at other women over the years? Wondered what it would be like to upgrade? To move on? It isn't 'new' anymore," he said, making the quotes with his fingers. "But that's what's rich, man. That's when it turns from puppy love to adult love. To real love. True love. You never give your relationships that chance, Noah!"

Noah was staring at his friend, speechless. In concept, all of this seemed obvious. But somehow in practice, he apparently didn't know it. Or wasn't living like he did.

"Dude, the fun part of love is not the feel of new skin, is all I'm saying. When you know every little sound and movement and pattern of the one you love, that's when it gets real. Then you have a partner. You should give that a chance, bro."

Noah breathed in deeply. Took a sip of his coffee and realized it was cold. He splashed it into the sink and dropped the mug behind it. "She left, man. I might have ruined it."

"Nah, man. No way. She's not going to walk away that easily. She's above that. But you do need to reach out. You need to tell her you were freaking out. Fix this."

Noah was nodding unconsciously. He looked out the back window. A deer stood at the edge of the treeline, appearing to stare right back at him. He scoffed. Doug looked over and saw it too. He smirked as if to say, 'there she is, man. Go get her.'

"All right man, I've gotta hop in the shower," Doug said after a time of silence. "I'm going to help Troy out at the shop today."

"Yeah? What's he got going on?"

"Fuckin' Red Sox pitcher just bought a Jeep. Wants the works. He dropped like sixty grand on upgrades. Eight-inch lift, forty-one-inch tires. The fuckin' works, bro."

"Slick," said Noah.

When Doug went to leave, he called Noah out to join him on the driveway. "You gotta see this shit, man." Noah followed him out onto the wet concrete in his house slippers and bathrobe. When they got to the Cherokee, Doug didn't even have to tell him what he was looking for. There was a huge dent in the right front quarter-panel. It looked like someone had tossed a bowling ball at it.

"Where the hell did that come from?" Noah asked, pressing his fingertips against the curve of the wound.

"No idea. It was like that this morning when I went out to the Jeep. Well, it could have been like that at the Sally last night. I don't know. But it definitely wasn't like that yesterday morning."

"Man, that shit sucks. Can Troy pop it out?"

"The other reason I'm going into the shop today," said Doug, pointing his key at Noah. He got in and pulled the squeaky door closed and Noah turned back for the house.

As he closed the door, threw the bolt, he bent down to pick up a wet leaf on the tile of entry hall floor that had hitched a ride in on his slipper. He pulled the door back open to throw it out and nearly jumped out of his skin when he saw someone standing on his porch about to knock. It was Trixie.

"Holy fuck," he said, grabbing his chest, the leaf all but forgotten. "You scared the life out of me. What are you doing here, Trix?"

She stood staring at him, cheeks red from the cold and tears in her eyes. "Can I come in, please?" she pleaded. Noah pulled the door open and stuck his head out, looking around. How had she gotten here? She could have been parked in his driveway and he wouldn't be able to see the car from here. But he knew he had not been in the house long enough for Doug to have gotten away without having seen Trixie. And yet, here Noah stood, alone, facing the girl. No bro-code here. He was on his own.

He sighed and pulled the door open. Trixie stepped inside and stomped on the rug, then unzipped her coat. "Brrr! So cold out there."

"Yeah. I know. That's why I'm inside. What are you doing here, Trixie?"

"Wow, Noey, I haven't seen you in weeks, and this is the welcome I get?" she said, dropping the coat off her shoulder and slinging it up onto an empty coat hook on the wall.

"Welcome? I'm not sure what you're doing here. This isn't a routine stop for you. Why would you be welcome here?" Noah said. He was losing patience.

"Come here, darlin'," she said, and raised her arms as if she wanted a hug. He didn't step forward. She closed the gap and wrapped her arms around him, standing on tip-toes. His arms were crossed, which made the hug awkward. He was okay with that. Not in the mood for her usual bullshit this morning.

"What can I do for you?" he said, still wrapped in her arms.

She looked up at him, close tolerance. Then she stood up taller and kissed him on his lips. Noah turned his head away, so she finally got the hint and backed away.

"Wow. Okay. Well, it's good to see you, too, Noah."

He turned and went into the living room, leaving his slippers on the tile. Without saying anything to Trixie, she took her rain boots off and left them next to his slippers. He dropped onto the sofa and looked back at her expectantly. The normal visitor would take a seat on the opposing couch so she could have intellectual discourse with eye contact. Not Trixie. She sat right next to him, feet curled up behind her on the couch, and immediately set about fingering his hair back from his temple.

"I haven't seen you since Joy died, Noah. I wanted to come give my regards."

"Trixie," he said, taking her wrist with his hand and turning to face her, "I don't need your regards. I'm fine. That's history. I'm dealing with it. Thank you."

She came up onto her knees, making her a good foot taller than him in his current posture. She gently excised her wrist from his grasp, and while he was still trying to figure out what she was doing, she took his cheeks in her hands. Trixie was staring at him through wide eyes, shaking her head. "Noah."

He shook his own head. "Huh?"

Then she swung her leg over him and straddled him coming to rest on his lap. Before he could object, she was kissing him, and grinding back and forth on his pelvis. It felt too good for him to immediately stop her. He realized peripherally that she was wearing some sort of yoga pant, so he could feel every pronounced curve of her through his boxers. She was quick with her will, and before he knew it, he was completely at attention.

Noah grunted and grabbed her by her upper arms, swinging her off of him. "What the fuck is wrong with you, Trixie?" he shouted, standing up.

She stared back at him with large puppy-dog eyes as if she were completely innocent. He could see her nipples poking through the thin fabric of her shirt and realized she was not wearing a bra. "What, Noah?"

"What the hell is your deal?"

"Nothing, Noah! Obviously, nothing is wrong!" she pleaded, coming up onto her knees again. Her hands were on her knees as she stared up at him.

"What the hell does that mean?" he said, shaking his head, a face full of frown.

"Well, look at yourself, Nono," she said, pointing her hand at his midsection. He looked down and realized he was fully erect, pitching a tent in his boxers, as it were.

And when he looked back up, she had whipped her shirt off. She was now pinching her nipples as she stared at him seductively. She raised up on her knees and took his hand. And that's when the front door opened.

6

It wasn't Doug returning for a forgotten wallet. It wasn't Alice or Lennie or Troy, coming to check up on him. Of course, it wasn't. And though Tanis wasn't the last person in the world Noah would have thought would come walking through his front door right at that inopportune moment, she wasn't at the top of the list. But whether or not she made the top or the bottom of any such list, it certainly was she who now stood at the threshold between the living room and the hall, staring wide-eyed at the display going on at the sofa.

"Oh, hi, Tanis," Trixie said. She still had hold of Noah's hand. "We were just getting started."

Noah looked down at her, shaking his head. But all the evidence she needed was below his belt line. He looked up at Tanis, face awash in desperation and exhaustion.

"I guess this isn't what I think it is, Noah?"

He was shaking his head. The full weight of loss and horror settled in on his soul as what had just happened began to truly sink in. What could he say? No? Well, it was worth the shot, at least.

"No. Of course not. But I understand there's no way I could ever get you to believe me now," he said.

Tanis shook her head this time. Then she turned on her heel and left.

"What the fuck is wrong with you, Trixie? Like, seriously. What the hell is with you?"

"What do you mean, Noah?" she said, leaning in and putting the hand she still held against her chest. "She's gone. Might as well fuck me now."

Noah was staring at the front door, shaking his head. The total weight of it all had now settled in on him. "What a wreck. What a huge fucking wreck," he said. Then he sighed and looked back down at Trixie. She was grinding on the couch as if he were beneath her. He had completely forgotten about his hand, which she was rubbing all over her breasts. In a normal universe, this wouldn't have lasted very long before he was on top of her. But here, he had no feeling for it. He noticed his male response had dissipated, as well. She had ruined him completely. Trixie was still staring up at him with her large brown eyes, made bigger by the situation, like an anime character.

He stepped forward. Took her head in his hands, then leaned down and put his lips right next to hers. Only a few molecules'-worth of air stood between them. She closed her eyes. "Trixie," he whispered. "Get the fuck out of my house."

As Noah stood back up, he grabbed her shirt and tossed it at her, hitting her in the face with it. Then he turned and went into his bedroom, slamming the door.

CHAPTER EIGHT
crescendo

From *WhiskeyNeat* Magazine

More than Just a Pretty Sound
by Codi Cohl

I have never seen One Last Orbit with human eyes. In my bio, I mention the fact that I have bionic eyes. Why would I do this? Because I'm seeking attention? Because I'm looking for sympathy? Well, as much as I would love to say, 'Of course not,' I realize you don't know me. At least not yet. So I can't say 'of course' anything. Not with any real power. We have to establish a trust here. You have to get to know me before you can respect or trust what I say to be true. Well, since I can't say 'Of course not,' just know that's what I'm thinking as I say a loud and resounding, 'No. Not at all.'

I mention in my bio that I have bionic eyes as part of that process of gaining your trust. I think the trust I'm seeking from you – much like the one you're seeking from me – will come from context. An understanding of who I am, what I'm after, and why I'm even doing this. Reviewing bands. In short, why should you take the word of a girl who can't even see the band she's writing about? Well, let's try this: because the best thing about bands is their sound. Right? Is not that still true?

I have bionic eyes. I can still see. I was not born blind. I had perfect vision up until my early twenties. Then began the quick and degenerative process that took my sight completely. I fell lucky into an experimental project where I was able to receive these implants and try to make some new sense of the world. They say a child born blind who knows by feel the difference between an apple and a pineapple upon receiving bionic implants, can not – by vision alone – then tell you the difference. Look it up. It's a real thing. And there is much written about it. This article is not about that. But nor is it about me. I just wanted to establish that context with you so that you'll know I can see, but differently than you. And getting used to this new definition of vision is a trial on its own. Sometimes I'd rather not see at all. But I will tell you one thing: it has made me appreciate my ears more than ever.

So while I have never seen One Last Orbit with human eyes – only robotic ones – I have heard them. And some might say my appreciation for this hearing is more profound than someone who has all five of his or her senses. My hearing has certainly improved. I can hear nuances I couldn't before. I can hear things I only used to see. I don't expect you to understand that. Not completely. Much less, believe it. But since this is my inaugural column here with *WhiskeyNeat* – or anywhere, for that matter – I feel like I owe you a broader explanation of why I'm qualified to review this band than would someone else who is equally qualified for the job.

I was at the *WhiskeyNeat* offices for my job interview when Tanis Ransom entered the building. I, of course, had no idea she had entered. I was in someone's office, answering questions about why I should get the chance to write to you, dear readers. But my best friend, a mentor, really, a remarkable woman named Rebecca, was in the lobby. So when Tanis Ransom came breezing in through the door, Rebecca stood up. She was the only one in the lobby, so making a scene was not a concern. My friend recognized Tanis instantly, and might have acted a little bit like a schoolgirl, as most people do these days. But instead of ignoring her, Tanis made a point of stopping down and talking to Rebecca. She actually sat on the couch in the waiting room and talked to her like an old friend. She then took a selfie with Rebecca and posted it to her own Instagram profile. You talk about a life-changing encounter? This is one of the things that makes Tanis a superstar. She walks among humans, but brings them up to godlike status with her during these brief encounters.

Well, Tanis was there for a photo shoot with the magazine. Not for this column, in case you were wondering. When she finished speaking with my friend, she came into the back offices, and I got the chance to meet her, as I was just finishing up. Tanis invited Rebecca and I to sit in on the shoot. We even got to take some pictures with her. They're on my friend's fridge door. (They didn't make it into the magazine, for obvious reasons. No one wants to see

Rebecca and me.) For someone who writes every song about being lost in orbit, or on a mission to another galaxy, Tanis Ransom is one of the most down-to-earth human beings I've ever met. I think most people who have met her would say the same thing.

When I turned this column in for review, I had initially not written anything biographical – because, again, no one wants to see me. You just want to use me as a vehicle for the delivery of the good stuff on the good people right to your greedy little eyes. And I'm okay with that. I'm good at it. But my editor tossed it back on my desk and said, 'Tell 'em who you are.' (Don't you like how I made it into a printed paper that I handed him?) So now that you know a little about who I am, and why I'm doing this – or why I think I am qualified to do this – let me tell you about what you came here to read.

I sat down with Tanis in her Manhattan apartment. This was several months after I had met her at the *Neat* offices. She was more than a good host. My friend Rebecca, who is normally available to escort me to such things, was unavailable. She has a real job, you see. So Tanis had her friend Carrie personally escort me from the curb to the apartment, which, without a guide, would be a confusing mess of mazes and elevators. Apparently a lot of celebrities live in this high-rise, so they don't make it easy to navigate.

As I sat on her sofa, she told me exactly what I was looking at. "I'm wearing a pair of blue jeans and a Porcupine Tree t-shirt," she said. "My hair is down today. I spent literally no time on it." She laughed. I laughed with her. From what I hear, Tanis spends quite a bit of time making her purple-streaked hair look like she doesn't spend any time on it. That is a talent I never learned. I can tell she is sipping from her glass frequently. She offered me the same – a bourbon on the rocks – when I entered. I declined. I'm a vodka girl.

On the heels of her recent breakup with her boyfriend from Bar Harbor, I asked her how she was holding up.

She took a sip, tinkling the ice in her glass, then sighed. "You know, it sucks. I'm not gonna lie."

It's very bright in here. I can tell, because natural sunlight at this brightness level sets my eyes to serious exhaustion. Everything looks blue and electrified. I have to wear sunglasses.

"We were a spark in the darkness. A shooting star on a night with no clouds," says Tanis. "A total one-in-a-million thing."

And though I can't make her out very well in this light – she would only be an amalgamation of boxes and pixels if I could make her out – I imagine her sitting with her elbow on her knee – that foot bouncing as she stares at the clock and thinks of what to say to me.

"I thought we were perfect," she says.

I don't know what to say to this. I just listen. Finally, she continues. I can hear the tears in her eyes. They haven't yet made it to her voice, but I can tell they're close.

"Anyway, I loved him very much. I thought it would be forever. Naive as all hell, right?" she says. I don't laugh with her. I think it improper. Because I know she doesn't want to laugh. She wouldn't be laughing about this if she had her way. She finally adds, "But all good things must end, I suppose."

"Why am I here, Tanis?" I ask. "Is this what you want me to write about?" I imagine her nodding. Then she confirms it by saying so much.

"I'm nodding. Sorry. Trying to remind myself to speak instead of using body language," she says. "Yes. You can hear my music on the streaming services. You can read all about me on the internet. But I want people to know who I really am."

But why is this important? Why now? What's changed? I mean, aside from the glaringly obvious. She just ended a very serious relationship with a man she thought was her soul-mate. But was this it? Is there some public service announcement to be made here? *Don't treat your woman like this, men!* Or was she just being down-to-earth? Maybe it's not my place to ask. But I do anyway.

"Why now, Tanis? Is it because of *him*?" I ask.

"No. No, no, no," she says. "I'm just so tired of nothing changing. We've become a sort of static society. We all do the same things and we don't see ourselves getting deeper and deeper into our ruts. We expect change, but we expect someone else to perform that change. To be that catalyst. To effect that change."

This seems to be completely off-topic from where we started, but I press on. "What changed for you, if not the loss of your boyfriend?"

"I realized that people will always take what's easiest to get. If there are options, they will always take the easier one. And that's what's changed. I don't think it used to be like that. I think we used to want to work for the things we loved."

I nod here. I feel like she has more to say. She does.

"Listen, I'm not – I guess I'm not saying all men are like that. But there are some of them who just get stuck going after that perfect thing. And that was his story. I think. You know? He was just chasing comets."

1

Troy and Doug were down in the ditch, hands on the truck. Doug was in the snowy mud on his back, trying to get the winch cable up under the chassis to a good hitching point, but the truck was too buried in the soft earth. Noah, meanwhile, stood up on the cracked and eroded edge of the pavement next to Twyla, waiting for his next direction. His rig stood idling behind him. He had recently had the winch put in and was excited to finally get to use it. The journal he kept in his glove box of all the pulls he had made was getting close to the end. This had been a busy winter.

Twyla was rubbing her mitten-laden hands together, blowing on them. Noah looked over at her, shaking his head. "Fuckin' people."

She smiled her agreement at him. An eager, toothy smile. She shook her head and said, "Hey, it keeps you in business, right?"

Noah made a face and shrugged. "I guess when you put it that way."

"Hey, if we got world peace, the entire military would be out of work!"

"Okay, I think the metaphor is a little extreme. But your point," Noah said, holding up a fist for her to knock. She did. He could see the giant sharp-edged stone trying to poke through the purple fabric of the mitten she wore. There was no glove going to cover up that rock completely. Troy had spent a new Jeep on the ring. Noah was happy for them. Twyla was the down-to-earth version of her sister, who spent her life practicing being down to earth. Noah understood this was no dichotomy. It was no fraud either. Tanis didn't fake anything. But being grounded as a celebrity was different than it was for the rest of us. Being grounded as a superstar was stopping to let people take selfies with you. Stopping and actually signing the little girl's cast or the boy's magazine cover instead of just walking by. Grounded for Noah was putting the money in his savings instead of blowing it on records. He had spent almost two thousand dollars on records this year already. And it was April.

"So why can't his truck get out, but Troy's can?" Twyla asked after a considerable moment. She was looking at Troy's Jeep, which was parked behind the truck down in the ditch.

"Lots of reasons," Noah said. "Troy lets a lot of the air out of his tires. That puts more of the rubber in touch with the ground. Add to that his Jeep doesn't weigh as much as the F250. Then add to that the fact that Jeeps have a lot more torque in the gears, and the fact that it's a four-wheel-drive, and you've got a vehicle that can just climb right out of just about anything."

"So why can't he just push him then?" she asked, still rubbing her mittens together.

"It would just push the truck deeper into the mud. I'm above up here. Upward angle. Raises the bumper toward the sky. Pulls him out."

"What if the rope snaps?" Twyla said, looking down at the synthetic cable, which did indeed look more like rope than it did cable.

"It just drops. No snap-back. That's the advantage of synthetic cables," Noah said.

"You're so smart, Noah. It's so neat talking to you. I learn so much. I can see…" she started, meeting his eyes sharply. She stopped and swallowed, but it was already out there. He knew what she was going to say. Thankfully, these slips were rare for her. She knew the story. At least Tanis's side of it. He had not found a reason to tell his side of the story. What was the point, anyway? It wouldn't change anything. It was easier just to let people go on thinking he had cheated. There was literally nothing he could do to change people's perception on that. He didn't think even Troy and Doug believed him that he had not invited Trixie to his house that morning.

"Thanks, Twy," he said, making a face that showed his disappointment.

Suddenly, she turned and wrapped her arms around him, burying her face against his chest. "Well, I'm glad

I have you as a friend," she said. It was a bitter-sweet friendship. She was nothing like her sister, but it was hard not to think of Tanis every time he saw her.

"Me too, Twyla," was all he could say.

After the pull, they sat at a booth in the back of the Denny's, trying to warm up over bad coffee and worse service. Weather notwithstanding, people were somehow always able to get out for breakfast. Twyla had ordered a huge stack of pancakes, and was spreading syrup over them with her mittened hand. Troy had his elbows on the table, talking a hundred miles a minute, dissecting and reviewing the current political climate. His omelet sat untouched. Doug was tearing into his breakfast sampler. Noah, meanwhile, hadn't even ordered any food. He had barely touched his steaming cup of coffee. Or rather, that's all he had done, was touch it. His hands wrapped round the ceramic for warmth, he had barely taken a sip of it. He was probably better off for that.

Lately he had been feeling a disconnectedness that could only be traced back to one thing. The obvious thing. Trixie had conveniently disappeared after he had told her to leave that morning. He had not seen her since, and was happy for that. She had ruined one relationship for him, and had almost ruined the other. Had Joy found out about Trixie's little stunt at the camping trip, she no doubt would have left him as well. Noah was not full of guilt, nor despair. Despair came from seeing the road ahead and knowing one didn't have enough to get there. He knew that wasn't true. No, it wasn't despair he felt. It was remorse. Remorse for having let that woman into his house that morning. Though his intentions had been pure, there was a part of him that he couldn't deny — that maybe

450

subconsciously he had wanted something to happen. But did that hold water, when at the end of the day, he had not let it happen? Didn't matter now.

But regret was definitely among the strongest of his feelings. Regret for having let her in. Regret for having even known her. At some point, he surely could have been stronger with her. A few less times putting his arm around her at the Sally; a few less twenty-dollar tips; a few less seconds of staring at her nakedness when he had entered that campground bathroom and seen her standing there in nothing but her boots. One of his interactions was that proverbial straw. One of them, undone, and with a time machine, could be used to reverse the changes it had effected. He was sick about the destruction she had caused, but knew he was powerless to change it. Because there was no undoing. There was no time machine. There was only pleading his case. *Yes, she was on my couch with her shirt off. Yes I was holding her hand. Yes, I was hard as steel, and standing tall like a flag pole. But no, I was not about to fuck her!*

There was just no believable recovery statement from a situation like that. So he didn't even bother to try. Just as marvelous to Noah at this moment, was the fact that Troy seemed to be completely oblivious to the pain Noah was in. Or was it his MO to talk like nothing was wrong, in an attempt to overcome the problem by ignoring it? Now there was a strong possibility. Well, not from Troy, it wasn't. With Doug, sure. Doug knew what discretion was. Doug knew when to tap dance and when to stomp. Troy had no such decorum. Troy was a robot. If he was rambling about politics, it was because that's what he was thinking about. Not because he was deflecting for the benefit of his friend. Noah could forgive him that. He loved Troy. Troy was as good as they came. And maybe he should celebrate Troy's ignorance. It might just be what was going to help get Noah through this mess in the long run. In the end, his attention to other things was what drew his attention *away from* Joy's death. And that's what had helped him get through it in a timely fashion. So people like Troy deserved high-fives from the open hand. Not slaps.

Doug, on the other hand, was deliberately being that guy. The one who used discretion, ignoring the obvious biggest elephant in Noah's life. They lived together. If there was an elephant in Noah's living room, there was an elephant in Doug's as well. Realizing this was a strong point to his attitude: the faster he helped Noah get through this shit storm, the faster the zoo would come take back their large unwelcome pachyderm. So Doug just acted like nothing was going on. If Noah brought her up in conversation, which happened frequently in the evenings while engaged with the whiskey, Doug was happy to listen and give whatever advice he could muster up. But if Noah didn't broach the subject himself, it just went away. Noah was thankful for this.

There didn't seem to be much point in talking about Tanis anyway, at least as far as Noah could see. All it did was make him bitter and put him in a dejected state. She was the greatest loss of his life – far greater than Joy had been – and he had allowed the tiny wedges to get hammered in until there was finally a gaping hole that Trixie could just walk into. Which is precisely what she had done. He knew, somewhere off in the distant regions of his thinking mind, that Trixie didn't really want him. Otherwise she would have cried. She would have pleaded. She would have hounded him. Pursued him. Called him. As it stood, she had accomplished her mission and disappeared. That spoke volumes to Noah. It told him that was all she had wanted from the beginning. Shortly, he knew this was all his to own. He wasn't worried what his buddies thought, because they knew the truth about Trixie. Though their knowledge of who she was as a flirt and a dare-devil wouldn't have helped him in the case of trying to win back Tanis. It still came down to the fact that she was in Noah's living room. Half naked. And he was holding her hand. Guilty by association.

It would take years for him to reconcile his own actions with himself – much less to those around him. If Noah didn't forgive himself, he couldn't expect his friends to pat him on the back and tell him it was okay. But now, as he sat here with his hands wrapped round a mug of weak coffee, he had an epiphany: this was perhaps what he had wanted all along. Noah was reminded of his teenage love, that mystical girl who called herself Stella. At only thirteen, his definition of love was that burning he felt in his chest every time he saw her at soccer practices. He and Doug played on the same team as her brother, John. So Noah saw Stella every week, usually twice a week. In his mind she held the place of an angel: a girl who would come to define what Noah looked for in a woman for the next twenty years. And maybe beyond. She was perfect. And it was all because he never even got a chance to kiss her. To hold her hand. Nothing could be ruined because nothing came to pass. Everything that could ever happen with her had only happened in his imagination. They had been boyfriend and girlfriend for about two weeks, but never got a chance to even see each other during that time. But at that age, just discovering that girls were not the enemy, and just coming into puberty, she attached herself to that desire in his mind like no girl had before. And he wanted her with the burning heat of a thousand suns. And just as quickly as she had said yes, agreeing to 'go with him', it was over.

Well, that want never died. Noah recognized the dichotomy of having the cake and eating it. Once you ate it, you no longer had it. He had never had Stella in any way, so she remained in the 'having it' category. She never lost any of her luster. So his want for her never died. An imaginary kiss was perfect. Or it could be. It could be whatever he thought it would be. But when his lips met hers for the first time, it would either cancel out or confirm his imagination. It would become the new standard. A memory rather than a dream. And having never kissed her, it still existed as that dream. Sometimes he just wanted to look her up on OuterCircle and find out where she lived. If she still lived anywhere near the same state, he would – in his imaginary trip – walk right up to her and kiss her long and hard. Then he would apologize and walk away. At least that way he could get on with his goddamn life and not burn for her for the next quarter-century.

If Stella existed in that realm of perfection for a teenage boy, then Tanis was the adult version. He had had her as an adult. He had experienced every bit of Tanis Ransom. From the kissing to the carnal, and everything in between. And the love. True, actual love, based on shared experiences and developing a closeness that came from being together. He knew exactly what he was missing now. *You don't know what you've got until it's gone.* Noah found so much truth in that now. Finally understood it. He had never *had* Stella. So he never really knew what he'd got. But now he did. Tanis was missing from him. So on this level, this adult version of the same desire, he stood at the same precipice. Truly in love when he lost her, now his vision and version of what being in love was would forever be locked in stasis with Tanis Ransom. It would, in short, never grow old. It would remain forever new in his mind. That *new car smell*, as Doug had called it, would remain in perpetuity. He had gotten what he wanted. Noah Wright could celebrate in the fact that he had a perfect love, and it would never age – never grow imperfect. It would never be subjected to the weather of time where it could be flawed and worn out. He had now in the prison of his mind, the one thing every human ever wanted, and it would never go away.

From *WhiskeyNeat* Magazine

More than Just a Pretty Sound (*continued...*)
by Codi Cohl

Hidden somewhere in those words of wisdom is probably a seedling of anguish. I don't purport to know the reason for her bringing up our 'static society', if not for the loss of this true love. I won't dare ask her what was taken; what was that *easiest to get* thing, to which she had referred? We can all speculate. But I think there's another answer: just look at her music. Tanis Ransom pours her soul out in her songs. Every song tells a story, and most of them use planets and quasars, long distances, far-away galaxies as the metaphors. But it's all in there. Every word of every song is telling us something she has gone through. She confirms as much.

WhiskeyNeat: "Do your songs speak for you? If we had a secret decoder ring to your superego, would we find all the answers about who you are? Would we know you on a deeply personal level?"

I can hear the smile in her voice as she responds.

Tanis Ransom: "I think that's a wonderful question, and I'm so glad you asked. Yes. The short answer is yes. I use space and the cosmos because that's how I think of myself. I'm a spacey gal. [laughs] But it's definitely all in there. I've written about so many of my deepest, most personal experiences, and some of my darkest secrets, too. But that decoder ring you mention – thank God it doesn't exist!"

WN: "So you've been doing this for some years now. But you were only recently picked up by a major label. It just happened to happen in the same era as your breakup. Surely, there's nothing to read into that, is there?"

Tanis laughs again.

TR: "No. That one is no conspiracy theory. It was just sheer, dumb coincidence. I had actually taken my boyfriend to the studio one morning as a surprise. We were recording our first album, and I thought he would be interested to see how it happened. You know, in the glass rooms."

Here, she pauses for a bit. I can hear her breathing change. I hear a tissue pulled from the box. I tell her to take her time. I hear her swallow. Tanis is very human. This being my first time to interview a rock goddess, I didn't know what to expect, coming into this room. So not only is it very sobering, it is terrifyingly real. You realize these are people just like us. We each have our own things. I can dance. I can write poetry a little. This

456

woman writes music. And she can sing. She is not so different from you and me. And maybe you can sing, too. But it's that perfect storm of luck, coincidence and knowing when to strike that combines all her little *things* into a soup that gets packaged up and served to the masses. That magic only happens to someone else. Never to us. But sitting here in this room with Tanis Ransom, I realize she is perhaps just as perplexed by it as we all are.

TR: "Anyway, a month later, we had an argument. I left his place. Got back to my own and found a package in the mail. It was several copies of the CD we had recorded. They were mastered. I was so excited that I was ready to go back and mend the fence. I didn't care about who was wrong or right the night before. I just wanted to share it with someone. He had a nice sound system, and he was my man. So I just went straight there. Well, I didn't like what I found."

I am not quite sure how to respond to this. Maybe after years of doing my job I will learn some of the tricks of the trade. I tell her this and she laughs and says I'm the perfect interviewer for this stage in her career. She needs to get used to being interviewed.

The manager for One Last Orbit, Josie Coker, had sent that CD to one of her friends who worked at a radio station in Boston. And here's another of those little recipe components that forms the soup we all love so much. Having a friend who can put his hands on the mixing board and blast your CD through the airwaves to ten million people is quite the boon when you're just getting started. Couple that with a well timed introduction to a certain magazine writer, and you're getting somewhere. Rod Agnew of *Front Row*

Magazine caught one of the last shows they performed on the local circuit. Though he didn't interview the band, he did write a column about them. He printed 6000 words I'm sure most of you have read. I've read it. *I subscribe to the online version, and am able to listen to my articles with special software.*

We all know the story from here. One Last Orbit went from packing the house at a local dive called the Sally West, to suddenly filling theaters and arenas. It happened almost overnight. When that CD hit the airwaves, phone circuits filled up with people calling the station asking who that band was they had just played. People who streamed the Boston radio station called in from all over the world. They demanded more of that smokey voice they had just heard. And, by the way *who was that?*

WN: "Can you tell me a little about that? Were you ready for this jump from obscurity to celebrity?"

TR: "It was a roller coaster, baby. Only it went straight up. We went up so fast I lost my breath. It's amazing how quickly everything has happened."

I agree. It seems like just a few months ago my friends and I were burning out on all the same old stuff on the airwaves. Then suddenly here was this new thing. We heard *Stardust Sunrise*, *Super Little Novas* and *String Theory* and it was very quickly the only thing we wanted to listen to. And the reality is, it *was* just a few months ago. All these things happened in the period of a season.

WN: "Is there anything different about it?"

TR: "Well, yes. Unfortunately, in another of those ridiculous coincidences, Mark, our beloved bassist, had to drop out due to health issues. We have Layne now, which is good, but Mark was with us all through the whole thing, and doesn't get to participate in the reward. It's like going to a casino and spending a week in front of a slot. Then you finally walk away, and someone walks up right behind you and puts a quarter in, and wins the jackpot. [laughs]

"We all love Layne though. He's incredibly humble about the whole thing. He doesn't believe he belongs there in place of Mark, but rather as a fill-in. He's not trying to take credit for all the hard work Mark put into the band. But it's all good. We wish the best for Mark and his family."

As do we, Tanis. Mark Watkins is an amazing musician and a genuinely good person. The kind of guy who would run into a burning building to save *someone else's* kids. In fact, that's what he used to do, as a fireman. We here at *WhiskeyNeat* pray for his recovery and good health.

WN: "So what's on the horizon for One Last Orbit? Should we be looking for a world tour?"

TR: "I wouldn't turn that down! But I think that might be putting the cart before the horse. We're going to tour the upper east for a bit while the managers work on getting things set up for the national tour, probably next summer. For now, we're back in the studio recording a full album. It's called *A Walk Through the Stars* and should be available by early next year."

I will be eagerly awaiting its release. "Anything else you would like to say? The floor is all yours," I say.

Tanis takes her time here. I hear her adjusting. Maybe crossing her legs. Chewing on her lip. She might be looking out the window as she puts words together in her mind. Then she answers, "Always test the tight wire before you cross it. You never know when you're gonna get stuck out there, and you might have to get out of your comfort zone to return to the world."

One Last Orbit, *the band.*

The music of One Last Orbit is now a real and tangible thing. You can find their albums wherever you stream music. As of this printing, their first two albums are available: *A Walk Through the Stars*, and *Makeshift Planet*.

I hope you will go give them a listen. The lyrics you read Tanis singing from the stage and in the iso booth in this book are now real songs.

To learn more about the band, you can visit their website at:

onelastorbitband.com

They also have an Instagram account where you can find pictures and videos of Tanis and the band.

@onelastorbit

AUTHOR'S NOTE

May 29, 2022

My sister Lisa sneaked me into my first real concert just a couple of days after I turned sixteen. I remember the date. It was December 5, 1989. She had worked at a local music shop in Denton Texas, right on Fry Street, selling records and CDs to the eclectic college crowd. This also put her in touch with a lot of the local talent. Ten Hands was one of those bands. She got me a CD and I just about burned a hole through it with the laser of my CD player. I kept that disc on repeat for months, I swear. I knew every word and every beat to every song. So when she surprised me that night by saying she was taking me to see Ten Hands live, I was on top of the world. I had been to many concerts before. But they weren't bands I pursued. And being only fifteen, I had only just *begun* to pursue bands at all.

The venue was a little hole-in-the-wall called *The Library*, and it was sandwiched between two other buildings. You had to go between these two buildings in this narrow walkway, much like something out of a horror movie, to get to the nondescript metal door that simply read LIBRARY on it. But inside it was so much more than that. I stood with my knees against that stage, less than two feet away from J Paul Slavens and the boys, who rocked my world for the next two hours.

Being a drummer myself, I kept my eyes mostly on Earl Harvin, the extraordinary percussionist who taught me so much. After the show, he signed a beer ad card and gave me a drumstick. I still have that drumstick today. He made me want to be a better drummer. I *am* a better drummer because of him. But not because I heard him on the album. It was because I saw him play live. Seeing someone performing his craft is an element that cannot be overstated in its importance to a music lover.

What Lisa didn't realize, and perhaps she did and I just don't know it, was that she was laying a foundation for how I would consume music for the rest of my life. Just this month, I attended a Pineapple Thief concert where I was leaning against the pit rail, twenty feet from Gavin Harrison, arguably one of the world's best drummers. And the whole night, I couldn't help but think of how I had come full circle. I couldn't stop thinking about how it had all started for me.

I grew up in music. My dad was in the business. He was a national sales manager for a record distribution company during the last twenty or so years of his career. He retired at fifty-five with seven or eight gold and platinum records on his wall. Needless to say, exposed is an understatement. I was *involved* like a fireman at a four-alarmer. My dad would bring home 45s and make mix-tapes for me before we had CDs. He would bring home CDs when they came out. Of course, there was the gigantic collection of LPs as well. I helped him close down Sound Warehouse stores and got to keep the posters and promo pinups. I had music everywhere I turned. And of course, he had a hi-fi in the den that we would listen to every Saturday night, my sister and I roller skating back and forth on the unfinished concrete floor. My earliest memories of music come from that room, before there was carpet in it. And as I grew up, my dad upgraded his hi-fi to the newer tech and passed down the still completely viable tube amps and turntables I had grown up listening to. I had a system in my room that would rival most adults' audiophile systems. And permission to turn it up. I installed speakers under the eave of the back patio so we could listen to music while we swam. I had a good stereo in my first truck. He would take us to concerts for artists whose records he sold, and we would sit on the side of the stage during the performance. It was insane.

I have tried to pass that down to my children as well. Not only the exposure to music, but the blessing of having a system on which to play it, and the permission to turn it up. My only rule has always been to make it sound good. I would rather hear them blasting music through their own hi-fi audio system, rattling windows and vibrating the floor, than to hear a tinny phone speaker squealing out music. It was meant to be played on matched speakers. It was meant to be enjoyed loud.

While I attended these shows and have lifelong memories of watching Carman and Amy Grant from the side of the stage, and getting to sit in their dressing rooms while they cooled down after a show, none of them counted to me as my first concert. But nor was the Tiffany show I bought a ticket to. I saw her play live at the Six Flags Music Mill Amphitheater when I was thirteen. And while I would have married her on the spot, it was not a life-changing experience. Even though New Kids on the Block opened up for her.

It was the show Lisa took me to that really sealed the deal for me. Because I loved those guys. True, I loved Tiffany's music, too. Not just her Amazon body and gorgeous freckled face. But let's be serious here, friends. Tiffany didn't sing anything that's gonna stick with you. Ten Hands did. I still spin that CD occasionally. And Lisa and I sing along to it. We dance in my music room to it. We *dance*. In our forties, this music is still good enough and sentimental enough to us that it makes us want to *dance*. That is something worth pursuing.

So being a musician myself – I play the piano, the drums, the guitar and I sing – I wanted to write about what it's like to be fully engaged to the music. But not from a musician's point of view. As you saw, Noah wasn't musically inclined at all. But he knew all about it. He consumed it in every way he could, every chance he got. During depressive states, standing in his den, too drunk to stand straight; in the parking lot waiting for his Jeep to warm up; in the middle of a crowd at a concert; sitting on the couch with his little sister, Lennie… We don't hear much about his other sister, Lisa. And my sister Lisa is older than me. But I think Lennie is pretty well based on her. I just reversed the roles. Noah introduced her to the concert life. I think that is such a special gift to give someone.

I took my oldest daughter to see Patrice Pike live at Poor David's Pub in Dallas a few years ago. This was a chance for her to stand with her knees against the stage and see someone bring down the house. And if you haven't seen Patrice bring down a house, you should start trying to remedy that. Afterwards, I introduced Callie to Patrice and got pictures of them together. You can see it in my daughter's smile – that life-changing thing that had just taken place. Realizing that musical bliss is attainable for just the cost of a concert ticket. Being close to a super star means getting in before they get too big to approach.

Having been the front man for a band in Dallas for several years, I have been on both sides of the stage. My band played to thousands at the White Rock Lake festival for three years in a row. Not to mention the other clubs around the area. Poor David's Pub was one of them. Club Dada. The Green Elephant. We had a pretty good following. I've had the blessing of looking down from the stage and seeing people singing my lyrics with me. That might be the greatest ever return on investment that music can offer. That means they consume it outside of the bar. That means they listen to it in their free time. They carry it with them. The stories you hear about how a piece of music might have carried someone through a difficult time are amazing as well. It's all very powerful, and I don't take any of it lightly. I was never arrogant about my talent. I know we don't choose our talents. We only choose whether to hone them or not. Or whether to engage them at all. I take no credit for the talent. Only the work I put into it.

But I know how powerful it is for a singer to see someone singing along with him or her. And I also know how it feels to have a musician stare at you from the stage – even for a moment – while you both sing the same lyrics. Both are almost equally amazing. The latter being where you give back to the artist – showing her you've done your homework. You've adored his or her music enough to learn it. That's a big thank you.

I tried to capture some of those feelings in this book. I hope I've done a good job with it.

I started this book in January of 2016, after having just spent a month putting down over 80,000 words to complete my fourth novel, *Into the Darkness*, which I had started in – shockingly – 2008. February, to be precise. I started *Darkness* with just over 3400 words, then didn't touch it again for over five years. In November of 2013, I finally got back to work on it again. But that only lasted a month, and about 25,000 words. Another almost 5000 in October and November of 2014. Then I picked it up again for a final run starting in December of 2015. Those 80,000-plus words I wrote in that month established a nice writing routine for me.

That routine carried through into this book, where I wrote like a house of fire over the next month and a half, putting down over fifty thousand words. But then I didn't catch it again until 2020, when I added another fifty or so thousand. All that to say, I don't stay dedicated to a project very well. In fact, what you're missing in this text is the fact that between 2016 and now, I also started and finished *another* book, called *Red Bell*. I got a few thousand words started on that one, then put it down for three years. Last month, April 4th to be exact, I picked it back up and stuck to a schedule of writing at least 3000 words a day. And I finished it in about five weeks. That's the closest I've ever come to starting and finishing a project in one swoop. Without that three-year break between the first 7000 words and the last 145,000, it would have been one quick stretch. Try as I might, I have never been able to stay focused on one project for any longer than a few months at a time. And you can replace the word 'project' with 'hobby' and it fits the same. My moods and hobbies change like the weather here in Texas.

My wife and I like to take little weekend getaways every couple of months, and having just finished *Red Bell* I was on a roll, and looking forward to coming out here to this little pool house and getting in some serious writing time. Yesterday, Friday, I wrote over ten thousand words, getting very close to the end of the book. I finished it this morning. This is my idea of a perfect weekend. A little relaxing by a pool, a few breaks for visiting local restaurants and bars, and a whole lot of sitting at the little station I assembled here as a temporary writing room. I have a lap desk across my chair, a big monitor on a TV tray and a bottle of Evan Williams on the side table. You can see a picture of this setup on my website. It's not the most comfortable arrangement, but it works. And it certainly achieved its purpose this weekend.

My goal was to camp here for most of the weekend while the wife hit the thrift and antique stores. My hope was to maybe get the book finished. Mission accomplished. Thank you for reading it.

- Brandon Spacey
Ardmore, OK

ACKNOWLEDGMENTS

Thank you to my Ideal Readers Group, who help me vastly during my editing process. These three people read all my books in advance of publication and look for anything that I might have missed. Grammar errors, misspellings, plot holes and continuity errors, to name a few. Without their help, this would be a lonely hobby. I get to talk to them about the characters and the stories at length, about which I am very passionate. Bless them for their time and energy. Thank you, Kellie, Paul and Jessica. You mean worlds to me.

Thank you to my wife, for always supporting my writing. It's a very selfish endeavor with a lot of time spent hidden away in an office with music blasting, occasional bouts of singing out loud and drumming on the wrist-rest of the keyboard, and the all-too-often repeating of a song over and over until I finish whatever scene I'm working on. It takes you two minutes to read a scene I spent twenty minutes writing. If a song is five minutes long, she might have to hear it four times in a row. Bless her heart. At least it's *good* music. Trust me, it's good. Thank you, Melody.